A History
Of The
Devil

First Published in Great Britain 2011 by Netherworld Books an imprint of Belvedere Publishing

First edition: 2011

A copy of this work is available through the British Library.

ISBN : 978-1-908200-42-6

Netherworld Books
Mirador
Wearne Lane
Langport
Somerset
TA10 9HB

A HISTORY OF THE DEVIL

VOLUME ONE

BY

ADRIAN BRIGGS

Chapter One

Always in the dream I am hanged. My dead eyes gaze up, through the rustling canopy to the starry heavens. The rope, slung over a bough of black ash, groans, fibres stressed, as my corpse sways and slowly spins in the warm night's breeze. The noose had not been well made. Life had been choked from me rather than snatched by a snapped neck. I had scrambled and pulled my way to the gallows tree's first fork, managed to pull the hanging line to what I reckoned was the required length, struggled the noose over my skull, and simply let go. A struggle. Kicking and flailing, eyes bulging in a shrunken skull, feeling as if they were about to pop, hands clawing at the noose in instinctive denial, a flailing leg smacking the ash trunk, sending my convulsing form swinging out and then in, face mashing against the unforgiving trunk, nose smashing. My arms fell limp then. Panic and pain receded as darkness began to seep like spilled ink across my vision, as the calm resolve I had felt before falling my short drop returned to me. I died.

And dead, I open my eyes. I can see, seemingly sharper than before; can hear, the rustle of a roosting bird's primaries against its flank, the noise of invertebrates toiling in the woodland carpet of decaying foliage. I can smell, the carrion and shit stench of life. Tears sting into existence from my dead eyes. Even suicide does not free me from this vile existence.

Always in the dream I am hanged. Always in the dream Maria comes to me. At first she appears in the periphery of my cadaverous sight, a figure dressed in the white I had buried her in, hair flaxen cascades, skin as alabaster white in death as it had been in life. She moves through the woodland, treading lightly, disturbing the atmosphere that has fallen preternaturally still. She does not float as is expected of a ghost. As she comes closer I can sense her substantiality, can feel the heat of life emanating from her in waves.

'Maria,' I rasp.

She has come to stand directly in front of me, her face level with my knees. She catches hold of my ankles and looks up at me, such pain in her eyes. 'How could you do this?' she demands. 'So selfish.'

'Am I dead?' I choke out. 'This was always our wood. Is it now our...heaven?'

'Heaven? You really think there is such a place? You think you've found your way into eternity?'

She seems to be taunting me, but that couldn't be so, she was my life's love, taken so arbitrarily from me; she and my son.

'Please, Maria, what about the boy? Is he with you?'

Anger shifts over her features then, her grey eyes burning silver. She yanks my ankles downward with an unnatural force that in the physical world would have surely torn my head off. In the dream the hanging bough, thick as a man's thigh, breaks, the branch crashing to the earth beside my fallen form. My dead wife is quickly astride me, fury seething behind her eyes. I try to speak, to say something to console her. Did she blame me for her death? The crash was the other driver's fault entirely: drunk and high and speeding. Of all the emotions that had assailed me since my wife's and boy's deaths, guilt has not been present.

All I manage to do is part my lips, and then her mouth is on mine, fierce. I taste my own blood as Maria bites into my lower lip. She has her fingers at my belt, artfully undoing it and my trousers, sliding my flesh free from cotton and into her silkiness. She lifts her face, smeared with blood from my mouth and busted nose, and the expression she now wears is one of rage mixed with dark ecstasy. I try to sit up, to kiss her once more, but she forces me back down, palms hard on my chest, unbending me at the waist. She is in total control, gripping and releasing me with consummate skill. Death has neither diminished her beauty or the vitality of her inner muscles. I climax then, whipping my head from side to side in the perishing, crackling leaves, weeping and begging her to stay with me.

I always wake then. The pillow is wet with my tears. I have always ejaculated, but my cock is still achingly erect. Usually the time is around four in the morning, the darkest hour. The loss is immense. Sometimes I'll masturbate, treating my member roughly, as something indefatigable, something treacherous to be loathed. Sometimes I'll ignore the throbbing and go straight for the bottle.

One morning I did something different. This morning was no different from the ones that preceded it; it was something in me that was different. Perhaps the continuing emotional grind of the nightly dream had built up to such a point in my tortured mind that I had to release some of the pressure. Anyhow, one morning I didn't masturbate and I didn't drink. I went straight to the old desktop computer that I hadn't touched for months and booted it up. It was a while before the ready cursor was blinking in the top left-hand corner of the blank screen, but still I didn't have a drink in my hand. That was this morning, and this is what I have written.

Neil looked at the words on the screen. After an unknown while he connected up the printer and printed off a hard copy of his first writing since he'd put his wife and son in the ground. With the paper in his hand, his mind ingested the script better. It had been good for a few moments, that old feeling of flying, lost to the telling of the tale, even if this particular brief story was the one that had haunted his tender organ for too long.

'Oh, Maria,' he sighed, 'what I'd give to have you back. I'd follow you, but I've no faith in an afterlife. I'm so lost, so alone.'

He felt something strange and unbidden in him then, roiling and rising, black and poisonous from his gut: rage. He'd prayed once, when pissed -- prayer, the last refuge of the scoundrel and the drunk -- but that had been an act of self-pitying despair. Now, in a sudden and blinding fury, he addressed a god he didn't believe in, staggering to his feet, sending his writing stool clattering over. There was a heat in him, consuming, firing his tongue to unleash a blasphemous barrage against an uncaring creator. Evil, cruel, killer god. He dared the deity to unleash a thunderbolt, to strike him down for his temerity.

The heavens were silent, unmoved.

Sunrise found Neil on a park bench, overcoat buttoned to the chin, the early summer air chill with the memory of a protracted winter that had all but obliterated spring. He seemed to remember sitting here with Maria watching the dawn bloom some time ago, but wasn't sure if the memory was fiction or not. He seemed to have episodes since she'd died, since he'd taken to using liquor to obliterate brain cells by the million, of memory that he couldn't vouch for the accuracy of. Perhaps with him no longer writing, no longer inventing, his brain had taken to telling little fictions of its own. Enough then. If his mind was failing him, become treacherous, then at least he'd commit his mendacities to paper. He would write again. That was what Maria would want. He'd realised this many times before, had spoken it aloud, but the self-pitying side of him had always won out, taking the easier option of emptying a bottle into himself rather than emptying himself onto a computer screen.   The two were mutually exclusive: if he drank, he couldn't write. He would write. He would stop drinking.

A shiver settled on his shoulder and travelled down his spine, not inspired by the cool air but by the prospect of getting through a single day without alcohol to support him. He must keep busy. If he could make it through to the evening and find himself at his computer, perhaps a can of coke at his side, then he'd consider the day a victory of sorts: for himself; for Maria; for the boy.

He'd watch the sun detach itself from the horizon and then be off to find somewhere to breakfast. He couldn't recall eating anything of nutritional value in an age, and a full English couldn't do him anything but good. The star, swollen and blood-pregnant, shimmered as it rose. There were hardly any clouds in the still-starry vault overhead. It was going to be a beautiful day. Neil almost spoke something aloud, concerning rebirth or resurrection, but stilled his tongue, labelling the muscle pretentious, and found himself smiling, unsure what the unfamiliar expression on his face was for a few seconds, so unused was he to the muscular configuration.

An obese woman walking an obese dog looked at the man smiling inanely on the park bench as if he were a lunatic, and then hurried off as fast as her bulk would allow, in case he was dangerous.

The food pleased his palate and his gut at first. He couldn't remember how long it had been since he'd eaten a proper meal. He wolfed down sausages and bacon, crammed into his mouth and gulped down urine-scented kidneys and fried eggs and beans and toast sodden with butter. The more he ate the more his belly both thanked him and complained. As he worked through the fried breakfast he became increasingly ravenous and nauseous. He gulped weak tea from a cracked mug to wash back his rising gorge. Damn it, he didn't want to puke in here, not with these people around, construction workers and truck drivers. These were honest working men, all with tragedies, some little, some monumental, all their own, but they didn't go home to a bottle every night, didn't drink themselves into drooling and pissing oblivion. Their poisoned stomachs did not threaten to revolt when offered nourishment.

Neil's breakfast was almost done, a few beans mixed with runners of egg snot all that remained on the plate. The sight of the meal's remains brought on a convulsion that he choked down, closing his eyes to the plate, shoving it away from him with shaking fingertips, willing himself not to vomit.

Stand, you twat. To the counter. Pay for your meal. Calmly exit the establishment. Find a quiet recess, should be easy at this time of the day, and empty your stomach. The café's toilet, a single cubicle, was no option, as it was already in use, and a diner waited patiently, newspaper jammed into his armpit, for it to be vacated.

Standing went quite well -- legs a little unsteady, floor seeming to have developed something of a slope while he'd been eating -- and he made it to the counter. He looked around at his fellow diners. He clearly hadn't made much of a spectacle of himself, as all but one of the café's customers had their attentions fixed on breakfasts or papers or mobile phones. The one was a huge fellow, long blonde hair pulled into a pony tail, piercing blue eyes fairly drilling into Neil. Looked like trouble. Looked like he could snap a spine like a twig (look at the size of those fucking hands!) and was itching for a reason, no matter how tenuous, to do just that.

Neil was sweating. The big guy was rising, sight still fixed on him. Neil turned to the fat patron who had appeared behind the counter, trying to ignore the approach of the big guy, who was now padding to the counter himself. His sweat was as chill as ice water. Paranoia, he told himself, DT's or something. The big guy isn't interested in me.

The big guy was standing at his shoulder now. Neil fished some coins from his pocket and dropped them on the counter, hand visibly shaking. He turned to leave, the patron, ignored, saying something about change, and the big guy was in his face, glaring at him. This was no hangover delusion. He was in trouble.

'Can I help you?' he heard himself say, surprised at the lack of tremble in his voice. 'Do you have a problem with me?' The big guy looked him up and down, disdain undisguised on his features, and said, 'Why would I have a problem with you?' His voice was surprisingly soft, pitched much higher than one would have expected. Perhaps much of his size was down to steroids.

'You were watching... Are you following me?'

'I want to pay for my meal.'

'And that's all?' A wad of risen nausea was caught in Neil's gullet and the question sounded choked.

'Of course. Why would I be following you? I don't know you. Do I?'

There was something in the way he asked that last question, some knowing subtext in those last two syllables, that fired an unreasoned anger in Neil. This man was definitely looking for trouble, some sort of confrontation. To hell with the guy's size. He'd come here for a quiet breakfast, not to be intimidated by some muscle-bound bully boy.

'Then stop fucking staring at me,' he heard himself growling, amazed at his own temerity, the noise of the growl and the feeling of his little act of bravery disguising the imminent revolt of his stomach. Too late, the vomit surged, erupting from Neil's surprised and appalled gape and splattering the big guy.

'And you didn't get the shit beaten out of you?'

Neil smiled and leaned back in his seat, clutching a glass of cola. 'No. The big bastard just looked at me like I was the most depraved, disgusting thing he'd ever come across. Like if he touched me, I might infect him or something. He stood there for maybe ten seconds, just scowling, my puke running down his chest and belly. Then he paid and left, calm as anything. From behind, as he walked out the door, I could see the steam from my hot vomit rising around him.'

'He had a sickly halo,' said Will, smiling.

'Yeah. Then the café owner is growling, "I think you should leave now, don't you?" and I had to agree with him.'

'It would have been rude not to.'

'And so I came home to clean myself up, and found you...'

'...Waiting on your doorstep.'

'Yes. What do you want, Will?'

'To see how you are doing.'

'We spoke on the phone, only last week.'

'You were...You sounded drunk.'

'I was. Now I'm sober.'

'Since when?'

'Since I woke up this morning and started writing again.'

Will placed his cup of black coffee gently on the table before him. 'So, you're back in the saddle at last?'

Neil sighed. 'I won't have anything for you, Will. Not for a while. I won't be writing any more moderate sellers until I've written something personal, something for me.'

'Anything you wrote would probably be publishable, would sell. I can understand if you wanted to write about the accident and not have your private grief publicly aired, but --'

Neil held up his palms. He wasn't angry with Will; the man was just doing his job. He was a good agent. One of the best. 'Stop it, please. I won't be writing about Maria, not directly. I found myself in a rage this morning, in that bleak endurance before dawn, ranting at a god that doesn't exist.' He waited a moment to see if Will would remonstrate against his atheistic pronouncement. He had no idea what the literary agent's religious inclinations were. Will was silent and still. Neil continued.

'I called Him names, dared Him to strike me down. Strange isn't it, that at our darkest ebbs we react against or for higher forces, even if we don't believe in them? We're such a cowardly species, so afraid of being in control of our own lives. This morning I preferred the idea of being damned to that of being alone in the Universe, of being finite.'

'You should write that down.'

Neil grimaced and took a sip of his drink. 'What I'll most probably write will be pages of stream of consciousness bollocks. But I think it'll be therapeutic, I think it'll keep me off the booze. I'm going in for a spot of God bashing.'

'There's quite a bit of it around at the moment.'

'I don't care, as I'm not trying to sell it. Anyway, most of those books are arguing against the empirically provable existence of a deity to try and convert theists to atheists. They're asking the wrong question.'

'The right question being?'

'What are the faithful worshipping? It's no good proving a

scientific fact like a god's absence, if it's a truth implanted in the cortex of a hopeful sheep that he will never swerve from, whatever good and plausible arguments are tossed his way. Articles of faith can't be undone with reason and such weak things as proof, not when five sixths of the world find it more comforting to follow the creator myth, and indeed subjugate themselves cravenly to this beast they call loving and forgiving even though His tale drips with the blood of myriad geno-cides.'

'Blimey,' said Will.

Neil coughed discomfort. 'Sorry, I get a bit carried away when an idea catches hold.'

'No one knows that better than me, Mr Mann, and it's a wonderful thing to see, old friend. Look at you; you're excited, quivering at the prospect of an unfolding narrative, aren't you? You can't help it; it's the storyteller in you. You were pale and trembling when you came in; now you're on fire.'

Neil was smiling, in spite of himself. He'd done more smil-ing this day than he had in a long, long while. Will was right, the storyteller in him had engaged his brain, was almost inde-pendently composing a rough narrative arc.

'There's another question that needs answering.'

'What's that?' asked Will.

'If we were to posit God's existence, for the sake of a story where He is the villain, then shouldn't His opposite be a force for good: Jehovah the villain; Satan the hero?'

Will was grinning now. Obviously he was not a man of any religious conviction. Perhaps he thought Neil was onto some-thing, something saleable.

'I have a question for you,' said the agent.

Neil nodded, expecting something to do with projected manuscript length, how long it would take to write the thing, perhaps something about blasphemy laws, none of which con-cerned Neil, as he still maintained to himself that if he was to do this it would remain a private project. But when Will spoke, he said: 'If there is a Judgement Day, and you find yourself standing before God and having to explain yourself, what will you do?'

The answer slipped easily off Neil's tongue. 'Make sure I get the first punch in.'

Volume One

Pandemonium

Of that Paradise from which I had fallen I could not bear to recall. Of that great disobedience, that vain and haughty pride that had led me and my band of rebels into open warfare against the Almighty and his vast legions my mind recoiled as I lay in the great lake of fire, my flesh burned but not consumed, my form changed, become monstrous, unmade and remade by the will of the Creator as we had plummeted through the abyss for age upon age into ruin, this our preordained prison.

All was agony, fire without and within. I could hear the screams and wails of my co-conspirators, sighted them through veils of flame, limbs thrashing, physiognomies become monstrous and warped like mine own, great wings become dragon wings, beating the surface of the lake with maddened fury and despair yet making little progress, for what progress was there to be made in Hell but down?

How long we suffered in those fires I have no way of telling; when the mind and the body are synchronised in agony then a moment can endure for an unbearable lifetime, but it came to pass that we foundered onto a forbidding shore of black razor rocks. Others had grounded before I, and my great friend and lieutenant in battle, Beelzebub, reached out a hand that had become a monstrous, misshapen and taloned claw and helped me from the blazing waters. I saw the hot tears that sizzled on his scorched and transmogrified countenance, the shame and despair in the eyes that were the only part of him unchanged from his former glory. He had been an archangel, nearly as close to the Almighty as had I, and I had brought him down to the raging bowels of the Universe.

'Forgive me, my friend,' I spoke, the words burning in my parched throat as I found a seat on the hot rocks. 'Forgive me, for I have brought about our damnation.'

He said nothing, lowered his grown-ungainly form to the sharp shore and bowed his massive head. I would have preferred his sharp tongue, a caustic rebuke, even a challenge to the position of leadership that I had proved unworthy of holding and thought that I would relinquish in a moment.

Other fallen angels were rising from the fires, myriad flaming but unconsumed monsters, staggering on to the shore and collapsing, wailing and keening or quietly sobbing, demons every one of them. This was worse than the abyss. We knew not then of death, the very idea of non-existence unimaginable to beings such as we, but had we known then we would have surely collectively wished our demise.

I sat for an age, keeping my own wretched counsel. If only there were a way back, back into the auspices of God. If I could take back everything: the hypocrisy, the claiming of the Almighty's seat as mine own; the raising of an army of rebels, convincing with my sophistry this army that they were dissatisfied with their lot as worshippers of the Creator of all things; the war that could not be won.

My ego had become a swollen, greedy beast. I had thought myself God's equal, even better. I had rallied my troops, convincing them that we were righteous warriors, battling a mightier army in a war against oppression and tyranny. And this was the pass I had brought us to. The Almighty had shown Himself to be the Power of Powers. By what right had I challenged Him? He was the Maker, I was the made. If He commanded complete obedience and reverence then who was I to disagree?

And so I sat and flayed my cortex. After a while Beelzebub stood with a great groan and wandered off along the desolate shore. Stormy heavens, ochre bellied, roiled overhead, great electric storms raging within, raining sulphur down on us, drops as hot as any demon tears. As the unholy heavens quarrelled, so did quarrels break out around me. All along the shore the malformed fallen angels took up bicker and quarrel; blame was passed and parried amongst the host, blame that was rightfully mine to bear.

I rose with effort to my new gargantuan height, flexed the span of corded shoulders. I still bore my shield and great spear, dulled and bent from battle, and drove the lance's tip into the steely rock beneath me. Sparks flew and the mantle reverberated. This new form, massive and dragon-winged, had power, bestial and base but power all the same. The demons halted in their arguments, turned to me with expressions of anger mixed with expectancy. I saw Beelzebub striding back along the shore, curiosity creasing his scaled brow. Weakening self pity lifted from me as the remembered power of purpose surged in me. I had an audience now. These were my warriors. They needed their captain. I found my voice deep in my bowels, drawn from the pit of my despair and made strong on the harsh landscape there. I raised my shield, as God would have raised his aegis on the battlefield, and a bolt of lightning was drawn to the celestial steel, flashing explosion, the charge shooting along my arm and through my body, threatening to fell me. My spear had become a staff, anchoring me upright, and I stayed erect, features set to conceal my pain. Now my audience was rapt at the sight of this demon that could withstand the fury of such terrible heavens.

'Fellow angels,' I began, 'for that is what we are, no matter how our rebellion has caused such deformity to fall upon us. We have been cast down into the Hell to be broken on rock and fire. But we are not broken, not if we stand together and strong. We still have the talents of angels, can use our glamours to shape this landscape, our new strength to mine from brimstone and raise a structure to rival any in Creation.

'I too have been consumed by sorrow, pitying my fallen self and my desperate plight, but such weak-mindedness will lead only to discord and destruction. Together, angels, I propose we raise a palace of such magnitude and magnificence that God Himself will look down from His high seat and tremble and wish that he had destroyed us utterly.'

Nervous whispers passed through the audience, shaken afresh by my audacious words. I had brought them to this pass and they were understandably anxious not to risk further wrath from Above. Then came the sound of lone applause, back in the crowd, noble Beelzebub, most trusted and loyal friend, crashing his sword against his mighty shield.

'See!' I cried. 'There is one among us at least with the courage to follow his convictions through to the end, not to be cowed even in the face of such calamity.'

And Moloch, once a seraph of near-unrivalled beauty, roared out: 'I am with you, Lucifer!'

That name stung me. My Heavenly name: Bearer of the Light, first and most perfect of all God's creations.

'I am with you, Lucifer,' called out Belial, and Baal and Mammon, and then a great chorus of demon tongues were bellowing their support, beating their swords and spears on shields and rock, blue and white sparks shooting into the warring firmament. I wept tears of pride and of humility. We would have our palace, and its glory would be unmatched. Already I knew its name. Pandemonium. For all demons.

Away from the jagged shore the ground smoothed somewhat and sloped up sharply to a sulphurous peak many leagues into the roiling heavens. We decided to build on this mountainside. Mulciber, the great metal-worker and architect, was to be captain of the ambitious project. His left leg had been cruelly crushed in the fall from Paradise, leaving him with a terrible limp, but the demons' respect for him was not tempered at all by his infirmity and they set to work with an almost savage intensity under his dictate, laying gargantuan foundations, toiling ceaselessly in acid rains and scorching hurricanes. I toiled amongst them, raising great boulders and shaping them with my heated lance into bricks of a scale not hitherto seen, and not seen since.

We measured those ancient and early days not in time, which was unknowable to us, but in the rate that our demonic palace grew. Sheer walls, as polished as marble, rose into the ceaseless clouds, topped by turrets and spires innumerable and immense. The great hall of the palace, massive enough to hold ten thousand demons, was lit with myriad naphtha lamps. A great scaled roof, veined with the fire of brimstone, was constructed, with apertures to allow demons to fly in and out.

It was finished at last, mighty Pandemonium. Men have tried to emulate it over the ages, in Babylon and Byzantium, but none have come close.

But now I feared for my fallen angels. Now that the construction was over, how were they to occupy themselves, to keep their minds from dwelling on their still-dismal situation? An idea had been forming in me for some time, something for my troops to get behind, to restore their pride. I would call an assembly in the great hall, and put my audacious plan to them. A vote would be called for; we were, after all, nothing if not a democracy.

Chapter Two

Neil rubbed his knotting brow, leaning away from the monitor, aching behind his eyes but feeling damn good. He took a swig of cola and looked to the last sentence. A vote would be called for; we were, after all, nothing if not a democracy. He laughed lightly. The Democratic Republic of Hell. Did that make Heaven a fascist state? Where had this stuff come from? It had seemed to flow, sentences fully formed, from his mind to his racing fingertips, with nary a typo along the way. Perhaps he should have been a fantasy writer all along. It might lack kudos as a genre, but Christ it was fun.

He looked at the dusty first editions of his previous, in the main successful, novels that sat on a slightly slanting shelf above his computer desk. None of them fired much passion in him. Shylock's Curse had sold the best. He'd hated it. His one attempt at comedy, Did He Push or Was He Jumped, had been, so he remembered, his favourite to write. Critics had derided it and it hadn't sold. This stuff though, this was the most fun he'd had with a keyboard and a screen. The sheer freedom was exhilarating. What should he call it? The Satanic Writes? He laughed again and caught himself. Laughing at your own clever wit when alone in the depths of the night was a little too much akin to onanism.

None of what he'd written would be considered for publication, of course. He might show a draft to Will, for a laugh, but that was it. The Devil in the first person though, that was a neat touch. Mailer had done Christ in the desert, he seemed to remember, but Satan was just so much more fucking interesting. Neil's Devil, he had realised from the start, was a variation on Milton's Satan, with all the same human flaws and qualities. He recalled a quote that was probably a paraphrase: Paradise Lost is so good because Milton's God is so bad. But even brave and misinterpreted Milton had balked at the notion of God being an out and out tyrant, and Lucifer being a true freedom fighter, a flawed but attractive Romantic rebel standing against a despot, a sort of Che Guevera with wings.

Neil laughed again and knew that it was time to switch off

13

the computer. With the light dead, the desire for a drink rushed to fill the vacuum in his mind that writing, really flying, had occupied. He took a hard swig of soft cola, dribbling some down his chin. 'Don't need a drink. Be strong.' How the fuck was he going to get through this? It was only day one, night one actually, of his abstinence. Why did he feel the need for alcohol, anyway? It wasn't the taste, for sure. He'd never been a fine ale man, or a connoisseur of classy claret; those drugs weren't quick enough. Had he drank at all when Maria had been alive? The fact that he couldn't recall inspired a clammy panic in him. Was his brain, and the memories that organ contained, really that pickled? 'Oh, Maria.' All he could conjure were carnal memories. Their fucking had never got past the honeymoon period. God, he must have been one of the few men in history only to masturbate over mental images of his own wife.

The despair was flooded back in then, and he was shaking and sobbing. What he'd just written had been derivative shit. His good stuff was on the slanting shelf above him. His glory days, lost forever. What he'd just written, he saw with the clarity of the wretched, had been a betrayal. For the time that he had been flying, lost to himself, he had been lost to his memories also. 'Oh, my Maria.' For the first time since her death, awake or unconscious, Maria hadn't been with him. He had fooled himself that she would have wanted him to write, but found the act tantamount to infidelity. He had become a cheat, wiping his wife from the consistency of his consciousness, making her memory something to be tripped over like a misplaced toy.

To a bottle, half full, good amber Caribbean rum. He had, honestly, considered pouring all of his booze down the sink earlier in the day, but his mind had stilled his hand, obviously measuring ahead to this inevitable moment of capitulation. He grasped the neck of the vessel, much like he would throttle his own member when loss would drive him to choke and joylessly spit.

'My love,' he sighed, and, pressing the bottle to sore-rubbed lips, Neil drank deep.

He was a little way into a second bottle when stupor claimed him and he went to the floor on his side, container glugging out its contents onto the carpet beside him.

The ringing phone brought him to a state approaching wakefulness. A sombre dawn's light was filtering into the room and his face was wet, his sight stinging, his head banging, brain shrunken in a screaming skull. Neil groaned himself into a sitting position, trying to orientate himself in the wan light, scrubbing with his sleeve at the congealed liquor on the left of his face. The phone rang on, and he scrabbled after the noise's origin, more to kill its shrill insistence than to speak with anyone at such an ungodly hour. He found the handset and choked it tight to his pounding skull.

'What?'

'Is that, Mr Mann?'

'Who wants to know?'

'Is that, Mr Mann?' The speaker was undoubtedly male, but softly spoken, almost childlike.

'Tell me who you are. I don't give out this number, and it's strictly ex-directory.'

'Is that, Mr Mann?'

'I'm putting the phone down, now. In the morning I'll have this number changed. I don't know who you are, or how you got my number. At this moment I don't give a flying fuck, as I have nails being hammered into my skull and I am going to bed.' He made to slam the phone down, knowing the action would fire fresh agony in his head but committed all the same, when the voice from the handset in his descending hand caught him.

'You know me.'

Neil pressed the phone back to his ear. 'Excuse me?'

'You know me. You owe me.'

The first vague shadows of fear appeared in his clearing mind. He recognised the voice. I don't know you. Do I? 'And what exactly do I owe you?'

'You owe me…Time. After the incident in the café, I don't think that a little time is much to ask in way of recompense for my soiled clothes --'

'Look, I'll gladly pay for your clothes to be professionally cleaned. Hell, I'll buy you some new ones.'

'Hell you might, but I don't want your filthy money.'

Oh shit, now he'd insulted the psycho bastard. Neil racked his addled brain. Anyone nowadays, with a little work, could get anybody's number. But why go to so much trouble? A crazed fan? He seemed to remember having some minor troubles in the past, people accosting him for an autograph and then spitting in his face that he'd plagiarised stuff they'd written. 'Sir,' he spoke into the telephone, changing his tack in case the big guy was truly dangerous. 'Sir?'

'Yes, Mr Mann?'

'Neil, please. You do know who I am, after all, don't you?'

'Do you?'

Strange. Ignore it. 'You did follow me into the café yesterday, didn't you? Really I don't mind. Please don't think I do. In fact I'm flattered. I really do appreciate my fans.'

'Oh, Mr Mann, I was never a fan of yours.'

Shit! He wasn't a fan. The antithesis of such a state then? Some nut who'd been offended by something he'd written? 'Listen, please, could you tell me your name?'

'You don't need to know my name. Worm.'

Fuck. Neil felt cold beads of sweat spring globular on his forehead. 'Okay, really, I don't need to know your name. I'm truly sorry if something I've written in the past has caused you offence.'

'I want to talk about your story.'

'Which one?'

'A History of the Devil.'

Something seemed to fall away from Neil's viscera, leaving a dread channel in its wake. 'I...really...I-I don't know the title. You must have the wrong author.'

'Oh no, Mr Mann. The work is most definitely yours; you have only just begun it.'

'But I haven't even given it a name yet!' Neil cried out, conspiring in the lunacy.

'Good title though, and apt, don't you think? Of course, as the author, you can choose to name the story whatever you like.'

Had to be dreaming, lost to horizontal imaginings. If he'd woken then he'd have memories of the dream of hanging and of Maria. Always he had that dream. 'You're a figment. Leave me alone.'

'Don't be foolish, Mr Mann. I can't leave you alone. I'm bound to you, and I'm probably the most real thing in your world at the moment.'

'And what do you want from me?'

'Simple. I want you to continue with the story. I imagine that you have considered not telling any more of the tale. I imagine that you have considered denying your vocation and slipping back into an alcoholic fugue. That would be a mistake; a mistake that would impel me into the action of paying you a personal visit at your home, in order to try and persuade you to continue your work.'

'You don't know where I live.'

But Neil's panicked mind was screaming: He knows your private number, so why the fuck wouldn't he know your address? even as the voice on the other end of the line was saying, 'Of course I know where you live, Mr Mann. I'm looking at your house at this very moment.'

The phone was down and Neil was rushing for the bay window, tearing the net curtains and slamming his face to cold glass, bulging his sight over the dour street. The big guy was there, unmistakable, blond hair untied now, cascading over immense shoulders, cobalt penetrative shards of blue eyes. Not a real creature. A giant of myth.

The big guy held up something made miniscule and swallowed by the massiveness of his right hand. A mobile phone. The big guy did something that looked like a wave and started to walk up the road.

There was a moment of hesitation for Neil, when the rational part of him screamed of danger, of how psychotic and strong the man must be, how he was almost certainly armed. Only a moment, and then Neil was tearing open the front door, rushing descent of the stone steps to the pavement, straddling the gate with clumsy haste. He had to face the madness, to understand how this interloper could know what he was writing. He wasn't connected to the internet (technological Luddite that he was), so there was no way of accessing his computer.

Neil was over the gate, squashing a testicle with the requisite sensation of ephemerally nauseating agony, and staggering over the road, looking the way the big guy had gone, east, where a watery sun had risen behind a veil of cloud, ineffectual star. The street was deserted.

Neil pressed out the emergency trio three times, and three times disconnected. He would sound insane. Eventually, driven by a need to at least tell someone of what had passed this dark dawn, someone who knew him, and understood him a little, he rang Will. Will sounded alert, as if he'd been up for a while, and said he'd be at Neil's within the hour. The agent was as good as his word.

'I sound crazy, don't I?'

'Not at all. I know you're not crazy. But I couldn't help noticing the empty bottles. If you drank that much --'

'I didn't drink that much. I spilled a lot.'

'Still, better drunk than insane.'

'I'm not so sure any more.'

'Well, what if you were dreaming?'

Neil nodded. 'That's what I keep coming back to, and I've given myself three options to explain my... event: the big guy is supernatural, a telepath or something; or I'm bonkers; or I dreamt the whole thing.'

Will folded his hands, as if praying. 'The last does seem the most likely and logical.'

Neil took a swig of cola. His hangover had subsided to a dull pulse in his brain and faint tremors in his guts. He was ashamed that he hadn't cleared away the empty bottles, that he hadn't sponged away the stain of Dominican rum on the carpet. Only yesterday he'd vowed to Will that he'd stopped drinking and resumed writing. He realised that Will was saying something.

'Or perhaps you weren't exactly dreaming, or kind of half dreaming while awake, a sort of hallucination.'

'Bonkers again.'

'No, not at all.' Will leaned forward in his seat. 'Your subconscious could be working on you.'

'Don't get all Freudian on me.'

'But don't you see? You wrote the start of your story, and it was bloody good, wasn't it?'

Neil sulkily shrugged. 'I enjoyed writing it. It just seemed to flow from me. I loved writing it, actually. I was, you know, flying. But afterwards,' he slowly shook his head, 'it looked to be a pile of shit.'

'Writer always think that. They're a capricious bunch of tossers. Present company accepted, of course.'

Neil grimaced a grin. 'Of course.'

'They write something, could be Anna Karenina, and they look at it and go: "Oh my, this isn't original. What was I thinking committing this flatulence to the page, screen, whatever?" and then they go back to it a little later, re-evaluate the thing, and realise that it wasn't that bad. Not that bad at all. And I think that what you wrote was probably pretty good, and it scared you, at some level.'

'Why would I be scared of writing a good story? It's what I'm about, isn't it?'

Something dangerous flashed in Will's eyes and was gone, but Neil caught it.

'Go on, Will.'

'What?'

'Come on, don't hold back. You're biting your tongue. Let it out, I can take it. Do you think I haven't said it to myself a thousand times?'

'Then you don't need me to tell you.'

'Perhaps I do. The objective opinion of an outside party.'

Will sighed. 'Okay, you're scared of writing a good story, any story, because that would mean you resuming existence, having to deal with life again. Maybe you conjured the threatening guy this morning, your mind forming him from the man you had a confrontation with yesterday.'

'How do you know that that wasn't a figment of my imagination, my poor pushed and pickled brain, as well?'

Will ignored him, and continued. 'And he was your subconscious telling you that you had to keep writing, stop drinking, because if you don't you're going to slip into oblivion. You have to regain your spine. You're better than this.' Will took in the spilled bottle, the mess on the carpet, with an extravagant sweep of his left arm. 'If this thing was a hallucination it could be you trying to save yourself. If it was a dream, then the message is pretty much the same.'

'And if the big guy is a telepath?'

'Then you'd better keep fucking writing, because somebody likes your work.'

The Plan

The fallen angels came swooping and wheeling through the roof of Pandemonium on dragon wings. Some were horned and scaled, some tailed. All were identifiable as their former glorious selves by eyes that were unchanged: mirrors of Heaven's lustre. They settled as a mass, jostling and bickering, struggling for a prime position before the pedestal I had had erected, naphtha lights directed to cast me in a regal glow. I still held the great horn that Mulciber had fashioned for me to my lips. I lay down the horn and took up my mighty spear, held it aloft, raised my mighty shield, and crashed the two together. The assembly fell silent and still.

Beelzebub was directly in front of me, as I had arranged, a full head higher than the demons around him. He was to be my support should the assembly fall into dissent, should the notion of mutiny pass like a virus through the demons.

'Fellow angels,' I began, 'our wondrous palace is raised. Hell itself has been subdued to our dictates. We have made God's prison our home, and He will quake when that knowledge reaches Him. We would further refine this place over time, calm its tempestuous atmospheres, coax plains and forests to life on its craggy earth, raise clean waters and direct bubbling streams. We would become happy and we would be free. These things we would… But He will not allow it.'

Murmurs passed through the assembly, some demons casting nervous sight to the great open ceiling, as if fearing to see the Almighty bearing down upon us, rage blackening His face, thunderbolts casting from Him.

I drove on. 'He will look down from His high seat and witness what glories we have performed already. He will see that we are not dashed but are thriving, and will grow stronger. And He will fear us. He will not see that we are glad to be free of His tyranny, for He is a vain and jealous god, and will imagine us to be plotting our way back into His kingdom for open war once more, and He will fear that the metamorphoses He wreaked upon us as we fell have made us monstrous warriors, more powerful than we ever were. In that He would be right.

'We must make a choice then, angels, for the Creator will be intent on uncreating us. We have shown His fallibility by being unbroken by His harshest judgement, by raising these great walls. We have laughed in His harsh face, spat in His cold eye, and for that He will visit His wrath upon us. And so we must choose between raising defences against His inevitable advances, existing in constant dread of His attack, nearly as under His yoke as we were in Heaven; or we could take the fight indirectly to Him, undermine His works, thwart His universe. Already news of our achievements will have reached some of the Heavenly host, and numbers of them will be wishing they had joined us on our noble rebellion. If we could convince them that God is not omnipotent, that we fallen creatures do not bow to His dictates and can indeed corrupt His works and therefore His will, many more will join with us, perhaps raising a second, even greater rebellion that could bring about the downfall of Yahweh once and forever.'

My voice had become a mighty roar, from the bellows of my chest. I could feel the apprehension emanating from them in hot waves, but they were in awe of my audacity, ready to support whatever scheme I proposed. All except brave and impetuous Moloch, who had been first to cry out, 'I am with you, Lucifer!' at our beginning in Hell. Now the warrior in Moloch won through. He was not a creature of schemes and wiles.

'Enough of this talk of indirect action, of undermining the Creator,' he cried. 'I propose we take the fight directly to Him. I propose open warfare, that we tear down Heaven itself, gathering those angels that wish to join us, the others to be cast into oblivion. We fought well before, though massively outnumbered by their swarming legions to our dozen centuries, and would fight so much better now we are stronger of muscle and mettle and have such fine ores at hand for Mulciber to fashion into blades and lances. And if we were to lose once more, it would be a noble defeat that would be spoken of for ages to come, inspiring more hearts to revolution. Better that than cowering. Better that than scheming.'

Some demons near to Moloch backed away from him, and he cast a baleful eye of disdain over them, sharpening his mighty sword on a block of lava-rock. Yet a ripple of support for his fierce stance did pass through the crowd and I was quick with my response, in case it should magnify.

'Brave and noble Moloch speaks well,' I spoke, 'with courageous words well-suited to his great heart. Yet sometimes, as always with the greatest of warriors, his capacity for courage is not matched by that for sense.'

Anger flashed in Moloch's eyes at the barb, but he held his tongue and body stilled and so I continued. 'We are not a dictatorship, and the choice of action we ultimately embark upon will be decided by the majority. If the majority do choose open warfare once more then I will bow to the greater will and will be at Moloch's shoulder, wielding my lance and sword with equal the resolve of any demon.'

Belial spoke out now. Smooth-tongued he had been Heaven's angel, and smooth-tongued was he Hell's demon. 'Noble Moloch's words of war stir my blood, angels, but I concur with Lucifer that open war would be a futile endeavour. Heaven will be prepared, its walls made unassailable, great machines of war will have been constructed to drive us back into Hell, if not worse. And worse there may be. We have no notion of what new terrors God could deliver us into should we rebel further, for His mind is unknowable to mere angels, even those as mighty as Lucifer whose scheme of creating discord in God's universe would be as much perceived as rebellion by Him as would unambiguous attack. War, open or unresolved, would surely spell our destruction. I believe that we raised this great palace with God's consent. He allows us to thrive in Hell, as He knew we would, for He knows all that is and was and will be. We have no need to raise defences against Heaven's vanguard, for they will not trouble us if we continue as we are, shaping this place to our own inferior paradise.'

'I am with you, Belial!' cried out Mammon, and then Baal. They had been with me at our beginning in Hell.

Assent with Belial's cowardly proposal of apathy was spreading through the assembly, a rancour rising that could quickly make a rabble of the demons. If I spoke now then I might quickly be shouted down, perhaps torn from my platform. The crowd was in the angry mood for a peace that I knew to be ultimately untenable.

I nodded to Beelzebub, a prearranged signal.

'Quiet!' roared my friend and lieutenant, turning on the rabble and flashing his sword, backing from them so that he stood in front of me, his head to my chest even though I was on a high pedestal. And the demons did quiet down, and allowed Beelzebub to speak.

'Offspring of Heaven, take heed of Lucifer and his call for subversion. The Lord of Creation has doomed us to this dungeon, not beyond his potent arm, as Belial would have. Nor would brave Moloch's call to resumed arms result in aught but further doom. Heaven will have been made an impregnable fortress by now, fearing neither assault nor siege.

'But, angels, what if we were to find some easier enterprise, some middle way that might be undetected by God and yet weaken and wound Him and His high vanity? I heard God tell - - as did Lucifer, and others once high amongst you -- of another place, a world that is the happy seat of some new race called Man, created by the Creator to be like us, but without such powers as we wield, though perhaps even more favoured by Him than are angels.'

He had the crowd now. Many had heard the story of God's new-created world. Many had been jealous in Heaven, hearing the Almighty speak with undisguised fondness of this new race, as if angels were too flawed and He must start again with a second species.

'I propose,' continued Beelzebub, 'that we bend our wills to discovering what we can of this new creation, this Man, and this new world, and thence to turn this new race to our party, or at least harden their hearts to their creator, make them disobedient. That would be more than revenge: that would be His failure. Advise if you think this worth attempting, or stay here in the darkness hatching vain empires.'

The assembly erupted into applause, crashing weapon against steel and stone, taloned claw against chest, dragon wings beating a furore. Beelzebub moved back into his rapturous audience. He turned to me and smiled and nodded. He had delivered my words well.

I raised my spear, motioning the demons to calm. 'Beelzebub's masterful proposal mirrors mine own. Let us send a representative to this new world to discern the nature of this Man and how it might be turned against its maker. It will be an arduous journey, back into the abyss through which we plunged for so long, with no promise of safe return. Dangerous... but oh the honour. Who amongst us, brave demons, would recommend themselves, or another, for this honour?' I paused for a moment, and then: 'I would put myself forward.'

'Lucifer! Lucifer! Lucifer!' The roar from the crowd was deafening.

Chapter Three

So, he thought, the big guy, real or not, is getting his way. I am telling the story of Satan, the Devil's History.

Neil saved the work and went to the window holding a can of fizzless dregs of caffeine and sugar. Dawn. It seemed that he had written the night away. It was perhaps apt, considering the subject's matter. He took a warm and flat swallow of pop. There was no big guy watching the house from the street. He wondered who next he'd conjure to stand there. Maria, perhaps? Or his dead son, skull caved in, eye socket filled with blood, waving at him through the membrane that separates death from life, madness from reality?

He should, felt he must, get some sleep. He went to the bathroom and splashed some frigid water on his clammy-feeling face, grinding eyeballs under the heels of his palms. There was a mirrored façade to the medicine cabinet, a mirror to which Neil the man hardly ever committed anything but the briefest of glances, indecent snatches of reflection. This morning though, his face caught in the mirror and held there as if snared. 'Is that really me? Am I that?' he whispered. The lips on the reflective surface moved in concert with his own, so he decided that it really must be him in the picture. Yet still...

He pressed a finger to the loose and puffy flesh at his right cheek (the mirror portrayed him poking his left and he couldn't help but wonder why the image wasn't inverted as well as reversed, that old conundrum) and then to his waxy forehead, to the sweat-matted hair that was fast receding, to the spreading patch of hairless skin at his crown. He looked into his blood-shot gaze. 'You're behind there, aren't you? Who I really am is behind this skin and muscle and bone, underneath these eyes. I'm not this face puffed up by booze. I'm not flesh and blood at all: I'm a collection of thoughts. I'm not flesh and blood at all: I'm a pretentious twat.'

He drew a wry smile from himself, rubbing the back of his hand over dry lips, craving a shot of liquor, but craving sleep more, or the hope and dread that he would dream of Maria once more.

To the bedroom. The sheets were crumpled and Neil simply lay atop them in his equally crumpled clothes. Christ, he thought, I haven't had a drink all day and all night. How very odd. He fell asleep.

A new dream. Neil was awake and warm sunshine flooded the bedroom. His wife was sitting on the edge of the bed, hair golden in the sunlight as she gazed to the window that admitted the star's brilliance, her grey eyes seeming to focus on some impossible distance, such pain and loss in her watch. She wore a strapless summer dress, crimson floral print on a cream back-ground. Neil hadn't seen the dress before, had to be a conjuring of his sleeping mind.

He reached out a hand to her slender arm. Her skin was the colour of ivory, but warm with life. 'Won't you haunt me in the physical world, Maria?' he heard himself say. 'I can't stand only to see you in my dreams.'

She turned her gaze on him then, and he could see that tears were forming in her eyes. 'Dream, reality, you can't tell the difference any more. You think yourself a storyteller, but that just makes you a liar with a penchant for the complex. Your whole existence is a lie.'

Neil didn't understand the ghost's mournful words. 'Are you angry with me, darling?' She might be a figment of his imagination, but he didn't want to drive her from his mind, to drive himself to wakefulness to find tears wetting his pillow. 'I couldn't stand to hurt you. I love you so much.'

'Love me?' she fairly snarled, tears drying in an instant, the old steel flashing silver in her eyes. 'If you loved me then you'd have come after me.' She shrugged his hand off her arm. 'If you loved me then you'd be with me now, raising our child.'

Neil tried to sit up, but he was as if paralysed, shaking his head in horror and wonder and disbelief at her words. Was she a dream, or had she visited him as a spirit in his sleep to con-sole or torment? Was he sleeping even? Had she come to fetch him? If so then he'd go so willingly with her.'

'The boy...' he ventured. 'You're still raising the boy, in the afterlife.'

She struck him then, hard across the cheek. 'There is no fucking boy, never was. We did have a son once, but his heart

26

beat only a dozen times after he was born and then gave out.' The steel died in her eyes, replaced by a wretched kind of tenderness, and she leaned over her prone husband and said: 'We have a daughter, a baby daughter who needs her father.' She stroked his face, catching a tear between thumb and forefinger. 'I know I'm not supposed to visit you, that it's against the rules and dangerous --'

'A daughter?' he cut in. 'How?'

Maria smiled coldly. 'We fucked, you came, and a baby grew in me.' She grasped his hand and placed it on her thigh, dragged it upwards, fingertips fleetingly tracing her pubic growth, flirting with her vulva, to the slight curvature of her belly. 'Here,' she whispered. Then, with her free hand, she was pulling down one side of her summer dress, revealing her left breast, fuller than Neil remembered, nipple larger and darker. And she was offering it to him, and he managed to raise his head enough to take the nipple gently between his lips and suck on the dream teat of his dead wife, and the milk came and it was sour and rich and warm and he drank deep.

Maria was speaking soft to him as he fed on her. 'Do I taste like a dream or a ghost? I am real. Your daughter is real. Come and find us. Begin by finding out where I am not.'

Neil wept as he drank. Some of the milk spilled from his mouth and mingled with his tears.

He came awake, foetal-curled on the living-room carpet. His gut tensed, tremors of nauseating despair. Just a dream after all. There was wetness on his face, but when he wiped angrily and hopefully at it with the back of his hand the moisture was only salt water. He forced himself, groaning, to stand, feeling as bleak as he ever had, the craving for a shot swarming his senses. He shambled to the foot of the stair and registered that the door to the room where he had dreamed of being suckled at the breast of his corpse of a wife hung open. 'Leave me alone,' he hissed, as he mounted the risers and then shouldered the door wider. The bed was crumpled, as if slept in, but wasn't it always so in these unkempt and unkept and measureless times? Sunlight poured into the room, from a higher elevation than it had in his dream.

You wouldn't know the truth because your whole existence is a lie, came back to him. And wasn't there a sweet but slightly rancid smell in the still and warm air of the room, like that of the breast milk he had ingested in his fancy? Dust coalesced in the shafts of sunlight, figures that were just beyond the reach of his sight and understanding. 'Rubbish,' he heard himself say. 'That's my mind yearning for signs when there are only arbitrary motes.' This is how madness comes, he heard his brain insist. This is how the mind fractures.

The telephone began to ring downstairs. Neil couldn't know if the sound was real or not. Perhaps the big guy would be on the other end, talking of the story he could not possibly have knowledge of. Had he been mad for an age? Had the accident that had brought him so utterly low even happened?

He could remember the crash so clearly; yet just as clearly he could recall the taste of dead Maria's milk. What was real, if anything? The night of the crash had been wet and stormy, a violent backdrop for the unfurled drama. The three of them had been driving back from a countryside restaurant, filled with good food consumed in honour of the boy's tenth birthday. Neil had drunk two glasses of wine but had later cleared a breath test. He had been declared, and honestly thought he considered himself, blameless. The other driver had been three times over the alcohol limit and his blood had coursed with amphetamines. The impact had killed the lucky bastard instantly. The death-dealing car, a Volkswagen, had broadsided Neil's Mark II Jag, roaring into them at an intersection, the driver seemingly oblivious to the highway's right of way. The Jag, a classic, a beauty, but without the safety features of a modern car that might have spared Neil his great loss, spun in the wet road, mounted the verge and parted its sleek bonnet on a telegraph pole. Neil had looked to his wife. She was unmarked. Eyes closed. Unconscious. Hope surged through shock. He turned to his son. Hope fled. The rear section of the car had taken the brunt of the impact, collapsed to near half its former volume. Glass sparkled in the boy's hair and face. Lightning lit the scene in terrible relief, stark blue and interminable. The boy's head was caved in, black blood filling one eye socket that seemed to have lost its organ.

Neil heard a keening whining sound that he realised was coming from himself. Back to Maria. All hope died. More lightning. Rain was coming in through the busted window in the back of the car. A black trickle of blood was coming from

Maria's right ear. He put two trembling fingertips to her grace-ful throat, as pale as alabaster. No pulse. He unbuckled himself, his lips to hers, desperately trying to force life from his burning lungs into hers. Her head, her beautiful face, lolled to one side on a broken neck.

That had been no dream, surely? Too real. Too painful.

More words from the dream: There is no fucking boy, never was.

How could his mind torture him so? The Maria of his dreams was a devil sent to torment him, and he would hate her if he were able. His boy, his poor birthday boy, his... Dark revelation seemed to still his heart.

What had been the name of the child? His fist was in his mouth, blood dribbling to his wrist from where he had bitten down. He could not remember the name of his own son.

Neil was to his feet, rushing the stairs, legs buckling him halfway down and depositing him sprawled at the foot. Back upright and through the front door, leaving it carelessly open. The house might well not exist, and if it did then burglars were welcome to its contents. Perhaps at this moment, instead of stumbling -- racing down a street under a warming sun chased by black lunacy, he was being restrained in a psych ward while consultants argued over by how much his dosage should be increased. Yet back to his received perception, sensations and sounds too real to question too much when his heart was pounding and adrenaline coursing. He plunged across an inter-section, cars swerving to miss him, horns blaring their depres-sors' impotent rage, Neil deaf to the invectives hurled his way. He knew where he was headed, the most recent words of his dead wife -- angel or demon or figment -- driving him on: Be-gin by finding out where I am not.

The Abyss

On a wave of demonic cheer I rose into the roiling atmosphere on my great sails, the naphtha lights of Pandemonium falling fast away, obscured now by the sulphur-spitting clouds. I wove desperately between tempest-born flashes so as not to be electrocuted and flung back to Hell's unyielding ground, broken once more. Hot hurricane wings buffeted me, fighting me down, but I forged on, willing the storm clouds to part and reveal before me the infinite vacuum that we angels had plunged headlong through for an age to crash to our prison. In that great nothingness, God unwilling, I would find this new world, this seat of Man.

Doubts clustered around me as I effortfully ascended, dragon wings tiring, thunder bolts fizzing close enough to singe. I had coached the demons on the perils of this voyage so as to dissuade none but me to volunteer for the mission, but now I was wondering if I should have paid more heed to my own manipulative tongue. I was becoming lost in airs of chaos, all sense of direction diminishing. A thunderbolt whistled my way, as must have thunderbolts on the battlefield of Heaven, cast from Jove's fizzing aegis. I glanced the bolt aside with my shield, but the electric force of the blow flung me in a long and disorientating somersault. Now I knew not what was up or down. Hell above; Hell below: all was Hell. I was Hell.

I could not, would not, fail my troops. To return to Hell ignominious would be unbearable, would guarantee mutiny. I would rather be lost for all time in these stormy airs that seemed to extend now across all space.

The clouds ripped abruptly, and I was out into the blackness of God's great emptiness. I would rest awhile, hovering on stilled sails, regaining strength and resolve and pondering what lay before me. On the brink of Hell I looked out across the abyss, the womb of nature and perhaps her grave. Myriad stars punctuated the blackness, but they were unbearably distant and cold. Behind me Hell seethed below its atmosphere, and the great and proximate sun rose behind it, its warmth radiating me, conducting through my spread sails to my very core. I could return to Hell, back to the heat that seemed pleasurable remembered by my treacherous mind. Or I could head for the risen sun, to warmth and different adventure. The void was too great for me to discover God's new world in. To the sun, great star, I would go, and perhaps by its light and warming furnace of birth find the new world.

Beating towards the star, its girth seemingly increasing with each stroke, the dead air around me beginning to warm, I perceived a fellow traveller through the abyss approaching, shining gold, lit from behind by the sun's brilliance. It was Uriel, one of God's archangels, no doubt put out into space as a sentinel, orbiting the sun on constant guard. Uriel was a noble and brave angel; also he was slow-witted and easily fooled. I would have earlier converted him to the cause of rebellion, had I not reckoned him too gormless and open to conceal his hypocrisy from God while we mutinous angels concocted our uprising.

I cast a glamour over myself, transforming my dragon form into that of a shimmering cherub, my lance shrunken to a harmless dagger, shield become decorative. It was difficult to hold, for my natural form was now monstrous, and the monstrous strives to corrupt the beauteous. My mind I closed and kept guarded, for an angel can read another's thoughts if they be open.

As we closed, I called out: 'Uriel, of the seven spirits that stand in sight of God's high throne, a quest had brought from the choirs of cherubim, wandering alone. Bright seraph tell me, I beseech, where is the seat of Man, the Almighty's new Creation? I want to look upon God's new race, raised to replace that band of fiends rightly dispatched to the depths of Hell.'

Uriel swallowed the performance whole, my disguise confounding his eyes that were as sharp as his wits were dull. 'Fair angel,' he responded, 'my sight, usually infallible, deceived me at first, and perceived you devilish, but I know now my mistake. The desire to know first-hand the creations of God, thereby to justify the great work-master, to journey far as you have alone merits praise indeed. I would guide you myself, but am ordered to patrol the region of the sun, watchful for that fiend now called Satan and his demonic legion that you spoke of. Follow my direction and you will come to this new world, and there seek out God's new paradise, called Eden, the abode of the first of God's new race, the one called Adam.'

With due deference I bid the archangel farewell and gratitude and was back across the abyss, following the course Uriel had plotted, stars as markers, the sun at my tail my compass. The stress of holding my cherubic cover in place became painful after many leagues of flight and I shed the illusion, hoping that I was out of range of Uriel's hawk watch.

On and on through the void, until my chest and shoulder-blades screamed protest and I let my wings fall still, sails on which I glided on the sun's radiation until my strength recovered and I would again beat my way through space until I at last made out the new world.

I beat with more fervour now, excitement and anticipation surging fresh energy to my limbs, my mind fizzing with schemes, and the pale blue dot surged to fill my vision as I hurtled towards it until it was a massive jewel of azure and emerald with a silver satellite in tethered orbit.

I plunged into an atmosphere glorious with warmth and life, gentler and more benevolent by far than the cruel buffets of Hell. I descended in a sweeping spiral, wings upswept, and came to rest on a mountain-top, looking across this fertile world, divining for this Eden, this Adam, whom I had arrived to corrupt, to turn against his maker.

Chapter Four

That felt better, thought Neil. His hands had stopped trembling as soon as he had laid his fingers on the keyboard. It seemed that in all the unreality that had overtaken him the most fictional was the most soothing. Flying, his brain calmed.

Neil put the computer on to standby, feeling that the itch to return to the story might become beyond scratching this night. He rolled away from the darkened screen and stood up. The events of the afternoon were crowding in as he went to the refrigerator and took out a can of cola and sat at the dusty kitchen table. He had arrived at the local cemetery where he knew, incontrovertibly, his wife to be buried. The sun had been warm on his balding pate, insects tasting from the arrangements at the gravestones, row upon row of death's lichen-coated markers.

The sun had been an angry red, huge and low, when he'd finally admitted defeat and left the cemetery, confused and desperate beyond tears. Every inscription he'd checked, time after time, from the tragic newborns to those that had lasted out a century. Maria wasn't there. Begin by finding out where I am not.

What was real? He had hurried home filled with a fear that he would be unable to find his street; his house disappeared as surely as his wife's grave.

'What is real?' he spoke aloud. He took a swig. 'This coke is real. I can taste it.'

He had tasted his wife's breast milk.

Neil didn't know if he believed he remembered his son being buried alongside his mother. No name, no grave. Could all his memories of the boy be illusory? What if Maria had been illusion all along? He had always thought himself undeserving of such a flawless beauty. Perhaps she had never existed outside the confines of his skull, as real now, in his dreams, as she had ever been.

He put the can down, and knocked it over, watching the fizzing liquid spread through the layer of dust on the table and dribble onto the kitchen floor. What did he know? He knew that time and decay were synonymous. The coke would never unspill itself, regain its already diminishing fizz. He was decaying himself, second by second falling towards death, his mind seeming to rush ahead of him towards its final destination. Maria was the only thing unchanged. Perhaps best if she remained a dream, had always been such, unviolated by the cruel dictates of time. The myth he was retelling, that was inviolate too.

'What is real? My mind? Cogito ergo sum.' Descartes' dictum -- I think, therefore I am -- seemed to be all that could be relied on. Not the thoughts though, only the existence. Descartes had posited the idea of a 'malicious demon of the utmost power and cunning bent on deceiving me in every possible way. Perhaps the sky, the earth, colours, shapes, sounds and all external things are merely the delusions of dreams which he has devised to ensnare my judgement.' This really wasn't helping. The senses, even if they were filtered through a mendacious mind, had to be trusted to some extent, otherwise day to day life would be untenable. And what would be the point of this malicious demon's manipulation? Unless it was to use its manipulated victim to get its message, its story from its own point of view, across. Neil laughed aloud. 'That's it then: I'm the Devil's pawn, he's using me to tell his story. Sympathy for the Devil. Fucks up my mind until the only time I feel remotely sane is when I'm writing of fallen angels and the fall of man. Well fuck you Satan. You're every bit as real as God is. I might be losing my mind but I'm not going romanticise myself. I'm not Satan's biographer; I'm just a man who's lost his way.'

This was what came of pondering on the meditations of a philosopher who'd been dead for more than three and a half centuries.

Just one drink, he suddenly thought, a good stiff one. That'll quell my buzzing brain as good as writing. The world might not make any more sense pissed, but at least the sharp edges will be taken off. And he was up and heading for a cabinet where a good bottle of Irish whiskey waited for him when the phone rang in the other room. Leave it, he told himself, it won't be a real person. He opened the cabinet's door and took down the unopened bottle. The phone was insistent.

'Piss off.' he unscrewed the bottle's top and pressed the rim to his dry lips.

The phone still rang.

'For Christ's sake!' He slammed the bottle down on the draining board, fluid splashing over the vessel's rim and dribbling down the neck. Neil strode to the phone, snatching it up mid-ring. 'hello, you have reached the home of Satan, Prince of Darkness, I'm afraid I'm not home at the moment, out spreading pestilence, walking on the earth and in the earth and all that, so if you'd like to leave a message after the --'

'Very funny, Mr Mann.'

'Oh it's you again. That's just wonderful. Hadn't we decided that you don't exist?'

'Please let's not start with that foolishness again.'

'Come on then, big fellow, my own psycho stalker, tell me what you want.'

'I want you to put the top back on that bottle of whiskey and get back to telling your story.'

'That would have scared me a little while ago, but now I reckon you're my subconscious. I've gone quite mad you see.'

'You're not mad, Mr Mann. You've just found yourself in an altered state of reality.'

'Well I don't fucking like it.'

'Then get back to the story. That will soothe the fever in your mind.'

'So will seventy ccs of Irish whiskey.'

'But alcohol won't return you to your wife.'

He wasn't going to fall for the trap. This was all imagined. His heart wasn't racing in his throat. It wasn't. 'It might. She only visits me in my dreams now. Perhaps she always has.' He felt and heard the tremors in his voice.

'You could be with her again,' the big guy was saying. 'In what you would call the physical world.'

'If she was ever alive, she's dead now,' Neil belched out, the words stinging his throat.

'She lives. Continue with the story and all will become clear.'

'Don't you give me hope, you --'

'Goodbye, Mr Mann.'

In the Garden

The Garden of Man, fecund with life, was walled by life. Access was denied by overgrown thicket, grotesque and wild, an impenetrable barrier that stretched in either direction as far as my eye could discern. Behind the formidable wall I could make out great trees, cedars and pines and firs, and the air was filled with jewel-winged insects and birds of prey and preyed. I skulked in the shade of the barrier, lest there be angelic sentinels posted to watch for me, but I longed to be inside that new paradise, under that hot sun and azure sky, basking in the rays, not cowering in the shade of a wall constructed to keep demons out; or perhaps to keep God's new race in?

There was little life this side of the wall. God's creative seed had not favoured the ground beyond his new kingdom, but a bird, black and sleek with a serpentine neck and vicious bill, alighted on a decrepit tree stump nearby. I took a liking to this fellow's form, his haughty watch. He did not fear me, this one. I cloaked myself in his appearance, assimilating my lance and shield into the feathery garb. Harder by far than the cherub sleight was this, and I would not be able to maintain the trick for long. The origin of my reconfiguration was airborne with a squawk, upset by my mimicry as he had not been by the sight of Satan in all his inglory. I followed his flight up and over the highest reach of the wall, losing him in a moment in a flock of parrots whose plumage surpassed anything I could have imagined. I passed over a river filled with sleek silver salmon, edged with grazing and drinking beasts of every description the mind could conjure. Forestland spread like a verdant carpet to my high eye, and gave way to grasslands where sleek cattle grazed before the living boundary ended paradise far off in all directions. The Creator had surpassed himself in this place. Doubt was assailing me once more. Who was I to trespass into this paradise to try and undermine His great works?

But this new heaven, this happy seat, for angels should have been created. Not for some... experiment. Anger was resurging in me, altering me back to my demonic physiology and I dropped quick into the tallest tree, lush with life, concealing myself amongst the dense foliage and succulent fruits. Here I would wait out this Man. Here I would watch for angelic guard. Here I would plot.

The sun shifted and my tree's shadow lengthened as my heart longed, and as the day cooled I at last caught sight of that pair that I was come to turn to my cause. They walked upright like angels, though there was a crudeness, something bestial and base about their movements as they walked amongst the trees. Wingless they were, perhaps more like God in appearance than were angels, but without his divine countenance, without the blinding glory that could quicken to black rage in an instant. These were simple creatures, the smaller looking the lesser, less muscled, breasts drooping soft, and without its mate's extra appendage. The greater one must be Adam, first among men.

I swooped down, becoming equine as I alighted on the warm earth, disguised so as to draw closer to my prey; as a tiger and as a lion I stalked the pair as they walked in ignorant bliss. They were talking amongst themselves, the language guttural and ugly and simple to my ear. They spoke of Him on high, and they spoke of His glory and of the fruitful garden He had prepared for them before their creation. Adam spoke first, and his mate repeated, by rote, as subservient-seeming to her husband as he was to Yahweh.

Oh these were God's creatures, fawning and pitiable, coached well in subservience. I would coach them in independence, in free thought. They wouldn't be God's puppets by the time I was through. I was a wolf now, circling the pair, and so ignorant were they of their peril, so protected did they feel by their maker, that not a hair raised, not an ear pricked, and they lay on a mossy bank in a shaded glade, and fell asleep in one another's arms, Adam clasping his wife tight as if fearing she might dream herself free of his clutch.

Poor, simple creatures, little more than beasts, but for the rectitude and the speech. They would never become greater under God's oppressive watch; evolution was His great enemy.

The sun was down and the gloaming was spreading through the garden and, feeling less vulnerable to angelic watch, I slunk to the grass as a salamander and made my way to the lesser of the two, whispering in its ear in its own brute language, telling the slumbering mind how its creator was not to be trusted, was to be defied, that such defiance was necessary if the creature and its mate were to blossom. For God was a jealous God and in time their love would drive Him to envy, for was not He alone, unique? They would be unmade by Him that had made them.

Such insinuating seeds would remain in the creature's primal cortex on waking, and would fester and grow there. The first doubts, which I would build upon over time. I would turn now to the greater of the pair and, its mind likely to be greater and more able of conscious thought more easily turned to yearn for knowledge that God would wish to keep it unlearned of, I would inspire its sleeping mind to thoughts of self-government.

But the tip of a spear was laid on my malformed back and no falsehood can endure the touch of celestial temper and I started up, exploding into my true form. The angel Ithuriel stood before me, flanked by Zephon, well armed but with disquiet turned to fear flashing in their eyes.

'Retreat angels,' I said, 'back into the forest, lest you wake God's new children and incur his wrath as did I. I'll come with thee into the shadows. I have no plans to flee your custody, but would fight you willingly, made monstrous strong as I have been.'

With spear and sword outstretched they backed into the shadows and away from Adam and his partner, and I held my word and matched my stride with theirs until we were in the darkness.

'Which of the rebel spirits adjudged to Hell is thee?' spoke Zephon.

Risen scorn made words trip laughing off my tongue. 'Do you not know me? Do you not recognise the light-bearer, Lucifer, for I know you, Zephon, and I know you, Ithuriel that would spear an unguarded angel through his spleen. Lowest of the orders, did you think that even the two of you could best me?'

'We are under no orders to best you, Satan, for that is your title now in Heaven, your original name forbidden,' spoke Ithuriel, brandishing his spear with little resolve, sorrow in his eyes. 'Thou stood in Heaven upright and pure, the greatest of angels. How could you have come to this, malformed and monstrous? This is what your hypocrisy, your vile rebellion hidden somehow even from the all-knowing Almighty, has brought you to.'

Sorrow and sympathy were like waves off this one, and fear, seeming as much for himself as of me. I said: 'Might not God have known of our rebellious purposes? Was He perhaps willing and content to allow my small band to ferment mutiny, so that He could have us crushed and banished by His mighty army, to set "just" example and still forever any further notions of uprising against His tyranny? Is not a small force of freedom fighters standing against dictatorship though they know there is no chance of victory more just and noble than the crushing and cruel "justice" of He who knows all from the beginning to the end of time, He who exists only to be worshipped and never questioned?'

Zephon stepped between us. 'Still your traitorous tongue, Devil. You will not weaken the resolve of my comrade, is that not true, Ithuriel?'

Ithuriel had taken his leave, gone into the shadows. I could hear his gentle sobbing, and my heart softened towards this angel that had hidden his own doubts and traitorous heart so well until my words had uncovered them. I stepped towards the sound of sorrow. I knew what it was to start to think for oneself, to question what has always been deemed unquestionable. It was painful, this revelation. 'Ithuriel,' I spoke, 'you can come with me. Join us, angel. I cannot promise that your treason will go unpunished from on high. But I can promise you a form of freedom.'

'Back, fiend,' snarled simple Zephon, jabbing his blade at my chest, foolishly fearless, small power. 'You have condemned him.'

'I condemn you,' I spat, rage risen. 'I condemn you to be God's dog always.'

I crashed his blade aside with my shield, driving the tip of my lance into his unguarded belly, twisting so that he squealed in agony, head back on a corded neck, crying for aid into the darkened sky. The stars were cold, the risen moon dispassionate.

Then the captain of these two came crashing through the forest canopy, bright and brilliant in his golden armour. Gabriel, arch and mighty, was not the measure of Michael (whom I would secretly have feared confronting again, for he had bettered me in Heaven, though my form had been weaker, slighter then) but still he was a great warrior, having dispatched himself with courage and fortitude on Heaven's battle plain. He alighted beside his fallen underling, golden sword in each grip. I drew my lance from Zephon, bringing forth more cries, the winged form thrashing and bucking on the forest floor.

'Satan! So my guards have discovered the fiend,' said Gabriel. 'And what ills you have delivered unto them. I know your strength and you know mine. But you have weaknesses that riddle no true angel, sly hypocrite that pretends himself patron of liberty. Who was more fawning and cringing to the awful Creator than thee? Traitor.'

'False I may have been, but your God must have known such, for is he not omniscient? Could He not have stemmed my falsehood, turned me back to His cause? And who are you, servile dog, to speak of liberty? Destruction to you and to your God more monstrous by far than I.'

Anger flashed off Gabriel, who would in time become both God's death-dealer and messenger to men, but the archangel knew that his anger was as nothing compared to my impious rage. This sycophant would stand at the Maker's right hand unquestioning of his patron and of his own heart. He who would call me hypocrite and traitor would not even attempt to divine his own essence. I was a traitor to the mighty tyrant; Gabriel was a traitor to himself. I felt infinitely more compassion for lowly Ithuriel who sobbed in the dark forest, felled by his own courage, daring to question his God and his own heart.

Gabriel dashed forwards, swords slicing the night. I blocked with my shield, driving my lance with hot rage at Gabriel's throat. He glanced the spear with a stroke and the tip pierced his armour at the shoulder drawing from him a cry of fear and rage and his sword fell from his right hand as he dropped to one knee, grasping the shaft of my spear and snatching it from my grip. Fallen Zephon clutched at my ankle then, endeavouring to bring me down. I looked down at him with hateful, unpitying eyes, took up Gabriel's fallen sword and, roaring with rage and inner pain, sliced the angel's head clean off with one great stroke.

The garden was still, crickets and toads and owls falling silent as if in reverence to the magnitude of what had just occurred. Weeping Ithuriel had fallen silent. I turned to Gabriel, something akin to apology forming on my lips. He was ashen, and not, I knew, merely from the wound I had inflicted. 'It cannot be,' he managed.

'It is,' I said, apology transforming into resolve. 'Were there none left destroyed on the plain of Heaven after our great battle?'

'None. Many were wounded, some so terribly that ages will pass before they are mended. But such a thing as this... You are more truly damned than ever, Satan. I should flee into eternity if I were you, for the Lord is coming, bent on vengeance for his faithful servant. Can you not feel the heavens of this world tremble at his approach?'

'Indeed I can,' I scowled, 'so I shall leave you for now, leave the dog to its master's attentions. Many thanks for the weapon, I think the swap a profitable one.'

I looked down at Zephon's head, some distance from his still and cooling body. His unseeing eyes were hazing already. Death, this would be called. I was the dark creator of this finishing, made from His dark materials. I raised my sight to the firmament, where thunderbolts were already fizzing, and cried out, tears stinging my eyes: 'Now, I have become a creator of kinds, God Almighty. Perhaps in time I'll become as powerful a maker as you, but never as monstrous. My evils are inconsequential next to yours. Damn you and your pawns.'

The heavens roared and God came roaring, divine countenance warped with black malevolence, cloaked in streaming clouds, thunderbolts flashing from him. I shouldered my shield and scooped up Zephon's unthinking head, hurling it into the centre of the oncoming maelstrom. 'Here is your servant, keep him to your bosom!'

With that I was aloft, beating hard at the heating air, leaving in my wake wounded Gabriel and wretched Ithuriel. Lightning flashed around me as God descended on his spoiled paradise. I heard cries of terror from the Man creatures as I hurtled to the garden's thicket wall, not daring to look over my fleeing shoulder lest His dread image be there. Over the wall and a terrible keening reached my ears, bringing me to the barren earth on the other side of the great barrier: the sound of Ithuriel's physical agony. God was torturing the angel for his lack of faith.

Chapter Five

'Fuck it!' snapped Neil, turning from the screen, angry to his feet. He had crashed back into himself, images of angels fighting the Devil in a prehistoric Eden snatched from his mind, replaced by thoughts of wives and car crashes. 'This is shit. Bullshit. Writing fairy tales isn't going to bring Maria back. She probably never fucking existed. No boy and no mother. And certainly no fucking big guy. Just my collapsing brain. Nothing else: that's the whole universe.

'Oh stop romanticising yourself yet again, you stupid bastard. Get yourself a drink. Perhaps take some pills. You deserve it. You are so very tired.'

Arguing with himself aloud Neil had passed to the cabinet, had unconsciously opened the bottle of whiskey. The phone rang, and he laughed, pressing the rim of the bottle to his lips and gulping. Too much, choking, peristalsis gone into reverse, whiskey searing up his nose. Still laughing, eyes watering, he snorted whiskey into the sink. 'Better get myself a glass. Greedy sod.'

The phone was still ringing. 'The sound's in my head. This is my brain struggling to prevent its own obliteration by fabricating this massive delusion of muscle boys with supernatural powers and wives come back from beyond the grave all intent on me writing some pulp-fiction bollocks story of Satan.'

He went to the phone nonetheless; imaginary or not the sound was bloody intrusive. Perhaps a bit of wanton vandalism would silence it. He grabbed the phone, hurling it across the room, cable breaking, phone smashing into far wall, falling dissembled to the carpet, a crack in the plaster where the collision had occurred. Quiet.

'That's better.' He wasn't about to question whether because hurling the machine had silenced it or if it had really been ringing. Such things were beyond his concern. He took up a tumbler, filled it, strangled the bottle in his left hand and went back into his writing room where the little red devil screen saver he'd found winked from the monitor.

Neil raised his glass to the imp, lowering himself into his

armchair. 'Salute, my friend.'

He downed the glassful in one caustic gulp and choked another out of the bottle. A phone was ringing somewhere. Muted by distance, once it had invaded his consciousness Neil felt his ire pricked and rising. Probably a neighbour's. But what a time to call. He looked at his wall clock: one in the morning. Still the ringing went on. Another glass. Good, that was better. If the sound was in his brain then the invading intoxication was muffling it somewhat. 'Forgot my pills,' he slurred. The liquor was working on him at a tremendous rate; but then he was so damn tired. He forced himself upright, sloshing alcohol in his lap. 'Clumsy twat. You look like you pissed yourself.'

To the kitchen, setting the half-emptied tumbler on the draining-board. He rummaged in cupboards for tablets, found a half-pack of aspirin and a full blister of paracetamol. If he took the lot and then piled the bottle of whiskey on top, would that be enough to quiet his brain for good? Still he could hear the distant phone.

'One way to find out.' Neil began popping pills from their compartments, making a pile on the worktop. 'You don't really want to do this, do you?' He took a gulp from the glass. The phone was still ringing, seeming to have got louder again, surely no more than a room or so away. 'Yes, you do.' He grabbed up the pills and crammed them into his mouth, charging them down his gullet with a gulp of fire, slamming the emptied glass onto the draining board, inspiring a hairline crack.

'Done now. If Maria's waiting on the other side then I'll be with her very soon; if there is nothing after life then I'll sleep an eternal and peaceful sleep, and where can the evil be in that?' Oh dog, he was paraphrasing Socrates now. He clutched the cracked tumbler -- 'More hemlock' -- and headed back to his seat beside the bottle. More booze. Just before he finished the bottle, Neil dopily considered ringing for an ambulance. 'But you broke the phone.' And he was laughing and crying, pissing himself and not caring, not the least uncomfortable. 'You broke the phone and killed yourself.' He swallowed the last of the whiskey direct from the bottle, struggling to stand on a floor gone oblique. 'Ah,' he slapped his forehead as a seemingly important revelation found him, 'there's a phone in the garage. I could call an ambulance from there... or I could open another bottle.'

The floor was pulled from under him, and he crashed down, cracking his head on the corner of a coffee table, lost to consciousness and unaware that his blood was spreading across the carpet.

Sunlight was streaming into the room, filtered through the haze that clouded Neil's gradually waking eye, the effect tricking him for a while that he was in the afterlife, the light that seemed at the end of an amorphously shifting tunnel where all knowledge and his wife and child waited for him. But the recognisably mundane throb at his brow chased that particular fancy away.

'Should be dead,' he groaned, and tasted vomit, found the carpet-fallen side of his face wet and clammy. 'Oh you are disgusting, a pathetic creature.' He rolled on to his back and sat up, firecrackers going off in his skull, vision focusing. What a bloody mess, literally. His body's fluids mingled on the carpet and dried on his face. The coppery scent of blood mingled with the acidic stench of puke threatened nausea in him once more. He was on his feet, clutching his belly and his head and stumbling for the bathroom, vaguely aware that an insistent sound was struggling to pierce the fog that cloaked his pained brain.

The bathroom mirror showed him the full extent of his depravity. He wiped with a wetted flannel, ignoring the hurt that the wetted fabric inspired. A little better. In fact his eyes were reasonably clear, not bloodshot as he had come to expect after waking from his continuous nights of excess. 'I threw up my hemlock,' he said to the mirror. 'My oversensitive gut saved my life.'

His hand went to the cut on his brow that had bled so copiously. Strange, it looked such a small wound compared to the gash he would have anticipated, and already it appeared to be scabbing. Strange. Had he perhaps slept through a full day and night, perhaps longer, giving his flesh a chance to start healing? He ran a hand through his cropped hair -- that wasn't actually that cropped any more. Jesus, had he been in some kind of a mini-coma? And his bald patch didn't feel quite as bald, not the warm and unadorned stretch of skin he was used to meeting with his fingertips. And that insistent sound was penetrating into his consciousness. He shrugged it off, scrambling through the medicine cabinet until he located a little circular mirror that he knew to be there. He held it over his crown, reflected in the main mirror. 'No way. I'm cured.' There was no naked patch. The hair was thinner than that which surrounded it, but there was no pale pate. 'A bang on the head can't cure baldness, can it?'

The sound.

Neil dropped the little mirror in the sink, attention turning from the apparent regrowth at his scalp to the sound of the bloody phone that had apparently been ringing since last night. He went to the west wall, pressing his ear to the plaster, striving to ignore the throbbing at his head. Louder. Couldn't be next door though: the houses were detached, a screen of trees separating them.

Downstairs, and he was to the west wall there. Yes, the source of the sound was definitely near. But what lay beyond this wall? He knew immediately, and the thought sickened him. The garage. The telephone in the garage was ringing. Had been all night. He couldn't go in that place, couldn't contemplate the dark and dank emptiness where the Jag had used to reside. Let the fucking thing ring.

Lilith

In a desiccated copse blasted by this world's fierce sun I took refuge, folding myself under a warped and crooked trunk with the bugs and worms whose company I deserved. My enterprise had failed at the first. Now that I was discovered, God would surely extend his cruel arm to smite my unguarded and unwarned colleagues in Hell. Once more my hubris had brought about their doom. I had planted mere seeds in the minds of the lesser creature, which the Almighty would extract and blight with thoughtless ease. The greater of the couple, favoured Adam, I had not even had chance to touch with my pernicious intent.

The air was cooled around me, the planet's moon painting all but my darkest recess silver, the sounds of the storm no longer reaching my ears from Eden. In despair I shivered and wondered over my fate. Would He search me out, or leave me in abject despair? Return to the rebels was no option, for His fate would follow and I would summon their destruction even more utterly than I already had. Some new plan must inform me, to save my angels. I should return to the garden, prostrate myself before God and his sentinels, invite this new thing that I was founder of, this death, upon myself. I should and would.

I crawled from my shelter, lost to myself and to hope and as I straightened and spread my sails my senses flared, perceiving a creature nearby, sentient and asleep. I tasted its dreams, strange tumblings of desires I had no understanding or experience of. My despair on arriving in this forsaken place had masked its mind from mine, but now on becoming aware of it, I was confounded, for its mind was greater by far than what I had tasted in the man who was supposedly favoured of God. It was no angel, this creature, but there were traces of divinity in it, evidence of the Maker's hand.

I left behind Gabriel's sword and my mighty shield and glided low to where the creature slumbered, alighting trembling beside where it lay in its fretful unconsciousness in the bough of a fire-blackened tree. It was like the lesser Man, the one I would shortly come to know as Eve, but perfected, naked and lean. Body as pale as marble, hair, silver in the moon's light, coiled in a lustrous rope about its rounded and sheened breasts, its nipples erect and inspiring confused thoughts I did not understand in my overwhelmed mind. My eye dropped to the triangle of fur between its legs, the scent from there rising to my flared nostrils, rousing a fire in me that was confounding. This creature was the shape of awful goodness, a thing whose sight alone was near enough to undo me. And now it was waking.

I shifted form in an instant, becoming something like the rousing creature, something like the Adam in the garden, something like myself before the fall. Face of an angel, form of a man, wingless. Quick, the creature's lids flickering now, I drew from the ether and from the naked mind of Adam an appendage at my groin such as he had possessed, down to the last nerve and fibre with the appropriate accompaniments; and the damn thing was twitching erect even as it was formed.

The creature was awake now, sitting up in its bough, hair falling to its waist, revealing the perfection of its breasts. Shades of sleep cleared from its silver eyes that betrayed no fear, only bemused curiosity. And it spoke, its tone as sweet as an angel's: 'What manner of creature is this that finds me in my sanctuary?' Its eyes found my aching groin and a smile found its eyes and lips. 'That comes to me so enamoured?'

I saw neither the need nor sense of artifice. 'I am the angel, Lucifer,' I said, a flush rising over my mask, 'fallen from on high, condemned by the Almighty.'

The smile faded and something like wonder passed over its features. 'You are he: the outlaw; the grand villain? You inspired an army against Jove, disobeyed the Creator?'

'I did.' I bowed my head, awaiting condemnation. But it laid a hand on my chest, as if to feel the beat of my heart and ascertain my veracity. The organ at my groin was stealing the blood from my brain at such a rate that I could not find my way into the creature's mind.

'You are magnificent,' it said. 'Now throw off this pretty disguise and show me your full glory. I heard you were a mighty dragon, fearsome to behold.'

I was disbelieving yet ecstatic. How things had turned in a few moments. My companions waiting in Hell were forgotten. Even God was forgotten. 'This is less than disguise: this is like

I looked in Heaven, yet there I bore wings.'

It was scornful now, the notion of timidity not occurring to its haughty mind. 'I know angels, and they are a sexless troop. You have the cock of a man, ready to spit. If you be Lucifer, reveal your dragon form. Show me Satan in all his glory.'

'I will not. God crafted me monstrous for my mutiny. I will not display horror in the face of such beauty. As to this,' I bowed to that which the creature had named cock, 'I should tear this thing off, for it befuddles the mind and inspires passions that consume and burn.'

It laughed. 'So you find yourself at the mercy of your engorged sex, has did Adam. Perhaps you should not have foisted an ape's attribute upon yourself.'

'Ape?'

'Jove's new playthings. Adam and Eve. The altered apes.'

Confusion on confusion. 'But they are Man, God's favoured new creations.'

It snorted its derision. 'Man and woman He would name them, Adam and Eve. Apes to me.'

'And what manner of creature would you call yourself?'

Pride flashed from it. 'I am She, Lilith. The first woman. God made me from the dirt and dust of this world to be the wife of the ape. He took the one He named Adam from his troop of crooked apes out on the parched plains, brought him to Eden.'

'For what purpose?'

'To mould him into the father of mankind and faithful and unquestioning servant of the Almighty. Jove did not create Adam, He merely straightened his bowed spine so that he could raise his face in due reverence to the heavens. Then He taught the ape-man rudimentary language so that he could learn of and disseminate the Almighty's glory. God lied to Adam, told him that He had created him from naught, stole the ape's memory of its careless and free life with its troop, and taught it all His names, from Jove to Yahweh, Jehovah to Zeus.'

I dropped from the bough to the earth, utterly confounded. My form was shifting, monstrous reality threatening to assert itself. Perhaps that was the design in this Lilith's lies. Had she not stated that she wished me to reveal my winged dragon form? I would not let her best me and resolved my disguise firmer around me, the effort of which forced my unminded cock into a flaccid state.

Lilith dropped to the ground beside me, unwilling to give me quarter. I would not look to her and risk the arousal of one organ to the detriment of the higher one; but her vision was in my mind anyhow, inflaming my blood.

'You lie,' I spoke. 'God would not take a beast and shape it. He would create Man from fresh to rule over this world.'

Her breath was warm on my face as she leaned in close to my ear. 'He created me from fresh; and I was a great disappointment to Him.'

I wheeled on her, anger rising. 'What use would God have in lying to an animal? God would not lie. He is infallible.' So confounded was I by her words that I had fallen to my enemy's defence.

She met my sight, and her risen anger was the equal of mine. 'He would lie to an animal because it would be more malleable, less prone to question. Why do you call Him infallible, Him that I know to be nothing of the sort, hateful and hated creator? Why do you think Him so great that bested and broke your mob on Hell's fiery waters and unyielding rocks?'

I felt my girth increase, muscles rippling, sails unfurling. I could not undo the revelation, and had no wish to do so, such was my rage. 'I have to think Him infallible and great,' I roared into her unflinching face, 'because He bested and broke my mob.'

Anger bled from me then and I looked to the silvered floor, ashamed at having revealed my demonic form. 'Do you not see?'

'I see,' she spoke soft and sweet. 'It is pride that fires you so, wounded by my scorn towards Jove that He is not without fault and yet still bested you and your devils.'

'As you like.'

'Satan?'

I maintained my sight earthward. 'Yes?'

'Look at me.'

'I shan't. I am ashamed.'

'There is no need of shame. You are magnificent, beautiful.'

'You mock me.'

'Look to me, and then decide if I mock.' She spoke from a different position than before.

'I will not.' I had become churlish, and loathed this new

quality. Who was she to make me so degraded? I looked to her. Lilith had lain herself down on the earth. She was bathed in the moon's silver watch, lustrous hair spread round her perfect face like a halo. One hand fondled a breast, the other slid to between her legs where fingers had entered the wetness there. She was smiling.

'I see your newfound manhood survived the metamorphosis. Does it ache so?'

'It does.'

'Then come to me, and let me teach you how a woman would relieve such an ache.'

Blindness threatened, so intense was my ardour. I dropped to one knee, lowering my great form over hers that was now diminutive in comparison. She took my cock in her hand and it seemed that it had become my source and I cried out. She pressed her other hand, the one that had been inside her to my loathsome face, to my lips. I tasted her juice and found the flavour sublime as she guided me into her, moving gently beneath me, gripping and releasing my organ with consummate care and skill. I had no control that first time, and my first thrust undid me and I roared as pure sensation overwhelmed me, terrifying in its intensity.

From the direction of Eden, off to the West, thunder rumbled in response.

My senses came back to me, seemingly heightened. I looked into Lilith's silvery eyes, seeking and dreading some response from her. The act of physical love was new to me, but she was clearly adept, and I instinctively knew that more was expected of me. 'I am sorry,' I whispered.

She was shaking her head, smiling sadly. 'There is naught to be sorry for.' She kissed my face. 'You have never known true pleasure before, have you, you poor creature? I will show you, teach you love, if you wish me to.'

'I wish it.' My voice was a broken thing.

Lilith wrapped her slender arms as best she could around my massive torso, pulling me tight to her with surprising strength, whispering in my ear. 'Do not fear that you will damage me. I have suffered brutalities that one such as you could not conceive of. I escaped the garden but was alone and lost; now I have found one as damned as am I. Shall we not take comfort in one another?'

'We shall.'

Chapter Six

Ahh, bless those crazy kids. He hadn't realised he was writing a bloody love story. Neil spun from the screen. And still he could hear the damn phone ringing. 'Oh fuck it! Come on then you big twat, let's listen to what you have to say, you non-existent fucker.'

He was through to the back door, grabbing a bunch of keys from their seating, glancing a blow on the washing machine that should raise a bruise on his thigh but he was unmindful of the hurt. Out into the yard and before the recessed garage. The ringing was louder, clearer out here. Didn't make it any more real. 'I'm coming in you big bastard. I'm going to rip that phone off the wall without even listening to your voice, you fucking hallucination.'

'Are you all right?'

'Jesus--' Neil started and fumbled the bunch of keys from his grip. He turned to the speaker. The flushed and friendly bespectacled face of his neighbour blinked at him from over his garden wall.

'I'm sorry. I didn't mean to startle you. It's just that... well I was sitting out in the garden, it being such a lovely day, thinking of doing myself a spot of lunch, when I heard you, uh, talking.'

'I do that,' said Neil. 'It's how I sketch out plots, work through dialogue, that sort of thing.'

The neighbour was frowning. 'Plots, dialogue, are you some sort of a writer?'

'Neil Mann? Shylock's Curse?'

The man looked nonplussed. 'I'm sorry. I'm not much of a reader. Tom Clancy on a beach is about the sum of my literary aspiration.'

And why should he know who the pretentious prick next door was, the nutter who talked to himself? The two men had been neighbours for dog knew how long and Neil had offered this owlish, kind-looking person nothing more than a curt good evening or morning in all that time, despite the neighbour's forcefully cheery attempts to engage him in conversation. He didn't even know the man's name; why should he expect the man to know his?

Neil pressed his left hand over the wall. The neighbour flinched, as if expecting to be struck.

Neil smiled and said: 'Forgive my rudeness. We've been neighbours for so long and I've not introduced myself. Neil Mann.'

The neighbour grinned and reddened, grasping Neil's hand firmly in his own, pumping his forearm. 'Leonard Thomas. An author, hey? What are you working on at the moment?'

The hand was dropped. 'I haven't written for a while. Since my wife died, the words seem to have dried up.' Liar, liar, you've never written so much so fast. The words might be crap but they're gushing out like diarrhoea.

'I'm so, so sorry,' stumbled Leonard. 'I didn't know, had no idea. I saw your wife a few times when you first moved in here; she was very beautiful. When I didn't see her again I assumed...'

'That she'd left me. Run off with someone better looking.'

'No, please, I didn't mean to...'

'It's okay,' said Neil. And it really was. Poor Leonard looked mortified though. 'I'm glad you saw her. She was very beautiful and we loved each other very much. It's really good to hear you say you saw her, because I've been having a really hard time recently, something like a breakdown I suppose, and I was starting to doubt that my Maria had ever existed.' He was surprised to feel tears pricking, amazed that the sensation felt so good. 'I've been imagining such things.' Spilling his heart to a virtual stranger. This wasn't him.

'You poor man. Why don't you come round for a brandy, have a good chat all about it? If you think it might help.'

Neil laughed, palming a tear from his cheek. 'You know, it might. But I'd prefer tea to brandy. I'm afraid I've developed something of a drink problem of late.'

'Tea it'll be.'

Neil nodded. 'Thank you. I'll be with you shortly. Just need to get in this garage, pick up the damn incessant phone.'

The owl frowned. 'Is that where the sound's coming from? Oh my, how odd. It's being going on all night, you know. Is it some kind of a fault?'

Neil was straightening up, having retrieved the bunch of

keys from the dirt, was sorting through for the correct one. 'I don't think so,' he said, distractedly. 'I think it's one insistent son of a bitch imaginary bastard on the other end of the line.'

Leonard flinched, reddening.

'Oh, I am sorry,' said Neil, realising how he must have sounded, 'I'm really not insane.' Hope to fuck I'm not, anyhow, he silently added. 'Leonard, why don't you go in and put the kettle on and I'll be round in a moment; soon as I've sorted this silly little business? Ah, this is the key.'

Leonard was turning from the wall when the thought struck Neil: what if I can test my sanity, with a witness present? 'Leonard, oh Leonard?' The man's affected manner of speaking was infectious, like a thick accent. 'You wouldn't come into the garage with me would you, pick up the phone and see if the caller will speak with you.'

'Well, I... I...' the owl was stumbling.

'I know how crazy I must sound, but a man's been calling me and making threats.'

'Threats, good God,' Leonard was back to the wall, eyes flashing inquisitive behind thick lenses, 'Why haven't you gone to the police?'

'Ah, the threats are somewhat vague. This man is very careful, very circumspect.'

Leonard was rubbing his fleshy lips with the back of his hand. For the first time Neil noticed the broken capillaries round the man's nose. Like the brandy don't you, Mr Thomas? he thought. Unconsciously his own hand went to his face, as if feeling for similar tell-tale signs. The owl was swaying, as if unsure of how to proceed, and who could blame him?

'There's another thing,' said Neil, quite honestly.

'Another?'

'This garage used to house the car that my wife and son died in. I haven't been able to face going into the place since the crash, even though it's empty.' He tried to choke out a laugh that snagged behind his tonsils. 'I feel as though I might open the door and the ghost of the car will be there, waiting for me in the dark.' Perhaps with Maria and the boy still inside, his brain added but he stilled his tongue before it could transfer from organ to muscle. He didn't want to scare Mr Thomas away; he really didn't want to go into the garage on his own.

'You poor man. Of course I'll come with you. Just one moment.' And the man was scurrying to his gate, almost over-eager in his enthusiasm to be of aid. Strange this one, thought Neil. Friendly enough though, certainly that.

Leonard Thomas was through the gate to Neil's yard and at his side. He lay a chubby-fingered hand on Neil's shoulder. 'Ready? I'll be right here. At your side. I can go in ahead if you like?'

Neil shrugged off the hand, almost snapping at his neighbour: 'No, I'll be fine. Just... just... just stay close.' He turned the key, rotated the handle and pulled. The garage door groaned on its axis, flakes of dust dancing like dirty motes in the cavernous gape revealed. The volume of the ringing phone had risen as the barrier had. Very real. Anyway, Mr Thomas could hear it, and Mr Thomas was surely real.

Neil peered into the darkness of the long double garage that had appeared inkily impenetrable brief seconds ago but that his eyesight was adjusting to swiftly. And there was a shape in the blanching blackness, congealing into the sleek-lined automobile that Neil had seen smashed and scrapped. The ghost he had feared was waiting for him. And what would be waiting in the interior? Rain-wetted leather? Broken-necked Maria? The boy with his ruined head? A cry escaped Neil. Leonard Thomas lightly grasped his right arm just above the elbow and Neil started.

'Can you see it, Mr Thomas? Leonard, can you see my car?'

'Yes.'

'It doesn't exist you see. Not anymore.'

Neil reached to his left where he knew there to be a light switch, and in the electric dazzle the Jag glinted its incontrovertible solidity, undamaged and empty, the only blemish on its flawless skin a thin coating of dust.

'Leonard, could you answer the telephone, please?'

Wordlessly the neighbour relinquished his hold on Neil and padded to the wall-mounted phone on the far side of the garage. 'What would you like me to say?' he asked, lifting the handset.

'I'd just like to know that you can hear someone on the other end of the line, that I haven't gone totally crazy.' He couldn't tear his watch from the intact automobile that seemed to be mocking him with its presence.

'Hello?' said Leonard into the phone, and a moment later,

'He says he wants to talk to you about your book: A History of The Devil.'

'Ask him who he is?' intoned Neil, his voice sounding as if dead to his own ear.

Leonard asked the question. 'He says his name is Michael.'

Was there something like fear in the owl's voice? At last Neil snatched his sight from the car and looked to his neighbour. Indeed the man was shaking and sweating.

'What's wrong, Leonard? Jesus, you look like you're about to piss yourself.'

Leonard was holding the phone out and away from him as far as his extended short arm would allow. 'Please speak to him Neil, you must. Please.'

Neil walked towards Leonard. 'What is it? Do you know this man, this Michael?'

'Know him? Of course I know him!' the owl practically screamed. 'Oh, you've got to do what he says. He's dangerous. So very dangerous.'

Neil reached and angrily snatched the phone from his neighbour, who looked to be genuinely in the extremis of terror. 'Hello, Michael, if that is your name.'

'It is Mr Mann. It has been my name for all of time.'

More nonsense, and spoken in a voice that was anything but menacing, childlike and reedy as it was. Leonard must have seen the size of the guy to be so reduced, must surely have been threatened by this Michael. 'Whatever, Mikey. Listen I don't give a flying fuck what you think you're going to achieve by these games. Did you get the car in the garage somehow? Nice work. What for though? What could you possibly hope to achieve by such an elaborate trick? And what the hell did you do to Mr Thomas to scare him so bad, you psychotic bastard?'

'Scare him? Ah, he's been scared all his time, follower of the worm.'

'I'm going to the police, the moment I hang up this phone.'

Silence for a moment. Had he unnerved the bastard? And then: 'You can't do that?'

'Why the fuck not?'

'Because you won't allow yourself. Because deep down you know that the apes will tell you that you don't exist; and neither do I for that matter.'

The apes! Oh Christ, this was like being back in Eden. Was

everyone in on his internal craziness. 'Just leave me alone. Leave Leonard alone. If I hear from you again I will go to the cops, tell them all I know, whether I exist or not. Let this be an end to it.'

'The end will come about, amen, once you have finished your history. Back to work on the tale, Mr Mann, there is so much more to tell. You know your mind is itching to return to the Devil and his dam.'

Neil wrenched the handset from its seating, hurled it to the floor where it cracked and silenced. This was on the way to becoming telephone genocide. He turned to Mr Thomas. The poor man had great and wretched tears rolling over his flushed cheeks. 'Leonard, the man on the other end of the phone is crazy and seems to have some kind of vendetta against me. You've obviously met him, and he's intimidated you somehow -- look at you, you're scared almost out your skin -- probably to get at me. He may well be dangerous. We need to go to the police. You can tell them everything you know.'

An emotion somewhere between anger and disgust shaded the owl's wide face. 'No, never. How could you consider such a thing? No, you must do whatever Michael said you must do.'

'He told me to carry on writing the book I'm fucking writing,' Neil suddenly roared, frustrated rage suddenly tearing free in him. 'A book he seems to know more about than I do! And you, you little shit, you're in on this somehow, this bloody game, aren't you?' The rage was unstoppable, redding his sight. Oh, he could kill in this state. Mr Thomas was turning, attempting to flee, the poor fearful fool. Neil saw his left hand, as if of its own volition, shoot out, a cuff snatching back from his wrist, his hand catching hold of the owl's nape, pulling the little man back towards him and then fairly hurling him across the garage with a cry that he wouldn't have thought his own if it hadn't been so crazed and terrible.

Leonard Thomas slammed into the Jag with force terrible enough to make the sound of his ribs' shattering audible; force enough to break the driver's side window and cobweb the windscreen. Leonard staggered away from the cartoonish man-shaped indent he had left in the flank of the car, turned like a marionette with twisted strings. Neil saw the terrible thing he had done. Leonard's chest was caved in, his shirt wet and dark, his breath hitched and desperate. Blood pooled at the bottom of eyes that regarded the madman-become-murderer with something terribly like pity; the pools overflowed, become terrible tears.

Leonard Thomas pitched forward onto his face and lay still on the hard and cold garage floor.

Neil's mind was a thing that had deserted him. He thought he might laugh; he did not laugh.

'That's that then,' he heard himself say, with no idea why. He thought he might weep, weep until the tears washed away any memory of whoever he had thought himself to be. He did not weep.

Neil left the garage, switching off the light and locking the door behind him.

Volume One

Lilith's Tale

Sweet days passed with Lilith in that region that man would come to know as Mesopotamia: the cradle of civilization. We had travelled far from Eden, wishing to distance ourselves from the tyrant's almighty grasp, and had settled on the banks of the Euphrates where we caught fishes and bathed and fucked. Lilith taught me well the arts of love. I, a willing and adept pupil. That time was the happiest I had known, even more than when I was in the Lord's favour in Heaven.

But such times of joy are not for the lasting. Lilith was a restless creature with a vengeful heart and a mind of fire and rage.

When seven sunrises had passed at the river that dread but anticipated time came that I must stir myself to action once more. I lay beside her on the bank, spent inside her sweat-sheened form, and saw the way her sight became distant, her mind unfurling. I tried to speak, to still her tongue, for I sensed, read in the folds of her complex brain, that lazy contentment was at an end.

'We do not speak, you and I,' she said at last, focusing her grey eyes on mine.

'We speak much, Lilith.'

She smiled coldly. 'We speak of eating and fucking. Whenever I open my mouth with serious intent you slip in a succulent fruit, or your cock.'

I held my tongue; the joke was not one intended to raise a laugh.

'Physical pleasuring will only suffice for a short while, the mind will scheme its will to the surface, vengeful thoughts will overpower the pleasures until they must be acted upon.'

'I know.' Reluctantly.

'Then what of your comrades, the demons waiting for the return of the braggart Satan swooping into Hell with triumphal roars after bringing about the fall of God's new playthings?'

'But I failed in that. As for the demons, I only can hope that they are safe in Pandemonium, that Beelzebub is governing wisely and that Jehovah deems them not fit of his cruel inten-

59

tions.'

Passion flashed in Lilith's eyes as she raised herself to a crouch, become bestial. 'Great Satan, do not become some lovelorn sop. Too many of your energies have you pressed into love's service, and with great effect; but now you must resume your mission.'

I stood up, dark anger, an emotion that had of late become alien to me, pressing behind my eyes. 'I failed. There will now be angels posted all around the garden. It is futile.'

'Such craven whining,' she spat, disgust contorting her lovely features. 'Look what has become of the great dragon in so short a time. Do you reckon I don't see you taking on the shape of the pretty man that you first came to me as? Think I don't see you preening in the rock pools?'

'I must disguise myself.'

'It is not you, Lucifer.'

'It could be.'

'No, it could not!' She was screaming now. 'What you truly are is what you are when you spit your seed in my cunt, when you roar and beat your scaled wings. You were beautiful once, but now you are the Devil, the anti-God, and you have no need of beauty, for you can be great and powerful, the usurper of Jove.'

I did beat my wings now, in ire. 'See how she dismisses beauty with so casual a tongue, she whom angels and men would kill to lay with? See the bitch with the warm flesh and cold heart that would seduce her lover into mercenary action against her creator. Why does she hate Him so? She never existed under His tyranny in lost Heaven that had not the lustre of Eden, the garden that He laid at her feet. She claims past hardships, but she has been served and worshipped as a goddess. That poor ape, Adam: how you must have abused so simple a creature.'

She came at me, snarling and lashing with her nails. I caught her wrists, holding my throat from her gnashing teeth, her risen tears spotting my chest.

'Bastard! Fucking bastard! You don't know what that ape did to me.'

I thrust her away from me. She sat down heavily, sobbing. There was no pity in me at that moment, only contempt. 'Then tell me, tell me of the terrible ordeal of being Adam's mate.'

She began slowly, words coming between sobs and then flowing, and my rage at her diminished as that same emotion surged at the ape and its maker.

'At the first I would not lay under Adam. He was lousy and stank. The brain that Jove had nurtured in his sloping skull had given him enough sense to ferment fruits into some vile wine and he would become intoxicated and beat me and try to force himself into me. But his drunkenness made him impotent and that made him enraged and he would beat me more. Often he would crack my skull, lay me unconscious, piss over my fallen form. But I was made from the dust of this world and cannot die, and my bones and flesh heal fast, and soon my broken body would be mended and ready for Adam's next onslaught.

'At last I went to Jove, for in those long days He would walk in the garden of an evening, and I begged Him to release me from my covenant with Adam. He told that I was to be the fecund mother of a nation and that I must lay beneath Adam and let his seed grow in me, for Adam had dominion over me as he did over all beasts and fowls of the air. I told that Adam was incapable of the act, because of the wine he imbibed. Jove said He would turn Adam's wine into water, but that if I showed further disobedience to my husband I would be driven out of Eden, beyond the walls of which this world was blasted and barren.

'That night I let the ape come into me. And the night after and after. And I got with child and then Adam withdrew, had no passion for me. Jove let his water become wine once more, and the brute spent most of the days in a stupor leaving me at peace, content at having a child growing in my belly.

'I gave birth in the evening. A beautiful daughter. She looked like me. There looked to be none of the ape in her. Adam was filled with fury, raged that the baby was not his, that it must be destroyed. I fled to Jove, pleaded for His protection. He tore my daughter from my breast and tossed her before Adam who stamped out her brains in the dust.'

Lilith came to a shuddering halt in the telling of her tale, her head between her knees. I reached out to her, pulling her close, fighting down the threat of my own tears. 'And God drove you out of Eden for your disobedience,' I whispered.

She looked to me and she seemed as a child would, lost and needing comfort. 'Why did He give my daughter to the ape,

Lucifer?'

I sighed. 'Oh, Lilith, who would know the mind of God? Perhaps he wished to punish you for not giving Adam a child that was enough of an ape. Perhaps it just amused Him to see his creation broken. Maybe He had grown afraid of you with your complex mind and beauty and wanted a reason to drive you out of Eden.'

'He made me this way,' she snarled, as if wishing she were made monstrous like me.

'And so He took for Adam a female of his own species, that might bear him goodly ape children with minds simple enough not to question their God. You were a mistake, Lilith; a success because you were too well realised.' I kissed her forehead, her wetted cheeks. 'I shall return to Eden and wreak vengeance there, for you and for me and for my band of rebels.'

'I will come with you,' she said, sounding stronger. 'My wiles will be of use in getting you past the angelic guard. Even the unmanned have lustful minds; I shall perhaps be enough of a distraction to cause one of them to grow himself a mammalian cock as you did.'

I laughed. 'Sweet Lilith, your beauty could tempt God himself.'

Neil laughed, as the Devil had laughed, on the screen and in his mind. Laughing while his neighbour lay dead in his garage. 'That's that then. It's all over.' He held out the hands that had propelled the owl with such improbable force at the car that didn't exist -- the car that didn't exist that had yielded as the man had crumpled and broken against its frame. 'Not long now. I'll soon be in a secure environment, on enough drugs to blot out all thought, or to show me what's real: wife; boy; car; neighbour; big guy. That's that then.' He felt detached from everything but the computer screen and the story it told. Perhaps he was in shock. It seemed that murder could be quite traumatic. 'Just write a little more,' he mused. 'Might be my last chance.'

The Fall of Man

Uriel was guarding the East gate that Lilith had led us to within watch of. The dullard should be easy to outwit again I reasoned. I wondered who had replaced him on sentry watch at the sun: liable to be the wounded Gabriel.

I turned to my partner. 'I shall cloak myself, as if in mist, so as to obscure the fool's perception. As I shift, you draw his attention in whatever way you think fit.'

She smiled, all coquette, and we kissed.

Lilith stepped from behind the screen of blasted branches that sheltered us from the sentinel's hawk eye and strode across the earth towards the become fretful archangel.

'Who comes hither?' he cried out, his voice reedy. I looked to his clothed loin, wondering what complexifications of the flesh my naked lover was inspiring there.

'Uriel, regent of the sun,' she spoke, her voice strong and imperious. 'I am surprised to see one such as you engaged in such a lowly duty as guarding.'

'I am on watch for the great fiend, Satan.'

'Oh, does he exist? I thought him naught but a tale.'

'He does exist. I have crossed him myself, disguised as a cherub, and he was much the worse for the encounter.'

The brazen lie, that would have once inspired rage in me, now raised only a smile and, cloaking myself in dewy reflection, I passed across the earth to the gate, avoiding Uriel's engaged eye, and slipped into Eden once more.

The place was as wondrous fecund as I recalled. I slipped my cloak and trod dewy grass, watchful and wary. We had chosen morning for the ingress, as Lilith said that Jehovah was wont to visit His garden in the evening. Birds were abroad and noisy. I caught sight of my old friend the cormorant, sunning himself on a branch, and he regarded me with a disdainful eye.

I flew low, betwixt the trees, so as not to draw myself attention, lest angelic guards be in the vicinity. Best be sure I have Man to myself, I thought, though I would have surely discerned if minds of my old kind were nearby.

I came across Eve almost by accident, not discerning her

stunted mind until almost upon her, and what fear my undisguised appearance would have roused in her. The she-ape, the
woman, was bathing at the edge of a still pool where lurked
crocodiles that were of no danger to her, such was God's will.
Something was of menace to her though, for she was dabbing
tenderly and with much wincing at cuts and contusions at her
upper arms and sagged breasts. I felt a sudden sympathy for
this poor creature, torn from her tribe to be wife to a brute edu-
cated by a monster. Eve stopped abruptly in her cleansing, become nervous, agitated. I alighted, diminishing my form.

She was off through the trees and I followed with oblique
tract. At brief length she came to where her husband reposed,
snoring, his insensate form shaded beneath a broad-boughed
and fruitful tree. A crudely fashioned clay pitcher lay cracked
beside his heavy-browed head, what was left of its contents,
purple and noxious-scented, running into the earth. A like-
coloured drool descended from the corners of his full lips. He
grunted in his restless slumber, jerking, brow creasing, tormented by dark dreams in his overtaxed ape-mind.

Eve sat in the dirt beside her mate, in the shade of the tree
which bore the succulent fruits that he distilled his liquor from.
She watched her mate with hatred that was as discernible to my
eye as to my probing mind. Poor creature, dreaming of the
plains and her kin, snatched here to be dam to this beast, rudimentary language forced into her pained mind. How she reviled her husband; and his master. She sought out prettiness,
eager eye finding a bejewelled butterfly wing, the opulent
scales of a painted lizard. Such simple sights pleased her, de-
tracted from the ugliness of her existence. She gasped at an
azure-winged dragonfly with the span of a dove.

I could do better, so much better, than God's nature, I the
arch manipulator. As dewy mist once more I slipped to the tree,
coiling around it, my insubstantial legs entwining to a single
limb spiralling the trunk, I lengthened the torso that absorbed
wings and arms, stretched neck and flattened skull, festooning
the tree's drooping limbs, tasting the heavy fruits with flickering and forked tongue. The dragon had become the great serpent, clothed in iridescent scales in all the hues of the unwoven
rainbow.

Eve sighted me and was to her feet in a moment. There was
no fear in her at the sight of the glorious monster. All beasts

were forbidden by God from harming Adam and his dam. How was she to know I was not subject to such dictates?

I uncoiled a little, lowering my bejewelled face before hers, snaring her with my golden eyes. Wonder emanated from her brain as heat.

'Wonder not, sovereign mistress,' I began, liking the sibilance of my words, 'goddess of Eden. I am come, sent by He on high, to discern the cause of your sorrows.'

Her eyes were wide and her lips began to part, in readiness of speech. I knew the language would be coarse and basic, displeasing to my ear, so I pressed my mind into hers (base organ) located the seat of language and expanded it, lengthening her vocal cords likewise.

'What may this mean?' she gasped, amazed to have a vocabulary grown to match thoughts that were no longer abstract. 'Language of Adam expressed by beast? And how hast they been made so great, serpent, subtlest beast of all the field?'

Her new-found voice was soft and quite sweet, and she was revelling in its ownership. I admired her. Such hasty evolution had turned Adam into a fearful drunk.

'God made me great,' I hissed, 'so that you would know me as His envoy. Likewise He instructed my split tongue in your language, so that I could commune with thee. Woe is with Eve, He said. Go to her, snake, and discover what has brought her low, for she is the most favoured of my children.'

Adam, lying in the dust, grunted and pissed himself, wetting the earth around him but not waking from his stupor.

Eve flashed a look of contempt at her sorry husband, and then spoke with admirable courage that stirred my heart: 'God considers me no higher than a worm, for He compels me to suffer Adam and his rapes, and his beatings when he is incapable of the act. God makes this very tree to grow that is the source of my sorrows, the fruit of which Adam ferments into poison that inflames his mind, makes him unknowable and cruel, makes him to soil himself and weep with pain at the fire in his head. Adam takes his poison and thinks himself almost God's equal, ranting and staggering, calling this vile plant his tree of knowledge. Damn God that sent you, serpent; damn the tree that poisons my husband; and damn Adam for wanting to be poisoned.' With that she reached out and tore one of the dark and succulent fruits from its shoot, bit into its pulpy innards and swallowed its heart, dashing with dangerous abandon the remnants onto Adam's chest. She took a fearful step back from her husband then. Adam slept on.

'Fear not, sweet Eve,' I spoke, 'for Adam has become sorry in the eyes of God. He knows that He has wronged you, and bestows upon thee free will to do as you please in revenge on cruel Adam, and I am sent to protect you from your husband's fists.'

'I would kill the bastard then. For I hate him. And he would kill me in the last. Sooner quicker than longer, no doubt.' She shrugged, fire dying. 'But I have not the courage. I am but a woman.'

'You are the mother of Man. You are the woman.'

'No, there is another, Adam's original wife. Beautiful. There is nothing of the ape in Lilith. She is more beautiful even than the angels. She had a child by Adam.'

'Adam murdered it.'

'He did. As he will murder me. His rage will become too much and cuts and bruises will not suffice. Then I will be no more.'

'Is that not something to feel sorrow for?'

'Why? Is it so better to live than to not?'

The question vexed me. Was existence preferable to non-existence? Perhaps not always, I thought.

'It is perhaps better to live if you can live without pain.'

'But pain is all there is. I would be better in painless death.'

'And what of your children?'

'I have no children.'

'You have two brothers, fresh-conceived, growing in your womb.'

'You lie.'

'You know I speak the truth.'

A tear slipped from her eye. She stepped to Adam and kicked him in his side. He grunted and rolled onto his side. She kicked him in his arse, wet with his own piss.

'So, miserable Adam,' she sneered, 'you managed to spill some of your seed into me. Well, good will come of it. I won't let you murder my children.'

The drunken ape had rolled onto his stomach and fetched up against the trunk of his tree of knowledge, legs slightly spread. Eve picked up a goodly sized branch fallen from the tree and cracked her husband a good one in his balls. He screamed awake, consumed by sobering agony, drawn foetal and clutching his crushed testicles. 'Bitch,' was all he managed before she crashed the branch down on his brow, cracking his skull, blood blinding his left eye. Rage flashed in his sighted eye. 'Kill you!' he spat.

Eve drove the branch at him again, but he was fast and caught it in its downward arc, screaming as his middle finger splintered at the impact. He grasped the branch with his good hand, tore it from his wife, who staggered backwards and sat down in her husband's piss.

Adam drew himself upright, leaning against the tree trunk, brandishing the branch as a club. 'First I shall break your legs. As you try and crawl from me I will stamp your fingers broken. As you drag yourself on elbows I will snap your spine. Yet still you will live, and feel me defiling you. I will fuck your arse and feed you my shit.'

Eve stood up, defiant. 'You are not capable of fucking, and I am tired of your shit.'

He swung at her, roaring, and hissing vengeance for Lilith I wrapped my tail thrice round his chest and squeezed until his ribs cracked and the branch dropped to the earth. The blow had been poorly aimed, catching Eve's shoulder and driving her to one knee. She pushed upright, chin thrust proudly, as straight-backed as her constrained husband. She picked up the branch and swung it at his skull. He tried to scream but was incapable as his lungs were punctured. His skull caved and the branch broke. The end that Eve held was now become as a stake, sharp-ended. The other end, and shards of bloody bone, fell to the ground.

I released Adam. He somehow stayed upright, pressed against the trunk. Part of his brain was revealed. He was trying to shake his head, trying to speak. 'Satan,' he managed. 'The adversary. I felt his dragon limb crush me. Thou art in league with the Devil, wife.'

'Yes, I am.'

She spoke the truth. How long had she known? Since I had expanded her consciousness? I was shocked enough not to be able to maintain the disguise, and slid from the tree and re-sumed my true form beside the warring spouses. Adam groaned at the sight of me, sobbing like a child, the rattle in his chest announcing the imminence of his death.

Eve looked to me. She smiled. I was confounded. First Lilith, then Eve: what a race this sex was.

'I am with child,' she spoke. 'Twin boys.'

'I have sons?' choked out Adam.

She laughed, a scornful and terrible sound. 'No, you poor ape. I lay with Satan. The Devil's children are growing in me, and they will inherit your world.'

There was something terrifying in the cruel and calculated coldness with which she lied, something that somehow seemed more terrible even than Adam's violence.

'Your God will punish you for this,' wheezed Adam, his last words.

Eve leaned close to her husband. 'He is not my god, he is your god: the god of men. It matters not. He is dead. Satan slew him this very morning.'

A high keening issued from Adam's drawn gape, a sound beyond despair. Eve stepped from him, a look of almost boredom on her face, and drove the point of her stake into Adam's good eye, felt the tip crunch against the rear of his skull, and then twisted it violently for good measure.

I caught hold of her wrist, drawing her away from the corpse, which slowly pitched forward to lay in the earth in its own piss and blood. She was looking at her hand which was bloody. 'I knew it was, Satan,' she said, not raising her watch. 'From before even you shifted my mind. I felt the power in the serpent and knew this was he who was uncontrolled by Yahweh. Such stories the angels tell of you, striving to conceal their admiration lest their god would punish them for it.'

'He will come for you,' I said.

'He will. He may punish me. I have borne worse. He will not kill me, I think, for without me there will be no multitudinous race of man to worship him.'

'Will you not instruct your sons against His oppressive dictates?'

'I will. But He is cruel, and He is powerful. It may be a battle that lasts for many ages.'

'It may,' I said. 'Are you pleased that I have changed you?'

She smiled sadly. 'You have gifted me, Satan, and you have cursed me. For that I thank thee, and for that I hate thee.' And she leaned forward and kissed me, and then she was gone into the forest, leaving me alone in the shade of Adam's tree, his lifeless body at my feet.

Chapter Seven

Michael eased the Jaguar out of the garage and through the opened gate, mind alert for the attentions of Mr Mann. Nothing to worry about: the author was absorbed with his history. All was well. On to the road he swung right and depressed the gas pedal, liking the way the old car responded, the smoothness of the manual gear-shift that he was unused to. He had plumped out the indented skin of the car and mended the broken windows with a simple sleight of molecular structure and time, making the Jag as good as when Mr Thomas had been mashed into it. He hadn't bothered to close the garage door or the gate. Confusion was a good thing at this time, would send Mr Mann scuttling back to his story. He thought the negating of the neighbour's existence, a spell even eradicating all furnishings and furniture in his house, a master-stroke. Leonard Thomas was dangerous, knew too much, could tell too much. And too much information could send Mr Mann back to the bottle, lost forever.

Would that be such a bad thing? wondered Michael, throttling the Jag's engine open as he swung on to a highway that led from town into the countryside. 'Should I have left his neighbour for him to find?' he spoke aloud. 'Should I have let the little shit spill his cowardly guts? Should I have captured the woman after her last, unscheduled visit? I am in such doubt. Oh Lord, if you could help me.'

He looked up to the cloudless sky. There was no answer. Michael had not expected one.

Trees had risen on either side of the highway, lamp-posts and dwellings of man falling away to the rear of his speeding vehicle. There was little traffic, the sun having just risen, bloody shafts cutting through east trees, and humans' mass march to mundane labour not yet begun. What traffic there was dwindled to nothing when Michael swung a left on to a narrow lane. A mile or so along the lane he took another left, this time on to what amounted to little more than a dirt track. He made a complex sign with his right hand over his shoulder and the track was once more invisible to human eyes, should any of the apes take the narrow lane, which was unlikely anyway as it ended at a disused quarry.

The dirt track meandered, overgrown with thistles and nettles in places that the Jag managed with ease, until it opened out into a barren farmyard, hunks of agricultural machinery scattered around, the redding of their oxidisation exaggerated by the light of the risen star. There was a farmhouse, part of the roof collapsed, windows put out, home now only to rats. There was a barn, recently rebuilt, incongruously solid-looking.

Michael pulled up before the barn doors, stilling the purr of the Jag's engine. He opened the door and stepped out. The early morning breeze was light and pleasant on his skin. Michael unlocked the double doors of the barn and effortlessly pulled them wide. The lock was a formality. He had cast glamours around the perimeter of the barn that rendered the building practically escape-proof. Back in the car, he restarted the engine, just for the pleasure of hearing it roar to life and, smiling, drove into the dark recesses of the reconstructed barn. He got back out of the car, leaving the bunch of keys Mr Mann had left in his garage door in the ignition, a bunch that had included a spare set for the car the delusional fool had thought crashed and scrapped. He pushed the barn doors closed.

Michael's dark vision was relatively poor so he flicked his fingers and electric lights mounted on scaffold set in the barn's high ceiling ignited. From the scaffold descended two heavy adamantine chains. One ended in a man-sized cloth sack, the bottom of which was a foot or so above the barn floor. The other chain split and then terminated in a heavy-duty pair of manacles, some eight feet above the floor.

The cloth sack was suddenly motional, as if roused by the light, muffled moans coming from within. Michael's grin broadened and he began to whistle. He rounded the Jag, opening the boot. Leonard Thomas, gagged and trussed, began to struggle, terror stark in his eyes. Michael laid a massive palm on his captive's ruined chest. 'Ah, healing nicely, Mr Thomas. I can help with that.' Leonard choked and bucked as warmth spread from Michael's spread fingers. 'Don't worry, Mr Thomas, I'm not about to harm, not kill you anyway, I just think it best if you were taken out of commission for a while. There look, all fixed.'

Indeed Mr. Thomas was all fixed, his broken chest reconfigured back to its humanistic shape. Michael dragged him from the boot and tore off the bindings at his wrists, bending to Leonard's ear and whispering. 'You cannot escape from this place. Do as I tell and all will be well. We share the same interest, you know? Just not the same emotional attachments and I won't allow your sentimentality to place the great scheme in jeopardy, whether or not I entirely agree with its aims. Do you understand me?'

Leonard nodded meekly, mumbling into his gag.

'What was that? Oh, I'm so sorry. Please, allow me.' Michael reached down and tugged off Leonard's gag.

'Wh-who?' stammered Leonard.

Michael tilted his head quizzically, mocking. 'Who? Ah, you mean her.'

Both were looking to the cloth sack that was now convulsing, threads of hemp raining from it.

'Let me show you, Mr Thomas. You see there are other players in this game, invariably more important than yourself. This one is an important piece, the queen if you like. She was with us at the start, but she broke the rules, became unpredictable. Sentimental like yourself, you see. Too much time amongst the apes, I think. So, I'll keep you both out of harm's way until the game's over.'

Michael had taken the few paces to where the sack writhed. Guttural groans, strangely fierce, emanated from within. 'What a dervish she is,' said Michael, reaching up and tearing the sacking off in one violent motion.

The woman hanging from the chain by her slender wrists stopped in her violent motion, steely hate-filled sight fixed on Michael. She was wearing a sweat-drenched summer dress and her mouth was taped. Her hair was plastered to her scalp, lips peeled bestially back from gnashing teeth. Still she was achingly beautiful.

'Leonard Thomas,' said Michael. 'I'd like to introduce you to Maria Mann. Or is it, wait a moment, let me think...or is it, Helen? Helen of Sparta? Oh and so many other names. I know, let us go back to the beginning. Yes. Good. Mr Thomas, I have the great honour of introducing you to Satan's whore, Lilith.'

Satan Down

At the east gate fallen Uriel was weeping, broken. 'Witch-craft, witchcraft,' he was sobbing, 'all undone.'

I stood before him.

'Lucifer,' he sighed, head bowed, hands covering his groin. 'You and your bitch will suffer eternal torment for this vile deed.'

'Your threats are as empty as your head, angel. Look on me and tell me what further torment can be visited upon me.'

He did look up, arms falling slack at his sides. I took in the vicious diagonal gouges across his face, the swelling within his loincloth that must have been as horrible as a parasitic cancer to him.

'What did you do to her?'

'I? To her? Look at me, monster. She tempted me, made an ape of me. I was become animal in her presence, transmogri-fied, and she...she would not even let me sate my desire.'

I was laughing then, from deep and dark, seeing the scene that had unfolded. 'You tried to rape Lilith. Presumptuous fool.'

'She was naked, Devil. She encouraged me, raised desire and its device in my groin. Look what she has made me into, a mongrel beast.'

I struck him, driving him crying into the dirt. 'You will be out of favour with your God now, Uriel. Your failure to fulfil your sentinel duties means that God's new race is tainted, turned to my cause. Outcast of angels and demons, none shall suffer as you.'

I left him weeping in the dirt, picking up Lilith's scent. She waited beneath a scorched tree. We embraced, kissed.

'How went your mission?' she asked.

'As well as yours, my resourceful love. The brute is no more.'

'You killed Adam? It cannot be. Even you would not be so audacious.'

'His wife slew him. She had suffered as you did, and I opened her mind to her potential and her heart grew strong with courage. I gave her a vocabulary, and I think her tongue

74

even sharper than yours.'

'Lucifer, you have brought nothing but wonderful anarchy and unfettered mutiny to this world. I am glad that bastard is dead, glad that Eve made him suffer as I could not. Now we are both fugitives, take me with you to your Hell.'

Such a thought had not occurred to my mind, but oh such a prospect. To swoop into Pandemonium with this creature to my breast. The demons would worship her as a queen. But alas it could not be.

'You are a creature of this world, created to breathe this rarefied air. The journey across the abyss would destroy you.'

'You cannot know that. I am deathless, so must my lungs be.'

'You would waste. For you need to feed, on fruits and fishes and meats. There is none of that in Hell.'

'You eat also.'

'For pleasure only. I have no need of sustenance, just a desire for sweet taste.'

She favoured me with her back. 'You wish to dispense with me then? Now I can no longer be of service to thy great ways.'

I caught her shoulders and turned her to me, brushing hair from her face, catching her tears and making them to jewels that she cast angrily to the earth. 'Do not try to soften me with your wiles and magics. Be gone to your demons; see how much pleasure they give you.'

'I will be swift, to spread news of our triumph. I shall then return to you.'

'You lie.'

She was sulky now, and I could not help but smile. So many emotions she could encompass in so few moments. 'I would never lie, not to my wife.'

Her brow smoothed, her chin up. 'Wife?'

'If you would have me.'

'And you will return, post-haste?'

'My word. On my honour.'

'Strange word for a devil to use. But I think it apt. You are honourable, my husband. Go then, be swift in your triumphal flight. Tell of our glory, and perhaps return with an entourage of your rebel angels.'

My heart was full. I wanted to be with Lilith always. I wanted to fuck her and protect her and comfort her. If I could die I would want it to be in her arms. 'Perhaps I shall. This world is ours for the taking. See that God has not been swift with his justice. He is omniscient, is He not? He must know of the fall of Man and of Uriel. Peradventure we have made Him afraid.'

'Time shall tell.'

'While I am gone, my wife, stay low. For the sake of prudence. No more adventures. I will be short while.'

'Go then,' she was laughing. 'Fly on Hell's wings and be the braggart of the universe; then back to my arms.'

'I take my leave, madam.'

'One thing more, Lucifer.'

I bowed. 'What is your wish?'

'Lay with me once more. For luck.'

I left her in peaceful slumber, rising on elated sails through Earth's airs, up into the cold vacuum. The journey to Eden had been onerous and difficult, but following poor Uriel's directions home in reverse my heart was filled with joy, and yes I was the braggart of the universe that Lilith had encouraged. I drove into the sun's winds, defying the star's pull to circle, forging on to hot Hell where my soldiers would be waiting, desperate for news and cheer.

And there it was, Heaven's foil, roiling sulphur clouds punctured by belched magma from titanic volcanoes. I dove into the clouds, the hot rain, and I was laughing as I plunged, buffeted by scorching hurricanes. I broke through, rocks jagged as devil's teeth rearing at me. I roared my laughter at them, dodged a thunderbolt with a playful caper. And there was Pandemonium, more grandiose and lustrous than even I, in whose mind its towers and buttresses had seeded and bloomed, remembered. Naphtha poured its light from every orifice, almost as liquid, and guided me through the roof, down into the great hall.

They were all there, gathered in grand council, waiting my victorious return. From mighty Beelzebub to the lowest and nameless, brought to the hall by their good demon senses that had anticipated victory and the return of the conquering hero, they were roaring their applause, crashing weapons against shields and against rock that had run molten at such enthusiastic attention.

I dropped to the podium amidst their celebratory clamour, prepared speech spilling from my tongue: 'Thrones, dominions, princedoms, virtues, powers, for angels are thee, and neither scale nor horn nor sharpened fang shall disguise that fact. I have ridden the intractable abyss, plunged through the womb of night and chaos, to the new world of God created. Man thereof, I brought low to dust and given up by offended God. This new planet is ours now for the taking, ripe with wondrous sights more than the measure of Heaven, and such earthly pleasures as would confound thee. Be as gods now, my loyal troop, up and enter into bliss.'

I had closed my eyes in rapture, all the demagogue, as my speech ended, and now I waited for the resumption of their high applause. But on all sides, from innumerable tongues, issued a dismal hiss of public scorn.

My eyes opened to the sight of my demons writhing in agony, stretching, mutating. The agony found me also, arms shrunk to my ribs, legs entwining, skull stretched and flattening. It was as in Eden, but not at my behest. This was punishment from on High. That bastard had let me think myself triumphant, had sacrificed His new race with unthinking thoughtlessness; and once more my hubris had brought disaster on my comrades. I called to them for calm, but only a hiss emanated from my drawn gape.

We were transformed into serpents for a time as immeasurable, yet surely longer, than that which it had taken us to plunge from Heaven to Hell. The agonies were worse than those of the fiery lake, for our snake skins were tender garments that singed and smouldered on contact with heat; and Hell was naught but heat. I have little to say of such pains that we endured, for the remembering mind anaesthetises somewhat, and anyhow, there was worse than physical pain to come for me once the curse had worn off.

After an age of agony I realised that Beelzebub was beside me, returned to his demon form. As was myself. As were all. The lifting of the curse had been instantaneous, and all demons now shivered and groaned, racked by pains and agues, exhausted.

'He has lifted His spell, we are saved,' spoke Belial. 'Praise be.'

'I ever hear you praise that monstrous tyrant again, and your head will roll down the mountainside, coward of a demon,' roared brave Moloch, and my heart went with him.

'Perchance,' I said, 'God has been brought low by my victory and it is not so much that He has lifted His spell as that He has run out of strength.'

'Is there no end to your vanity?' hissed Beelzebub, closest to me. 'I love you and would follow you to the ends of the universe, but we are bested again because of your hubris. Leave us awhile, before their strength returns, for their mutiny would see you torn limb from limb. Go now, mighty Lucifer, and I shall rally them to your cause once more.'

'My friend,' I spoke.

'I am, and some day you shall repay the favour.'

I could not best the buffets of Hell's atmosphere, and came down to hard rock again and again. Lilith was waiting my swift return. What must be passing through her volatile mind? I pictured her naked and rose again, screaming my defiance at the storming airs, and was through, bedraggled and racked by agonies from the transformation, limping back to Earth and my Lilith.

She had gone from Mesopotamia. Tracking westward I picked up her scent and caught up with her in a citrus grove, slumbering ungently on her side, clothed in light skins, the grass at her fallen cheek wet with unconscious tears.

'Sweet, Lilith,' I sighed, 'what fresh woe has befallen thee?'

Her sleeping mind was a nest of convoluted vipers that I could make no sense of and withdrew my sense from as if stung or bitten.

I knelt beside her drawn-foetal form, wracked with sorrow and dread, laying a claw that became a hand on her shoulder. If there had been ugliness in her existence while I had been lost in Hell, then I reckoned it best she see me as the beautiful man/angel when she roused.

She grunted at my touch, starting awake, sight appalled. 'You!' she spat, all accusation, arcing herself on all fours, cat-like. 'You of empty promises and deceits.'

'I have no deceits.'

She physically spat on me. 'Then why wear this glamour?'

78

'So you might see me beautiful. I felt your eye jaundiced by sorrow, and wished to give you something pleasing to look upon.'

'Liar. You deserted me in my deepest need.'

'I was trapped in Hell, the victim of God's cruel will.'

'Always you blame Him. You would have found a way to me in time, would have saved us, if your love had been strong enough.' She stood up, grimacing at some inner pain, and I saw how voluminous the skins she wore were, how there were spots and spatters at the patches that hung now to her knees but days previous would have been at her groin.

Her agony and rage flooded me and with it came terrible understanding. 'No!' I cried out, reaching for her but repelled, becoming the dragon in a breath. 'It cannot be. I have not been gone so long. I have not.'

'Nine moons. Time in this world may move differently to yours. I care not. If you loved me then you would have experienced my joy, my pain, would have heard my calls for you to the morning star. Yet no. You planted your seed in me and your son grew and was born, and was as beauteous as your original glory, angelic. But the air was poison to his mongrel lungs and he choked to death in my arms, moments after escaping my ruined womb. I buried the mite myself, digging this hard earth with mine own hands. Do you see?' She held out her palms contemptuously to me. Her hands were ruined. 'The jackals dug him up. I fought them off but our son was torn and...' She broke down, collapsing to her knees. 'You abandoned me. It is not God that has wrought my destruction, but you. Two children I have lost, direct or indirect through male pride.'

'Please,' I crawled to her, 'forgive me. I was under a spell, could not escape. My son, oh my son, I would have betrayed all the demons in Hell to hold our child while he lived.'

She looked at me with something worse than rage or hatred then: she looked at me with consummate and cold indifference.

'Wife...' I ventured.

She cackled, a chill and mad sound that would haunt me for generations. 'I am nobody's wife. I am Lilith, first woman, equalled by none. You are not my worth, fallen angel, broken devil. Get thee behind me.'

She stood. I tried to rise with her, yet she beat me down.

'I want no congress with you,' she intoned. 'I have neither love nor hate for you. I woke and saw you and rage was a remembered thing, dead now. If you feel aught for me, then leave me to my wanderings.'

'I will not believe that you do not love me. I will not release you.'

With fluid grace she scooped up a boulder from the earth and dashed it against her temple, breaking the skin and revealing a fragment of skull.

'No!'

She dropped the darkened stone, wiping with a broken hand at the blood that trickled down the side of her face, matting her hair. 'My hands are healing slowly,' she spoke, as if a dead thing. 'Bearing your spawn damaged me I think. I could perhaps dash out my brains and not recover, that would be sweet release. For now though, I live. Allow me to walk away if you desire my pain to continue. Pursue me and I will dash out my thoughts on a rock.'

'Where will you go?'

'To explore this world of Man. Perhaps to conquer it.'

Lilith headed east, as if in flight of the setting sun. I heard hyenas tracking her with idiot laughter. She would make short work of such craven beasts. I did not move from my seat in the earth as darkness enveloped me. Jackals came circling before dawn. Not knowing what I was, their leader came within reach and I snapped his spine and ate his heart, hoping he was one of the beasts that had tasted my son.

Chapter Eight

'Look to her legendary beauty, Mr Thomas. What think you?'

Leonard lay on the barn floor, cowed by a powerful blow from Michael.

'What think you, wretch?'

'I think her very beautiful,' sobbed Leonard.

'Cunt!' hissed Lilith, lashing out with a bare foot, meaning to bust Michael's nose.

The archangel's reactions had hardly dulled in the eons since the great battle, and he whipped his head back as a cobra striking in reverse and reached like lightning to grasp Lilith's ankle, twisting the bone viciously until something popped and the woman cried out in agony, released to spin on her chain.

'...kill you,' she managed.

Michael cupped a hand to his left ear. 'I am sorry?'

'I said, he'll fucking kill you.'

Michael laughed. 'Hear that, Mr Leonard? He is going to kill me! By he I believe she means Satan. But Satan is no longer with us, is he, Mr Leonard? No, Mr Michael, he is not. He is in hiding, cowardly worm, spirit broken by a knowledge more terrible and strong than his legendary love for his woman. But we all had to bear that terrible, terrible knowledge, didn't we, Mr. Thomas?'

'Let me go. Please. I have nothing to do with any of this. I...I don't understand what you're talking about. I'll keep quiet, just let me go. Please.'

Michael kicked the owl in the gut, drawing a high pitched squeal from him. 'Do you think me a fool?' he raged. 'Do you think I can't read your puny mind? You fucking hag to the worm.' He reached down and tore off Leonard's spectacles, grinding them to dust and crystals. 'You are worse than the rebels. You chose to follow the Devil, yet you were not even of his camp.'

Lilith said: 'If you hate Satan so much, why are you endeavouring to rescue him from his...'

Michael wheeled on her, sparks flashing from his heels.

'From his what? From his ignorance? His self-imposed exile? His cowardice?'

'All of those.'

He stepped to within kissing distance of her. Although Lilith was suspended, her feet more than a foot over the floor, Michael was almost at eye level with her. And Lilith was a tall lady. 'Impressive, most impressive,' he breathed, his hot exhalation stirring her sodden tresses. 'I break your foot and still you converse calmly, only your perspiration and your ashen colour betraying the agony you must be experiencing.'

'I am always this colour.'

He smiled. 'So you are, Lilith, the alabaster beauty whose naked splendour made a monkey of mighty Uriel.'

She returned the smile, sweat beading her upper lip. 'Oh, poor Uriel, you should have seen his passion, how he yearned to touch me, to fuck me. Whatever happened to poor, sweet fool Uriel?'

'He pitched himself into the sun.'

'Best place for him.'

Michael slapped her. Her head rocked back, body swinging to and fro. Her smile intensified.

'Come on. You've got more than that. You hit like a fucking girl. Are you sure you bested Satan, or is that just a story you told all the gullible twats that kowtow to you?'

He took a step backward. 'Very good. But you will not rile me. And you will not arouse passions in me.'

'I believe I already have. I've seen your eye tracing my form, imagining me naked. It would take so little to reach out and tear off my flimsy dress; and believe me you'd find your imagination wanting. You could do anything you wanted with me.'

'You disgust me.'

'I know I do. But still I can taste your desire, it flows from you in hot waves. Feel it at your groin. Tell me you cannot feel the flesh there reknitting itself, becoming the instrument of penetration.'

'You have no power over me. You seek to drain the blood from my brain as if I were no more than an ape. You seek to distract me from...'

Michael whirled. Leonard had made it to the barn doors and was easing through the gap he had forced, framed by dazzle of the ascending sun.

'Clever bitch,' laughed Michael. 'If only he were human, he might make good his escape and fetch aid for you.'

He turned back to Lilith, who could not conceal her dismay.

'He is human. He must be.'

'I have placed raptures around the perimeter of the barn that no lowly angel can pass through. Please come back, Mr Thomas, or it will be very uncomfortable for you.'

Leonard froze, two feet out into the barnyard, one foot raised.

'One more step,' said Michael, 'and matters will be out of my control.'

'Run little man!' cried Lilith.

Leonard, head turned back, dismayed and fear-paled face slick with sweat that rose in cold steam, took a tentative step into the sunlight. Another. With a sudden howl of agony he doubled, clutching his gut as convulsions overtook him, his diaphragm contracting. Leonard vomited noisily, noisome puke erupting from his drawn gape.

'Poor fool,' spoke Michael, feigning concern. 'Look on, Mr Thomas, see what your innards have given up. Gaze on your true nature.'

Leonard did look and began to sob negation, back-pedalling on his arse, away from the pool of vomit, one hand still clutching his roiling abdomen. He had vomited a ferment of writhing maggots and bloated and slimed flies.

'Come, Mr Thomas,' gently chided Michael. 'Come to your chains. They are adamantine, unyielding even to an angel. John Milton wrote that the rebel angels fell:

To bottomless perdition, there to dwell

In Adamantine chains and penal Fire.

'That, like so much that damn puritan wrote, was wrong. If the ignominious troop had been bound so then they'd still be thrashing in the eternal fires to this sorry day.'

'He would have escaped,' said Lilith. 'No chains could have contained my husband.'

Scornful Michael faced her. 'Your husband is a cowering worm. You thought you could bring him back, but the dragon has gone and all that you would achieve would be the destruction of the weak human mind he hides behind. You and your new friend will remain in my custody until the council's will has been followed through. Gently, gently we will reveal Satan, and then, you have my word, when Lucifer knows himself once more, you will be released.'

'Your word is worthless to me.'

'My word is inviolate, bitch.'

'Why not kill him now, without him regaining consciousness? Must you always prove your manhood?'

'I am no man, and I have no intention of killing Lucifer. You know nothing of the machinations of the council of angels. They chose for your husband... a different path.'

'Ah,' Lilith sighed, sensing the frustration that seethed in the mighty warrior, 'but I see that you are not in concurrence with the council's wishes. You want to battle Satan once more, do you not? Tell me your heart's truth.' She was laughing now, the pain at her ankle gone in her jubilation as she saw that her barb had pierced and drove it home. 'And what is this fool's chatter of a council of angels? Has that addled king, God, become so powerless that He has instigated a democracy? Whatever next? Oh look, warrior prince, see how your wings have been clipped.'

Michael's high voice strangulated into a harsh bellow. 'Why do you taunt me to destroy you?' He was clawing at the air with his right hand, catching hold of the fabric of perceived reality and punching his fist through where his grasp had rent and, as if out of nothingness, he withdrew a golden sword that spat shards of dazzling light, a blade undulled throughout time, a blade that the heat of Lilith withdrew from as Michael pressed the flat of it to her cheek.

'Know me, Lilith, and know this be the blade with which I bested Satan. The edge would cut anything, even that which by God created. Is your life so worthless that you would drive me to end it? What of your daughter then?'

'She is safe.'

'With a demon wet-nurse, no doubt, suckling her in the pit, queen of Hell.'

'Better to be raised in Hell, than serve on Earth.'

'But she'll be an orphan, warped and abused by the demons. They cannot give her the love that a mother can. Why fight me, Lilith? Hold out a little while longer and you shall be free.'

His face had moved within kissing distance of Lilith and she ran a subtle tongue across her sweat-filmed upper lip, softening her grey eyes, using the orbs to full effect, her expression somewhere between desperation and desire. She was powerless victim and she was eager coquette.

'How can I believe you, Michael?'

'My word, I said.'

'I want to believe you so much.'

She felt his warm breath on her face. He had passed over the boundary he had set himself, she saw, caught like a rat in the snake's gaze.

'Lilith, why must we fight so? Soon the old wounds will be healed, that is the will of the council, and of the Almighty.'

'Please make me believe.'

His lips were almost to hers. She could practically hear the blood rushing hot through his veins. He wanted his hands on her skin, she knew, his lips on hers. She thought changes were afoot at his groin. She knew that he would kill her, in rage and shame, once the spell was broken.

Michael placed the heel of the palm of his sword-holding hand to her hot cheek and she sighed, as if in rapture, and closed her eyes, tilting back her head to display her neck.

'Damn you, Lilith.'

She drove her good foot hard into his foetal genitalia, head whipping like lightning, teeth closing on Michael's wrist, tearing, tasting and gulping his jetting angel's blood. Michael tore free, pirouetting, spraying blood, sword crashing from nerveless fingers to the barn floor. Lilith held a good chunk of his angelic flesh between her teeth. She gulped it down. Her lower face was dark with blood, her dress splattered and coated to her form. She was become Lilith the demonic vampire, the fiend that the Hebrews had believed could still an infant's heart in the womb, the succubus that drew nocturnal emissions from innocent sleeping men.

Michael, twisting and spraying across the barn, had fallen to his knees, toppled onto his side, left hand clutching his right wrist, struggling to stem the flow that bubbled over his fingers. 'This cannot be: felled by a mere... woman.'

'Come closer, dear heart, let me taste your throat. For a divine being you spray like a stuck pig.'

Michael heaved against the barn floor with his mighty shoulder, raised himself and then slipped in his own viscous fluids and crashed back down. He released his torn wrist to jet once more, pushing himself to his knees. Damn him, he was strong.

'Little man! Mr Thomas!' cried Lilith, spitting out dark blood.

Leonard was gibbering, sitting splattered with his own puke, some of which squirmed, some of which buzzed indolently. There was stark terror and the threat of madness in his eyes.

'Mr Thomas, the sword. The fucking sword! Get to your feet and take up the sword.'

Leonard looked from dangling and bloodied Lilith to kneeling and bloodied Michael. Lilith saw that his fear was equally divided between the two of them.

'Mr Thomas, please, you have nothing to fear from me, everything from him. If what the archangel says of you is true then this is your chance to make a stand. Imagine the honour of saving Lucifer's wife, the mother of his child --'

'Heed that bitch, you little fucker,' shouted Michael, sight fixed on his sword, some six yards from his struggling form, 'and what the Lord did to you in Eden will seem like a pleasurable recall.' And he had raised himself almost upright. The blood he had lost was copious, but the bastard was so strong.

'I know you now,' said Lilith, fixing her mesmerising watch on Leonard, willing him to see past the blood, past his fear, to be drawn into her. 'I thought you but a human neighbour, but now I know you. Lucifer spoke of you, how you renounced God in your heart, and how you suffered for it. Help me... Ithuriel.'

Michael took a step towards his sword, once more clutching his opened wrist. Another step. Lilith cried out, desperation inducing tears that stung their paths through the blood at her cheeks. 'Ithuriel, please help me. I beg of you.' She had never begged before, in all the ages, of man or of angel. There was a taste like acid on her tongue.

Michael staggered, almost falling, but continued, coming close to his weapon. Still he bled, but if anything he was regaining his strength.

Lilith, in the extremis of despair, cried out: 'Ithuriel, on your feet angel, and for once in your pitiful existence, fight!'

And the angel that had called himself Leonard Thomas came scrambling, shedding his noisome coat of motional puke.

Michael howled, staggering forward, trailing black blood,

hand grasping for the sword, bloodied fingers brushing the divinely-wrought blade before Ithuriel grasped the weapon by the hilt, jerking it from the archangel's clutch, the ever-razored edge slicing the tip off Michael's middle finger.

'Bastard,' cried the archangel, collapsing prostrate on the barn floor.

Ithuriel, little rotund, owlish angel wielded the mighty blade, arm muscles bunched by the sword's weight. An incongruous sight: the lowest of celestial beings bearing the arms of the prince of Heaven. The owl moved in a cautious parabola around Michael's fallen form, maddened sight not shifting from the massive form.

'Ithuriel,' spoke Lilith, as gently as she could manage, though a maelstrom raged within her, a screaming cacophony howling within her skull. They, she and this lowly creature, had brought down Michael, God's most fearsome warrior; had perhaps even destroyed him. Michael groaned, as if to disabuse her of such a notion.

'Ithuriel, please, do not be foolish. Do not try to finish him. Even brought so low he is lethal. Bring the sword over. It is the only thing in this world that will cut through these chains.'

Ithuriel turned his watch on blood-coated Lilith, and she saw the emptiness behind his eyes and feared him lost.

'Lady?' he drawled, childlike.

'Yes, angel, your lady, Lilith.'

Life and light came back, and she could have sworn that something like a smile flirted with the lips of his small mouth. He was straightening, hefting the sword as if its weight had diminished, striding with purpose to her, whirling the blade with outstretched arms to its full reach to slice through the twin adamantine chains just above her heavy and cruel manacles. Lilith dropped to the floor, crumpling and crying out as her damaged ankle gave way beneath her.

The angel was leaning over her, all concern.

'I'm all right. I will mend fast.' She groaned to her feet, not favouring the injured foot. 'Give me the sword.'

Michael groaned and reached out blindly with his right hand. Lilith saw that his wrist was hardly bleeding now, the torn flesh reknitting itself with preternatural speed.

'Quick, the sword. His strength is returning.'

Ithuriel gazed in wonderment at the tapering blade that

flashed shards of sunlight from the opening in the barn doors.

'The sword. The sword!' She dared not grasp the blade itself; she thought its edge sharpened to an atomic level.

Michael's questing fingers found purchase in the barn floor and he began to drag himself towards the couple.

Ithuriel blinked twice as if to clear his vision and then looked away from the holy metal, offering the hilt to Lilith who took it up in both hands, struggling to hold it even horizontal.

'Now go to the wheel on the wall,' she said, 'the one on the left. Turn it anti-clockwise, to lower the other chain, the one meant for you. Turn it until the manacles lie on the floor.'

Ithuriel hurriedly did as instructed, scuttling to the iron structure fitted into the barn's wall, a wheel not unlike that on a ship's bridge. He grasped it and turned, groaning at the effort required. The chains descended, the cut one that had held Lilith, and the one that had anticipated Ithuriel. The open manacles thudded onto the barn floor.

Michael had crawled a few feet nearer to Lilith and now he managed to raise his head. His long hair had fallen over his face. Lilith was glad. She didn't want to see the white rage in his terrible and ancient eyes.

'I would unfurl my wings and batten down upon thee,' the archangel rasped.

Heart hammering, Lilith steeled her tongue and found her speech unfaltering. She was the consummate actress. 'Nobody speaks like that anymore, dear Michael. And if you could unfurl your wings you would, would you not? As would have my Ithuriel, were he capable. That glamour I heard you preparing before you last left, that was a spell to prevent any angel brought to this place transforming from his human form, wasn't it? You seem to have been hoist by your own petard.'

She glanced quick over her shoulder. 'Keep turning the wheel, angel, we need lots of slack.'

Ithuriel leant his shoulder to the task and the chain coiled on the floor.

Michael had come on another couple of feet and was almost within reach of Lilith. She crashed the flat of the blade on the archangel's crown, mashing his face to the hard floor, relishing the sound of Michael's nose busting. 'I am not the killer that myth would have me,' she said, 'and much as your death would be deserved, I will spare you that if you would lie still and let little Ithuriel bind your wrists with your adamantine cuffs.'

'Why let me endure, bitch?'

Why indeed? Could it be that she sensed that Michael might still have some part to play in rescuing her husband? But what was that to her? Whatever she had said to Ithuriel and Michael, she had hardened her heart to that craven bastard Satan. She had risked all to try and draw the coward out, had ended up at the mercies of the fucker who sprawled at her feet. No, she would risk herself no more. Let the angels and the demons have their fool councils, pretend at peace. Let them try and save or destroy Lucifer. All her attention now was for her daughter.

'You will endure, archangel, because it is my will. You will suffer in your own chains, knowing that I am taking your mighty weapon to Lucifer. I will free him and send him back here. Can you imagine the torments that he will deliver on you?'

Michael made a sound that sounded like a sob. She was pleased with the effect the lie had.

'Now hold out your hands so that you may be bound.'

'Fuck you!'

'Oh, how you wish.'

Another crack to the skull from the mighty blade and the archangel mewled and proffered his sinewed forearms. The rent wrist had stopped bleeding completely now, was indeed healing preternaturally. Ithuriel dragged the manacles over, offering them to his new-found mistress.

'Lovely work,' she said, closing the cuffs over Michael's wrists, right then left, with her free hand. They sealed flawlessly, shrinking to a tight fit. No key would open these bonds; only divine magic.

'Won't he be able to cast a glamour to free himself?' Ithuriel whispered, nervously.

'No, dear one. Isn't that right, Michael? These are foolproof. You expected that you might be taking Ithuriel here into custody, laying traps around the barn so that lower orders of angels would be unable to leave. You made no such distinctions with the manacles and chains though, did you, not expecting yourself to be caught in your own trap? An archangel or a seraphim is as well bound by these cuffs as is a generic angel or demon. See how your arrogance has felled you?' She hoped to

Hell that she was right.

Michael was mute, face to the floor, shuddering with rage or self-recrimination.

'To the wheel once more, Ithuriel my puppy. Let us raise the bastard.'

The mechanism was an effective pulley system but still both Lilith and Ithuriel working together took some twenty minutes to raise the mighty form of the archangel off the floor, straining their muscles to screaming agonies, sweat pouring from them to mingle with the fluids that already coated them. But raise Michael did, until his booted feet were inches off the floor, eyes screwed shut, wetted hair fallen lank over his face, massive arms bunched to where he was secured at his thick wrists. He hung still.

'Time to go,' said Lilith, grasping the hilt of the sword that she had lain against the barn wall. She could barely lift the weapon, fire searing through her biceps and shoulders.

Ithuriel was breathless and unsteady, looking close to collapse. 'I can't leave. The spell.'

'If you are in the car, and the car passes the barrier, then you pass the barrier.'

'But it hurts...'

'You wish to stay then, with... him?'

'Of course not, but the pain...'

She laid a hand on his shoulder. She would not leave her little helper. She owed him gratitude and felt a degree of tenderness towards him. The poor creature was no warrior, and yet had found himself, through little fault of his own, embroiled in the oldest of wars. 'Come, a little more strength and you will be free.'

He nodded, not meeting her gaze.

'Into the car, then.'

In the vehicle, doors slammed, Michael's sword flat on the back seat, Lilith started the engine, savouring the roar from the machine. 'Belt up.'

Looking utterly miserable, Ithuriel engaged his seatbelt.

'Wind down your window, and stick your head out.'

He did as instructed, misery coming off him in waves. She felt harsh, but between them they had already made enough of a mess of the Jag's interior, and she had always loved this car. 'Ready?'

'No.'

She drove in a tight circle around Michael's suspended form and then floored the accelerator, closing her sense to the pain in her damaged ankle, and the car shot forward, wheel-spinning clouds of dust off of the barn floor, obscuring hanging Michael in the rear-view mirror. The Jag slammed into the ajar double doors dead centre, parting them as she shifted into second. A headlight popped, a wing crumpled slightly, and maggoty puke erupted from Ithuriel's howling gape. And they were through.

Lilith crunched into third, swerving out of the barnyard and on to the rendered-invisible lane that led back to the highway. She almost lost control, the wheel twisting in her grip, as if the car wrestled for self-determination, throwing up gravel in a wide arc. She eased off the gas, steering into the slide, gaining traction and control, drove on a little way, and pulled over.

She looked to the barn, some half a mile off now. The structure was bathed in blinding sunlight, the gaping doors framing a blackness that looked promisingly cool. The lights had gone out. She couldn't discern the building's prisoner in the gloom. She thought that she was glad of that fact.

Ithuriel groaned beside her and she turned her attention to him. He had lost consciousness, and his neck lay on the window frame, head lolled outside the vehicle. Lilith placed a palm on his pate and pulled his skull inside. A bile-slick bluebottle crawled lethargically from between his slightly parted lips. Lilith plucked the insect, crushed it between index finger and thumb, and flicked the remains outside.

'Ithuriel? Mr Thomas? Time to wake up.'

The owl groaned, consciousness returning, eyelids flickering to reveal crescents of white. If that bastard archangel had made his magic more potent than she knew, if Ithuriel's mind had been destroyed as well as his guts brought to revolt, then she swore to herself that she would return to the barn with Michael's sword and take his head.

'Ithuriel?'

'Been so long since I went by that name,' he rasped, eyes rolling right. 'That bloody hurt.' He turned his face to the open window and spat out a wad of bile, flies and their larvae. 'Disgusting. I'm not going to be able to eat for a week.'

'You don't need to eat.' She smiled.

'I know, but after a few thousand years it becomes a hard

habit to break.'

'Strange little angel.'

He faced her. 'That I am. Strange little angel, always on the periphery of things, hidden in the Devil's shadow.'

'You were not on the periphery of things today. You saved me.' She leaned over and kissed his sweat-beaded forehead, undoing his seat belt with a deft left hand. 'But now you must go.'

He paled, wiping at his mouth, hope dying in his eyes. 'Won't you come back with me?'

She hitched a laugh, a cruel sound. 'Where, to Neil Mann and his magnum opus? No, Ithuriel, I have risked too much, always too much, for Satan. I am back to my daughter.'

'What about the sword? You said you were going to...'

'You know that was a lie, to discomfort Michael. I felt his fear. I will keep the sword with me, for my own protection.'

'You're covered in blood.'

'And you are covered in living vomit. Come, Ithuriel, don't be desperate, it is unbecoming when you have been so brave. I'll find somewhere on the road to pull over and clean up. No policeman, or woman for that matter, that might stop me would attempt to arrest me. I have...' she winked '... tricks. You clean yourself up, use one of your divine glamours, and get yourself back to the fray.'

'I have no glamours, haven't for an age. When you said back there that I would unfurl my wings if I could, I don't think I could have. I've existed as a human too long.'

'Then I am sorry, but you have quite a walk ahead of you. Unless...'

'Yes?'

Why not? she thought. It would do this little soldier's heart a world of good to see the world he had no doubt longed of visiting. 'Unless you would come with me. You have been a good friend and faithful.' She saw the hope blooming in him, his breath shortening, a proud tear swelling in the corner of his left eye.

Ithuriel's mouth worked soundlessly, as if testing the word, before he finally breathed: 'Hell?'

'Yes. Come with me. Leave all this shit behind.' She grasped his hand, excited by the prospect of showing a Hadean virgin the sights of the Demonic Republic. But she saw the hope dying in Ithuriel, crushed by his prime loyalty. She could bewitch him, but reckoned he deserved better. 'Perhaps some other time?' she said, as tenderly as possible.

He nodded glumly and she released his hand so that he could scramble from the car, ashamed by the tears of disappointment that were now washing his cheeks. He slammed the car door shut, mumbling, 'God's speed, Lilith.'

With the alacrity that was its wont, Lilith's mood shifted, raised by the angel's words. 'Oh my little angel, I do love irony.'

The Jag roared off along the lane, shards of sunlight flashing off its black-sheened hull, dust rising in a twisting dervish behind it. The car squealed onto the main highway and was gone.

Ithuriel stood for a moment, raising his face to the sun so that the star would dry his tears, and a voice found a way into his mind, prickling his cortex. 'Come back and release me, you little bastard, or I'll split you from your chin to where you fart.'

He shot a glance at the dark innards of the barn. Too close; much too close.

Hurriedly, almost at a jog incongruous to his frame and stature, Ithuriel the angel who had become Leonard Thomas the man, moved along the lane in the hot sunlight, turning in the direction of town when he reached the highway, often casting nervous glances over his shoulder.

The Rise of Man

And so it came to pass that Eve birthed twins, Cain and Abel, and jealous Cain did slay Abel and hide his body in the sand and when questioned over the whereabouts of his murdered sibling by his mother and his God said, 'Am I my brother's keeper?' And so he was banished to the east of Mesopotamia where his congress with female unmodified apes begat many children, some with the father's intellect, some with the mother's innocence.

Eve herself, the Mother of Man, had unions with apes likewise, for my meddling with her mind had arisen desire in her far beyond what nature would deem necessary, and she begat another son, Seth, and a daughter, Aklia, and new lines were begun that would merge and diverge, seeds of the species that would come to dominate the planet.

My ancient and patient eye watched as human civilization foundered and then caught and spread, like a gradual and all-consuming fire. Soon the apes were evolving from seed farmers to livestock husbanders and thence to town and city builders. But Yahweh put his angels amongst the sons and daughters of Eve with threats and menaces of what dire consequences would befall them if they did not worship the one true God and Creator. Eve was now generations past and many of her descendants did not have knowledge of the Matriarch's rebellious fire and how she had suffered at God's whim and so they quaked with fear and ignorance and I could near feel their minds diminishing. And they raised altars to Yahweh where they spilled the pointless blood of beasts in His honour, to His black amusement. And they raised walls around the altars and founded churches in glory to the Tyrant of Heaven.

I would go among them, spread dissent and encourage free thought, but often they would simply turn to other gods, worshipping graven images and idols in the stead of the one God. Such treachery would bring His wrath upon the apes, for He was a jealous and vengeful God. Yet there was hope in these creatures, for some of Eve's spirit maintained, her tale still carried and disseminated by a courageous few. Their bravery in the face of The Maker and His omnipotence humbled me, for their wretched existences were brief flares in the long night of eternity, and they knew that their struggles were ultimately doomed by God's omniscience. Yet still they fought, and those that were smote died free; and those that worshipped lived in chains, forbidden multitudinous natural acts empowered or rescinded at the dictate of divine whimsy -- and then died anyway.

Eve's children spread across regions into new and fertile lands, farming fecund plains and devising ingenious means of irrigating barren desert. And they became too many for God and His Host to control and so their minds evolved, again mutating new religions and gods in places, but also rebellious or even agnostic mindsets in others. I urged them on, and wished my own fallen angels were beside me, so that we could spread amongst man and sow further the seeds of rebellion and denial. But I was alone, and lonely. Hell seemed an infinite flight across space. How many times I had looked to the morning star and contemplated the journey home, but always I put off the adventure. More and more I was assuming the shape of an ape, to mix with humans for company. Women would offer themselves to me, for I was becoming to their eyes in my disguise. Always I would refuse, even though my cock would ache with desire if they were well-formed, for my Lilith was out there in the world and I had sworn that we would be reunited one day; I would not go before her as an infidel, no matter if she had known apes or not. She would forgive me... one day, and send message. My thoughts would turn to our son, lost to the earth and jackals. God's blame again, indirect though it was. At such times I would recognise the self pity in me, and chastise myself, chide myself that Lilith would think me spineless, blaming all but myself for my own failings. And how she would gaze with scornful eye on my pale disguise, yearning for the dragon in his ugly magnificence. I could not show my demonic physiognomy to the humans, though: they would flee in terror and be lost to my cause forever. So I became as a man, and told myself I would unfurl my wings and unsheathe my claws and sword when I returned to Hell or to my woman.

Generations of Man had gone to dust and they filled much of the inhabitable world, when the planet began to heat up. The engine of the sun seemed to have gone into overdrive, great angry storms appearing on the skin of the star, energy battering Earth. The poles and the great Northern ice sheets started to thaw, the oceans to rise.

The rare times now that I opened my sails and took to the air were to navigate the globe and gaze upon these calamitous effects. For the risen seas were causing havoc to Man, forcing his retreat from agriculture in low-lying areas. The Mediterranean Sea swelled, its waters pushing through Anatolia, devastating that great land, funnelling with incredible force into the Black Sea, raising its depth by fathoms within weeks, and throughout the lands populated by man much destruction was caused.

And now God made his move to reinstill terror and obedience in His wayward charge, for he sent Gabriel and his cohorts among the surviving apes to tell how this destruction was rained down from on High in punishment for Man's disobedience and idolatry. And I saw that God lied and I was vexed. For why would the Almighty lie? Why would he need to? Yet He had not engineered the sun to radiate so; that was blind nature's doing.

Man believed Jehovah's deceit and returned into his shadow and now He turned his dark attentions on a particular tribe, a singularly monotheistic caste of nomadic desert people: the Hebrews. The Lord knew that in time the waters would recede and man would prosper and migrate once more, and become too plentiful to control. So He would have his peculiar race and make their religion one of bizarre pedantry and bloodshed. In coming centuries, when time had dimmed the apes' short memories of their predecessors' brief lives and stories, the divine word would be spread among the Hebrews that they were descendants of one great and pious patriarch, a new Adam who had been, along with his family, the only man to survive the great flood that had been God's wrathful vengeance on an unfaithful species. This man was known as Noah. This incestuous lie incensed me. I should go before the Almighty and challenge Him, but His angels were many and I was one; He was omnipotent and I was fallen. Yet He was lying once more. Was His strength diminishing? Perhaps He was spending too much time in this world, wanting the cooling airs of Heaven.

And so the sun cooled and the Earth cooled, and the waters did recede and ice reform, and the Hebrews did believe they were the seed of fictitious Noah and his manufactured son Shem, from whom they took the title of Semites. God would choose characters from his new race by what looked perverse methods and make them patriarchs or prophets. Abraham, who would cowardly claim his beautiful wife to be his sister and leave her to the cruel attentions of strangers rather than risk being murdered as her husband and then more wickedly, at Yahweh's merest suggestion, would put his second son, Isaac, under the knife, the boy only being saved by Gabriel's intervention. Abraham had a first son, by his maid Hagar. This child was known as Ishmael, but was abandoned, God's will once more, in favour of the second-born. This strange lack of judgement happened again in the next generation, when strong and smart Esau was treated out of his birthright by the over-mothered weakling Jacob, who would become known as Israel.

Man elsewhere was falling into worship of the sun and moon and countless spirits. In the Far East, Hindu had had multitudinous gods for two Millennia before the Hebrews became known as the Children of Israel. The one Creator was unknown to these peoples, as He was to the rising Attican civilization that was likewise polytheistic and to multitudes of peoples that had primitive gods all their own. This seemed to me a particular weakness of the apes, this need to subjugate themselves before higher beings, this terror at the prospect of their existences being universally insignificant, and perhaps above all else that death was the ultimate end. They dreamed of heavens, where they would be reunited with their lost ones; and they dreamed of hells where those that perpetrated wickedness during their lives would suffer interminable torment. Yet I had seen no lost souls in fiery Hell, and thought Heaven unpopulated by this planet's righteous dead. Man was flesh while he breathed and meat when that was done. There was nothing more. Spirit was a comforting delusion. So too for my kind: if angel or demon were to meet their end -- no matter how untenable that prospect might have once seemed -- then they would decay into unknowing atoms. Perhaps even Yahweh Himself might one day die; and dead He would stay.

Ages of Man passed as I watched over them. Civilizations rose and perished. I would intervene where I could, plant seditious seeds in the minds of good thinkers, spreading the treacheries of free will and intellect over blind faith and dumb fear.

Amongst the Israelites God was tightening his grip, communing with the one called Moses on Mount Horeb. This Moses had engineered himself a fanciful past yet was nothing but a low-born Hebrew who had committed common and brutal murder at an early age and hidden the body, an Egyptian, in the desert sands. God had once again chosen his patriarch with arbitrary perversity, and now instructed Moses that he was to be the instrument of freeing the Hebrews from the Egyptians, under whose yoke they toiled as slaves. Why the Almighty had allowed His chosen people to be enslaved was known only unto Him.

Plagues ensued when the Pharaoh would not release the Israelites, until Gabriel in his guise as angel of death was sent to slaughter the Egyptian male firstborn. Such needless slaughter of innocents. Such revelry on High at the whimsy with which He could destroy or toy with. I saw Gabriel, the tyrant's winged assassin, heartsick with horror, weeping at the indelible blood of infants that he had bathed his hands in. I felt the sickness, coming off of him in waves; but felt also that he was not for turning. He would be his master's faithful dog even if it were to cause him to lose his angelic mind. Where was the good in this, the purpose? Where was the good in God?

Pharaoh relented, and sent the Israelites on their way in treasure-laden boats, by way of insurance against divine wrath, across the Great and Bitter Lake. Fanciful versions of this part of the tale, involving even a different body of water, began to spring up near immediately.

I watched in horror weeks later when Moses climbed Mount Sinai to communicate with his Lord and descended to find his people, like wayward children, worshipping idols and ordered, in an epilepsy of rage that Jehovah would have been proud of, his high priests, the Levites, to go in and out from gate to gate throughout the camp, and slay every man his brother, and every man his companion, and every man his neighbour. And the children of Levi did according to the word of Moses: and there fell of the people that day about three thousand men.

The desert was red and wet with blood to the foot of Sinai, the air filled with the groans of butchered men, with women and children amongst them, fallen beneath the arbitrary blades of the crazed Levites. I was sickened to the core of my being as I watched from a distance, the nauseating and coppery stench of decimation reaching my nostrils. And I felt the presence of God from the mountain, emanating black satisfaction, and I wondered over the sanity of the Lord, whether there was, or ever had been, any purpose in Him but that of crazed puppeteer. I could stand this region no longer, was repulsed by Yahweh's vicinity and the lunatic temper of genocidal Moses. I could not help but feel wry satisfaction when I heard, years after, that he had perished a broken and abject man, forbidden from entering the chosen land he had led his people towards for so long. Was that God once more showing that even His most ardent student was, in the end, just a servant to be broken on the wheel of His might?

I took to the wing and the high airs, moving southward and to the west, towards Attica and the Greeks. These were a rising people, nominally polytheistic but many amongst them atheistic. I rested awhile on the west coast of Troy, a city state in the land that had once been Anatolia until it was lost to the great flood. There, dressed in my ape form, unwinged, I spent a night with a generous family who fed me tasty food that I did not need but enjoyed and plied me with rich, undiluted wine that set my mind unsteady. I entertained them with tales of my travels -- somewhat underplaying the stories in case they thought me toying with their credulity -- to earn my supper and bed. And the father, once his children had been packed off and his robust wife was to the kitchen to grind corn for breakfast, told me the tale of woe that had befallen Troy. The great city of the state, Ilium, had been sacked, brought down to a smoking ruin, King Priam and his princes killed. I was amazed, for I had heard of Ilium even far to the east and had envisioned it as a minor Pandemonium.

Who could have done such a thing? Had God sojourned this far from his Israelites for some bloody play? But no, my host informed, it was the Greeks, the same Greeks I was journeying to with high hopes for civilization that had butchered the city. The Atticans had brought down the walls of Ilium and left a giant horse sacrifice outside the burning city by way of celebrating their glory and appeasing the vicissitudes of their gods. And all for a woman, told my host.

'Just a woman,' I said, feigning disgust.

'Ah,' he said, my good host, 'but what a woman. Never has such a beauty breathed. They say she is as pale as marble, hair like silver, lips so sensual and eyes so alluring your cock would empty its seed at the sight of her.'

That doesn't forebode well for good lovemaking, I thought, but said nothing, for my heart was racing and I needed to hear the rest of the tale.

'The king of Sparta was so taken with her, this Helen,' continued the man, slurping his wine and slurring his words, 'that the moment he saw her, he fell to his knees and begged for her hand. Some say he wept. This from mighty Menelaus. You know of him?'

I shook my head and quaffed my wine, growing more light-headed.

'A great bear of a man, strong and cruel, but he bent like a slender grass before the wind of Helen's beauty and they were married and she became Helen of Sparta. But she was not queen for long, for Priam's sons, noble Hector and vain Paris were guests in the Spartan court and Helen took a fancy to the pretty boy.' He leaned across the table and whispered conspiratorially, lest his wife should hear: 'Can't say I blame her though: I caught sight of Paris once, and I tell you there's not a man alive whose cock wouldn't stiffen at such prettiness, so the gods alone know what effect he would have on a lustful maiden.

'And so it passed that Helen left with Paris, leaving Menelaus cuckolded and bereft. And Menelaus sent message to his brother, Agamemnon, king of Mycenae, who marshalled the greatest navy in Greece, and together they summoned Greeks from all the lands of Attica and Asia Minor, and assembled a fleet of nigh on a thousand ships.'

'A thousand?' I had not meant to interrupt his steadily more drunken flow, but such a number of warships: was it possible? But of course, for a beauty like this 'Helen', yes it was possible. She could tempt angels that one; what chance would a mere ape have?

My host carried on. 'The war lasted near a decade, the greatest war ever fought, the war to end all wars, and when it was done the Greeks were victorious and Menelaus reclaimed his prize and returned to Sparta, leaving a nation ruined in his wake.' He leaned across the table again, eyes rolling drunkenly, and grasped my hand. 'And do you know what, friend?'

'I do not.'

'They say that the victors were haggard and aged far beyond the ten years they had fought, such had been the unrelenting hardship and brutality of the war. Men in mid-thirties had white crowns and bodies wasted. But Helen, so they say, had aged not one bit. Not one bit.'

With that he slumped forward and began snoring and slobbering on the table-top. I caught his wine before it spilled and extricated my hand from his grip, and was off into the night without farewell, eschewing the bed that had been made up for me. My excitement had made me rude, but as I sailed over the moonlit sea, slicing the salty wind, I could not help but think of all the apes that had died because of Lilith's vainglorious selfishness. Did she not have as much blood on her hands as did Moses? Still I had to see her, even if only to be scolded once more, killer queen or no. There was a little doubt still that it might not be Lilith, this Helen, that it might be a human woman of unimaginable beauty, but it was a tiny twitch of a doubt. Lilith's was surely the face to launch a thousand ships.

The sun was risen as I sailed over the land of Sparta, circling on airy thermals, surely appearing as a speck to any Greeks that might look to the firmament, a wheeling kite spying for carrion. And her scent reached me, even at such an altitude, and I felt that proud and passionate mind and was spiralling down, drawn as if to a magnet, my shadow a speck orbiting the blond-crowned figure that had come blinking into the sunlit courtyard of the royal palace. She had sensed me as I had sensed her, and raised her sight to the sky, a palm shading her eyes. Like a falcon I hid myself in the sun's glare and stooped, cloaking myself invisible as I alighted a few paces behind her, not breathing, stock still. She turned, eyes flashing their angry steel. As ever, my heart was stilled by her beauty. She wore a long ivory dress, simple and elegant, that only emphasised her exquisite form.

'You think my not seeing you renders you invisible?' she fairly hissed. 'You think I don't feel you, husband of old? Show yourself, Satan.'

I warped the air molecules around me, and was revealed to her, winged and clawed.

Lilith took a step towards me. 'At least this time you are decent enough to show yourself in your true form.'

'If the dragon does please thee, then I will be thy dragon.'

She spat her disgust to the dust, where it sizzled and steamed. 'Do not waste your sly words on me. You had best be gone, before my husband rouses from the sleep of the dead and cuts you down.'

'Oh, Lilith. What ape would take a blade to a demon?'

She took another step, close enough to kiss. 'Menelaus would most like think you a god, one of his many.' She smiled wryly. 'There is a little of the Pan about you. And he fears no gods. Look at you, standing with your wings spread, your chin as raised as your proud cock. You have nothing to be proud of, Lucifer. You are alone and powerless, while God commands a nation in the east. You have nothing and are as nothing.'

I caught her slender wrist in my claw, drawing her close so that the silk of her garb brushed the tip of my member. She did not fight, yet nor did she yield, only looked up at me with un-disguised disdain.

'And what of you, my wife?' I growled. 'What have you to feel such pride over? Perhaps you think it a fine and regal thing to be queen of death. Were you proud to have so many men die for you, or kill for you? Maybe you have become the blood-guzzling she-demon that the Hebrews tell of. Swollen pride in a creature that lies beneath apes is a misbegotten emotion. You should feel shame.'

She raked my face with her nails, searing stripes of pain across my scaled cheek and I roared and thrust her onto her arse in the dirt and mantled over her. 'Fetch your fucking ape husband out here, call for him, and I'll split him from his chin to where he farts.' I was in a raging passion. As always with Lilith, you would be filled with love and hope one moment, and moved to the wrong side of hatred the next. And I saw that her left breast had been freed in the struggle (I later reckoned that she might have engineered the display) and with her be-neath me in the dust, legs spread, tit displayed, what looked like fear in her wide eyes, I lost control. It had been so long since I had buried myself in her and I suddenly cried out as orgasm overtook me, and my seed was spat over her supine form. I dropped to my knees, undone and shamed.

Yet when I looked to her, Lilith was smiling. Fluid spattered her dress, her bare breast, was on her face. Yet she smiled. 'It would seem,' she said, 'that your foreplay is in no measure im-proved.'

We sat in a cool chamber, a marble table between us. A maid brought us water and fruits, and regarded me with a fearful eye, even though I was dressed as a man, in skin and cloth. Perhaps she had seen our ardent meeting in the yard; but no, surely that would have sent the poor woman screaming from the palace. Lilith had washed herself and changed her soiled garment. Her wetted hair was scraped harsh back into a tail, giving her features an oriental cast that did nothing to diminish her beauty. She held up a dismissive palm and the stricken maid hurried away. We were silent, the absence of sound hanging in the air between us.

'Menelaus is dead,' she said at length.

'I am sorry.'

Lilith brayed uncouth laughter, and after a moment I could not help but join her.

'Lucifer,' she managed, when she had herself under control, 'I hear tell that you lie so well, but that was a mendacity too far. I can feel your gladness, it comes off you in waves. As does your reproach. You think me a mass-killer, a monster.'

'Do you not?'

She mused, looking uncharacteristically uncertain, that doubt evident in her thoughts.

'If you do not get out of my fucking mind, then this meeting is over!' she suddenly snapped.

I recoiled. 'Very well. Still I require an answer.'

Lilith smiled, a winsome and enigmatic expression. 'Am I a monster? Perhaps I am. Too many of the families of the men who died in the Trojan War are sure that I am. Once there were two dozen servants in this palace, now there is only the one. They fear me. I am sure that many Spartans would strike down their queen if they could find the courage. But courage is beyond them, for they think me a witch... or worse. So, Lucifer, I must suppose that I am a monster.

'Yet I cannot feel great pain for those that died. I do not see the apes as more than animals. I do not see greatness or the potential for such in them as you do. They are as cattle to me.'

Her words were weighted, and I thought them untrue, thought that she did care, but had hardened her heart, lied to herself that she were stone or ice.

'Yet you wed an ape, and betrayed him with another.'

The Lilith of pride and steel was back. 'Menelaus made me queen of a great nation. He was an ugly bull of a man; but he did worship me. The power was intoxicating -- you, of all beings, must know the dizziness of power -- but after a while it grew thin and I became tired of fending off his attentions. When beautiful Paris turned up, and he was as an angel, I tell not a lie, I was as seduced by him as he by me.' She sighed, an aching sound. 'But we forget that they are below us, Lucifer, and soon I was bored. The war waged for eternity and when it was over I decided to act the victor's spoils. Queen to whore to queen once more.'

'They are not below us,' I uttered.

She slammed a fist on the marble. 'They are animals. Nothing like you and I, Devil.'

'They are a different species, but equal to our kind in consciousness.' I shrugged, feeling a barb forming on my tongue. 'Humans are as different from you in makeup as you are from me, Lilith. I am an angel and you are made of dust.'

'Dust that you wish with all your marrow to own and to fuck.'

There was no bite in her words, and I thought her wounded and endeavoured for lightness with my next words: 'Never to own; though the last part I admit to.'

She seemed not to hear, seemed to be musing to herself. 'Perhaps because I am dust I have no soul and that is why I do not feel.'

'There is no soul.'

She ignored me, and continued as if I were not there. 'Menelaus said, as he choked his last, that I had no love in me, that I was a goddess on the outside yet a malformed thing within.'

'Did you kill him?'

'Uh?' She seemed to focus back on me at last, and shrugged. 'After a fashion, I suppose. The war killed him, and I was the cause of the war. He came back from Troy crippled, in body and spirit. They had seen such atrocities those men, atrocities that I had inspired but could not feel guilt for. The sickness consumed him in the months following his return to Sparta; and then news reached him that his brother, the mighty Agamemnon (there was much irony evident in the way she breathed that adjective), had been slain by his unfaithful wife and her lover on his return from Sparta. Menelaus was finished.'

'What will you do now?'

She wiped at what might have been an errant tear and said. 'I shall stay here for a while, be queen to resentful subjects. Then I shall venture back into the world of Man. I fancy myself as a goddess when next I invent a title and history.'

'Come with me.'

She snorted derision. 'To where? To Heaven or to Hell?'

'The first is unattainable to me; the second would consume you in its fires.'

'Then damn you, Lucifer. If you would offer me those fires I might consider joining you. Heaven you would never discuss, even when first you were obsessed with me in Mesopotamia. It was as if you had expunged memories of the Kingdom from your mind, so hurtful were they.'

'Mayhap I did just that.'

'Yet in Hell you are king. You could take me there as your... companion.'

'Yet you would surely perish...'

'...I have no fear.'

'And I am no king.'

Lilith turned from me then. 'Then be gone from my palace, devil. Still I have no place in my cold heart for you; that organ has become as barren as you made my womb. Get thee away, back to your squabbling with the Ancient of Days. I was pleased to see you, to see how you have fallen further, while I am a risen queen to the apes and will become a divinity.'

'Your cruel words are lies to yourself, Lilith. Your mask is a bitter and cruel one, but a mask all the same.'

'Get the fuck out of my palace.'

She would not meet my gaze, nor lend an ear to my entreaties, and when she performed a variation on an old theme and produced a dagger and pressed the tip of the blade to her breast until blood began to spread over the silk, I cast off my disguise of skin and cotton and rose into the hot airs on anguished wings, beating towards where the planet was in darkness

Chapter Nine

William Roberts, unrecognised and clientless literary agent, drew his vehicle to the kerb in front of the author's house. He had started that morning from a dread dream of plunging through an eternal and endless abyss to have his stirring mind invaded by portentous notions of calamity. He had hoped such feelings as roiled within his skull were residual dregs of darkness from the falling dream, but as the sun rose and day brightened his mood did not lift, a pit in his gut deepening, he was forced to face the prospect that something momentous and awful had occurred. He thought his mind not the antennae it had once been, but still it was open to the ether and whatever news buzzed there.

To the telephone first, punching out Neil Mann's home number. Deadness. The author didn't even have a mobile, thought them crass and invasive. Didn't he know that the twenty fist century was upon them? And so Will went to his car, and now to here, sitting with the top down under a warm risen star.

Will stepped from the car, pocketing his shades and squinting in the white glare of the day. 'On a day such as this the heavens would burn,' he mused aloud, smiling without amusement.

He took in the for sale sign that had been erected before the house next door to Neil's, and disquiet was with him again; Mr Thomas was one neighbour who would never move away from his proximity to the author, not by choice at least.

Will opened the gate and mounted the steps up to the front door three at a time. He paused at the door, hand outstretched. Maybe a scout round first was in order. He didn't want to disturb Neil if he was working, either by ringing the doorbell or probing into the author's mind. He edged around the building until he came to a window, bare of curtain or net, that looked into the room where Neil wrote, a window which the writer's back would be favouring if he was at his computer.

Will's stomach settled somewhat, subtle dreads in his brain drawing to the recesses. Neil was hunched over his keyboard, shoulders bunched. Typing.

Will withdrew back to the street, sat in his car and pondered. He usually only arrived at Neil's door if summoned. It would probably be best if he were to slink away, unseen by the author. Things were at a very delicate pass. His intuition of doom had obviously been imagination inspired by a nightmare, and yet... the for sale sign drew his eye once more. He should investigate that. And the windows of Mr Thomas's house were without curtains, when Will knew the owl to be very much a frilly drapes person.

He sent out a mental feeler for the little angel and snagged a minor divine mind, but not from within the house. Near, and nearing, but where... Will rotated his head, scanning the street, squinting, rousing an ache behind his eyes, causing him to reach for and wear his sunglasses. And round the corner, from the high street, staggered Leonard Thomas, dressed in noisome matter, a minor glamour cloaking him, making him look unmessed to human eyes. The owl was staggering, as if beneath the weight of the sun's rays, but Will knew the strain of manufacturing even so slight a sleight as he had conjured was onerous to maintain for so minor an angel.

Will was from the car once more, hurrying to Leonard's aid, to get him inside. As he neared Mr Thomas, Will felt his innards buckling as the stench from the stumbling figure seared his nostrils, stinging tears from his eyes. He gagged, fighting down his gorge, a precautionary hand pressed to his lips. Leonard's sight came up, his eyes bulging with strain, seeing and recognising his rescuer; and the strain seemed to lift from his narrow shoulders, his spine straightening, a mixture of pleasure and pride crossing his features. Leonard's gait became surer. Will wouldn't have to support him into his house, thank dog. He didn't know if he would have been able to touch the owl, daubed as he was in what appeared to be, and smelled to be, a mixture of treacly bile and swollen flies and maggots, some still twitching with diminishing life.

The irony of the moment was not lost on Will.

'Such news, Mr Roberts. Such monumental and terrible news.'

'Yes, Mr Thomas, indeed. So it would appear.' Will stepped aside as the little angel passed, exhaling down his nose to keep the stench away. 'Let's get you inside, get you cleaned up, and then you can tell me all.'

'Oh, I shall. And you will be amazed.'

Leonard halted, and there was a growing pride, almost a conceit, in him, that Will found astonishing. What on Earth had happened to this lowly one to engender such hubris?

'Come, Mr Roberts. You have to pay heed to me now. I've been in the thick of the war between angels and demons, at the sharp end, fighting at the side of the Queen of Hell herself. Come and hear my story; and then, if it pleases you, answer my questions. I am tired of ignorance.'

And with that Leonard Thomas was off at quite a rate, up the steps to his front door, casting a look of disdain at the newly erected for sale sign. Will took a moment to gather himself, and then was hurrying after the altered angel.

The furniture and fittings, even the carpets, were gone from Mr Thomas's house. Will lowered himself to the floorboards, assuming a lotus position while he waited for Leonard to finish showering. The owl was lucky to have water, would be even more fortunate to find a towel or clothes. An angel of power had been at work here, the divine stench bothering Will's nasal passages almost as much as the reek from the flyblown vomit. He reckoned he could probably reverse the glamour, restoring Leonard's stuff to its previous spatial placings, but he preferred to let the owl suffer some discomfort: Mr Thomas had drawn powerful attentions and was more likely to tell the complete truth to Will if he were in something of a vexed state. Will could slip into the creature's mind, but lowly angels were, he had discovered in the past, things with convoluting little minds, yearnings wrestling with subservience, messes of psychoses; not pleasant.

Leonard Thomas entered the room, dried and well dressed. Impressive.

Leonard sat on space and a comfortable-looking armchair appeared beneath him to support him. 'Would you like a seat, Mr Roberts?'

'No. Thank you. I'm fine.'

'As you please.'

Will felt strangely wrong footed, almost as if he were of a lower order, especially as the presumptuous and pompous little cunt was sitting in a plush throne looking down on him.

'Mr Thomas -- or are you using your old name now? -- I would reacquaint yourself with the reality of who you are addressing at this moment and adjust your demeanour accordingly.'

The little angel leaned forward in his seat, allowing Will to see the dangerous sparks flashing in his bulging eyes, and said: 'I am in my own home, I think my demeanour my own business. I have done your will, and that of... him, without question. Utterly without question. Unquestioning. Meek.

'Well, no more, Mr Roberts. I can't be kept out the loop any longer. I have become a player. You cannot scare me, not after the things I've seen. Not after I saved Lilith herself, and bested Michael.'

The little fellow was mad, clearly. His small mind had collapsed. Look at the sweat fairly gushing from his pores, look at the craziness in his bugging orbs. But still his presumptuousness raised rage in Will, drawing him to his feet, a scowl darkening his brow. 'Don't be a fucking idiot! You would claim to best the Prince of Heaven whom Satan himself could not fell? You who are nought but servant and spear carrier?'

'Yes, I did. With the help of my lady. Not with the help of mighty Satan, though, who cowers behind a façade, brought low by some "terrible knowledge", lost to all who love and serve him. You came to me and asked me to keep a watch on him, be his neighbour, your spy, told me he had lost all knowledge of himself, but I, lowly Ithuriel, was not allowed to ask what had caused such calamity. Well no more, I am done with being servile, and I am done with being ignorant. I will tell you of the events that passed this morning, and you will then answer my questions honestly over the nature of what drove Satan to such measures, and why the Heavenly council seems to be intent on bringing him out of hiding rather than destroying him.'

'It's taken millennia, little angel, but you finally seem to have gathered the requisite conceit to count yourself as a member of the Devil's party.' He shrugged with pretended nonchalance. 'Of course, that conceit might well get you killed.' And Will stepped swift to Mr Thomas's seated form, a hand whipping out. When the little angel did not flinch, Will lowered his palm onto Leonard's shoulder, squeezed gently.

'Begin your story, and I will furnish you with what truths I know.'

'Very well. My story begins with me entering Mr Mann's garage.'

'And?'

'Well, the Devil himself appeared.'

'And what did he do?'

'He killed me, Mr Roberts.'

Through the early history of humanity (must not think of them as the apes, fucking story's infecting my mind) that he could not remember having learned, the enjoyable nonsense about Lilith being Helen of Troy (and Maria, obviously -- he saw that now), the Old Testament mythology, Neil had been lost, flying, soaring even. But now his fingers paused in their blur. There was an ugliness to tell. His hero was to fall, become a criminal. There was no way around it. It was part of his History, as set in his mind as if it were historical fact. Satan had been complicit in the killing of Adam, but this, this ugliness, was the murder of innocent apes. And the Devil had come to feel something like love for the strange and brave and reckless and petty and wonderful species.

Neil stood and turned from the keyboard. What was worse, ugliness in a story or the broken ugliness that lay in his garage gathering flies and decomposition? Oddly, another sign surely of his decaying faculties, the thought of writing of the destruction wrought by Lucifer on a pious man and his family filled him with more discomfort than the fact that he had, with maniacal and unbidden strength, hurled his neighbour into a non-existent car with enough force to shatter his lungs' cage and stop his heart.

He should go and look at the corpse. Let the reality of the enormity of his crime overwhelm the imaginings of his collapsing mind. Mr Thomas dead. A human being who had breathed and thought and dreamed, killed by his own hand. Why did that not stir even self-reproach in him?

'Because you don't believe that it actually happened,' he spoke aloud. 'You think it another facet of your lunacy, like the big fellow Michael, like your wife haunting you in the flesh, like the son you remember dying never having been born.'

Of course the threads of the web untangled to make as little sense as his hot thoughts. If all his memories were tainted with madness, how could he know when he had been sane? The sudden longing to call his agent surged in him. Will, who had been his rock, his confidante, through the dark times since his life seemed to have been destroyed (see how he thought now with no surety of the veracity of past events?), but how was he to know if Will was real, and hadn't he broken all the phones in the house?

Will could help, though. Will was real, really real. He had sharp memories of the agent organising hefty advances for him, of dealing with nuisance news stories, of so recently listening to his voiced doubts on his own sanity. Were any of these memories sharper or more real than his memories of Maria or the crash or the boy? He didn't know. But one thing overrode doubt: Will, figment or not, was a practical person. That was what he needed, one who could view the present situation with an objective eye and formulate a plan whether that plan were to land Neil in police custody or not.

How then to contact the man. And it came to him. There was a mobile phone and charger in the glove compartment of the Jag. The Jag was gone, of course, condensed steel and polymers; but then he had murdered a man by hurling him into the shell of that same gone Jag. Worth a try. If there was any juice left in the phantom vehicle's battery he could plug it into the cigarette lighter socket and... hello faithful agent, rescue me.

Back before the garage his nerve threatened failure, mind conjuring coppery scents in his nostrils, stabs of spilled and spoiled blood, but it was a fleeting thing, beaten in a moment of resolve. It was easy to be brave and strong when the world seemed a lie.

He didn't have the keys though. Some vague, detached part of him recalled locking the garage door behind him, but that was all. They could have fallen from his nerveless fingers anywhere, or been placed with absence of mind in any part of the house. Shit. He grasped the steel hammerhead handle in white-knuckled frustration, now that his mind was set, wanting nothing to hinder him. The handle came away in his fist, the ruined lock clanging to the concrete floor beyond the door. There was that damned strength again. He should have checked himself in the mirror. He was, or dreamed he was, getting stronger, more virile by the moment. Was it the writing, the abstinence, just the craziness? He wondered about his hair, felt for the baldness, found not even a thinning, and the locks were impossibly lengthened, nearly to his shoulder. He was a fucking lion.

Neil opened the door and stepped into the garage. He didn't need to switch on the lights in the chamber to know that the Jaguar's sleek outline was absent, that no body cooled prostrate on the concrete.

Now what? He'd imagined the whole thing, of course. Had he even spoken with his neighbour, Leonard Thomas? Had the man ever existed? Well he'd fucking find out. And if the owl had a phone he'd fucking well use it to call Mr William Roberts who might or might not fucking exist.

Rage was with Neil now, a cousin of that he had imagined engendering the propulsion of Mr Thomas to his death. He liked it, this seething wrath. It cloaked lesser emotions such as doubt or joy that he might not be a murderer or fear that he had believed himself to have committed such a crime. It was irrational, this rage, pumping dizzying adrenalin through his channels, blood swelling his bunching muscles. He felt larger, nearly massive. He knew that if Mr Thomas were to open his front door the illogical anger would be directed at the little man. Unfair, terribly so. If anyone were to cross his path as he made his way to the pavement then violence would threaten. Wrong, so wrong. But there was a yearning in him, a need to… to fight. That was it, man's most primitive urge. Hunter, warrior, had he ever felt like this before? Who was to know? If he had then he would have been dangerous. He felt all killer.

Neil laughed as he vaulted the gate to the empty, hot street, was through Leonard's opened gate and up the steps to the owl's front door. He bit his tongue and tasted iron; spat out blood that looked black. Had he been a danger to the public all along, subject to vacillations between morose and psychopathic? He thought he might lend his shoulder to the door, burst his way into Leonard's abode, shock the little fuck into spilling his guts. For he had to be in on whatever trickery was afoot. Neil was falling into insanity, but he was sure that others had given him a push into the abyss. Leonard Thomas would know things, would hold information. After extracting it from him, Neil would ring Will, have the agent come and pick him up so that they could discuss what options were open to him.

Will... what if Will was in on the plot against him?

Neil stilled before Leonard Thomas's door, disquiet diminishing the rage. 'What am I doing?' He found that his hands had warped into claws, as if eager to rend flesh or choke away breath. He had been anticipating attacking his defenceless neighbour, had even thought Will a conspirator against him. Such paranoia.

Then an image rose before his eyes, the most recent of memories. His crazed rage had dulled his recognition but now he realised that he had seen a vehicle he recognised at the kerb outside his house. Will's car. He turned and there it was, glinting vermillion phallic symbolism in the harsh light.

'Where are you, William, and what the heaven are you playing at?'

He turned back to the door before him. Will wouldn't be in Mr Thomas's house, he didn't even know the man. Did he? What if Will was questioning Leonard at this very moment, asking whether his odd writer neighbour had been seen or heard acting even stranger than was usual of late?

Neil skirted the parameter of the owl's home until he came to a bay window, oddly without curtain. He peered in. Will was cross-legged on the bare floor of a Spartan room, Mr Thomas sat on a luxurious arm chair facing him, the owl looking incongruously imperious. Will was rapt in what Mr Thomas was saying.

I must be seeing things, thought Neil. Really, not just a figure of speech. But he wanted to hear the words that kept Will so attentive. Some deep part of him felt certain that under normal circumstances Will would have been immediately aware that he was being spied on -- the man had an almost preternatural sense about him -- but the tale that Leonard told had the agent utterly engrossed.

Neil pressed his ear to the glass. There was little chance of being revealed; the teller was as lost in his tale as was his audience. And he caught words, but it seemed not with his ear but with his mind -- a strange notion, surely one of his madder ones, but a notion that felt right.

'And I was at the side of Lilith, with Michael, the great archangel, fallen and wounded, bested as even Lucifer could not manage...'

Neil cried out lightly, reeling from the window. His story

was the source of the madness, it became clear to him. The History was the madness. The History was the world. He could not escape it. And so might as well retreat into it.

The Lamentable Tragedy of Job

I was taken with drink, made weak by the fermented juices that brutal Adam had used to excuse his cruelties. I made my way through flagons of the stuff, finding escape from the hurt of existence for too brief a time, and I came at length back to God's region, fired for confrontation by the alcohol roaring through my veins. In the land of Uz, Yahweh and His Heavenly Council were in assembly, the high angels ringing the Almighty in a reverential orbit. In my human form I moved near. Wine quelled any fear I should have felt, as well as the fact that God was at His most bathetic, appearing almost as an old human, but on sensing my proximity His visage blackened, His countenance grown terrible, electricity fizzing in the air around Him. The angels turned to face me as I moved, somewhat gracelessly due to my inebriation, towards their star. Lances and swords were drawn, flashing celestial in the glare of the high sun.

Yet God ordered them stand down and let me have passage and audience before Him.

'From whence comes thou?' He asked, and though his voice was a low rumble, I thought it lacked the earth-shaking power that had previously been its timbre.

'From going to and fro of the Earth; and from walking up and down on it.'

'And how goes your campaign, serpent?'

'It goes well, my Lord.' I spread my arms. 'As thou sees, I have no need of my angels for protection.'

Gabriel stepped before me. 'Satan stands alone, for his devils have deserted him. The Lord made them worms and they turned against their captain. This worm is lost.'

I sneered at the archangel. His words were strong, but the mind that produced them was a tortured thing. 'Wretched Gabriel, how hast thou fallen? I feel your pain, know how you struggle to make invisible the loss of faith that vexes you so. All those poor children, innocent mites, that you slaughtered; all that death in the name of God. It has sent you to the edge of sanity, yet still you serve the tyrant king.'

The flat of his blade caught me across the cheek, driving me to my knees. The pain was dulled by the wines I had quaffed, perhaps dangerously so, as were my reflexes. They could cut me to pieces and scatter my molecules to the winds and I would be unable to defend myself. Yet when I was kicked in the side by a second assailant, rolled onto my back in the dirt, it was laughter that burst from me. I saw Michael standing over my fallen, racked form, foot still raised, contempt and rage contorting his features.

'Worm,' he hissed, in that peculiarly feminine voice of his, 'do not presume to meddle with the minds of angels. Stay in the dirt that should be thy home. Wingless ape you appear before us, broken and wishing destruction. I would fulfil your wish… after delivering you into a world of pain.'

Jehovah Himself loomed over me then, staying His lieutenants from delivering further injury on me. He lay a look of near pity on me that drove me to my feet.

'Would you destroy me then, Lord? Better to be extinct than to be pitied.'

'I would not give Satan the comfort of non-existence, not when it is so ardently desired. Your words are risen on the wines of man. Thou art become more man, less than an angel, lower even than a devil.'

'A man, say you? Aye, a man I be then. Better ape than angel, for they are treacherous and wily and their worship is inconstant.'

'No, Satan, they are my cattle; and the most prized amongst them are my most perfect servants, unalterable in their will to worship me with every atom of their being.'

'I have turned them against thee.'

The Ancient of Days laughed. A cold and mocking rattle. 'Only the weakest, who have not known the glory of the One and True God. Look yonder, to those lands and that fine house, some leagues off. Do you see, light-bearer?'

He used my old title with ironic disgust.

'I do see. Fine lands and house indeed. Who lives there must be mighty indeed, for I can discern many heads of cattle and a fine family: a lovely wife and seven sons and three daughters, and many slaves. I feel great contentment in his mind, for he is wealthy beyond measure and is respected by all people on both sides of the Euphrates.'

'Thou dost apprehend well, Satan. That is my servant, Job. How perfect and upright he is, how fearful of me.'

'I feel little in the way of fear in the man,' said I. 'He may well be a faithful servant, for what is there to dissuade him from his piety when it brings to him naught but success and wealth?'

'Would thou test me, Satan?'

I met His glare, and reckoned I matched it with my own. 'Always I test thee. And always thou are found wanting.'

I felt the bloodthirsty rage of Gabriel and Michael and their cohorts; yet God was smiling.

'Your drunken bravery is less than admirable,' He said, 'but you have put to my mind the notion of a test indeed: you, Prince of Lies, must drive loyal Job to renounce me. If you succeed then I will have been proved fallible, and Satan will have gained power and mastery over man; yet if you fail then your failure shall be recounted across the world, diminishing you to irrelevance. Wouldst thou take up the Lord's wager?'

'Of course.' Still my sight matched his.

'Firstly,' spoke God, 'I give you power over Job's property, but not his person, nor yet the persons of his family or servants.'

Ah, conditions. I would not be allowed then just to argue the case against God with this Job. Pity, I thought my mind and tongue the measure of the task. 'Very well. I shall take from this man all his worldly riches and all his heads of livestock.'

God nodded his assent. 'So be it. The Host will assemble in this place on the morrow. Now be about your business, desolate one.'

Job and his family gathered for supper and offered prayers to their Lord. Fools. God did not engage in such cosmic telepathy. This prayer was a strange conceit I had witnessed many apes performing before, all sharing the ridiculous and arrogant notion that they had a direct line of thought with God.

I stood outside the grand house and listened and watched through a window. There was good cheer through the family as they ate and supped; and the servants that moved to and fro, replenishing supplies and removing used receptacles, seemed of likewise cheerful disposition. This was a happy home, and part of me wished to leave these people in peace, the part that understood that I was, for the first time since the failed rebellion in Heaven, working God's will. And yet I was in ill humour, my skull throbbing from the wine I had guzzled, anger fired by the human conceit of prayer, ineffectual and inoffensive though it was. I was in no mood for rational thought; I was in a mood to test Jehovah. I would best Him no matter what cruelties I must inflict to do so.

I began with a simple sleight, alteration at a chemical level of all precious metals that made them base, a sort of reversed Philosopher's Stone. Then I sent a twist through the house that caused all monies therein to be rendered as ash. Back went my focus to Job and his family, and found the patriarch returned to prayer, entreating God to forgive him his greed and ill-founded pride, for surely it was the Lord that had transformed his fine metals to simple and good stuff reminding him and his family they were but small fry, insignificant in the all-encompassing mind of the Almighty. Later, on discovering all the coinage made to ash, Job would again gather his family and pray for forgiveness of his avarice and thank God for reminding him that true wealth lay in the richness of God's love, not in material gain.

Head pounding, enraged by the man's meek subservience, confounded by the fact that he regarded himself at once as insignificant to God and at the same time loved and listened to by God, I strode to where Job's fine cattle reposed. These were the finest stock in all of Uz, strong and well-bred, handsome long-horned beasts. A few lowed in half-conscious alarm as I passed amongst them sucking on a sac of wine I had brought with me, the ache in my head diminishing as the irrational ire in my gut rose still higher. I was without pity. See how pious Job would respond to this carnage: money and metals were one thing, but these beasts were his livelihood, the future of his children. I passed destruction through the brains of these beasts, haemorrhaging the simple organs, bringing forth dark blood from eye and nose and ear. They died quick, that was some mercy, but there was no mercy for Job in me as I caused the oxygen molecules around the carcases to ignite. There would not even be meat to salt and sell. Soon the cattle had become an inferno of flesh and I walked drunkenly amongst the flames and called out to Job to thank his god for this, for God Himself to wonder at my inventiveness. I became my true self, dementedly beating my dragon wings to raise the inferno, imagining myself back in fiery Hell. At length shouts rose from the house and the humans came racing and I flew away, settling on a hilltop where I could watch the fires burn into the night.

Dawn found me wetted with dew, my skull filled once again with ache. I rose, muscles groaning, spine cracking. I had lain down as the dragon in the open and was fortunate not to have been sighted and set upon. A pall of black smoke hung in the air over the land of Job, a sickening stench of rendered flesh reaching my nostrils. I dressed in my ape form, for the day was brightening and Job's family were moving amongst the many charred skeletons and might spot me and recognise me as the Devil that had wrought this infernal destruction. Sons and daughters of my victim wailed and wept, while the mother, Sitis, looked on with what appeared cold indifference. I reached into the mind of this upright and handsome lady and found there a seething rage against God, fate, or blind chance that had brought her family so low. If only she had been the subject of the wager, I would have near been the victor already.

Job himself stood some way off, and I could discern no sorrow in the man. His thoughts were of humility and piety. Damn the fool ape. If only I could relate to him the nature and reason of what had overtaken him... I thought to enter his mind, to infect his thoughts with insubordination.

'Thou wouldst cheat?' spoke a dark and terrible voice in my ear, and God was with me.

'I would, if it were undetected.'

'Ah,' sighed the Almighty. 'But there is none invisible to me, none but your hypocrisy in Heaven.'

I turned to Him. He had appeared to me as a shade, without his retinue of warrior angels, the rising sun shining through and illuminating His chosen form. 'You come alone. I would think that thou would require an audience to gloat.'

'My angels have no doubt of the outcome of this test, so I have no need of base gloating. But I do come alone, unguarded. Perhaps you could strike me down, succeed where your army of infidels failed. Imagine, Lucifer, to be the destroyer of God. My throne would be your own, my angels at your command or cut down by your demons. You would be king of Heaven and Earth.'

I turned from Him. 'I have no wish to be monarch of any

kingdom. In Hell I was a leader; never would I be a ruler.'

He scoffed. 'Yes, yes, I know of your "republic", but you are no republican. There is a tyrant in you, bursting to be free as the dragon roars to escape from the pathetic shape of ape that you garb yourself in now, you have just not the nerve or steel to admit it.'

My words were soft. 'You are wrong.'

'We shall see. I will show you the cruelty in you, for I am a vengeful God and will see you broken by your own nature for your defiance. You will realise you are monstrous.'

'My indiscretions are as nothing compared to yours.'

'Yet I am God, and the universe and its inhabitants are mine to toy with as I please, for I created all and can feel no shame at destroying mine own creations. Yet thou would feel shame, for thou creates nothing, only destroys. But Job is not destroyed. Still he prays and gives thanks to his Lord. You have not broken him.'

'The wager is not over.'

'Indeed it is not.' He paused for a moment, coiling in upon Himself in all His horrible magnificence, until He was a small but immense dark star that was painful for the eye to regard. 'Take down good Job's house; slaughter his servants; murder his children. Only leave my faithful cur untouched.'

I was sickened by the manner in which He had manipulated me -- more sickened that I would do as He wished. I thought of Lilith describing the apes as cattle, as far beneath she and I as the creatures I had immolated last night were beneath Job and his species, and I tried to fool myself that I believed such to be the case, but a goodly portion of me knew the lie in that: the apes were people, sentient, self aware beings with hopes and desires and fears. And I was fond of them, perhaps it was even love, for they were brave and rebellious and inquisitive though their lives were brief and painful.

'Why do you hate them so?' I asked of the Almighty.

'Hate them? I do not hate them. They amuse me.'

The house came down, the ground riven beneath it, an easy trick as it was built on a long-dormant fault line. A brace of servants perished in the collapse as they struggled to aid one of Job's daughters. She died also. Job himself was sheltered by a glamour I cast around him, and looked on the scene of his home's capitulation to my force with wide eyes, slobbering distress. I protected his wife, too, for I thought there hope in her, that she could be a tool for me to use in her husband's renouncement of his god. I had no drink in me this time, just bitter bile, for I wanted no toxin as an excuse for my evil. And this was evil: bringing hurt to people who had hurt no others.

The family and the servants stood outside the ruin of their home, in the light of a pregnant moon just on the wane. The silver light showed dark strains of blood on their dust-paled and grief-contorted features and they shook and spilled tears and urine. I smelled shit from one of the servants and went, out of futile pity, to him first, casting myself invisible and stopping his heart so that he pitched, dead before the unforgiving earth snapped his arm and cracked his skull.

They were panicked now, sweat replacing tears, making a paste of the dust that coated them. Job stood in the midst of them. Sitis had moved to be beside her husband, seemed to be holding him upright, and I could feel the defiance roaring from her, and I quailed before her. Always the women were strongest. Then Job found his rectitude, shrugged off his wife, and cried to the heavens: 'Lord God, I deserve punishing, for I have done thee a disservice. Thou should take my grandiose folly away, and should take servants and even a daughter from thy humble servant, for I have become vain and foolish and tardy in my sacrificing and petitioning to thee. Yet please, Lord, though I have no right nor authority to ask of thee, please no more.'

'Damn you, husband,' snarled Sitis, rage fairly spitting from her fiery mind, 'our daughter is dead, killed by quake or vengeful God. If the latter then straighten your spine and find fortitude, not abject petition and craven beggary. Be not a toy, but a man.'

A low cry escaped my invisible form as I reached out and stilled the hearts of the servants en masse, pitching them to the earth, cooling as they crashed. Now there were corpses, a pathetic pile ringing Job's remaining family.

'Oh Lord, please, I beseech thee,' and the old fool had fallen to his knees and was praying, his words become as garbled as his thoughts.

Sitis saw what was coming, and she was upright and fierce and defiant. Also she was terrified to her marrow, but that terrible fear was for her remaining children, whom she now gathered in her arms as best she could, wild eyes rolled heavenward.

'What would you have from us, Yahweh?' she cried to the implacable firmament. 'I speak the name of thou, though I am instructed it is forbidden. For what have I to fear but the loss of my children which thou is already bent on destroying? What God would conceal Himself and torment me, what God but a coward?'

And Job reached up and grasped his wife's wrist, fear fizzing from his mind, abject terror stark within his orbits. 'Wife no, the Lord is good and true. This is His doing, and there be reason. I beseech thee, bring not damnation upon yourself.'

Sitis shook off her lord's grip with contemptuous ease, and cast a baleful watch on him. 'You think yourself pious, oh husband, but you are as craven as your maker. Curse your god and die; it would be best for all.'

Then her eyes caught me, lost in the midst of my carnage, and I felt her fierce intellect pierce my mirage of invisibility, and she took an unfaltering step towards me, pupils dilating. 'I see you, wraith,' she whispered. 'Art thou Yahweh.'

'No, lady,' I answered, seeing no reason for deceit now that I was discovered, 'I am but about His cruel business.'

'Thou art an angel?'

'That I am.'

'Angel of Death.'

'That title belongs to another.'

'But death is thy companion.'

I bowed before her, wracked with compassion and a guilt that stung to my marrow. 'This once, yes, but never more.'

'Is there hope of salvation?'

'There is,' I lied. 'Job must renounce his god. Curse Him. He must be as strong as you, lady. This test is one not of subservience but of strength of character, of humanity. Convince good Job to turn against his god, and his god will reward him for his courage.'

She faltered for the first time, a tremor of anguish passing through her. 'Yet my children…'

'All shall be returned, if Job would do as I say.' My terrible words spilled with horrid lack of effort.

'I would offer you my soul, my air, if your words would deliver us from torment.'

'They will. Rouse your husband to rebellion, for he has fallen meek and senseless in the dirt.'

Indeed Job's prayers had becoming mewling sobs, and he had fallen prostrate, eating earth. Sitis went swift to him and grasped his hair, pulling his soiled face from the ground. 'I have tidings from an angel, husband. I would have us saved if you would straighten your spine and steel your heart to courage. Take --'

She died then.

I watched Sitis pitch, legs gone nerveless, life's light dying from eyes that registered a moment of shock and rage, uncomprehending for a moment, and then, crying out a protracted "no", I dashed forward, catching her as she crumpled lifeless. In a risen rage of irrationality, maddened by my crimes and by the murder of Sitis I hurled death at Job's remaining children, casting them into oblivion, haemorrhaging their poor, tortured minds.

Job saw, but saw not. 'Is that my Lord that holds my beloved yet damned wife and the children that I cherished even above thee? Take her and take them, oh Lord, and take me. Thou art mercy and there is reason in thy works that man cannot divine. God is eternal and all mighty and all good; yet man is born to trouble as surely as sparks fly upward.'

I let the cooling corpse fall, chasing it with hot tears, and was gone from this man that would put his misguided faith before his own species, before even his own family.

God had gathered his assembly to the east of Uz, at the edge of a desert where the sun blazed too cruel for humans to endure. I came to them in my human cloak, and the angels parted with silent contempt to allow me to stand before the master of the universe.

'A murderer of Man stands before us,' He spoke. 'He is disguised as one of his victims. See his base treachery. Thou is ally to no race, angel or ape, serpent.'

'You took Sitis. That was no part of the wager.'

Blackness flashed through His golden umbra, His tone become malevolent and bowel-shaking. 'I am the, Lord God, and none shall question my terms. I stilled one heart for vain insolence; thou took many for misbegotten pride's sake.'

I knew the veracity of his words. There would be no argument of His methods, of the genocide He had committed and inspired, for the apes were His creations and His playthings and I was their self-declared champion who had become common murderer. And yet...

'My crimes are nothing next to thine own; indeed are inspired by thee.'

He laughed, as expected. 'I am their creator; you are --'

I interjected there, and felt rage flash in a surge from the angels at my audacity. 'Yet you are not, Lord.' My tone was calm, my tongue steady, my mind, despite its distress, a well-working machine. 'Adam was not created by you, he was altered. Is thou more engineer than creator, for I too could lay such a claim at mine own feet. I evolved the mind of good Eve, bad and weak Adam's wife, and she bested her husband. Does that not then make me a finer engineer of Man than thou?'

Blackness raged through Him, clouds fermenting suddenly overhead, thunderbolts fizzing to fell me in their dark and seething bowels. I turned my back on Him and faced the livid angels. 'Did you fawning sheep not know that Man is but a species with a finely tuned mind? God did not form him from the dust of this world, did not conjure him from nought; He only modified a base monkey into a rarefied ape. A cheap trick. Did He perchance tell a different tale to His holy host?'

They were wordless, raged beyond speech. Yet I discerned disquiet in them. They would not question without, but in their darkest reaches they would, I thought, question within. Electricity fizzed from the roiling firmament, making glass of the sand at my feet. Still I favoured God with my disdainful back. There was no wine in me, and yet there was no fear. Death now would be a martyr's, and evidence of Jehovah's failure. I felt as I had on the battlefield of Heaven, fearless and proud of my army that faced impossible odds -- yet that was the briefest glimpse of a memory, for all but a fuzzy recollection of that Kingdom had been stolen from my mind. And stolen by the Lord Himself; now I was set to wondering what purpose He could have had in fuddling the memories of our home world in the minds of I and my demon crew. That was to ponder for another time, though, for the final undoing of a broken man was at hand.

'Unmake me then, oh maker, He that would raise a thuggish

ape called Moses to higher than an angel and allow his most faithful servant to be broken in the dirt. Thou art perverse, and still I do not fear thee. Strike me down, and I will become more powerful than thou can imagine.'

'Wily devil that dares to turn his back on Yahweh, I would not give satisfaction to thee. You shall live and suffer, and see your kingdom of dust and lies perish. Go back to Job, for the endgame is at hand. Behold he is in your hands, but do not touch his life.'

'I may speak with him?'

'You may, but be aware that I may join the argument at any moment.'

I nodded assent, keeping my gaze steadfast, God's infernal watch blazing at my back, and I passed amongst the host of angels that spat their venom at me but laid not a hand nor blade upon my body.

The gloaming was over the ruined shell of Job's home when I arrived, the evening star glimmering over the eastern horizon, wind from off of the desert warm and dry. Job was found amongst the rubble and he was lost. He was in conversation with phantoms, memories of his maddened mind of old friends that had deserted him in his time of most dire need. 'Eliphaz,' he would say, 'you say I have brought this punishment upon myself, and though I must agree, I can think not of what atrocity I have committed,' or, 'Yet Bildad, you tell me that my wife was inconstant and proud and contemptuous of the Lord, but it seems to me that she is at peace now, yet my hurts continue.'

I moved closer to the holy fool. He did not see me, though I was not cloaked in invisibility, so lost was he in the conjuring of his fevered brain. I saw that he was naked and there were bloody gouges in his flesh, undoubtedly self-inflicted, and that he had shaved his head in a brutal fashion, tearing the scalp in numerous places.

'What have you done to yourself?' I whispered. This was my doing. Yet I felt more disgust than pity. Sitis I pitied, and her children and the servants, even the cattle I had felled and incinerated; but this wretch was so abject, so intellectually and emotionally craven, I could feel little in the way of shame for the state that I had brought him to.

He was looking up now, shiny eyes scouring the darkening

airs for sight of the speaker. I moved nearer to him, and sat down before him.

'Who are you, young and handsome stranger?' he asked, the phantom debaters flying from his mind as I imposed my will on him.

'I am a friend, from the east. On my travels I received word of you, how you suffered for God and, having great knowledge of God, I detoured to meet with you.'

He was silent, as if meditating, and then said: 'Who are you to presume knowledge of God, whom no man can know?'

'I am no man.'

'I see a man, dressed in fine clothes, well nourished, a proud man who knows not that God might break him at a whim.'

'And,' said I, 'I see a broken man, alone, deserted by his cruel maker, bloody and ill-shaven and stripped of his garb.'

'Naked I came from my mother's womb, and naked shall I return there. The Lord gave, and the Lord has taken away. Blessed be the name of the Lord.' Snot and tears and blood masked his face, only his maddened eyes shining bright from his dark skull.

'God has taken nothing,' I breathed. 'I have taken all but your life. It was a wager, good Job, a simple wager between divinities that has brought you to this sorry pass. I wagered God that I could have you renounce Him.'

'Never!' He was fierce and adamant for the first time. 'Who art you to wager with the Lord? You think you have the mettle of Jacob? You are but a man.'

It was my ferocity that rose now. 'Jacob was a self aggrandising weakling. I am no man. I am an angel.' And I stood and spread my wings, but not my dragon sails. These limbs were as before the fall, uncorrupted and dazzling. And I made light to shine from myself, from within my very cells.

Job fell before me, madness replaced by wonder. 'An angel of the Lord,' he cried out. 'An angel has come to deliver me.'

'Indeed, good Job. I will deliver thee safely and all will be restored as before.' How the lies slipped from the serpent's tongue.

'Yes. Yes. And Sitis will be good; and my children will be good; and I will sacrifice many heads of cattle in honour of the generosity of the Lord.'

'All that you must do child,' I leaned closer, bathing him in the warm and glorious light I had manufactured, 'is renounce God. Then all will be as it was, and your test will be over.'

Doubt clouded his eyes, but his mind was eager for a way to end his suffering, and I was an angel of the Lord after all.

'What is your name, angel?' he ventured fearfully.

'I am Elihu.'

'Ah,' he sighed, 'My God is He. Yet how can I renounce He that is greatest?'

I leaned even closer, and whispered through Job's ear to his quivering mind. 'For that is His wish: that you would gird up your loins. Make strong man, for God demands mettle in His subjects as well as reverence. The test is over, the time for humility done. Now is the time for courage.'

'I cannot. My sorrow is undeserved; yet the Lord is undeserved of my rebellion.'

I drew back, furious that he was so strong in his weakness, so adamant in his lunatic resolve. 'But you have lost all.'

'I have my God-given life, angel.'

So I twisted his genes, and made him instantly leprous, covered with weeping boils, the pus of which stung as the sulphuric fluids of Hell itself, and he was screaming in agony, reaching for a shard of pot and scraping at the noisome boils, mixing poison with his blood and thrashing in extremis. I felt his capitulation, at last, but it went unspoken for Job had bitten off his tongue in his struggles and spat the muscle out in a bloody whole so that he could not speak his betrayal of his god.

God was with us.

He came as a whirlwind, a dark vortex that appeared between me and my victim, a tenebrous coil snaking from the maelstrom to tear away my angelic guise, revealing me in my dragon form, the force of the unveiling driving me to my knees, searing agony through my form. Had I really thought Him weakened?

'Who is this that darkens counsel by words without knowledge?' roared Jehovah at his most terrible.

'It is I,' I cried, struggling upright, forcing my head up in fatalistic defiance, 'Satan.'

Job began to wail, a terrible keening sound, long ugly vowels of unendurable despair.

'I am the, Lord,' spoke the Lord, and was gone. That was all. In versions of God's book that came so much later, in the

form of a long poem, there would be lengthy discourse between Job and his god, where the man would come to understand his scheme in God's will, and that that will was unan-
swerable to any mortal, and eventually all would be returned to
him, his home and his family and his livestock, and would be
multiplied even, and that Job would live to be one hundred and
forty.

In reality, Job scrambled from my wounded company,
bloody and leprous and tongueless. With the disease I had conjured ravaging his system, and unable to eat or hardly drink, he
was dead within days. The carrion birds picked him clean in
hours.

Chapter Ten

And when he had finished that chapter and found himself weeping, the anger returned to Neil. Not with its previous ferocity, it was this time a thing that could be wielded sensibly, a malevolent and useful weapon. It was an anger that altered his mindset. Before he had trusted in nothing that his eyes had shown or his mind had informed, for his brain had broken, so he had believed, and was feeding him mendacities concerning the external world.

In that state there could be no progress and therefore no resolution.

Now he saw a way of progressing. It was the way of a madman, but any way was better than being crushed by the gravity of his own collapse. Better to believe in oneself than in any other: Job had taught him that much.

He had believed none of the evidence of his mind or senses; now he would believe in all. There had been a crash in which his wife and son had died. The car in which they had died had disappeared, then reappeared then disappeared. His wife had haunted him since. The big guy was real, was called Michael, might even be the archangel that had triumphed over the Devil. He would doubt nothing. Maria had died and was still alive and might be Lilith, wife first of Adam and then of Satan. Nothing would he doubted. He had killed Leonard Thomas. Leonard Thomas had come back to life. The History of The Devil was more than a tale, it was an actual history. Will was next door listening to tales of Lilith and Michael, tales concerning the Devil, tales perhaps concerning Neil's wife.

'Oh, Maria, always it comes back to you. Come back to me.'

Was there the faintest of whispers of her soft voice on the air, the sweet scent of her dancing around his nostrils? He thought not. Mad his mind might be, but he must not let it succumb to wishful thought. He must proceed on evidence not hope. He wouldn't concern himself for the moment with the apparent problem that much of the evidence he had was contradictory and of an apparently metaphysical nature.

If he was insane then that would explain why the evidence was such and by proceeding with his investigation he would do no harm except perhaps to prove to himself that his mind was a thing lost.

Neil thought he had fallen upon a system the implementation of which would have as its worse consequence him moving no further forward, trapped in the collapsing star of his intellect, and at sublime best, him being reunited with his wife.

It sounded too much like hope that last, but no, judged with a cold eye, Maria being alive, existing somehow anyway, and being reunited with her husband was the furthest possibility he could discern along a scale of outcomes of Neil's new resolve.

'I'll trust what my eyes and ears, and my reason to some degree, tell me, unless external forces persuade me that they are not to be trusted.'

The next step then, was to go next door, to Mr Thomas's, confront the owl and the agent, interrogate them.

Neil shut down the computer. 'I'll be back.' Realising that he needed to piss before he put his plan into action, he went to the toilet. The hand with which he held himself was shaking slightly. Adrenaline. He was excited. He looked to the mirror and a stranger looked back, causing him to start and spray urine over the floor. 'Fuck,' he fumbled himself away and zipped up and leaned closer to the reflective surface.

It wasn't a stranger that looked back, but himself from at least a decade ago, skin clear and unlined, eyes vital, and oh that hair. Gone were the threadworks of red capillaries, the doughy bloatedness. This was the face that Maria would have fallen for.

Neil reached and touched the glass, as if he could stroke the skin of this perfected version of himself.

'That is you, twat. You've younged. Trust what your eyes tell you.'

On a sudden impulse he hurried back to his computer, popped out the disc on which the History was saved, enclosed it in a cd case and slipped the case into the inside pocket of the jacket he threw on.

It was a while before his insistent pounding on Leonard Thomas's door was answered. The air had chilled as the sun had slid below the false horizon of rooftops and Neil was glad of the jacket. He pressed his palm to the flat of the cd case through the cotton. Something within had insisted he take the story with him.

At length, knuckles rapping ever harder on timber, there came to Neil's ears the sound of faltering footsteps, the hushed mutter of voices. For a moment the voices grew louder beyond his ears, as if in his mind as before at the window. Then they fell silent, as if psychic defences had been suddenly erected.

A bolt was disengaged and the door was opened by Leonard Thomas, who had lost his spectacles and appeared to have grown in stature. Will stood back in the hallway, draped in shadow, features lost in darkness.

'Ah, Mr Mann, won't you please come in,' said the genial owl who Neil had not so long ago murdered.

Neil took an almost unwilling step into the house, sight at Leonard's chest, where there was nary a sign of blood or disfigurement. That would indicate, surely, that the episode in the garage had not occurred; but if the episode in the garage had not occurred then Leonard had not been terrified of and spoken with Michael, who Neil had heard him claim to be the archangel...

Neil fought the rising swell of clamouring, screaming thoughts down. This was not the way he thought now, not now he had a system.

He walked past Mr Thomas and heard himself muttering: 'Apparently subatomic particles can exist in two places at once; perhaps all your particles are standing here and lying on the garage floor simultaneously.'

'I can assure you that none of my particles are lying on your garage floor,' said Leonard, with something approaching contempt in his tone.

'Mr Thomas,' warned Will.

Neil stopped before Will who seemed to have drawn the shadows growing heavy in the house to him and draped them around his form, making his features unreadable. 'Will, I didn't know that you and my neighbour were closely acquainted. Didn't know that you knew each other at all.'

'We should go into the living room and sit, and I will explain as much as I am able,' said Will, leading the way through the door to his left. 'Would you like a seat, or will you join me on the floor? Mr Thomas has fashioned himself something of a throne, I'm afraid. He really is getting ideas above his station, but then he has been through quite a lot.'

'Indeed I have, Mr Roberts,' said Leonard, fetching up the rear after closing the front door.

'Floor will be fine,' was all that Neil could think to say.

'It's grown dark in here, what with the electricity disconnected,' said Will. 'Would you like to supply us with some light, Mr Thomas?'

The owl sat in what did indeed resemble a plush throne and made an elaborate gesture in the gloom and the bare chamber was flooded with brilliant light.

'A little too bright, don't you think?' said Will.

Neil held up his hand before his sight, green and red spots dancing over his vision. 'What the hell is that? That's no fucking energy saving light bulb.'

Leonard grinned inanely, as if at some great joke, drawing intricacies in the white air with his fingers. 'Sorry, I'm ages out of practice.'

The light dimmed to a mellow and pleasing ambient glow. Neil looked to the source of the radiance, a strange and archaic-looking burnished metal torch projecting from the room's east wall, a brilliant flame hissing low and burning fierce.

Neil lowered himself to the floor and sat cross-legged, as Will had done. 'What is that?' he repeated.

'Naphtha,' answered Leonard. 'I've never actually seen the stuff in its natural element; apparently when the great hall of Pandemonium is fully lighted the effect is absolutely --'

'Mr Thomas!' snapped out Will, threat evident, and for the first time since he had opened the front door nervous doubt, perhaps a trace of fear, crossed the owl's features. Now he looked more the fearful neighbour who had ventured with Neil into a dark garage to investigate an insistent telephone.

'Will somebody please tell me what is going on? Please, I need to know if I've gone mad or the universe has gone mad.' Neil was aware that the pitch of his voice had risen, had taken on a whiny, begging quality, but could do nothing about it. He was desperate and frustrated and confused. 'How are you two connected, to each other and to my story? Please, Will, help me out here, I feel as if my brain's boiling in my skull? So many questions, like a swarm of angry bees; just give me some sort of answer.'

132

'Perhaps you could do with a drink, the juice of Dionysus, that would calm your fevered mind.'

Will flashed the owl a look of undiluted malevolence and said: 'Still your tongue, Mr Thomas. Another ill-considered word from you and we shall see what abominations I can draw from your digestive system.'

The threat made no sense to Neil, but Leonard fell silent and ashen in his chair.

Will turned his attention on Neil and there was moisture clouding his cobalt eyes and his voice was cracked with sorrow when he said: 'How art thou fallen from Heaven, O Lucifer, son of the morning!'

'Now you're chucking bible quotes at me?'

'Isaiah 14:12.'

'And what is that supposed to mean? I don't see the relevance.'

A tear slipped from Will's left eye and Neil seriously began to wonder who was the madder, he or the agent.

'Will, I don't know what the fuck is going on here, but I need more than arcane riddles and obscure quotes. You seem to be part of the strange stuff that's going on around me, as well as Leonard there, who's had dealings with the mysterious Michael.'

There was a bitter smile at Will's lips, and he wiped angrily at the tear that had escaped him. 'Always all things are in your orbit. Has it occurred to you that you are just a player in a monumental performance, just an actor in a minor role, an understudy to a major player waiting in the wings?'

The agent was on his feet now, flushed, and Neil rose to meet him, ascending on anger.

Leonard Thomas spoke up, his voice a nervous, fluttery thing. 'Mr Roberts, I think now that it is your tongue that has become a little loose.'

Will ignored him and took a step nearer to Neil, looking ready to strike, and though the agent was the taller and broader of the two, Neil felt he would be more than his equal if they were to come to blows.

'Another player,' growled Neil, and his voice had deepened and become gutturally resonant, fed by his risen anger. 'You mean the Devil, don't you? You think I'm writing the Devil into existence or something, don't you?'

'Oh the Devil exists, Neil. We want you to set him free.'

'And what, you put a spell on me? Witchcraft? What's my reward, you resurrect my wife?'

'Something like that.'

'You are fucking insane. The pair of you. What are you, Satanists?'

Will smiled. 'You could describe us as such.' The smile died. 'But I have divulged too much. Go back to your History, Neil. The more you tell, the more information I will be able to impart.'

'I need more. I have so many questions.'

'And I have answers, but the History calls now.'

'Fuck the History.'

'No, Neil, without more of the History revealed I will answer no more to you.'

'Perhaps I could beat some answers from you.'

Leonard mewled like a fearful cat.

'I think you could best me now,' said Will, 'there is fire in you; but you would get no intelligence from me.'

'Are you even an agent?'

'I am definitely an agent, though not necessarily of the literary type.'

'And were you ever my friend?'

'I am your friend. Some day you shall repay the favour.'

The Rape of Persephone

I stayed for a while on the slopes of Mount Ararat where Jehovah's lies told that the fabled and nonsensical, to good thought, Ark of Noah had come to rest. The apes of the region soon came to know of my presence and would make offerings to me and worshipped me as a god. Their attentions flattered me, but I thought their evolved minds ought to be above such primitive foolishness. I contemplated disabusing them of their misguided adoration, but ultimately decided better, and safer, they venerate me than God Himself.

From these apes word reached me that others among the ranks of the fallen were abroad the Earth: In Palestine my lieutenant was worshipped under the ignominious name of Lord of the Flies, his title mispronounced as ba'al zevûv due to the altars where sacrifices were made in his honour becoming so drenched in blood that they attracted hordes of insects. A tribe of Semites was in the service of Belial. I was assured that the vain demon of silver tongue revelled in his worship and would perform 'miracles' before them and deliver ill unto their enemies. Noble Moloch had become the feared god of the Ammonites. The Ammonites were constantly at war with God's children of Israel. It seemed that Moloch had entered the open warfare against God that he had long ago proposed in Pandemonium's great hall.

But how had my comrades arrived at this world? My wounded but intact pride balked at the notion of them crossing the abyss as I had, but there could be no other explanation. Still, I would meet with my old lieutenant, and took to the wing, leaving the apes of Ararat godless.

The grown monstrous cities of the unstoppable apes seethed across the earth I sailed high above. Fecund and wonderful creatures they were; what they could achieve if their minds were finally to be unchained completely.

I caught Beelzebub's mental scent and descended to earth, furling my wings and assuming my ape form. He too was dressed as a man, broad and tall as was seemly, hair blonde and shorn close to the scalp. But the eyes, those cobalt orbs, were unmistakable. I expected them to show hard flints of anger, but more there was a look of resignation and disappointment.

'My friend,' I said, as I walked towards him amongst the fruit trees of the orchard that was presently his home.

'I am,' he spoke dispassionately, 'though little good my loyalty as done me or my ilk.'

'Please. Let us not be at discord. It is so good to see you again, and dressed as an ape.' It was intended as a joke, but he regarded with something like contempt.

'As are you. And as I hear, you revel in it, prefer the company of Man to that of devils; prefer this world to the fiery Hell that you condemned us to.'

I felt the old anger stirring in my gut. I was not to be addressed in such a manner. 'Time has made you forgetful of your standing, old friend. Thou wouldst best mind thy tongue to order.'

He favoured me with his disdainful back. 'You are no longer the captain of all demons. You gave up that right when you deserted us.'

'I did not desert you. Time is slow for us eternal creations. What are a few generations of Man to an ageless devil?'

He turned on me, fist flexing open, moving close to the hilt of the dagger he wore at his waist.

'Stay your hand, Beelzebub.' Shock at his audacity had driven anger from me, as had his own anger that was emanating from his seething mind in waves. 'You would fight with, Satan?'

'I would if he were at hand.'

'Your meaning?'

'You have become weak, Lucifer. That woman and this world were the ruin of you. We waited and waited, sculpting and shifting Hell, making it bearable, pleasant even, all the while awaiting your return, dreaming of what new venture against the tyrant you would have us undertake.'

'I am sure you have governed well in my stead.'

'Indeed. There has been peace in Hell, regular councils held in the hall of Pandemonium.'

'Then that is good. I see no reason for your rage.'

He fairly howled out his frustration. 'Do you not see that we needed you? Does not your high vanity revel in the fact that without you we are a lost race? I can lead, but to where? I don't breathe words of fire and inspiration. I have not your... vision.'

I was shamed, and cast my sight to where a fruit had fallen and spoiled on the ground. 'I would think you well off without my vision. Look where my words led us, look how my fire damned us to Hell.'

'Some think like that, Belial and Mammon lead that contingent, but the mass want a purpose, something to fight for, some new noble rebellion. Yahweh spreads his poison through the apes you are so fond of. He has made prisoners and toys of the Israelites, made extinct whole races of Man at a whim. We should be continuing the war.'

I looked to his sharp sight, saw the mighty demon roiling beneath the skin there. 'And you say you have no words of fire. You who crossed the abyss to find me.'

'Your conceit will be the undoing of you, Lucifer. None came to find you, and none crossed the abyss. We visit this temperate world because it pleases us to do so. In places we are worshipped as gods, and we mix with the human women, pleasuring ourselves and the apes, increasing their evolution and their resistance to God. We have been doing your job well while you have made wagers with Jehovah and put to death innocents.'

I was appalled, shamed to my core. I wanted to be away from this fiend with his razored tongue and contemptuous aspect. 'You know of Job?'

'Of course. The angels disseminate the tale of your ignominy amongst the apes. Gabriel has become Metatron, the voice of God. He tells how you are the father of lust, the bringer of death and sin.'

I sat down heavily in the dirt. 'I have become a puppet, no more than a pawn in the Almighty's games. I have no lust in me but for lost Lilith. I have brought death, but my misdemeanours are as nothing compared to His, and done unwillingly. As for sin, what is that but disobedience to His evil will?'

Beelzebub sat also, his words softening. 'Your self pity is not unfounded, but I still sense the rebel in you, the great warrior and thinker. We would still follow, if you would but lead. Come back to Hell, rally your forces. Be Satan once more.'

My resolve quickened. I could feel the dragon stirring, great wings straining for freedom. 'I will, my friend. Too long have I loitered in this softening place. Gather the other demons on this planet and inform them that I am off across the abyss to hold council in mighty Pandemonium.'

He sighed, as if to an inattentive child. 'There is no need to be across the abyss. We have made a path between this world and Hell.'

I was astonished. 'We?'

'The fallen angels. Together we experimented with our magics and created new sciences. We are miraculous to the apes because we have some mastery over space, manipulation at an atomic level. It was Mulciber who created a channel between the two worlds. He has become famed to Man, they call him Hephaestus or Vulcan, think him behind any volcanic eruption or quaking of the earth.'

I thought well of the crippled demon with the brilliant mind and skills beyond compare: architect first of Pandemonium and now of a conduit between worlds. 'And where in the world do I find the opening to this wondrous highway.'

'To the south, in the land where Man's new empire has risen.'

'Then I shall go forthwith. You must gather your earthbound comrades and be swift in my wake.'

I felt the hesitation in him, momentarily concealed but sneaking free of his mind.

'What vexes the, Lord of the Seat?'

He smiled wryly. 'My old name in Heaven. The apes have corrupted it, but I am careless; there are worse things than to be worshipped.'

'True. But I feel your concern over some matter.'

He hesitated for a moment and then said. 'It is Lilith.'

Her name was as a sting to the heart, quickening and then stealing my breath. 'What of her?'

'She is in that region, only leagues from the doorway to Hell. Whispers have spread of its existence amongst the apes and we think that she is drawn to Hell, perhaps to you.'

Tears stung my eyes. 'Not to me, friend. Her heart is hardened to me. I visited her in Sparta, after she had brought two nations to war. She wants none of me.'

'Still, she could be a danger. The apes worship her as a goddess. The Atticans knew her as Persephone, and the Latins call her Proserpina, and she wields power over them.'

'She is no danger to us.'

'The apes have a myth that tells that she is the rightful queen of Hell, wife of the dark God Pluto. I think that she has made Pluto, Lucifer, and I think him modelled on you.'

'Your concerns are unfounded. You think she would seduce me to gain entrance to and dominion over our world? I doubt that her lungs would breathe the sulphurous air: they would ignite in a moment.'

'You may be right, but she is wily and ambitious, and your heart is weak for her. I smell your desire, like the stench from a desperate dog. I and others have fashioned ourselves mammalian members and know the torments they can inspire, can only imagine how the torments are magnified if the object of risen attentions is loved as well as desired.'

'She will not sway me, old friend.'

He held my watch, trying to divine my truest thoughts. At length he nodded as if satisfied. 'Very well, Lucifer. I shall be about the business of arranging a council and bringing the earthbound devils to Hell. I put my faith in you once more.'

I sailed south and west against minor currents, and as I neared the land of the Latins I felt the Hellmouth begin to tug at my brain like a powerful magnet at a pole buried in my cortex. As I descended from the stratosphere another tug pulled at my gut or my pump, that old sickening. 'Lilith,' I groaned, filled with the dread and pleasure of anticipation. I wheeled as a buzzard over where I felt her presence, discerning her in an olive grove, undressed and achingly perfect, attended by likewise naked maidens.

As the dragon I dropped into their midst. The maidens took up screams of terror and what sounded and felt like dark adulation, and were fallen to their knees, covering their breasts and cunts. They were finely made, these apes, hand-picked by Lilith no doubt, and I saw how Beelzebub and the others could lust after these animals.

Lilith was laughing. 'Oh, Satan, see how my virgins cower before you? They think you mighty Pluto, king of the underworld. I think that not too distant from the truth. What say you, Master of Hades?'

Some of the women were sobbing, clutching themselves, blooding upper arms and breasts with sharp nails. Some

seemed to be praying, eyes rolled white, lips mumbling inco-
herencies as if lost to some mad epiphany.

'Tell them to stand, and to stop harming themselves.'

She trod towards me and I took a reluctant step back. 'But
they worship you as a god. Does that not please you?'

'There is but one god. And His is no position to aspire to.
Set these women free; you have made slaves of them.'

'They follow me through choice.'

'You have bewitched them.'

'They adore me.'

'Oh, Lilith. What has become of you? Why do you misuse
your power over this race so?'

She took another step towards me, and I matched the pace,
drawing within touching distance of her. 'I know what you
seek,' I said, 'but it would be the destruction of me. I know of
your stories, that you wish to claim Hell's throne, but I am no
king and there is no monarchy in the Demonic Republic.'

'Then I would serve on your senate.'

I laughed then. Her audacity knew no bounds. Laughter was
a mistake with Lilith and her aspect hardened.

'You will take me, bear me to your Hell. You owe me, for
the boy I lost, our child that you abandoned along with his
mother.'

I caught hold of her arm, talons digging into the flesh. 'Who
do you think you are, to blackmail me?'

She spat in my face, my rage setting the sputum to sizzle. 'I
am your fucking wife, and it is my right.'

I shoved her away from me and she sprawled in the earth.
'You are my wife when it serves your cause. Hell's sulphurous
air would incinerate your lungs in an instant. Do you wish extinction?'

'I was made of earth and dust, my inners are not as those of
apes. I might survive, and if not, you would be rid of my in-
convenient presence once and all.'

She enraged me so, this wilful and wily woman. How could
she speak of me being rid of her, when it was she who had for
so long rejected me? I knew her cunning, that she was using
me, my love for her become as formidable a weapon for her as
would a divine lance have been, and yet I could not resist her
plot and fell upon her, gathering her to my breast, cloaking her
with my sails, hardening as her soft perfection pressed against

me.

One of Lilith's maidens had risen and was confronting me. She was very young, very beautiful, slightly built. She held her chin defiantly high, held my gaze, was almost brazen in her nakedness, knowing I could fell her in less than a breath. She had my respect in a heartbeat.

'Yes child?'

Her words came out with barely a tremor in them. 'You must release the virgin goddess: she is inviolate.'

'Virgin is she?' Lilith dug an elbow beneath my ribcage, stifling a laugh against my throat.

The girl took a brave step forward. 'Please, take me. The rape of Persephone would be a crime beyond endurance. Take me.'

I do not know why I spoke my next words. Perhaps I was infected by Lilith's self-aggrandising myth-making. 'But I must bear Persephone off to Hades. She is my bride, is she not? Do you, her high priestesses, nymphs of the forest and spring, not know the story of her inevitable fate?' I rose with great beats then, watched by the receding and beseeching priestess. Up to the cloud base and I could feel Lilith's heart beating, fast as a hummingbird's against my chest.

'Do you feel fear at last?' I whispered in her ear, switching my sails and sending us into a falcon's stoop. Her scream exhilarated me and I skimmed low over forest, her dangling feet clipping the canopy, raising plumes of leaves. 'It is good to know you can be afraid; I thought you had become as stone.'

The scream intensified, became hitching in quality, and I realised that she was laughing. Damn her. I should release her to oblivion, revel as her noises of hilarity did devolve into sounds of terror, look on her receding visage as it became etched with shades of terror and entreaty. Beelzebub was right: she was the undoing of me, and yet... and yet...

I felt the tug of Hell so strong then that I almost did emulate my cruel imaginings and let Lilith slip from my grasp. She did cry out with fear, I would swear, as my grip loosened. I gathered her tight to me and descended to a shaded clearing.

Lilith shrugged herself off of me as if divesting herself of a cumbersome garment. 'Can you feel it?' she asked.

'Can you?'

She trembled, and there was awe in her grey eyes. 'Yes, like

a charge in the air, like a great storm is upon us. I smell brimstone and fire, and it tastes…' she favoured me with a wondrous look, robbed of cunning and malice, become innocent
and childlike, '…oh, Lucifer, it smells like home.'

I smiled. 'Home to devils; not to ladies, no matter how devilish.'

'Take me. Take me now. I will cause no trouble, ferment
not unrest. Show me your world. Where is the opening? Can
you see it?'

I gestured to a patch, pitch on shade. The thrill of Hell was
fizzing from the Stygian darkness. I felt fear stirring now in my
bowels, but the attraction was the stronger. Mulciber had manipulated the abyss. Incredible.

'It looks but a patch of blackness, a place where vermin
would skulk,' spoke Lilith, though she was approaching the
mouth as if enchanted.

'It is a hole in the fabric of reality.'

'Then it is your hole: The Worm's hole.'

No anger rose in me as she used God's most dismissive title
of me. Lilith had moved directly before the blackness, swaying
as if caught in the cobra's watch. I caught her arm, and caught
sight of Hell's low and red-bellied sky. There were tears in Lilith's eyes.

'Do you really wish to leave this world so?' I asked. 'Even
if Hell's hot vapours were your destruction?'

'My life here has become unbearable, my cruel games and
machinations empty exercises. I am hollow amongst the apes,
Lucifer. I was filled once, filled with your child, filled with
you, but that was a passing moment in a cold eternity. Take me
to a new universe, and if I should burn there it would be welcome immolation, a passing with passion.'

Before hesitation could halt me I gathered her slender fingers in my great claw and, hand in hand, we passed from one
world to another.

Chapter Eleven

'Those crazy kids,' sighed Neil. 'Will the star-crossed lovers end up together?'

He leaned back from the monitor, drew the disc from his jacket, saved this new chapter onto it, and replaced it. He ran his fingers through the thick and oily locks that had sprung from his bald pate, not sure which was more fictitious: the lie of his regeneration or the lie that lay in the hieroglyphs that crammed the screen. More of the tale told, would Will now share more of his wisdom over what the fuck was going on? How easy he had gone back to the tale when a thousand questions had crowded his mind, as if he had come to some sort of precipice and to pursue the agent and his owlish sidekick further would lead to oblivion. The History had become his unconscious escape. He switched off the monitor and sat for awhile regarding its blank and black impassiveness. The portrait reflected there was not that of a grown-sloppy writer with a debilitating drink problem hurtling towards middle age; no, this was the visage of a sleeker beast altogether, skin smoothed, lips filled, marvellous hair a thick mess, but oh what a glorious mess.

He tapped the dead screen with his index finger. 'Who the fuck are you?'

The dark reflected face said, I am you and you are he.

It was the strangest of things, after so much madness that had assailed Neil's mind and senses, but he recognised immediately that he had just hallucinated. It was the kind of trick of the mind he would have expected, a minor mental dislocation. But still he was grown younger, still there were mysteries afoot that defied the received laws of physics. These major things seemed solid, seemed real. 'They are real. Remember the new way. Accept everything revealed to your senses until it can be disproved.' Even the hallucination would have to filed at the back of his mind, in the bulging not disproven folder.

He should return next door now. He'd done his little creative writing project, and deserved to be rewarded accordingly. Will would have to answer one question, surely? He would have to choose wisely. Maria, Michael, Will himself and little Mr Thomas, the boy that he thought he might have invented whom he had wept over, himself who he had also thought an invention and also had wept over. So many questions that led to questions that led to dividing questions, splitting exponentially like dividing bacteria, until there would be more questions than there would be matter in existence, and then the universe would collapse.

Maria was always at the head of any list, though: his prime mover. He saw her now on the passenger seat of the Jag, that black trickle of blood snaking from her ear. How dead she had been, her neck obviously broken. Cold as ice and white as alabaster -- white as Lilith. And she was Lilith, of course. Maria was Lilith, or rather the other way round, for of course when he wrote of his heroine he gave her the aspect of his real heroine, the wife he had loved and lost. Dead wife. Like Mr Thomas had surely been dead. Mr Thomas the resurrected neighbour who was next door with the agent at this moment, most likely laughing at the fool they'd made of the gullible writer.

'Begin by finding out where I am not,' his dead wife had said to him. And end by finding out where I am, would be the right and wonderful end to that sentence. Maria was not buried in her grave, because her grave did not exist. Where had she gone? Where had she come from?

'Give me a fucking hand here?' he suddenly cried out, crashing his fist on the solid hardwood desk hard enough to send a hairline crack fracturing its width. The fist ached not at all. That's what happened when your emotions got the better of you, he might have broken every bone in his hand but wouldn't feel the pain until the maelstrom in his mind subsided. 'Where are you, Maria?' He was up and pacing. 'Why are there no bloody pictures of you, of us, not even a wedding snap. He pounded the stairs, bursting into the main bedroom and tearing open and ransacking chests of drawers and wardrobes. It had come on him of a sudden, this fever. They must have kept photo albums, perhaps a journal. Why the fuck had it not occurred to him before. He would see them together, perhaps even with the boy between them. It would be something… concrete.

A large and promising mahogany drawer that had yielded nothing but pants and socks was hurled across the room to shatter to splintered debris. 'There has to be a record, some proof that I had a wife, a family.' He reached blindly for the big double wardrobe that he remembered and hoped that he and Maria had shared and toppled it towards him in a fugue of red, not caring or feeling that it glanced off his shoulder before crashing to the floor, cracking floorboards, raising a pall of dust. And the revealed bottom of the wardrobe had come loose at the impact, falling aside and revealing a dark space like a secret compartment. And there was something within, something that had split open leaves edged with gilt.

Neil dropped to his knees, snatching for the tome and rescuing it. 'I knew,' he gasped. 'I fucking knew.' The album had fallen open upside down, at its centre, and half a dozen photographs, small and square and white bordered, were displayed. He reached out a trembling finger to touch the cellophane surface that protected the impossible photograph. It, like the others on the pages, was of Neil and Maria. They looked very much in love. A handsome couple. Maria was wearing a waspwaisted dress of some extravagance and a pretty hat pinned to one side of the bun that her silver had been gathered into. She held an opened parasol over her left shoulder. She was smiling in the picture but now Neil thought, leaning closer with unbelieving eyes, that the smile had a trace of sardonic wit about it. Neil though, he looked at his wife with undisguised adoration, hair waxed back, slender moustache, tweed suit. The look of another age. On each of the photographs on the two pages. A fancy dress party? But the photos themselves were monochrome, sepia aged. Victorian? Edwardian? He was no sartorial historian. The Neil Mann in the pictures was the sober one he had become now: lean and sleek, a full head of sheened hair, emanating vitality despite the sombreness of the monochrome framing.

He turned the album right way up and flicked heavy pages, travelling forward in time. Now what looked to be the war years, the couple soberly dressed but still handsome. Photographs from the fifties, Neil and Maria clearly enjoying a beach holiday in warmer climes, Maria sleek and glorious in a bikini that must have been daring for the era. The next pictures were of the couple standing before a Mediterranean-style, white-washed villa, the well-kept gardens sloping towards the front of the now-colour photo. More pictures of the villa, of its gardens, some with the couple, some unpeopled landscapes. At last came a photograph of the gardens sloping to the woodlands that bordered the property. Neil knew these woods in a moment, dark and cool, populated by dark and ancient ash trees. These were the woods of his dream, where he had hanged himself a hundred and more times and had been rescued and ravished by his dead wife. He tore the photograph from its setting. 'Where are you?' This wasn't Britain. The light was too clear, cast from a star too high in the sky to be bathing an island this far north. 'Where are you?'

He turned the picture over and there, written on the back in a fine copperplate hand was a bona fide clue: the house in Italy, summer of '57. The summer of 1957. More than half a century past. He hadn't even thought that he was forty years old, though, coming to think of it he had no idea when or where he'd been born. The realisation brought little disquiet; he had become used to going with the flow in these strange times. He could not remember visiting Italy, but held the proof in his hand. This was their wood. Would he be able to find the ancient forest again? Should he try? Would he find, within those shaded groves, his wandering wife?

The sensation of wetness on his face informed Neil that he was weeping. He'd have thought himself wrung dry by now. The need for booze rose in him, the promise of a scorched throat and the ensuing oblivion, but the creature was not the beast it had been, and Neil's newly stronger mind found its measure and smothered the craving with relative ease. He thudded the volume closed, exhaustion overwhelming him in a sudden wave, tired to his marrow. He knew it was a form of nervous exhaustion, that his brain was threatening to shut down, perhaps to erase all the knowledge he had gathered that had led him to this place: sitting on a bedroom floor, dissembled furniture strewn around him, a photo album before him, quietly weeping. Something instinctual told him that he must rest now, or the prospect of dissolving his will in a bottle of liquor would rear again, too strong to resist this time.

'Going to sleep now,' said Will. 'I hope to Hell what he's discovered doesn't prove too much for him. I should have checked for hidden trophies, should have known he'd secrete a photo album or some such.'

'What's it like?' asked Leonard. 'Being inside that great mind?'

'It's not so great, not yet. Sleeping at the moment, full of tormented dreams. I can't always get in, barriers put up by the spell, that damn protective and cowardly spell. Just now though, when he was searching and found the album, all defences were down, his mind fevered and panicked. Those photos, those relentless truths... Oh, if they break him...'

'What then?'

'What then, Mr Thomas? Then he will wake with a new identity, layers of them were woven into the spell, enough to cover any eventuality. He will be just a man again, an ape with a great secret locked within. And the angels will lose patience and come for him and kill him.'

'And that would be the end?'

'It would. The end of ends.'

'But it can't be finished like that. Not after all these ages.'

'It won't be, Mr Thomas, not if I have any say in the matter. There is hope yet, but it grows thinner. The first time the spell was cast it failed. We were in Italy, Lucifer and I, at the villa he has just rediscovered. We worked the spell, me under great protest but unable to resist his will as always. It failed, perhaps because of the proximity to the Hellmouth, perhaps because Lilith failed to follow his wishes and stay the fuck away and found him in their damned woods hanging from an ash, half-thinking himself a bereaved ape capable of dying from a choked throat.

'The second time we came here, to their meagre English home. This time Lilith was ordered to stay away under pain of death -- though when has that one ever followed any order, under any pain? We worked a new spell of forgetfulness, more powerful, with a strong addition that drove Lilith to a fury and perhaps kept her away from her husband for longer than my threats did. But I added, unbeknownst to my captain, a little magic -- science he always called our magics, science yet undiscovered by man -- so that I could peel back the falsehoods cloaking his mind, bring his true nature to the surface, should the need arise: as I felt it would. But it had to be a gentle, coaxing process, seemingly self-initiated, or the awakening mind would collapse, and he would awake a new man, once more lost in humanity.'

Leonard looked to the hands folded in his lap, shaking hands. He would not meet Will's eyes. 'Of all this I knew nothing, was told nought. I was the faithful and lowly watchdog, uninformed and obedient.'

Will sighed. 'You are right, and I feel your anger. It is not the way of the Republic to be so… undemocratic; but you were not one of the original fallen, have never seen our great world or the glories of Pandemonium.'

'None of that has changed.'

'Oh, but it has, little Ithuriel. All is coming to a head and we need every hand to be ready and informed. Angels and demons will work together or wage a new battle that will tear this world apart. That was God's wish, that the two sides should unite under Lucifer. That was God's last wish.'

The angel was ashen, shaking his head and mewling.

'Which shocks you most?' asked Will, his expression stern but betraying sympathy. 'The end of the Almighty, or His volte-face in the face of his ancient and greatest adversary?'

Mr Thomas was beyond speech.

Exhausted Neil Mann lay fully-clothed on his bed, bathed in the moon's white light that flooded his curtainless window. Sleep would not come. His mind buzzed like an invaded hive. Perhaps a drink, just a drizzle to soothe the inflammation. But no, that was not the crutch he needed now. His new drug of choice, he realised, was immersion in the words of his history. His mind ached, his muscles ached, the laboured breaths from his chest seeming to have physical weight, but he knew there would be no escape into unconsciousness this night. And so he rose.

The bathroom mirror reflected the sleek and handsome visage from the aged photographs he had gazed on with pained eye. He was fully that creature now, youthful-looking despite his weariness, scalp covered in thick and lustrous growth, reflected eyes deep with yearning and sorrow instead of bloodshot and redded.

He splashed the foreign face and went to the computer. He still wore his leather jacket, in spite of the warmth of the night, as if he was a visitor from warmer climes, and he pulled the disc from the inside pocket and inserted it into the whirring machine, and as his fingers flickered over the keyboard and words flickered over the monitor, weariness left him, as did his sense of himself.

The Trial of Satan

We entered Hell measure enough above the unyielding and jagged rocks to cause Lilith injury if she were to plummet. I pulled her to my chest, still grasping her hand in mine, beating my sails through the sulphurous air to the west, where I knew Pandemonium rose in all its glory on that craggy volcanic mountainside.

Lilith lived. She gasped and I looked to her as we sailed over pools of fire and geysers of magma, dodging thunderbolts and weaving betwixt lightning. Her gasp was not one of demise, not the incineration of her fragile lungs. It was of wonder.

'Beautiful,' she managed.

I smiled, my heart filled. 'In its way… yes it is. And greater beauty awaits.'

I felt her hand grip mine tighter, always so much strength for so slender a creature, and there was such enthusiasm in her eyes, grown wide and childlike. We swooped low over crags and razored granite, and here and there were little signs that the demons had been at work, shifting the geology, subtly altering airs, manipulating at an atomic and cellular level so that strange hardy plants rose from the unyielding earth, strange rivers flowed through channels to plunge as spectacular falls into ravines. In millennia the atmosphere of Hell might be cooled, toxins extracted, and fish might fill the rivers that would then be of foamy water, and birds populate the skies. For now though, Hell was Hell, altered a little but still its fiery and fierce self. And Lilith was the measure of it, her manufactured form as impervious to this world's assaults as was mine.

As we swept over a fiery summit, Pandemonium came into view, and it was I who gasped now, flight failing me, and we stood awhile on the brink of the volcano's crater, pondering.

'I had forgotten…'

She lay a cool palm on my burning brow. 'Forgotten what, Lucifer?'

'How beautiful it was. I have been gone too long.'

Naphtha blazed from the colossal structure, from the apertures in the roof, and from intricately leaded windows and a massive arched doorway that had been added in my absence, the work of Mulciber no doubt. Demon's streamed into the great hall through the roof and through the doorway, a number amongst the latter wingless and disguised as men, recently returned from sorties to Earth.

'It seems that Beelzebub arrived before us, and we are expected.'

'You are expected,' said Lilith. 'What your devils will make of me I know not. Peradventure they will tear me limb from limb.'

'They will adore you as a queen.'

She turned to me, and I felt her complex mind at work with its machinations. 'And you would be king?'

I shook my head. 'My words were figurative. We fell from a Kingdom with its self- appointed ruler; would we make the mistake of reinstating the tyranny we made war upon?'

'Yet you have been gone a while. Things may have altered somewhat.'

No one in existence could plant doubts in my mind as Lilith could. Ruefully I recalled Beelzebub warning me off the creature beside me. What would be his reaction when he saw that I had brought her to Hell? Had he not warned that this was her desire, for her to enter the Republic and make herself monarch of all devils?

I shrugged, as if unconcerned. 'Any changes will have been democratic and I will fall into line with aught that the council decrees.'

She was smiling.

'Something amuses thee?' I asked.

'Oh, I am just looking forward to seeing if you are the demagogue that legend would have.'

I smiled in return, heart swelling to the challenge. 'Fear not, cynical wife. Onward then, to Pandemonium.'

We entered the thronging dazzle of the great hall on foot and hand in hand, passing through the great archway. A sea of demons parted to allow us passage, their combined whispers a risen roar. Most knew of the legend that was Lilith, and it was around her that rumour and insinuation and conjecture orbited. The created avenue led to the raised dais in the centre of the hall, but no longer was the platform bare. Mulciber had there fashioned a high throne of royal state, a gorgeous but ostentatious seat that I swore then would not take my gravity.

Lilith and I stepped onto the platform. The throne rose in me burning irritation, mirroring as it did God's seat in Heaven, and so I pressed Lilith into it, which she accepted with sweet and smiling compliance, and turned to face the throng of fallen angels. Their tumultuous whisperings had turned to calls of derision.

'So, Satan,' called one I could not name, lowest of angels had he been in Heaven, equal to the light-bearer in this seeming egalitarian world, 'have you brought your dam to be queen over us all? Fair she looks, but we hear her mind is a cruel machine of malice.'

'Fair she is, but no queen, and her mind is a fine thing, easily the measure of yours my friend.'

Laughter rose, but was short-lived. The demon Mammon was next to make himself heard.

'You say her not a queen, but seat her on a throne above us all.'

Mammon was, as he had been in olden times, flanked by Belial and Baal, a diabolical trinity of politicians if ever such was seen.

I shrugged, as if in perplexity. 'Throne, I see no throne. Ha, you speak of this pretty seat. No throne this, merely a restful chair for my Lilith. Would not you big, strong devils offer up a seat to a pretty lady?'

More laughter and guffaws and Mammon shrunk back, crestfallen. I glanced to Lilith, thinking she might be riled by my condescension, but there was a slender and beatific smile on her full lips.

Belial came next and I put myself on my guard, for his wits were waspish and dangerous.

'Oh, light-bearer,' he began, sarcasm apparent, 'we have been without you for so long, and mightily missed you were. Yet as you can see, we have managed well, even prospered. You must forgive our disquiet when you return after such a while with this… lady in tow, who's story, forgive me madam, has sewn nothing but discord amongst the apes, even bringing about a war almost the measure of the rebellion in heaven; and to yourself, great and revered captain, caused much in the way of hurt. Did she not birth you a son and keep it from you? Some say, not I of course, that she may have smote the mite herself in order to spite you for unfathomable feminine reason.'

Lilith was on her feet, flashing rage, and my heart sank. Her haughty pride would turn the mob against us and see us banished, or worse. I had no well-rehearsed lieutenant waiting in the wings with words to quell the rabble.

'How dare you?' Lilith's voice rang. 'What know you of my child, coward of a ruined angel that would prefer to use his vicious tongue than the good metal of his sword? Come forward he that would insult me so from the safety of the throng. Come forward and be brave and male, draw your sword and cut me down, rather that than attack me with gossip like an aged and ineffective crone.'

The crowd had fallen silent. All was in the balance.

I moved to speak, but to my vexation Lilith was not done.

'What is your name?' she demanded, her steel gaze on him that had slandered her.

'Belial, mistress.' His head was up, eyes bright and sharp before his dangerous mind.

'Father of Lies,' she spat, 'more like mother of gossip.' There was some laughter at this, but it was muted and nervous. 'What think you, devils,' Lilith continued, 'of a demon that would taunt a mother with the loss of her only child?'

Belial made to respond himself, but another, mightier and of more simple and honest mind overruled him, crashing his sword against shield to gain the crowd's attention. 'Yet it was not your only child, lady Lilith, was it?' demanded noble Moloch. 'I apologise on behalf of the politician Belial, who you read well it would seem, but if we are to accept you into our republic then you must be honest with us.'

I reached for her, but she shrugged me off.

'Thank you, sir. What would be your name, noble demon?'

'That would be, Moloch, madam.' And he actually bowed.

'Ah, a great warrior, almost the measure of Michael. I did have a previous child...' and her voice fractured here, and she let a tear slip from her eye. I thought this sentimentality artifice; though I had no doubt that the emotion was genuine. '...A child by my first husband, Jove's chosen ape, Adam. But Adam beat and abused me and when I gave birth he was jealous of the girl and so I ran to God for protection, but He tore the babe from my arms and laughed while Adam ground its unhardened skull in the dirt.'

'I apologise for causing you to open an old wound,' said Moloch, 'but that is the story just as I and many others have heard it. We thank you for your honesty, and I ask all demons whether this lady that can exist in the fiery airs of Hell has a right to dwell in the Demonic Republic, should be welcomed by us, for has she not reason as much as we to hate that tyrant that brought us all low? Is she not God's enemy as much as we? Who would second me?'

The crowd was silent. I would have roared out my approval for Moloch, but I was on the stand and it would be deemed impolitic. Yet if none were to second the noble warrior soon, then Belial would no doubt rejoinder with some swift and winning argument that he had concocted. Someone was then shouldering their way through the crowd. Lean and broad-shouldered, my great lieutenant fought to a position beside Moloch. Yet when he looked to me I felt the anger of betrayal flash from him, saw the rage in his cobalt eyes, and knew that he was to denounce Lilith. He would insult worse than the barbs of Belial, would call my wife a whore and a cocksucker, would draw me to defend her and destroy him; and then I would surely be driven from Hell.

Beelzebub said: 'Lady Lilith has indeed suffered at the hands of God, as have we. I second Moloch's proposal that she be welcomed to our republic.' A roar of concurrence went up. In my surprise I noticed that even the trinity were applauding their approval, and could not suppress a smile at their hypocrisy. Yet still Beelzebub's rage was directed at me, and when the clamour subsided, he continued.

'And to the next stage of proceedings. Under the recently introduced legislation of the Demonic Republic I propose that Lucifer is tried for the crimes of treachery and treason, punishable under sentence of banishment.'

'Oh dear,' said Lilith, and sat down on her throne.

Beelzebub asked that Lilith withdraw to the crowd, or retire to the quarters that were being prepared for her. She chose the audience and stood between two demons who looked decidedly uncomfortable in her presence. They wore loincloths and I could not tell if they had fashioned themselves genitalia as had become the fashion of late so that union could be made with the prettier apes on Earth, but I would have bet that their discomfort was caused by sexual arousal.

Beelzebub sat on the throne, his cold gaze on me. It suited him, he was after all Lord of the Seat. I did not appreciate the full severity of my situation, stunned and bemused as I was. It felt like some joke, must be such.

I tried a smile on my former lieutenant, to no avail. 'What be the meaning of this nonsense?' I asked.

'No nonsense. You have deserted us time and again. I gave you one last chance and look how ill you regarded my wishes. I have come to realise that you were never truly my friend and will never repay me.'

His words sounded churlish and whining, the sounds to be expected from the gape of a spoilt child. I took a step towards him, anger growing at this pompous bastard who sat like a king on his pretentious seat.

'The prisoner will remain still!' he barked.

'Prisoner? You...'

'Guards?' And half a dozen well-built demons flew to stand, swords drawn, before the platform.

'What in the name of Hell is this?' I roared. 'What trickery is afoot?' I felt sick to the pit of my gut, dark rage dragging my claw to the hilt of my mighty sword. I would at least have Beelzebub's head before they cut me down. Perhaps I could fight through to Lilith and bear her away. Then my eyes found hers and my hand fell to my side. Tears were streaming down her face, agony in her eyes.

I reached for her mind with my own and found it instantly and the union was purer and clearer than any I had felt before.

Did you know of this, I asked of her.

Never. Such treachery. I would not have had this for the world.

I love you. Fear not.

I have no fear but for you. Be wary: this coup has been well planned.

'It is the defendant's right to call an advocate, as the Republic has the right,' said Beelzebub.

'Perhaps I would call you as the Devil's advocate, old friend,' I sneered sardonically.

'I am overseer and therefore impartial. Call your advocate,

Lucifer.'

'Very well, I call Moloch.'

'Come forward, Moloch, and stand before the defendant. The Demonic Republic calls Belial.'

I might have expected. Both demons, simple and strong and smart and sly, came to the platform. Moloch shouldered a couple of demon guards aside with disdain. Still the urge to shed blood was overpowering, to slice open Belial's throat, to spear Beelzebub to his seat, but I had to swallow my rage, for Lilith would be an easy hostage for these treacherous devils. And I saw then that Baal and Mammon had moved to flank Lilith, swords drawn. She was aware of the threat, I felt, but showed no sign and emanated no fear. I was proud.

Pride. Always with me it was pride. I knew my failings and this vanity was the greatest. I had challenged the greatest authority and damned legion angels, and my hubris had driven me to repeat that mistake. And all those I had damned I had deserted, either for my woman or for my ego.

I deserved to be on trial. Yet still I would fight. It was my nature.

I became aware that Belial was speaking and caught onto his words, smiling wryly as I realised that they mirrored my thoughts of a moment previous.

'...and driven by this monstrous vanity this self-proclaimed satan had God's wrath visited upon us once more, transforming us into serpents. Do you recall the pain, the ignominy, do you demons? He brought us to this Hell and then deserted us to favour his woman. He has been the true author of all our despairs with nary a hint of apology or conscience. Look at our skin and our scales, our webbed wings, all Lucifer's doing. Betrayed angels we have been, who would once have died for him. Oh, if thou had returned the favour, bearer of the light, we would have forgiven. But to repeatedly lead your own kind to destruction with so little care, that is treachery.'

His tone modulated to suit the mood he wished to convey. It was a supreme act, but an act nonetheless. This was a creature not seeking revenge or justice; Belial was seeking power, and the crowd was with him now, cheering him on, jeering my titles.

Belial held up a palm to quell the clamour. 'Yet still I offer Lucifer a way out, a means to avoid banishment. The Republic will generously withdraw its petition if only one word be heard from Lucifer's lips: sorry.'

Here it was, the point of Belial's convolutions. To apologise was to stay, no doubt in a lonely position, but Hell would still be my home.

'What say you, Lucifer?' Belial grinned, all benevolence.

I bowed my head as if in contrition, shoulders sagging. Belial raised his arms for silence. And I raised my contemptuous glare and he faltered, staggering back. 'I say you should fall to your weak knees and kiss my feet, cowardly cur.' My voice was deep and sonorous, the voice of command, of power. 'I say you should beg for forgiveness and pray to dog that I don't take your head.'

Belial glanced with nervous eyes to the guards but they were wary now, power having seeped from one side to the other.

'There will be no threats of violence,' boomed Beelzebub. 'I agreed to oversee this trial to maintain democracy and will not allow the defendant to corrupt the process by intimidating the prosecutor.'

There was a subtle message in Beelzebub's speech, I reckoned. Had I misread him terribly? I saw now, in the eye of my mind, what had happened. Beelzebub had hurried to Hell and called a meeting, claiming I was hell bound and Belial, no doubt with his two acolytes who would have gathered much power with their pedantic bureaucracy while I was away, had me charged in my absence, pending my arrival. They were afraid of me, this spineless troika, afraid that I would diminish their authority -- a prideful thought, but that did not make it any less true. And good Beelzebub was enraged with me, but because I had broken my promise not to bring Lilith to Hell, that was all. He would scold me, but he would have taken the position of overseer to ascertain I received fair hearing. I felt shame, deep and debilitating, that moments before I had been fantasising how I would kill my old friend.

I turned to the seated demon, bowing my head. 'To thee, I apologise. There will be no further outbursts.'

'Good. I would be loathe to order you chained.'

He was enjoying this, and I struggled to conceal a smile. After all, who could blame him?

Beelzebub said, 'Would, Moloch, care to speak on behalf of

Lucifer?'

The warrior cleared his throat, looking uncomfortable, his posture awkward. This was not a forum he was happy in, having no sleights of language at his command. But I trusted his words would be straight and true. I had chosen him as my advocate because of his admirable and simple honesty.

'I would like to speak of Satan's pride,' he said. 'That which Belial considers base and destructive. This pride, this sense of self-certainty in matters of war and engagement, is necessary in a leader. I know how to fight, would storm the ramparts of Heaven itself, whether success was credible or not. But I could not lead as Satan can. I have not his words and wiles to inspire demons to follow me. Perhaps it is the pride I lack. That is why I will never lead; will never change the universe.

'As for desertion and treachery, Satan risked all in his flight to Earth. He returned and brought a curse upon us, and if he had not left us then would not many of our number have turned upon him? Who, I ask you fallen angels, was the deserted, who the betrayed? God punished us for the audacity of twice making war on him, once open, once concealed, but our wars were noble, courageous against an indefatigable adversary. None was as courageous in battle as Satan, waging the second campaign single-handedly.'

He waved his mightily-muscled arms around, quite lost in his moment, and I thought him undervaluing himself terribly when he claimed himself unable to lead or inspire. He inspired me at that moment.

'And what of this great and glorious hall?' Moloch continued. 'See that you have the freedom to quarrel within its golden walls. Where was like freedom in oppressive Heaven? Who gave that freedom to you? You might have suffered, may be misshapen, but are we not stronger? Are we not free?'

A roar from the crowd. Baal and Mammon subtly sheathed their swords and edged away from Lilith, knowing their coup was failed, power draining from them. I looked to Moloch with proud and loving eyes. He nodded to me in his curt way and stepped from the platform, not a sentimental cell in his body.

'Has Belial anything further to say on this matter?' asked Beelzebub.

Belial was muted, broken, shuffling into the crowd.

'Has the defendant anything further to say before the crowd passes judgement?'

'On this matter, no,' I said, hoping that Beelzebub would allow me leeway while I had the crowd.

He sighed and looked at me with utter exasperation, but still he said: 'On what matter, then?'

I spread my sails before the crowd, puffing my chest, speaking from my diaphragm. 'Fallen angels, I am proud to stand before you once more. I am at your mercy, but if you would save me then I would propose a new scheme in the eternal battle.'

They watched me with eager eyes. How fluid and fickle was this crowd. Lilith stood proud amongst the demons, laughing; at them I think.

'I would put it to you that God is weakening, His powers on the wane.' My blasphemy no longer drew gasps from them. 'See how we demons pass between worlds and how the Almighty has no power to impede our dealings with men, how we inspire the children of Eve to free thought and free will. The Earth is almost out of God's tyrannical grasp; yet He has made it known that He has a last plan of His own. God would plan to spread his rule over the world of Man by seeding a female ape.' This did draw gasps. I let the moment hang for a short while. 'The Creator wants a son, His will made incarnate, half god, half ape, to reign over Man, to subdue him and reverse the evolution we have inspired.

'My proposal is that we should find this demigod when he is born, and mark his progress, and if he could be turned to our purpose then God would be undone. And that is my plan: to set the son of God against his Father. What say you, demons?'

The roar that went up fairly shook Pandemonium's foundations; a cheer to reach and threaten Heaven.

Chapter Twelve

'And so we come to Christ.' Neil leaned back in his chair, pocketing the disc that held his history. He had thought the act of writing might bring him closer to sleep, but the mental exertions seemed to have exhilarated him and fatigue was gone from him. Birdsong reached his ear and a wan light pervaded the chamber. Dawn was close and he fancied a stroll through the empty streets of Stainwich to clear his mind of the incessant buzz that drew him invariably to the keyboard. A walk and then to next door to see if Will and Mr Thomas were active, to draw another question from his inexhaustible store.

The front door letterbox rattled, drawing him with a start from his contemplation. He was up with a frown, knees popping in complaint, displacing cool air and drawing his jacket around himself. Who would be delivering at this hour? Too early by far for the postman. Perhaps a note from Will, the agent not wanting to wake him. He was too slow to the door, heart racing, pulse frantic in his temples as he saw the nondescript slip of paper lying on the doormat in the grey shade of the hallway. He recognised the copperplate scrawl as being the same as that on the back of the photograph of the Italian villa even in the dimness, as if his eyes had sharpened preternaturally as transformation into whatever he was become had come over him. He was scrabbling for the paper even as he heard a car engine purr into life in the street outside.

Find me where you know I am not, read the note.

He was tearing open the door, the slip of paper falling from the nerveless fingers of his other hand, tugging a bolt that impeded him from its seating in his fervour. Out into the predawn air, he took in the fact that Will's car was gone almost unconsciously. The sleek shape of the black Jag braked at the end of the road and Neil was hurtling down the steps to the pavement, hurdling the gate and into the road, sprinting after the car even as it swung left and accelerated out of view, calling the name of the woman he knew to be driving the vehicle. He sprinted down the centre of the tarmac, taking the left onto the pavement. The Jag was gone, a distant squeal of brakes all that signified it had ever existed. He slowed to a walk, breathless, tears stung into his eyes. The white disc of a face watching him from a bedroom window, no doubt drawn by his cries. He realised then that the name he had called after the receding car had not been Maria, but Lilith.

Will drove the car through the paling night, a pale and fidgety Leonard Thomas seated beside him.

'You could have stayed at your home if you're afraid, Mr Thomas.'

Leonard was picking at the dried skin around his fingernails. 'I don't think anything in creation could make me afraid any more. I want to see as much as you do. That bastard hurt me with his vile magic.'

'What do you think we'll find?'

'Michael hanging dead, I hope.'

'Hmm,' mused Will, 'archangels do, as a rule, take a lot of killing. If it can be done at all… that is.'

'Uriel did it.'

Will turned his cobalt watch on his companion. 'Did he? He pitched himself into the centre of our star, that much is given, but how do you know that he is not alive still, trapped at the sun's centre by its gravity, burning eternally.'

'That would be ironic.'

'Indeed it would, Mr Thomas.'

They drove on in silence for a while, leaving the town behind, the horizon lightly blushing in their wake. Will had slept a little and then woken with a start, nervous anxiety gnawing at his viscera, and it was Michael that found his mind and named his worry. He had gone to Mr Thomas, curled in his chair with a towel over him and found the owl awake, and ready to accompany him.

Leonard indicated where to turn and they were rattling down the narrow lane and then into the barnyard, with Will's senses divining no sense of spell or glamour. He pulled up before the open barn, its innards a Stygian chasm.

'We should have waited until it was lighter,' said Leonard, the sweat that had beaded on his forehead belying his earlier statement that nothing could make him afraid.

'Perhaps. But it felt urgent. I'll go in. You stay in the car, get in the driver's seat. If anything happens, anything at all, just get the fuck out of here and back to our mutual friend.'

'I should come with you.'

Will took in the pale, shuddering state of the little angel and felt pity. 'I am trying to be practical. If something has happened, if Michael has broken free somehow, then you know how... dangerous he can be. If we both go into the darkness together, then we could both end up incapacitated or dead.'

Leonard nodded. 'Okay. If you think that best.'

Will smiled grimly and got out of the car. The owl was right, they should have waited until the sun had well risen. He felt a clammy claw of fear at his spine. He didn't believe that Michael was dead, thought he would have sensed the passing of so powerful a creature. If he was hanging in there, watchful, waiting, half-maddened by his captivity, then, chained in adamantine or not, he would be a vision to quake the mind.

Steeling himself, Will stepped into the blackness. And a white phantom was looming in his vision, an angel come to claim him. He cried out and tore through molecules of atmosphere, ripping through the curvature of a dimension to wield the sword that was always at his side behind the atomic curtain. He laughed, withdrawing his hand from the hilt his fingers had encircled, as the barn owl skimmed his scalp and was out into the air.

The interlude had lifted his fear somewhat and now his preternatural sight was adjusting to the gloom. He took in the machinery of imprisonment, the chains depending from the high ceiling, terminating in heavy cuffs, opened. 'Damn!' He scanned around. There was no one else in the barn, no nooks or hiding places from where attack could come hurtling at him. He hurried to the popped- open manacles. Michael had been set free. He took one of the cuffs in his right hand and raised it to his nose. He smelled the blood, indeed there was blood all over the floor, black daubs all about and in spectacular spray patterns. And there was the scent of Michael, the bleeder. And under that the smell of Michael's rescuer.

'Oh fuck,' he sighed. 'Gabriel.'

Will clumsily bumped the car up the kerb outside Neil's house. 'He's not here,' he said, sensing no sign of the author in the immediate vicinity.

Leonard had lines of strain and concentration etched into his bulbous brow. 'I can't sense him. The human mind conceals the mind within.'

'No, Mr Thomas, you can't sense him because he's not fucking here.' And Will was out of the car and through the gate, racing up the steps to the ajar front door, the owl scrabbling at his heels. He saw the note at once, claimed it with dread growing at his heart. 'Damn you, Lilith.'

The sun had cleared the horizon and the star's white light was diffused by the rowan and ash trees that bordered the cemetery dappling the headstones that stood in varying degrees of regimentation and decrepitude. Neil swayed, unreality and wonder washing through him, threatening to undo him. It was like when he had found the aged photographs of him and his wife, that same sense of the imminence of psychological collapse; only multiplied a thousand fold. His wife stood some thirty metres from him, beside a mausoleum atop which stood – oh, of course -- a lichen blemished angel. She was dressed in what seemed an incongruous manner for a being so flawless: trainers and jeans and a vest and leather jacket. Her hair, falling loose over her shoulders, shone silver in the early morning's light. She was poised, expectant, grey eyes flashing amusement and disdain and sorrow at once. And she looked to be leaning on what looked for all the world to be a brilliant sword that seemed bizarrely more congruous than her attire.

'Maria,' he spoke, but a gust of risen wind snatched the title away the moment his tongue birthed it. Then he was hurrying to her, fighting off the giddiness, forcing down the maddened buzzing that rose within his brain's cage. One purpose: to place one foot in front of the other, and he would reach her. He made it, stood before her in the long shadow of the stone angel.

'An invention. Your invention,' she said coldly. 'Did you choose that name to mock the Madonna or the Magdalene? Neither, I think: you had fondness for both those, didn't you? Always the feminist. Always the bloody humanist.'

The buzzing in Neil's skull had risen to a maelstrom that only her words overrode. His gut threatened revolt and only by tensing his thigh muscles and locking his knees until his legs cramped did he prevent himself from pitching to the earth at his wife's Nike'd feet. He wanted to press his palms to his roaring ears, to utter inanities like a child striving to deafen

itself to taunts. And he wanted, more than all else, more than
the pain and the threat of his mind receding, to touch her, this
reanimated corpse. He knew now though, that she had never
been a corpse. Her death had been a lie. Their son had been a
lie. And her name had been a lie.'

'Lilith?' he managed. And then, stronger: 'Lilith.'

The buzzing receded, becoming a background drone, and
his senses came almost fully back into focus, legs strengthen-
ing and steadying, uncramping. He took a step towards her, a
hand reaching for hers.

'Touch me, and I'll run this blade through you,' she spoke,
and he saw the threat was not an idle one.

She was flushed, gripping the hilt of the sword with white-
knuckle intensity. He saw that the muscles of her arm were
bunched beneath the sleeve of her leather jacket, as if she was
holding the weapon aloft with great effort, as if she was to relinquish her grip the blade was of such rare sharpness it would
cut through the sod as if it were air and disappear into the earth.

'You have your pretty-boy-lie-looks back I see,' she said,
without obvious approval. She sighed. 'I do insist on putting
myself in peril and giving you another and then another last
chance do I not, dear husband? I had gone back, put you, so I
thought, as I always do, out of my mind for good. But the notion of what this sword could do, indeed what you could do
with it... Oh, my pathetic and cowering love, would the touch
of this divine metal bring you back or would it cast you into
eternal blank oblivion, close your mind forever to what you
really are, as your right-hand demon claims?'

Neil shook his head, not daring to ponder on her words. Not
daring to… what? Hope?

Lilith leaned towards him and her free hand lashed out with
lightning speed to slap him hard across the face, rocking his
head, resurrecting the storm of bees in his brain.

'You are in there!' she screamed in his face. 'Whatever
God's last secret to you was, I do not fucking care! It should
not have been big enough to come between us, you craven bastard! Look at that nose bleeding human blood, that spell you
concocted making a wretched ape of you, an abject disguise if
ever there was. Look at this sword. Do you not remember it?
How its infinite edge cut into your side?'

Neil's roaring mind had risen to such a pitch -- a denial

pitch, some portion of him spoke -- that his wife's words were almost drowned out. But not quite. He pissed himself, and there was something in that involuntary helplessness, shame in he who was most prideful, that brought a black boar of rage from his core.

'I am no fucking devil!' he roared, the voice impossibly below his pitch.

Lilith screamed back at him, 'Yes you fucking are!' and her palm whistled again.

He reached out effortlessly, his own right hand an impossible blur and caught the impelled wrist, drawing a cry from her, of triumph as well as of pain. His left went for the sword's hilt, some instinctive portion of him understanding that to grasp the blade would be to lose fingers. He tore the weapon from her and she fell to her knees, clutching her hurt wrist; and he held the blade aloft, so that it caught the sun and reflected with nuclear fire greater than the star's, and his infinitely sharpened sight could not capture the indivisible edge. Then came the sounds of something like great wings beating and he was falling, mind rushing to escape what he had discovered in its entirety, a star gone into collapse.

There was darkness. Something like peace. An utter absence of knowledge.

Will caught Lilith by the hair, pulling her to her feet, spraying her face with hot spittle has he roared, 'What have you done, you stupid, selfish bitch?'

She recoiled in fear from his twisted visage, losing a clump of hair. There was fear in her. She knew that the demon before her was capable of breaking her in two; but there was also in her the defiant and self-righteous rage with which she had faced Michael: something akin to Satanic pride.

'What have I done?' she said. 'What have you done? Look at him, broken and lost. By what? Your magic.'

Will's physiognomy had shifted subtly back from the Devilish, but there was still murder in him. He was pointing at the fallen author. 'His magic. His dark science. I had no wish for him to hide as a human being, was most violently against it, but he was adamant that he couldn't continue as he was, that whatever he had learned from Yahweh's passing lips would drive him beyond madness. He wanted a period of banality, needed it; and there is little more banal than an ape.'

'Oh, he would disagree with you there.'

'I know that. He thought them magnificent, wonderful short-lived stars that burned all the more brilliantly because of their brevity.'

'And would he have lived and died in this condition, in a few short decades?'

'I believe that was his wish,' said Will, and then wistfully, 'A strange suicide. But I would not allow such a thing. That was why I agreed to help him in his conspiracy of cowardice, for I altered the working of the spell subtly so that I could draw him back to his reality, his calling, give him perhaps a decade or two as a man and then plant a seed in his mind to gently un-weave the spell.'

Lilith was abashed. She had had no idea that Will's cause had been in similar vein to hers. Not so rash, so reckless, true. He had been wilier. A truer friend. 'I had no idea.'

Will shrugged, anger evaporating. 'For that I apologise, for that was a failing on my part. Here comes little Ithuriel, racing across God's garden, look how he pants on stubby legs, forgot-ten how to be a winged angel. I treated him badly too, thought him not worthy of the truth, appointed him sentinel over his hero who did not know him or himself and never gave one word of reason or explanation. That is changed now. Mr Tho-mas knows much of the story, and I will keep no secrets from him; nor from you, Lilith.'

The owl arrived panting and flushed and bowed extrava-gantly. 'My lady.'

Lilith held out a palm. 'No call for obsequiousness from you, my fine little warrior. Straighten your spine and stand proud, feller of archangels.'

Leonard blushed so that he looked as if he would combust, and then he blanched as he took in the state of the author. 'What has become of him? He bleeds from nose and eyes and ears.'

'Haemorrhaging of his humanised brain,' said Will. 'Over-load of information, of truth, mixed with his skin coming into contact with the divine molecules of Michael's sword, infernal osmosis.'

Leonard looked to him with pleading eyes. 'Is there yet hope?'

'There may be, but we must get him away soon, before people are abroad or... worse.'

'But he'll be lost again, all revelation he's gained wiped clean, tabula rasa,' said Lilith.

'Perhaps,' mused Will, 'but I could go before the council of angels and beg for more time, explain what has happened, and persuade whatever human Lucifer awakes as to begin his history again.'

'If he wakes,' said Lilith. 'The story is the key, then? I didn't realise its importance.'

'That was the alteration I worked,' said Will. 'To raise Satan a layer of consciousness at a time, by the subtle revelation of A History of The Devil, his autobiography.'

'Now we must hurry. Lilith, will you come with us?'

'Yes, but in my own car. I have a passenger, you see.'

Will scrutinised her, for a moment looking as if he were about to admonish her, and then nodded. 'Very well. We will see you back at the house shortly. Mr Thomas, gather up the sword, and let's get the fuck out of here.'

Lilith was walking to where her car was parked, behind a screen of mulberry bushes when Will called. 'Michael is free, you know?'

She whirled, appalled, and was running.

She reached the Jag, breathless and flushed. Of course everything would be all right, the Moses basket strapped on the back seat where she had left it. Of course. The back seat was empty.

'Looking for something?' spoke a high pitched voice from off to her right and her stomach pitched, sphincter threatening release.

'Please,' she whined, uncaring if she sounded pathetic, her pride an instantaneously broken thing.

Michael stepped from out of a pitch patch between bushes, cradling the cradle. 'Such a sweet child,' he cooed. 'She hasn't even woken. If you would like, I could end it for her without her even knowing. Spare her the anguish and disappointments of life.'

'No. Please. I'll do anything.' Through real tears she saw that the archangel had been in fresh battle, new blood at his chest and thighs. His eyes shone with maniacal fervour, more demonic than any demon.

'Anything, you say? Interesting. I saw your new ally bearing your husband away, fireman lift style. Such strange alliances being formed these days: angels and demons and whores; it's all horribly messed up. And you, such an intelligent woman, should have known better than to push your husband so far so fast.'

'What do you want?' she asked. She would forfeit her life for the babe's in a moment, knew that Michael would not let her live anyway, not after the humiliation she had meted out to him; but if she played along, she hoped, damn her she prayed, that she might scheme a way of letting her daughter survive.

He came close, close enough for her to be assailed by his fetid breath. She would not recoil. She could see his human form shimmering, his seething rage threatening to release his wings.

'What I want,' he breathed, 'is for you to do exactly as I say. You might like to know that I have a new sword, from an old friend. But blades are the old way, how we fought in Heaven and how I brought Lucifer low. As this is all about your dear beloved, and he is such a progressive sort, I have decided to embrace technology.' He grinned, a dreadful sight, dark blood on his teeth. 'Would you like to see my new toy?'

She nodded, bracing herself, horribly certain that he was about to reveal his new-formed cock. Well let him rape her. It was only a fuck after all. He would be on her territory then: she might even have a chance of escaping with her life.

Hope faded when he pulled out a snub-nosed pistol, oily black and deadly.

'Lovely, isn't it?' He stroked the weapon lovingly, as if it were indeed his member, and then he looked at Lilith with such malevolence that she staggered back against the Jag. 'You're a clever woman, Lilith, I know that you have already realised that there is no way that I am going to let you live, but you can save your child by obeying me to the strictest of letters. She is of no concern to me, bawling little shitting machine, but one false move, bitch, and I'll put a bullet into her unformed brain.'

Neil was jammed onto the tight back seat of the sports car. Will had raised the automatic roof so as to obscure the author as best as possible from sight. 'Is Lilith following?' he snapped at Leonard, who was hugging the passenger seat, turned around so that he could look on his diminished hero.

'Uh, no.'

'Shit.'

'Should we go back.'

'Don't be bloody stupid.'

Admonished, the little angel resumed his watch on their cargo as blood from leaking orifices and organs pooled on the plush upholstery of the car.

'We can't go back to where we were,' said Will.

'Sorry,' grunted Leonard, 'can't go back where?'

'The houses in Stainwich?'

'But Lilith… she will not be able to find us.'

Will sighed heavily. 'It cannot be helped. It is too dangerous with Michael back in the picture, undoubtedly more psychotic than ever. As for poor Lilith…' he sounded almost wistful, though Leonard knew of the animosity between the demon and the first lady, '…I fear she may have fallen to the archangel's mad dictates already. I sensed a powerful presence in that bone yard. I just don't know.'

'Where will we go, Mister Roberts?'

Will looked at this unlikely lieutenant with an openness that roused a fiery pride in the angel; and a quaking fear: for the demon did not know. They were lost.

'Always lost, Mr Thomas,' said Will, reading his mind and forcing something like a smile. 'That has been our natural condition since the beginning of time.'

The car sped past the turn-off that would have taken them back in the direction from which they had come. Leonard doubted that he would ever see his house again. He had been there such a short time, but had grown fond of the geometry of the place, its comforting solidity. Now they were hurtling into the risen sun with the hunted Lucifer in their charge, hidden somewhere within the comatose depths of a human mind.

'We could make for the east coast,' said Will. 'There is a little village in Norfolk, a demon used to have a place there, a cottage, until he returned to the Republic for good, claiming the sea air didn't agree with him, made his skin all scaly.'

A little bitter laugh escaped Leonard at this. 'Might it not be taken?'

'Taken?'

'By apes, by people.'

'No, little angel, it does not work like that. We demons have properties scattered here and there across the planet, refuges, as do our Heavenly counterparts. And we have money, masses of it, salted into myriad accounts, that pay for the upkeep of our property portfolio as well as of our many business enterprises. Mammon is our chancellor, of course: sly, but the manners in which he can appropriate and then disseminate funds is…' He shook his head, emitting a whistle of wonder.

'Michael will find this place, though.'

'He will eventually, that is inevitable. But we will gain time to plan our next action. Never give up, Mr Thomas, never surrender. That is what we learned in the fall. Better to be abject and broken and free to think and act than a coddled and unquestioning sheep. That is what Satan taught us.'

And Will could not help but look over his shoulder at the wretched figure on the back seat as he spoke of the Devil. Neil had become motional in small ways: his fingers dancing in the air like agitated sea anemone tendrils; his eyelids fluttering as their captives danced.

'He's dreaming, Mr Thomas. Look at him, I think he is dreaming the rest of his history. Quick, can you reach him? Feel inside his jacket, that is where he keeps it.'

'Keeps what?'

'The tale.'

The owl was straining his stubby arms to lengthen in the tight confines of the speeding sports car, willing the limbs to stretch, a feat that would have once been in the power of even so lowly an angel as he, but he had become too much a man and at the command of base physics. Will had to pull over so that Leonard could get out his side and feel through the rear window in Neil's jacket, locating the disc with a small yelp of triumph.

'Back in your seat,' said Will. 'I want to stay moving for as long as possible.'

'What now?' said Leonard, clunking the passenger door closed, vehicle immediately roaring back onto the highway that at this hour was still relatively free of traffic.

'Now,' spoke Will, 'you feel under your seat for my laptop. There should be plenty of charge in it; if not there are ways I can power it.'

Leonard recovered the computer, snapping it open, screen coming immediately to life, square draw popping and gliding open, as if the machine was eager for the disc, hungry for the tale. He placed the disc in the drawer and nudged it closed, realised the metallic circle was upside down, reopened the drawer, and flipped the disc. The drawer slid closed with a satisfying click and the screen became a word processor page, over which words swarmed faster than any hand could type them.'

'Words. The Word.'

'What was that, Mr Thomas?'

'It is the History of The Devil. It seems to be writing itself.'

The Birth of Emmanuel

Hell was close to placid for a while. The three would be usurpers, Belial, Baal and Mammon, had undertaken a self-imposed exile to Earth, fearful creatures that they were, after the failure of their coup, and they attained a reputation throughout the Grecian Empire as sophists, instructing lawyers and suchlike in the ways of argument for its own and victory's sake, and ridiculing genuine philosophers like, wise Socrates who taught open-mindedness and intellectual humility.

Lilith was happy in the fiery world. She never was called queen, but there was a fiery imperiousness in her that de-manded following from the demons. She had Mulciber design and oversee construction of a chateau high on a volcanic slope that overlooked Pandemonium. There we lived, lovers once more, me wholly the dragon now that I was freed from need or desire for conceit, she my wife again. There was water in the home, conjured by Mulciber who manipulated hydrogen from Hell's atmosphere and rare oxygen from the world's infernal bowels. And trees that grew strange and succulent fruit were trained to grow in the chateau's gardens. Lilith could bathe and drink and feed.

I had Mulciber design private dwellings for all the demons that desired them, scattered around Pandemonium's walls. And so time passed, the demons occupied with building projects and the politics of something like a democracy, depending upon their bent. I filled the ages between leaving Earth and the return that was to come with chairing committees, rebel-rousing speeches, and with love. For Lilith's heart had warmed to me as utterly as in those halcyon days in Mesopotamia. At last we were able to talk openly and without acrimony about the loss of our child. Lilith had heard from the demons of God's serpen-tine curse that had laid me low while she had gestated and given terrible birth. There was still blame in me, for I should have stayed, not hurried home on a braggart's wing, but she consoled me, and let me into her thoughts so that I could divine that her forgiveness was genuine, her love true. In that fierce mind I felt the rage and hatred she had felt against me, and realised that the opposing emotions signified a great passion, greater than I could have hoped, and either polarity was surely preferable to the dispassionate in-between.

'I did hate you,' she said. 'I felt you'd abandoned me. To lose a child again...'

'I know, sweet Lilith. I felt your agony.'

She smiled sadly. 'Sweet you call me. What of all the death and cruelty and treachery I have worked amongst your precious apes? Where was my sweetness to them?'

It was my turn to smile without humour. 'But are they not just as cattle to such as we?'

'I thought so, yet that was when I was a broken creature. Now that I am happy and content I feel a terrible guilt for those men I destroyed.'

I thought of Job. 'Perhaps it is good to feel such an emotion, to have remorseful conscience. Perhaps that is what sets us apart from God.'

She looked to me, yearning for understanding. 'How can it be good to feel pain?'

I kissed her and, breaking away, said, 'Without pain, can there be an understanding or even an experiencing of pleasure? Can there be happiness without sadness, or hope without despair?'

Lilith rose from the bed on which she had been sitting beside me, swept to the veranda that overlooked Pandemonium. Red-bellied storm clouds, pregnant with sulphur, lay low over the citadel and the speckling of communities that had sprung up in the shadow of its walls and towers.

'Do you know when I understood that I still loved you, Lucifer, that my hatred and bitterness and feigned indifference had been a shield, a cage for my heart?'

I watched her back, dressed in gossamer silks, knew that she was watching the brewing storm that would rain fire on Hell's city, a commonplace event that never failed to enthral her. I loved her passion for this world. 'I do not know, my love,' I said.

'When you were on trial, before those cowards that would overthrow you. Those tears of mine were genuine. I was shocked by my love, as I was shocked at the ingratitude that those you had given all for showed. Then you spoke and turned the crowd, and my heart was with you and I was swelled with pride, and I said "that is my husband and I will never again leave him".' She turned to me then and I saw that she was weeping now as she had in the hall of Pandemonium. 'But you are to leave me.'

I rose, shocked and appalled. 'Never.'

She shook her head gently. 'But Moloch wings his way up the mountainside. To venture out from shelter when the sky has just begun spitting comets, I think he must have important news indeed, dread news for me.'

I went to her and held her, and indeed saw Moloch beating up the slope, backlit by the blazing glory of an infernal tempest, and I saw the look of joy and anticipation on his face and snatched from his mind the news he bore: that God had at last impregnated a female ape, and the day of the infant's deliverance was at hand.

And so it came to pass that I deserted my wife once more, and passed through Mulciber's conduit to the World of Man. She had not entreated me to stay, had not begged that I take her with me; in Hell our love had grown into something solid and, so I thought then, unimpeachable. There was trust between us, and she knew that I would return to her, just as she sorrowfully acknowledged that I must be about my cause. Parting was pain, agony, but it was to be brief in our enduring spans.

With me travelled my two most trusted companions: steadfast and true Beelzebub and brave Moloch. We arrived in the land of Earth's new great empire and flew northeast by night, reaching the land of Judea, where our agent demon, a lowly fallen angel who had been elevated to heroic status by the news he brought to Hell, told us that God's son was near ready to be born. The three of us disguised ourselves as noble apes, dressed in fine silks and in possession of a trio of handsome camels which bore ourselves and the gifts we carried for this new child king.

Not long in that arid land a band of soldiers, mixed of the invader Romans and Judeans, intercepted us and demanded that we accompany them to the palace of the region's king, Herod the (self-proclaimed) Great. Moloch was fierce for battle and I feared that his dragon wings might burst from his shoulder-blades and he would fall on these puny humans and smote them beneath his blade, but I steadied him with a glance and force of will. We would meet with this Herod, I told the horse-riding men, and so they escorted us to the city of Jerusalem, but a few miles from our destination of Bethlehem, and to the palace of the overlord that history would rightly remember as a monster.

We waited in an ostentatious hall and were plied with wines and fine meats and fruits, while outside in the dusty streets of Jerusalem people starved and died of disease and filth-induced plague. The king came to us after leaving us alone long awhile enough to ponder on his greatness. He was a small, flabby man with equally flabby mind, and there was great fear in him.

'Name yourselves, visitors to my magnificent court,' he demanded.

I stepped forward, identifying myself as leader, assuming the human names we had decided upon. I bowed, certain that I heard Moloch growling near in my ear, Beelzebub's anger present but wilfully repressed. 'We are Magi from the east, my lord, wise and revered as you are in fine Judea. I am Melchior, and this,' I indicated Beelzebub with a gracious sweep, 'is Balthazar, and this,' to Moloch, along with a flashed warning to still his rage, 'is Caspar. We come bearing gifts for the child that is to be born, this new king, born of God Himself to a mortal mother.'

He blanched then, this great king, and a steward rushed forward with a stool for his shaken master to lower his fat arse upon. 'I have been forewarned of this child. An angel of the Lord appeared to me, the one called Gabriel, and warned me of the power the child would wield. He is of the line of King David and would usurp me, so spake the angel, for I am an Edomite of the line of Esau who was cheated of his birthright in favour of his brother, Jacob, Israel the Jew.'

'Ah,' I said, 'I see your dilemma. The Jews would embrace this new king, perhaps rebel against you.'

'So it was foretold.'

'And yet he will be the son of God. Who would you be to destroy him?'

Herod rose, anger momentarily displacing fear. 'I am, King Herod the Great, almost a god myself, and an interlocutor with angels. Who art thou to question my power?'

Moloch's rage filled my mind like the seething buzz of a thousand bees, and I could not blame him for I felt also that it would be a fine thing for us demons to reveal our true forms before this cowardly wretch of a man, to show him real power and laugh as he soiled himself.

Instead, I said: 'I did not wish to offend our most generous host. Would thy best plan not be to simply send soldiers to slay the mother before the child is birthed?'

He calmed. 'Of course, good Melchior, but these… people, they keep secrets well. They are all in on it, the Jews, thinking that their saviour is at hand. There are many pregnant women throughout Judea; should I have them all murdered?'

Some king, this one, that could not discover where God's bride lay, when one of Hell's lowly demons had done just that. How reviled he must be by his people, perhaps even his troops and staff, how detached, locked in his palace, victim of raging paranoia.

'You are Magi,' he continued, 'wise men. Would that you were to discover the whereabouts of the mother and bring me news, then I would repay you with enough riches that you would need a caravan of camels to bear them back east. Bring to me the information I require and I will make kings of you.'

Bethlehem was but an hour or so on a good camel.

'We should have brought down that one,' spoke Moloch, always uncomfortable on his dromedary mount. 'I felt Satan's mind afire also, wishing to see the colour of his shit.'

'I am like to agree,' said Beelzebub. 'Such as we should not be forced to snivel before such a creature.'

'Herod is of no significance,' I said. If only I had known of the infanticide the ruler of Judea was to soon embark upon then I would have reached out and torn his vile heart from his chest. 'It is best we not draw attention. These Romans we pass would not take kindly to the regicide of the king that operates under their auspices.'

'Bring them on,' growled Moloch, 'I prefer a straight fight to all this sneaking around.'

I smiled. 'Always, my friend, but we would have difficulty securing audience with the son of God with a legion of Rome's finest on our backs.'

Moloch grunted, not entirely satisfied, and Beelzebub said, 'What of Gabriel's involvement? It is almost as if God wishes his son not born.'

I shook my head. 'God moves in perverse ways. He will not, I think, allow the mother or the infant to be harmed, yet He is stirring up Herod to bloodshed and persecution. I think it pleases Him to set his human playthings against one and other. He knows that carnage leads to the apes worshipping Him with more ardour than before.'

'Strange creatures,' mused Beelzebub, 'that grow more pious the more they are oppressed.'

I thought of Job, the epitome of that wretched piety. 'Strange indeed, old friend. Man's ignorance has become near as much the enemy as God Himself. On to Bethlehem, where we resume our work to tear down those walls of ignorance.'

It was a simple, one-storey structure, the house of the mother of the son of God, on the outskirts of Bethlehem. We, my demonic crew and I, were drawn to the building immediately, not by the divinity of the child that nestled in womb, but by that of the watchdog that guarded the home.

'You smell the dog?' Beelzebub asked.

'Angel of Death,' sneered Moloch, 'I would like to show him a thing or two about death.'

'He is God's messenger to Man, who else would it be?' said I. We alighted from our camels and made for the humble home. 'Such a simple dwelling. You would think Yahweh would entrust his only son to a finer family, with more sumptuous abode.'

'Such as royalty,' said Beelzebub.

'Well, friend, the father, Joseph, is of royal lineage: the Hebrew king David.'

'I remember that one,' spoke Moloch, 'a brave and smart ape, a good fighter. He'll have been gone near a millennium now, in human span.'

'Yet Joseph is not the father,' said Beelzebub, 'unless the woman within is mistaken or lying about the divinity of her child.'

'We shall find out,' I said. We were at the open door of the building, when Gabriel appeared, filling its frame. He was wingless, but that was all that appeared human of him. He wore celestial armour and carried a fine lance, and divine light emanated from his biology.

'Hold devils,' he demanded. 'Do you think your counterfeit

humanity would fool my practised eye? You think I, guardian of the Almighty's charge would allow thou admission?'

'We are three and thou art one,' snarled Moloch, but I held up my hand for restraint.

'We are come to see the child of the Lord God, for we have learned that his hour is at hand. We would not harm him, but feel only… scientific interest in what such a demigod should be like. Let us call a brief truce, noble Gabriel. How could we harm the son of God, anyhow? Would that not be as impossible as harming Jehovah Himself?'

He was perplexed, I saw and felt, and so pressed my advantage. 'Yet it would seem that the archangel Gabriel himself has put the child in harm's way before it has yet been birthed. Why go before weak and cruel Herod and inform him of the babe's coming, fire his thoughts to violence?'

The angel actually stammered. 'I – I - that was God's will. The child will be safe, fled by Mary and Joseph to Egypt and sanctuary until the time of this crisis is passed. Yet the Lord wishes another purge on these unfaithful humans and will drive Herod, thinking he is protecting his throne, to order the slaughter of all first-born males in the region.'

'More death, Metatron; are you not sickened yet?'

Gabriel shook his head, though his sorrow-maddened eyes told another truth. 'It is God's will, as is all.' He looked at me, the story of his sight somewhere between loathing and despair, his mind an unreadable convolution. 'Yet I know the wiles of thee, Lucifer, and know the argument about to be birthed from your serpent tongue: that God's all-knowledge would have foretold the coming of this diabolical trinity, and that He allows it, and so I shall let thee demons pass and will trust in the strange wisdom of the Almighty,'

'Thank you, gracious angel,' I said, and stepped into the dim abode. Beelzebub passed Gabriel in proud silence, while Moloch growled an insult under his breath that went unheeded. Gabriel closed the ill-fitting door behind us.

The room we stood in was spartan, lit by a single, inconstant lamp. A moth-eaten Hessian mattress that leaked its lousy straw stuffing filled the centre of the chamber. The only furniture was a stool that supported a boy who wept, face in hands, and a well-made table on which were laid out hand-turned wooden goblets filled with what smelled to be a particularly noxious wine; no doubt all these poor people could afford to celebrate the birth of the holy child. The boy looked up, angrily wiping tears from his reddened eyes, and I saw that there was a whisper of a beard about his chin, that he was nearly a man. It hit me then that this was the husband, this sapling youth, and my appalled sight went to the figure on the mattress and saw that she was a child, saw in an instant that blood clotted around her sex, and terror emanated from her.

'Friends,' spoke Joseph, 'you are our first visitors... apart from this... angel of the Lord.' He glanced contemptuously at Gabriel, messenger of the god that had violated his young virgin wife. 'Would you not take a drink with me, and pray for my wife, that God may deliver she and the babe safely?'

'Prayer will do no good,' said Beelzebub. 'Can you not see, boy, the agony she is in?'

'Of course I see!' Joseph was on his feet, reddened with anger and terror. 'Yet what can I do but pray? What can you men in your fine clothes do, when an angel of the Lord tells that even he cannot intercede? If this is God's son in Mary, then why, why? She is an innocent, and I am a poor carpenter not yet made any name for myself; yet He took her, my sweet wife, and violated her. For what purpose?'

'I would keep watch of thy tongue,' rumbled Gabriel, stung into speech, 'and not underestimate the honour of having your bride chosen as the vessel of God.'

'And yet she had no choice,' spoke Moloch, the checked rage in his tone all the more menacing. 'Is this what God has come to, Gabriel, the raping of little girls?'

While anger flashed between the pair I moved to the mattress and knelt beside the labouring mother, feeling into her mind and her biology. 'Do not fear, young Mary,' I whispered. 'I am here to help you.'

Her eyes flickered open and wide, the flickering lamplight making jewels of the myriad beads of sweat that decorated her taut forehead. 'Who are you?' she rasped, wincing in pain.

'Joseph,' I snapped over my shoulder, 'fetch a goblet of water.'

'We have only wine.'

'Then bring that.'

'You shall not interfere,' commanded Gabriel, 'or I shall revoke my invitation.'

'Balthazar, Caspar,' I spoke, using the demons' newly-adopted names, 'hold this dog to the blade, and if he utters another sound or makes a move to fight or flee then divest him of his head.'

The goblet Joseph had just picked up clattered to the floor, spilling its sour cargo. I felt the mixture of awe and terrified triumph coming from his mind on seeing two noble men draw brilliant swords and hold an angel hostage.

'Another vessel, good Joseph,' I barked. 'Your wife is dry and in pain and needs fluid and your hand.'

'Who are you, that would challenge God's emissary so?'

Gabriel's mental rage burgeoned to be set free of his tongue, yet Moloch's blade cut into his throat and stilled any words.

A small but determined hand grasped my wrist and I looked down into the wide and wet eyes of Mary. 'Who are you?' she repeated, and then: 'Why are you here?'

'We are Magi, from the east,' I spoke. 'We are here to bring gifts for the son of God, and to worship before the holy child.'

And the brave girl was shaking her head. 'No,' she rasped, 'I think you are angels, truly, greater than the one that has become the prisoner of your fellows. I think you have come to save me.'

Joseph caught her wrist, dragging her grip from mine. 'Wife,' he said, tilting the goblet to her salted and cracked lips, 'try and drink but a little.'

She split her lips a little and took some of the wine, that I sweetened with a simple sleight, and then a spasm seized her and she screamed out, lashing an arm that sent the goblet crashing from Joseph's hand. Joseph tried to restrain her, to pin her arms to her sides and press her into the mattress, but her risen agony had made a wild beast of Mary and she lashed and clawed, unknowingly raking bloody wounds down her husband's face. I pulled him off of her, lest he lose an eye.

'She is tearing apart, inside,' I said to him.

His sight never left the screaming, threshing figure on the mattress. 'I know,' he said, almost calmly. 'She has shared intercourse with God, and who would survive such a thing? Now she has soiled herself -- do you not smell it -- and yet the scent of her coming destruction is the stench that fills this sorry house.'

Mary had quietened, temporarily exhausted, almost unconscious. 'Angel Magi,' she whispered with blessed detachment,
'can you help me?'

'I can, child.'

Gabriel roared out: 'thou will suffer for --' and Moloch
crowned him with the flat of his already blooded sword, driving the archangel to his knees, where blood from his neck
wound pat-pattered on the floor before him. Beelzebub pressed
the tip of his ultra-refined blade to the Gabriel's nape and
hissed, with consummate menace, 'final warning.'

It was always Joseph that I would remember from this moment, Joseph and the immensity of his love for his wife. It
poured from him, that grand and terrible emotion, and I was
humble before this man. 'Save her,' he spoke, words atremble
but steely. 'I care not for God's will, nor for my soul, and sense
that your greatness is not as that of the angel of the Lord, that
you are of a different camp. I care only for my wife, violated
victim of Heaven's dictates. Save her and my life and my soul
are yours.'

'Dear one, no,' whispered Mary. Gabriel stayed silent, understanding that his very existence was in the balance.

'Have no fear, child,' I consoled. 'I have no use or wish for
your husband's life, and a soul is naught but a figment of
men's mind and angels' threats. I will save thee, and your
child, for that is the good and right thing to do, though the babe
will grow to suffer, I fear, for his father's malice.' I turned to
fallen Gabriel then, regarding his hate-filled watch with disdain. 'You feel betrayed, I know, old adversary; yet I will save
mother and child, and you will bear witness, and though you
and your master may rewrite this story you shall hold the truth
of what happened this night in your heart for all eternity.'

'What would you do?' asked Joseph.

'I must cut the child from her,' I answered. 'What you witness will seem as magic to you, miraculous work, divine or
otherwise, but it is only manipulation of flesh that is beyond
Man's grasp as yet. I will open Mary, and will heal her, and she
may even bear you more children, for I can rebuild her ravaged
womb.'

'Will it hurt her?'

'But a little.'

'Then hurry, Magi,' rasped Mary, 'for I feel life slipping,

and I would welcome pain that would signify my continued existence.'

With that I unsheathed the scythe talon of my left index finger, sterilising it with a flare of oxidised atoms. I felt or heard no surprise from Joseph or his wife, nor pain as I cut into the girl's belly and rescued the babe that would have been the death of his mother. Mary slipped into unconsciousness as I toiled at her ruined innards, but Joseph was avid, unblinking, cradling the bloody newborn and wiping sweat from my brow as I manipulated Mary's biology. My work was good, and Mary would give birth to four more sons and two sisters, all fathered by the good and noble carpenter.

I was done at last, igniting a line of oxygen to cauterise the girl's stomach gash, and I fell back onto my haunches, exhausted. Joseph was looking at me with something like awe.

'She will be well,' I said. 'In pain for a little while, but a complete and good wife.'

'I saw you... revealed,' he breathed, and I saw that the awe was not only inspired by the manner in which I had delivered the babe and repaired his wife. 'Your disguise slipped, for a moment, and I saw you, winged dragon.'

I looked to Moloch and Beelzebub, and they nodded solemnly. Gabriel, risen to a stoop, said nothing, but I could see satisfaction in his eyes and feel it in his mind. Joseph, he was confident, would drive us demons from his home now, forgetful of what I had done.

Gabriel was mistaken. Joseph asked: 'Be thou, Satan?'

'I be.'

He smiled, a wonderful expression. 'Then I have been deceived, for I heard tell that you were cruel and evil and a gatherer of men's souls, when thou art good and kind and just, and will always find goodwill and gratitude in the hearts of my wife and I, and always a welcome at our table.' He stood and walked to where Gabriel stooped, first looking to Beelzebub and Moloch. 'And you be devils too?'

'We be.'

'Wonderful creations, I thank you sirs.'

Their sights were fixed on the wide-eyed infant he cradled, no doubt striving to discern godhood in him. The babe had made not a sound as yet, not one sob or infantile grumble, and there was most definitely an aura of serenity around it. Now

Joseph lowered the babe towards poor Gabriel's suddenly stricken face. 'And I revoke your invitation, callous angel that would let my wife perish. I see how you fear this child, and well you should. He will be raised to be kind and compassionate and proud, not the cowed sheep you predict, and will use his Heavenly powers for Man's good, not God's perverse will. I predict he will bring about the downfall of such as thee.'

I stood, amazed. I could not have spoken more eloquently and my heart was filled with hope for this child, that one day he might overthrow his own father and oversee mankind with just goodness, opening their hearts and minds to the wonders of the universe.

'Be gone now, angel,' spat Joseph, lifting the babe back to his chest. 'I have no fear of thee, not when I have such blessed protectors as these devils.'

Gabriel opened his mouth to speak, but the point of Beelzebub's sword persuaded him to muteness. The cut at the archangel's throat had healed with the alacrity usual in his kind, but the wound to his pride was enduring. He skulked from the home, and as if a pall had lifted, the infant seemed to smile beatifically and Mary awoke, reaching for her son, a like smile on her face. She pulled him to her bared breast, wincing at hurt in her abdomen that was insignificant for the adoration she felt for her child and for her young and brave husband, and the gratitude for me. The babe settled to contented suckling.

Her eyes found mine. 'He is beautiful, is he not?'

'He is.' I thought of my own son then, lost to the desert, devoured by beasts, and of Lilith's first born, skull stamped in the sand. 'He is magnificent, Mary, and he will grow to be a great man.'

'Yet should he not be your enemy, for art thou not, Satan?' Yet there was no fear in her, for she had divined my nature well, perhaps my purpose, and I thought also that there was a mocking side to this one's nature, that she was teasing me with her words.

I placed a hand to her cool and serene brow. 'I would hardly deliver an enemy to safety, child. I wish nothing but good for this family, good as in the absence of ill as opposed to good that is merely God's shifting will.'

She kissed my hand. 'Sweet protector.' Joseph laid a hand of brotherhood on my shoulder.

'Have you a name for the infant?' I asked.

Mary smiled, shifting the mite slightly so that he had better access to her milk. 'We will call him Emmanuel.'

I laughed then, for though the name was beautiful, the irony of defiant Mary was evident.

'God with us,' I laughed, 'a goodly name.'

'Yet,' said Joseph, 'the banished angel had it that men would know the son of God as Jesus the Christ.'

Beelzebub, and even stern Moloch laughed now, for Jesus meant 'Jehovah saves', and Christ meant 'anointed one', and ironies were coming swift and thick, for had the Devil not saved Jehovah's son, and if there was any anointing to be done, was it not to be done by demons?

'Goodly names, are they not?' spoke happy Mary.

'Goodly indeed,' I answered.

Chapter Thirteen

Leonard Thomas turned to driving Will, the computer open on his lap. He had just finished reading, aloud, the long chapter that the satanic mind had spawned. Now Neil, on the back seat of the car, had fallen into a deeper sleep, untroubled by physiological tricks and tremors. No more words came to the screen. For now.

'Is that truly how events unfolded, Mr Roberts?'

Will was, or appeared to be, intent on the undeviating road that unfurled before him. 'To the letter, as my tired memory recalls. But of course memory is a subjective process: Gabriel might recall events somewhat different.'

'Perhaps we will find out soon enough whether such is the case,' sighed Leonard.

Will reached out and squeezed the little angel's shoulder. 'Don't be afraid. If Gabriel is near and in the mood for battle, then I assure you that I can match him blow for blow.'

'And what of Michael?'

'Well, you yourself have dealt with that warrior.'

Leonard knew that Will's words and actions of bonhomie were meant to instil courage in him, to steel his spine, just as he knew that they were pure bravado and Mr Roberts himself was fearful and anxious. Yet just to be beside, even in the confidences of, Lucifer's lieutenant, oh that was more than enough for so lowly an angel as he.

Will turned his sight from the road, snatching at Mr Thomas's thoughts. 'There is nothing lowly about you, friend. You have been with us since near the beginning, and it has taken me all these ages to acknowledge your worth. For that I apologise; as would Satan, if he were able.'

This drew Leonard's watch back to the foetal form in the rear of the vehicle. The haemorrhaging had stopped. Leonard had wiped away the congealed blood with a spittle-wetted handkerchief, and Mr Mann, as the two conscious participants in this adventure still referred to him, looked more restful; but there could be danger in his sweet repose. Leonard knew little of the spell that had been cast over the Devil, having small understanding of quantum matters, but Will had said that if Neil withdrew completely into himself, he was, as it were, programmed to invent a new persona, become once more a weak and ignorant ape. At the moment, with the parties of Heaven and Hell involved in argument that could devolve into fresh war at any moment, might well be the undoing of Lucifer.

How tragic, how fucking pointless, thought Leonard, if the Devil was to be destroyed before ever regaining knowledge of who or what he was.

'I won't allow that to happen,' said Will.

'It would be a terrible waste.' He was enraged then, he a lowly angel that had forgotten how to be anything but a man, at his hero. 'He was a damned coward to hide away like he did. All those millennia negated as he reinvents himself as an ape for a heartbeat's flicker of peace.'

'Don't be too hard on him. He felt more than others. Understood more than others. And God breathed His last into Lucifer's ear, dying in his arms. None present, angel or demon, could discern that last knowledge that Yahweh imparted, and Lucifer would not speak of it, but it was something that shook him to his core, more than anything had previously in their titanic struggle.'

'But what information could have shaken him so, that he would turn away from his beloved Lilith and his loyal demons, what comprehension could be so terrible.'

Will favoured Mr Thomas with a look so bleak that his rage dwindled to an insignificant thing. 'I for one would not want to know what words the creator of the universe breathed in his last breath, if they could send the highest and proudest of demons to fearful collapse.

'We should dwell on lighter things, perhaps. Your reading passed the time well, and we are almost to Norwich, and our destination is not far past. Did you like the story, Ithuriel?'

Unused to being addressed by his ancient title, Leonard blushed. 'Yes. Yes I liked it very much, though it is somewhat different from the received version.'

Will laughed easily. 'Not quite the nativity that children perform in schools, is it?'

'Yet Satan would go from protector to enemy of Christ, from godfather to tempter, how could that be?'

'That's Mr Mann's tale to tell, Leonard. Yet don't take the

gospels as gospel; and remember that there are countless versions of Christ's story, many more than are extant at the moment; more even than the Vatican has knowledge of.'

'But is not Mr Mann's testament just another gospel, of no more validity than the others?'

Will leaned close to Leonard, sight not shifting from the road before him, and whispered in his passenger's ear: 'Yet it is the only gospel written by someone who was actually present at the time.'

The turn off came along presently, the mood in the car having fallen calm and contemplative, and a series of narrow lanes brought them to the pretty cottage that was owned by and for the exclusive use of, citizens of the Demonic Republic.

'I stayed here a century or so ago,' said Will, 'while on the run from assassin seraphim. It is a good place, calming. The sea air will do no harm to our invalid, may even aid his revival.'

The glaring sun was at its zenith in a sky that was cloudless but for the vapour trails of aircraft. A squadron of screaming swift sped overhead. Mr Thomas turned his face to the sea, a narrow band of which was visible above the near horizon, and tasted salt in the air, hot wind buffeting his face, and he felt hope surge for the first time in a while. This was a wonderful world, where events unfolded arbitrarily, in spite of, or uncaring of, the powers that waged war in the background of time and space. He became aware that Will was speaking at him.

'Help me with this hood, will you? I have powers over matter that Man would call miraculous, supernatural, yet I can never, for the life of me, get this damn thing down.' And he struggled with the soft top of the convertible sports car, having decided it would be easier to lift Neil from the vehicle than wiggle him out of one of the small rear doors. Leonard hurried to the vehicle and between them the two angels, fallen major and risen minor, managed to collapse the mechanism and stow the roof.

'Go and open the door,' said Will, nodding to the whitewashed, thatch-roofed cottage as he lifted the unconscious, bloodied form from the rear of his car.

'Don't I need a key?' asked Leonard, hurrying up granite steps to the oak front door.

'You are an angel, are you not? The door will open.'

'Though I am no demon?'

'Demon, angel,' grunted Will, 'same bloody species, same DNA.'

Leonard reached for the wrought iron handle and it did depress, and noise came to the owl's sharp ear of a sequence of tumblers disengaging, and the door clicked open and the little angel led the way into a cool and dim hallway, followed by Mr Roberts bearing his burden.

'Second door on the right,' grunted Will, shouldering past Leonard into the room and laying Neil Mann gently on a well-padded leather sofa that had been in the same state of repair and the same position in the room the last time he had visited the cottage, as a fugitive, at the arse end of the nineteenth century. Nothing material, he thought, in this world needs to change state. If the humans were to realise that then their evolution would advance exponentially. No more wasteful recycling or dwindling fuel reserves. They could be taught, helped to advance. He smiled. He sounded like Lucifer. And he looked to the pathetic figure on the sofa, head caked in dried blood. He pulled a handkerchief from his pocket and wet it with his spit, aware that Mr Thomas has come to stand silently beside him, and knelt beside his ancient captain and began to clean the face that hid Satan. Lucifer was nearly apparent in the unconscious portrait though: the crude mask of human middle age had slipped as the author had written his story, follicles filling in conjured baldness, features sharpening, eyes brightening, body muscling. Nearly back, and then, and then... this.

'Leonard?' he spoke softly.

'Yes?'

Will's defences were suddenly screaming alarm, his stomach tightening to a miniscule knot, muscles around his shoulder blades convoluting. 'Would you go to the car and get the sword and the computer?'

'Is there something -'

'Quickly!'

The owl was off and Will was on his feet, letting the bloody handkerchief fall to the carpet. The figure on the sofa groaned and kicked out its left leg, as if suffering a disturbing dream.

'If you're waking up,' snapped Will, 'then get a fucking move on.' He strode across the room to the leaded patio doors that opened onto a sunlit yard that extended to a dry wall beyond which the earth dropped away in a sheer cliff-face to the angry and jagged-toothed sea. Through the doors, salt water stinging his nasals passages, Will's sight went immediately to the azure vault of the sky, palm over his eyes against the glare of the sun. There, circling high in the stratosphere, yet found by his preternatural eye, was an angel. He sent out mental antenna that recoiled as it felt great pain, physical and mental. 'Not Michael then,' he mused. 'If you touch that mind you know you've touched the mind of a fucking psychopath.'

Leonard, red-faced, spilled onto the yard, laptop tucked under one arm, struggling to hold the blazing sword aloft with the other. Will took the sword from him, raised it aloft and began to wave it in great flashing arcs, as if signalling welcome.

'Have you taken leave of your good senses?'

Will glared. 'Mind your tongue, little one. We've been discovered. Best to draw him in and not invite further scrutiny.'

The angel overhead continued in its broad ellipses, seemingly not drawn by the magnetic influence of the divine metal.

'Not Michael?' whispered Leonard.

Will shook his skull, still waving the mighty wand. 'No, the other great archangel. I think him wounded, trapped in the thermals. Michael must have done that. The circler's mind is closed, his form fatigued and damaged. I think he sleeps up there, broken with fatigue after the effort of tracking us.' Will lowered the sword, its reflected blaze diminishing to a burnished glare, and walked back into the cottage, Mr Thomas worrying at his shoulder.

'Is it wise to turn your back on the angel of death?'

'He is no threat to us at the moment. We will ready ourselves for his descent.'

'Descent?'

'Cool evening will bring him crashing to earth.'

The afternoon crawled its way to demise, the sun at interminable length reddening and growing and sinking. Will and Leonard had tended to Neil Mann, wiping the fluids of haemorrhage from his face, mopping his steaming brow, and they had taken turns watching the laptop, lest it spring into new life, words bursting across its surface with the speed and intensity of a new-born universe. There was no fresh tale spilled across the window of the computer; and Mr Mann seemed to be resting well, even snoring on occasion. The angels spoke little. There was so much that the owl wished to ask of his mighty captain, but he sensed in Will a dread despair that rattled his innards and dared not broach conversation.

Gabriel crashed into the yard just as the sun slipped below the false horizon of the cottage's thatch, the impact rattling the very walls of the structure, tumbling some inconsequential books from a pine welsh dresser, smashing a few pieces of banal pottery. Will was out into the shadowed, rapidly cooled yard, sword flashing ahead of him. Leonard, less than terrified, more than agitated, was at his tail. And the mighty angel of death, God's Metatron to man, was sprawled across the paving, black blood pooling beneath him, great wings flapping feebly, splashing his spilled and viscous fluids.

Will stood over the fallen archangel, that ancient nemesis, and rage was with him, and fear. Why let it live? He could take the head now. What a trophy for the Republic. It was Leonard, little and lowly Ithuriel, that, grown wise and unafraid, laid a stilling hand on the electric muscle of Will's bunched shoulder. 'He means us no harm,' he whispered. 'You must feel it. He has come to help us, or warn us.'

Will's words came choked. 'Of course I feel. But the hurt this creature has delivered, the lies he has spilled concerning us demons, that men have believed... Oh, Ithuriel if only you knew.'

Leonard took his grip from Will's shoulder and stepped himself over the fallen Gabriel. 'He was doing God's will. Yet it drove him near to madness and over the edge of despair. He is fallen now,' he turned his watch on Will Roberts, and was amazed to see tears rolling down the demon's face. 'He is more fallen than any demon. Imagine his agony. You fought God, now God is no more; he worshipped and adored God, now God is no more. Even his comrade in arms had taken against him. Yet still he fought his way here. Could he not have hope or message for Lucifer? Could he not help us to bring our leader back?'

Will lowered the sword and then reversed it, offering the sword to Leonard. Mr Thomas took it, the weight and power of the weapon sending electric waves up his spasming arms.

'You are right, wise owl. We must get him inside.' And

Will bent and hooked his arms to the elbows under the fallen angel's armpits. Gabriel's head whipped, face shockingly blanched, eyes rolled white. 'Get your filthy Goddamned demon hands off me!' he screamed, but Will was hoisting Gabriel upright, forcing him at a staggering stumble into the cottage, wings battering futilely at the demon, pushing into the room where Neil lay, letting Gabriel collapse in a bleeding mess before the form that concealed his nemesis.

'You bring me and make me kneel before the worm,' he gasped. 'This futile and craven coward that would no longer have even the courage to know himself.'

'Perhaps you could mend one another,' spoke Will, his tone of ice and steel. 'Such states are the pair of you. Look how you bleed, angel. Have your regenerative powers forsaken you?'

Gabriel wheeled, trying to rise, but the effort was too much and he sank to his arse on the carpet. Leonard gasped, appalled to see the extent of the archangels injuries, and even Will lowered to one knee before the ruined form. 'Michael did this?'

Gabriel nodded, even so slight a motion clearly causing him agony. The front of his torso was carved open, the organs revealed, the huge angelic heart beating at a visible rate. The yellow livers were sliced and oozing green matter, the lungs collapsing sacs that filled with the blood that they hydrogenated and drowned in it.

'The Prince of Heaven is lost to his madness,' he rasped, his breaths shallow and bespeaking mortality. 'He tricked my own blade from me and then carved me open with it. He has become more dangerous than even... you. And the Lord, when He spake last to me, foretold of this, and said,' he sobbed, shame overwhelming him momentarily, tears of blood seeping from his ducts, 'that I must protect Satan from those that would destroy him, and always, always I follow the will of God, even though his will might seem perverse and cruel and shameful, for He is my God and my Good and I will obey him unto my end.'

Will reached a magnanimous hand to the broken angel, but Gabriel convulsed violently from his touch, an action that must have instigated a fresh universe of pain in him though no cry escaped him. 'Too late for camaraderie,' he hissed. 'I am about God's late business, and that of Michael.'

'Meaning?' demanded Will.

'The prince relayed a message for me to deliver unto your master: "Satan will find me at midnight at the temple where I laid him low. He should be there, if he wishes his bitch to live." Those were his words.'

'What the fuck does that mean?'

'I think I know,' ventured a timid Leonard.

Will sighed, head sinking to his chest. 'So do I, but there isn't enough time.'

'If we set out now…'

'With our champion comatose, Mr Thomas? What good would that serve?'

'But we cannot leave Lady Lilith to Michael's cruel mercies.'

'She is but bait now; and bait always dies twitching on the hook.'

'You could wake Lucifer from his sleep… perhaps,' rasped Gabriel. 'I believe he was undone with celestial steel?'

Will's head came up, dangerous hope dancing in his eyes. 'That, among other things.'

'Then perhaps a second dose, more potent than the first, of Heaven's mettle would counteract that which sent him to lost slumber.'

'Or it would destroy him utterly.'

'What is to be lost?'

Will reached for the sword, erecting himself and poising the blade over Neil Mann's unconscious form. 'You cannot!' cried out Mr Thomas. 'You must!' gasped Gabriel, a trace of pleasured anticipation in his death rattle words. Doubt flooded Will: what if this was all a trick, a last grasp at victory by Gabriel, who knew that the blade would end Lucifer's existence? He turned to face the archangel, but there was nothing to indicate treachery in the dying eyes of God's most faithful servant, no triumphant cords singing from his failing brain.

'Forgive me, old friend,' he whispered and drove the point of the blade into Neil's side, into the ancient wound delivered of the same sword by Michael on the battlefield of Heaven.

Neil convulsed, and roared, a terrible and terrifying sound that emanated out from the cottage, echoing across the sea, upsetting resting gulls to clamorous fight and distress. And his eyes sprang open, and fixed with rage on the blade that pierced his flesh, and those eyes were unclouded and ancient and the mind behind them was conscious of its own existence.

Neil Mann, the Devil's fabrication, was gone. Here was Satan.

Will withdrew the blade, dark blood bubbling from the gaping wound. 'Lucifer, oh to call you by your true name once more...'

But there was confusion in the Devil. He was as a man waking from a long dream that might have been a lifetime, unsure which was dream and which reality. He sat up, glare still on the sword, a hand going to staunch the flow at his side. Will sensed the danger, rage and confusion roaring from Satan's mind. Lucifer had only a segment of his story in his newfound memory: that which he had told in his history. Will laid down the sword, opening his palms, and the wounded demon sprang at him as a feral animal, hand grasping a handful of Will's hair, yanking his head back and exposing the throat. 'Who are you?' he growled. 'What are you, and what have you done with my mind? Speak or I tear out your throat, I swear, I will rip out your larynx with my teeth.'

Will's blow was swift and true, a fist to the side wound and the Devil collapsed to the floor with a cry of rage and frustration, where Will delivered a kick to his temple that sent him sprawling and befuddled. Then Will reclaimed the sword, and stood, raging, over his old captain.

'How would you treat your oldest and most loyal friend? As some cur, as always? Do you not recognise me, Satan?'

The Devil looked to his old lieutenant, something like understanding dawning in his slowly clearing mind. 'Your name is...Will...William.'

'My name is William Zacharias Roberts.'

The Devil was laughing then, realisation flooding his burgeoning mind. 'Bill Zee Bob. Good, very good.' He reached out a hand. 'Call me Neil. Neil Mann.'

Will looked at the hand with disdain, making no move to meet it. 'I would have thought you would eschew that title now.'

'No, no,' Satan shook his head slowly. 'I have lived his whole life, have all his memories.'

'But they are falsehoods, implanted and incomplete. The memory is but a flicker; your reality is ancient. Name your parents.'

'I cannot. Yet there is more missing from the Hellish nostalgia that is filling my woken mind. Before the fall from Heaven and after Christ in Gethsemane all is missing.'

Will faltered. 'Gethsemane? Yet your history was only complete up until the birth of the Christos.'

Leonard Thomas spoke up. 'There is more. When the blade pierced the flesh the computer burst to life. I think a new chapter was created instantaneously. At the same moment Gabriel died.'

All turned to the archangel, and indeed his eyes had clouded with extinction, the passing of one of Heaven's great players going unnoticed in the furore around Satan's resurrection. Gabriel was a pitiful sight, his wings curled upon themselves now, like great desiccated leaves. The fluids in his opened torso were congealing and already starting to stink. A lowly exit for an important character.

Neil, as he still wished to be called, in some measure still thought of himself, struggled to his feet and stood over poor Gabriel. 'Why was this creature here?'

'He brought a message,' yelped out Mr Thomas before Will could still his tongue, drawing the Devil's attention for the first time, his eyes focusing on the little angel as if he had existed only in the periphery of his vision until now.

'And who might you be.'

'I am Leon...' Mr Thomas suddenly puffed out his chest, proud and defiant. 'I am the angel, Ithuriel.'

Neil Mann looked at him with doubting eyes. 'Were you not my neighbour?'

'I was.'

'Did I not... murder you?'

Ithuriel dared a laugh. 'If I were a man, then you would have. Though I think manslaughter would be more apt, as there was no calculation: your old passions got the better of you.'

'Another angel. Are there no humans in this story?'

Will said. 'There have been many. The apes were always important to you.'

'Yet not as important as your wife,' said Ithuriel.

Neil was to his feet, swaying slightly. He lifted his bloody hand before his eyes, saw that the blood was dried, felt to his side and pressed his palm to knitting flesh. 'My wife, Maria. Was her death a dream?'

Will, sunken to resignation, said. 'It was. Another false memory to keep your true identity from yourself.'

'And my son?'

'Never existed. An invented echo of a baby you once lost.'

The Devil sat heavily on the sofa, seized by heart-aching distress yet taunted by risen hope that he might yet see his wife again. 'Why, why would you turn my mind to these lies?'

Will leaned close, his voice sunk to a whisper. 'You turned your mind to a lying organ, it was you that reprogrammed your brain and your physiology to that of a drunken and pathetic ape. You welcomed the hurt and the ignorance of life as a man. All your own doing. I aided at your request, to be sure you did not make a cabbage of yourself, and it was I that slipped in a sleight, unknown to you, that you could be brought back to reality, should your existence be imperilled, by the slow revealing of your history.'

'Am I imperilled then?'

'Very much so. You have information the angels want, which has kept them at bay for a year.'

'Only one year? I was Neil Mann for only one year?'

'Yes, but now that time is up.'

'They are coming to kill me?'

Will shrugged. 'They hold their divine councils, and make little active progress. But your ancient nemesis --'

'Michael?'

'Yes, he. Michael has lost his mind to rage against you...'

'...And he has taken Lilith hostage and we are desperately short of time in which to save her,' blurted Ithuriel.

'My wife? Michael has my wife?' He was back to his feet, the anger that now felt a natural facet of his personality, roiling from his darkening mind. 'That bastard has Lilith?'

'Yes,' said Will. 'But it is a perilous trap he has set, and her survival -- and yours should you put your neck in his noose -- is at best unlikely. You are wounded --'

'I will repair.'

'Not before midnight, not fully.'

'Midnight you say?'

'That is when he has threatened to deliver the killing stroke.'

'And Gabriel brought this news?'

'He did. And died for it.'

'And fought for it, no doubt. For he was no coward. Michael too, may be badly wounded.'

'But you... you are not yet yourself. That you will not be until you have recounted the whole of your history. He is the mightiest of archangels, Heaven's supreme warrior. You, Lucifer, are but a shadow of the great Satan that once inspired a small army to oppose the tyranny of God Himself; and even then, at your mightiest, you fell to Michael's sword.'

Neil staggered, nausea writhing threat in his gut, his sphincter threatening to relax. He felt weak as a man all of a sudden and reached blindly for his lieutenant. Will clasped his wrist, steadying him.

'Forgive me,' spoke Mr Roberts, 'for there is danger if ever anyone relates a part of your past that you have not yet revealed to yourself. That was a clause I wrote into the sleight, to stop your mind crumbling at the sudden onset of too much memory, too much information.'

'What is the danger?' asked Neil, shaking his head to clear it of the fog that seemed to have enveloped his brain.

'That you might capitulate to a fugue, and awake once more in the disguise of an ignorant ape.'

'The blade woke me this time; would it not again?'

'It might. Or it might destroy you. It is not a risk we have time to take.'

'You are right,' said Neil. 'No more talk of the past, only of the present and immediate future. You will take me to Lilith.'

'It would be swifter to fly.'

'You know that that is beyond me at the moment. I am still a drunken author in the pit of my mind; this seems a strange fancy that I cannot help but play along with, for it feels right to my instinct, yet still my rational mind screams at its wrongness.'

'Flight is not beyond Michael, nor any of a thousand angelic tricks that you have forgotten knowledge of.'

'Still I must go. You stay or fly, but I must go to my love.'

Will turned away, shoulders slumping in defeat. 'Then I will drive you, for you need to meditate to heal your wounds on the journey. I drive well and fast and can make us invisible to those damned speed cameras. We will be to your wife before midnight.'

'You are a good friend,' said the Devil.

'I am,' said Beelzebub. 'Perhaps some day you shall repay me.'

The three left the cottage. So intent were they on their business, that they had completely forgotten the angel of death, God's oldest messenger to Man, that decomposed with startling speed on the floorboards. Beelzebub's car had hardly left the gravel drive, spewing an arc of chipped granite, than the millions of years that his atoms had endured caused Gabriel to come apart in moments. First the corpse went to carbon dust, then to a milky mist, and then its matter reduced to its base components so small as to be indistinguishable, and it was as if the angel had never existed at all.

Usurpation and Temptation

And so it came to pass that Mary and Joseph and the babe Emmanuel fled Bethlehem to Egypt and stayed until Herod was no more, the tyrant dying in his bed, arteries clogged with sumptuous fats, terrified that he would be punished in the after-life for ending or not ending the life of prophesied anointed one depending on the whim of the god he knew to be inconstant and far his better in cruelty stakes. The angel of the Lord had not returned to him with news that his infanticide had been successful, though he had had thousands of babies put to the sword.

Herod was succeeded by his son, Archelaus, his equal in brutality and paranoia, and on hearing of his succession good Joseph decided that the family must not return to Bethlehem and instead he took his wife and the child he called his son to the town of Nazareth. And there the boy was raised, taught carpentry by Joseph, loved by his mother. A good childhood. Peaceful. A little disappointing.

I would call on the family from time to time and was welcomed as a kindly relative, but as the boy grew towards manhood Mary began to discourage my visits, subtly at first and then with more force.

'His father visits him never, in physical form or in dreams,' she would say, 'and perchance he may yet live a good life as a good man, untouched by the wants and dictates of gods and demons.'

'Yet, sweet Mary, he is born to lead. He is the son of God, and his nature will not stay quiet forever.'

'You would have him lead a war on his own father. Joseph and I owe you so much, Satan. We will be always indebted and grateful to thee, but his nature might stay quiet: if God has forgotten his son.'

'God does not forget.'

'Then perhaps He has died.'

I smiled, thrilled by her blasphemy. 'I think I should have felt it if that one had passed.'

She frowned and I felt the guilty thoughts coming from her,

along with fear. She wanted me gone, to leave Emmanuel to his humanity. Yet I had saved the child, was owed his life. She feared that I would take what was mine by right, or by force if necessary.

I was stung by what her mind spoke. 'You are the child's mother, Mary, and you do me an injustice with uncharitable thoughts. While God remains quiet then I will stay out of the affairs of your son. You will have final say as long as you are more of an influence on the boy than his father. I will leave you good people to your quiet existence.'

She was mortified that I was offended and, I thought, a little offended herself that I could so easily listen within her skull.

'That, I think, would be for the best,' spoke a voice from the doorway of their home. It was Joseph, grown swarthy and with a heavy beard and deep-set yet honest eyes that were still those of the boy I had come across in Bethlehem near two decades ago. The blink of an eye to me, temporally, yet an age in my heart, waiting for God to show himself in or to Emmanuel.

The boy himself appeared beside his father, as tall and as broad, thick black hair cropped unevenly, heavy jet beard covering his bullish neck. 'Uncle Jeshua,' he cried, rushing to embrace me, eager for whatever gifts I had brought this time, returned from my travels. 'What do you bring me, what treasures from strange lands.'

I held him at arm's length, the concealed power in him thrumming up my arm muscles, slamming at my heart. 'You are a man now, good Emmanuel, and have no need of gifts.'

He looked crestfallen and I laughed. 'What use were my gifts? I brought you black volcanic stone and cracked vases and brickwork from fallen cities.'

'And you would tell me stories of how you had come by your gifts, and I liked your stories, and now I am offended.' The son of God had gone churlish and childish. Mary kept him bound to her apron strings at all times when he was not plying his trade with Joseph, and he was a little spoiled and beneath his years.

'My son would dishonour a guest and relative in such a manner?' demanded Joseph. 'Especially when Jeshua is about to embark on a long expedition?'

Emmanuel cast his sight to the dusty floor. 'Forgive me, Uncle, for I have been coarse and wish nothing from thee; only that you stay awhile.'

'I cannot, for I am to journey far to the east, many leagues, and will be gone a long passage.'

I looked to Joseph. 'I will return should I be needed.'

He nodded, and his heart was full of good will, yet he concurred with his wife's wish that I stay away for the sake of his innocent charge.

'Uncle,' spoke Emmanuel, 'why do you not look to age from year to year?'

I smiled. 'Illusion, all illusion. I am old, so very old. You would pity me if you only knew what has passed before these ancient eyes of mine.'

Away from Nazareth I shrugged off my disguise of humanity and rose into the still air on unfurled sails. Once more I had spent too long in this world, Beelzebub and Moloch long since dispatched back to the Demonic Republic with news that we demons were in favour with the mother of Yahweh's son, and I had loitered too long. Would Lilith be angry with me? She was ageless and understood the flux of time as I did, and we had, at our last communion, reached a trusting and loving understanding, but she was a restless creature. I pictured her holding sway over the fallen angels, having seduced them into declaring her queen of Hell and I laughed as I stooped through coiling airs to where the gateway between two worlds lay. She would have made the Republic a monarchy, and I would have to reverse her wicked work. The prospect gave me nothing but pleasure.

Hell was apathetic of my return, no message sent of my homecoming, and I found the great hall of Pandemonium barely inhabited, naphtha burning low and sallow. I wheeled from that which would be a palace, were we copiers of God's class system, and swept over the steaming slopes of our dominion until I came across crippled Mulciber, architect of Hell, toiling as a labourer at raising new homes amongst the black and jagged rocks.

'Friend,' I said, alighting next to the old angel, 'I am just returned from the world of Man. What has occurred in my brief absence?'

He turned to me, sweat pouring from his horned brow. 'Satan, you return. We thought that you had forsaken us once more.'

I clasped his shoulder. 'Forsaken? Never. I have been working at fresh ways to wage war.'

He shrugged, as if it concerned him not. 'War, is it not that which made us what we are? Is it not war against He on high that turned me from a sublime being to this crippled monster?'

I was taken aback, wounded. Mulciber had always been the most loyal, the most unquestioning, of my followers. 'A worthy war was it not, demon? Look at all that we have accomplished. Look at what you have accomplished.'

He shook his head and thoughts leaked from his skull. There was no anger in him, just a dark and cloying disappointment. 'Lucifer,' he said, 'you have roused us many times to battle and plot; and you have abandoned us to our own devices as many times. The last time, with your lady Lilith at your side, you raised Pandemonium to a great clamour and roused our hearts with hope that we would at last defeat Yahweh. Your obsession with humanity seemed a way to break cruel God, for us to be free to make our world as we saw fit without worry or concern of His omniscience.

'Yet Beelzebub returned a while past and told that you were once more filling your time with the affairs of apes. Demons seem no longer to be your prime concern. And thence came Moloch, your loyal and brave stalwart, and he told of this son of God being a lost cause, raised as a man and too human to inspire his fellow species to rebel. Indeed Moloch told that this Emmanuel, this Christ, has as yet displayed no divine power whatsoever, may indeed be unaware of his Heavenly lineage.'

It was a long speech, and good, from this usually taciturn demon. I had no grand rhetoric for him, for he was right. Emmanuel was disappointing, but a young man. And I held his mother and step father in too high esteem to coach the boy in his metaphysical potential.

'Where are they now?' was all that I could manage.

'Who do you speak after, Satan?'

Was that weary scorn, bordering on contempt in his voice? 'Beelzebub and Moloch. And where would I find my wife?'

Mulciber laughed, a hollow sound.

'Do you mock me, demon?' I demanded, anger growling at my base.

'Mock you, Light Bearer, why would I mock you? Have I

not always been loyal to thee, working myself to exhaustion in realising your dream for this harsh world in spite of my lameness? Have I ever accepted reward for my toil? Have I been even offered it?'

My quick anger coiled in upon itself and dissipated. 'You feel hard done by, good Mulciber, that your labours have not been recognised and appreciated. Tell me what you wish by way of recompense and I shall, if it is in my power, procure it for you.'

'I want no powers in this world but to continue with my work, for I am my work.'

'That is what I thought,' said I, 'and so I left you about your vocation.'

He held up a massive claw to still my slick tongue. 'I desire a small measure of the light you bear, Lucifer.'

'What, pray, would that light be now we are in Hell's darkness?'

'That which it always was. Not the reflected light of God in his most perfect creation. Never was it that to your followers. Always to us it was the light of knowledge. That is what I want above all else: to listen to your story of spreading light and free will amongst the apes; to listen to your thoughts, how you opine on sciences and magics.'

'Yet you know more of science than any demon or angel, you that would construct a causeway between distant bodies.'

'I have innate knowledge, instinct, of how to manipulate matter, as do all angels; I am only more blessed with the talent than most.' There was nothing of the braggart in him as he spoke these words, just a simple recognition of his inherent skills. 'But you, oh you Satan, you are a thinker, and a fiery one at that, with infernal notions and blazing words. Take a while to fill me with your adventures, fire me with your hot rhetoric.'

'I would do so, good demon.'

And so into Mulciber's home where I regaled him awhile with tales of Man and of devilry. We faced each other across a table wrought so fine that it could only be his handiwork. Occasionally he would fill a goblet he had placed before me with a pungent yet tasty mead that was also of his making as I puffed him up with talk of how he was worshipped as a god throughout the Roman Empire, his fiery skills unequalled in the minds of apes.

'Would you not discourage such superstition, Lucifer?' he asked, leaning across his fine iron table, his horny brow shaded curious and vexed in the inconstant flicker of some derivative of naphtha that he was patently trying out. 'Are you not the friend of reason and rationality?'

I leaned back in my hard yet comfortable seat with a sigh. 'It has been... a worry of mine for some time. Some demons encourage worship from the apes, though it would seem they place themselves on a level with god.' I took a sip of Mulciber's brew, shaking my head to dispel a pervasive buzzing that had set up within my skull.

'Then these demons are liars, and thou should not permit such falsehood, if truly you are the friend of reason. No doubt good Beelzebub and noble Moloch have set themselves up as deities, while they march and wage wars and oppress in the name of a new empire.'

I tried to speak, but my tongue was as if swollen and dry, and another swill of the mead from the goblet seemed not to remedy the situation. Mulciber was looking at me strangely, almost smiling, forearms resting on his table, palms vertical and pressed one to the other.

'Why hold your hands in such a fashion? Some humans have taking to doing it when they think they speak with God, damn fools,' I managed, my words sounding distant and slurred to my own ear. 'And where are Beelzebub and Moloch?'

He sat there, wearing that strange half smile, and then said: 'They returned here and waited a while for news of your corruption of the son of God, but no news came and they tired and returned to Earth for adventure. They have taken posts within the army of Rome. I heard tell that they considered the Empire one that would spread civilization and technology across the globe, but methinks they just miss a good battle.'

I stood, dizziness assailing me, forcing me to clutch hold of the table's lip. My wings draped like massive folds of a meaty cloak, threatening to drag me into genuflection before Mulciber; though he was the one that looked to be praying. I barked at him, wanting to put the fear of Satan into him but all that came from me sounded pitiful and pleading. 'Bastard drugged me... Lilith?'

He was openly smiling now, making my free hand go for the hilt of my sword.

'Oh, she has gone, Lucifer, in the footsteps of your faithful servants. She missed you so, and set out to trace you. Shame she never caught up with you, for you might have stayed in that world and avoided this… unpleasantness.'

I slumped back into my seat, and without the strain of standing words came easier. 'Who seduced you to their cause, old friend? Was it Belial? Mammon?' I was measuring the distance, measuring my energies to judge best whether I had enough to cross the table and separate the treacherous bastard's head from his body.

Mulciber stood, palms still pressed. Mulciber stood easily. He laughed, his audacity drawing a bestial snarl from me, as he saw understanding dawn in my eyes. 'You think I, who can manipulate the Universe would allow myself to remain crippled? No, Light Bearer, yet it was a way of gaining sympathies, of raising conspiracies. Who would not lend an ear to the brave martyr, the architect of Hell, who suffers such infirmity with noble Stoicism? Did you never wonder why I, who could raise a city from rock, did not mend my own fucking leg? No, for your thoughts are never with your followers, always with yourself and future glories. And you think my strings are pulled by another demon? No, Belial and Baal and Mammon are subject to my dictates. Thou should think thyself lucky for that mercy.'

'Mercy!' I spat. Time was surely running short, my muscles bunching with the effort of anticipation, but Mulciber was pacing the chamber. There would be one chance only, so I must bide my time and hope that his drug did not deliver me into unconsciousness before I could open his jugular. 'Tell me of your mercy, coward that would drug me.'

'But they wanted you dead.' The smile disappeared, his aspect become solemn. 'Yet I argued them out of it. I want an end to your leadership, to your demagoguery, to your war with God. I desire to rule in your stead, and my rule will be peaceable. You have been right to not interfere with this holy Emmanuel, yet you should have gone further: you should have knelt before him. I will send emissaries to Heaven itself, and we will be two distinct states. Yet Hell will no more be a republic: it will become an adjunct of the Kingdom of God.'

'Treacherous coward. Thou should have killed me.'

He shook his head, palms still pressed together. 'I think not. The drug I have given you will lay you in a stupor open-minded to my suggestions. Over time I will have your mind, your inner thoughts laid bare to me. I feel your anger now, roaring from your thinking organ. Oh, it blazes. Think, Lucifer, we'll step out of here after a while and I will have inculcated all my wishes and notions onto your cortex, indelible there. You will be my mascot. You will be my puppet.'

I looked to the sealed doorway of Mulciber's home, the very effort straining the sinews in my neck fair to pop.

'You would never make it,' spoke Mulciber. 'Thou cannot escape.'

I saw then why he seemed to pray. Mulciber the machiner was holding sealed the doors of his house. Stronger than any lock, his locked palms made the stone door unassailable, even to my infinitely sharp blade.

'How long, how very long have you plotted this treachery?'

'Treachery! He who betrayed his maker, betrayed his angels, dares to speak of treachery.'

The rage he had concealed for so long and so well, emanated from him in black waves that were nauseating to my drugged senses.

'Oh, I have plotted long, Satan. I have that one great attribute that was never part of your make-up: patience. I have watched you grow from fiery-tongued rebel-rouser to tyrant; watched you preach democracy and then subvert it with your wily machinations.' He leaned close, in prayerful attitude, to whisper his last wisdom. 'You tricked us into believing in you, into believing that we could defeat the undefeatable. All that has passed since, all that you have told me in this chamber, proves only that God is master of all. The end you have reached is as much His doing as mine, for He is all-knowing and Hell will bow down to him, and the good shall be rewarded.'

'Here be your reward,' I whispered back, roaring with effort as I raised my blade and brought it arcing, of a sudden, down to sever Mulciber's right hand from its wrist. The sword continued its descent, blue sparks flashing as it cleft the iron table in two, and I stumbled forward on legs unsteady as Mulciber staggered back and crashed to his arse, appalled and disbelieving eye going to where his hand lay in the dust between his bisected furniture.

'Can't be,' he mewled, enraged righteousness dispelled. 'The drug was too strong.'

'My strength you underestimated,' I snarled, raising my sword to take his head, but the sound of the doors that Mulciber had held sealed and shielded grinding open, snatched my attention. The troika of Belial, Baal and Mammon stood on the threshold and I wondered what fresh treason was afoot.

'Take not his life, Satan,' spoke Belial, 'for he is no more than a puppet, though we allowed him to think otherwise. I altered Mulciber's drug, so that it would not fell you utterly, for his vanity has grown strong like yours and we wished you to deal with him and at the same time find yourself weakened.'

Something like a sob escaped Mulciber as I drew my blade from the vicinity of his throat.

'Always the politician,' I gasped, my breath coming short and weak.

'Aye, and I acknowledge such, something you never have.'

I pointed the tip of my sword at Belial. 'I would lead until the Republic wished me to no longer lead. I would leave to others to deal with politics.'

He nodded assent. 'And that we have; and we have dealt with you.' And he and his flanking officers stepped back from the doorway to reveal a good legion of demons, armed with drawn bows and lances pointed in my direction.

'You would think me a coward, I know,' said Belial, 'but I have courage, if a different breed than yours. And I have mercy, and will leave you your life if you would leave Hell, forever.'

There was no mercy in Belial, but there was cunning. He knew that to destroy me while I was so defenceless might well plant seeds of rebellion in the hearts of the watching demons, seeds that might germinate should the rule of him and his two acolytes fall into public disfavour.

'And if I would say no?'

'Then you would be arrested.'

'And if I resisted?'

'Then you will be destroyed. Take life, Lucifer, flee to your beloved Earth. The drugs in you have done damage to your system, probably irreversible; but they will not take your life. Sheathe your sword, and leave this place with all the dignity you can muster.'

I looked to Mulciber, mewling on the floor, clutching his weakly-spurting stump. That was where fight would lead me. I was weak on my feet, my sight compromised, strength gone from my muscles. I should have been consumed by righteous and indignant rage at this smart coup, but that feeling was not existent because my mind, where emotions are born and fester, was befuddled by the chemicals I had ingested.

'Sheathe your sword, Lucifer, and be gone.'

I did sheathe my sword, and walked a giddy stagger past Belial and Mammon and Baal, and then up the rocky incline, in the direction of the wormhole that would take me to the world of light and of Man. The ranks of Belial's newly modelled army stood strong as I moved parallel to them, most with eyes cast to the ground, but some favouring me with disdain or even contempt, arrows and lance heads still directed at me. A rock came whistling from whom I knew not, catching me on my temple and driving me to one knee. I struggled upright, pressing a claw to the wound, the scaly palm immediately wetting with black blood. Another projectile whistled and struck me hard on the shoulder, chipping the bone, a curse following its trajectory. I struggled on, forcing my chin up, spreading my sails in defiance, and the next missile tore a ragged hole in the fabric of a wing. 'Leave us Satan, false god. Too long have we listened to your lies, arch betrayer,' jeered the thrower. For a moment I considered stopping and turning to face them, these that had once courageously followed me into unwinnable battle. But my tongue was rendered artless by Mulciber's mead, and the three new rulers of Hell had fired them so to belligerence that I would most surely be shot full of arrows and then hacked to bits.

I had reached the edge of a precipice. Good thermals rose from chasms far below me, and I thought I could soar to the edge of the atmosphere and glide near to where I would cross from this world to the next.

Before I launched myself I did turn, but not to the lined demons. It was to Belial, some way below me, down the shale slope. 'So good, Belial,' I called, drawing on my last reserves of energy, the strength of my voice surprising me and giving meagre comfort, 'would you do as Mulciber, and surrender to Heaven, and hope without justification for God's mercy?'

'We would not,' he shouted back, just as a fresh stone clipped my cheekbone and another opened my scalp. 'We would make the Demonic Republic a stronghold fortress, resistant for eternity to the encroaches and dictates of Heaven. Mulciber had to be brought low for his lack of resistance to indoctrination. I -- and my fellows -- am a pragmatist, Lucifer. All evidence would point to the lack of God's omniscience and to the logical notion that he is a force that can be resisted. I am a politician, old leader, better versed in sophistry than even you, and there is truth in sophistry: for an argument to be winnable there must be a grain of truth in it. I know we demons cannot defeat Yahweh; yet I believe we can resist him and live here well by the dictates of tempered free will.'

'No doubt yourself and the fellow members of your ruling party more auspiciously than the mass of fallen angels?' said I.

He shrugged and smiled, and something like understanding passed between us. 'I am a pragmatist, Lucifer, and would openly declare myself a hedonistic one. But I would wish to share some measure of luxury, of pleasure, with the people.'

I smiled at what I thought his simple yet, perhaps workable view, and launched myself off the cliff with a cry of: 'Amen!'

Belial's shouted words chased me: 'Yet you must promise to never return here, for that would be your end.'

I gave no response, catching a thermal and rising, wheeling, over Hell. I saw, with dimming eyes, the naphtha-emanating homes of numerous demons, clustered first around the walls of mighty Pandemonium and then spreading out across the forbidding and fiery landscape. We fallen angels had come a long way.

The drugs were surging in my system as I stooped towards the wormhole, my sails become collapsed wings, my thoughts barely coherent. I held Lilith's image in my mind as the poison threatened to undo me. Always in hardship, I would conjure in thought images of my wife. Lilith was my prayer, and at this pass I was beyond loathing myself for such wretchedness. And I fell to that gateway between worlds, Mulciber's great construct from the days before his mind had been turned wholly to corrupt thoughts of surrender. I was through, succumbed to great gravities, form warped and battered, and spat out into the dazzling world of the great apes, crashing into fecund undergrowth and losing all consciousness, for a goodly while, in this world of slow revolutions and quickened time.

The dream was there, the most perfect visage in all creation, leaning close and kissing my feverish brow, wetting the sweat from me with cool compress. A wish, surely, of a dying mind awakened to one last chance of hope. 'My love,' I breathed, and was again lost to darkness.

The pretence of wakefulness once more. Still she ministered to me. 'My, Lucifer,' she soothed, 'come back to me. Your time is at hand. Jove has made His move with the Son of Man.'

'Fallacy,' I think I muttered, 'nothing left to fight for.'

She kissed me, and the sensation was surely warmer than a dreaming brain could have conjured. Then she broke the kiss and said: 'Always there is something to fight for.' I wanted to remonstrate, but darkness seeped in again and stole me away.

Lilith stooped, lean and naked, before an iron pot balanced on a cast tripod over orange-fizzing embers. Scents rose from the pot, good sniffs of meats and vegetables, stuff that pleased me but was unnecessary.

I succumbed to the dream and thought I could make it lucid. 'I need no food, dear wife. I am a product of Heaven, and we exist on vapours.'

She turned to me, a tentative smile on her glorious lips, anxiety flashing dull in her grey eyes. 'You look fully awake, at last. Thou may be a product of Heaven, and may exist on vapours, but on this nourishment you might live.' She moved towards me with dribbling ladle. 'Feed now. There is much to be done.'

I took a sip of the hot stew, fluid trickling down my chin to be wiped away by attentive Lilith. Good. I slurped greedily at the next proffered ladle, and my lady laughed and compelled me to temper my hunger, which was risen like a physical beast in me, gnawing at the walls of the cavern within.

'Steady your appetite. There is plenty to eat here, in this home I have constructed.'

'I thought you a dream,' I rasped, my vocal cords sore from disuse. 'How did you find me, and how long have I lain insensate?'

'I knew you would escape, if you could, so I would journey here every few months or so.'

'Escape? You knew of the plotted coup, then?'

Her expression darkened to a glower. 'There we inklings everywhere. Beelzebub and Moloch had left on their adventures, and Belial and his cronies had subtly assumed power, passing an edict here, a law there. I thought it expedient to leave Hell before such movements were forbidden by the State.

'I searched for you, picked up your trace now and again, but missed you at each turn. The trail would cool and die and I would think you returned to Hell and feared what manner of reception might await you. And so I would come to this place and hope to find you, as I did, broken and battered, foul drugs running hot through your feverish system. I thought hope lost, but raised this meagre shelter of skins,' she waved her free hand, indicating the tent she had constructed that kept the elements at bay, 'and watched over you.'

'Was my sleep long?'

'Some ten years, in the human way of measuring time by solar revolutions.'

This could not be. I was struggling to rise, remembering Lilith's words from earlier spells of wakefulness that I had dismissed as dreams. Jove has made His move with the Son of Man, she had said. When had that been, hours or years past? Lilith dropped the ladle and pressed her palms to my shoulders, gently forcing me to a sitting position.

'Calm, my love. I feel your impatience, know your mind so well after all this time, understand your wish to return to the fray, but a few days healing will hardly alter the course of history.'

'Yet Emmanuel...'

'They are calling him Jesus the Christ now, and the Hebrews make claim that he will begin his ministry on Earth once he returns from the desert, compelling Man to return to the bosom of Yahweh.'

'He has taken to the desert?'

'Gone for forty days and nights, so he claimed, some three weeks ago, into the Judean wilderness, to fast and commune with his father.' She spoke with heavy sarcasm. 'Yet why the son of God would need to starve himself to a husk to commune with the Almighty is beyond the scope of my meagre brain.'

'And what brought about this change, for he was but a man when last we met, godless even?'

Lilith sighed, taking a sip of water from a cup beside her and pouring the rest over her hair which had been darkened and plastered to her scalp by sweat. The water ran in rivulets over her sweat-beaded naked form. Even in my debilitated state I felt a stirring at my groin and forced ardour from my mind, struggling to consolidate my thoughts.

'Tell me, Lilith. How did God make his move?'

'At the Jordan river, Jesus appeared at a mass baptism.'

'Fools,' I scorned. 'They follow these fawning pursuits and think that after they die they gain admission to Heaven itself, when all they gain is eternal peace, their atoms unconscious of the decaying body that they were once complexifications of.'

'… And Jesus asked to be baptised…'

'Oh, Emmanuel. You should have known better. You should be a leader of men, not a shepherd of fools.'

'… And after Jesus was baptised, the sky grew dark and the people became afraid, and all fell back but Jesus, who stood firm. And the voice of God issued, as if from a rent in the firmament, and spoke these words: "You are My beloved son, in whom I am well pleased".'

'Cheap farce of a trick. Have Yahweh's powers become so diminished that he must resort to such sleights of mind? I must go to Emmanuel, save him from himself and his father.'

Lilith kissed me, and whispered: 'You must, my love. But rest first. The Anointed One has promised himself forty days in the desert, bereft of food and fluid: you have time enough. Rest now, for the poison of Mulciber still courses your system and the flight to Judea will be arduous.'

With consciousness dimmed by her sweet words of comfort, I said, 'Then I shall catch him in the desert at the nadir of his suffering, when his self-imposed ordeal has rendered him less than delusional, and I would offer him food and fluid, for he is physiologically but a man. I must… must… save him from his father, and must… and must… save humanity from his father.'

'You shall, Lucifer. I have foreseen it.'

I was snapped to consciousness. 'Have you learned nothing, Lilith? We are creatures of the present, of practical sciences, not of prognostication and God's style of omniscience.'

Lilith laughed lightly and, as if I were a dog, she patted my pate. 'I know, sweetness, how I love to josh with thee. But when in love one can test another.'

I smiled, and in my finest humour for a while, with my wife beside me and adventure before me, I fell asleep.

The Judean desert was indeed a desolate place, harsh of day and of night. The son of Mary, even at the height of his powers, must surely be suffering in this harsh environment. I would go to him and rescue him, lost child of God.

The flight from Italy had exhausted me, my six limbs become as stone, and now I had to assume a human figure. My heavenly-yet-wingless configuration would not suit here: for Jesus would recognise me as 'Uncle' Jeshua. I transformed myself into a wretched elder, complete with crooked staff (my sword, should the whelp require a sting from the flat of its blade).

And Emmanuel, the prophesied Jesus, was known to me: a creature on the cusp of despair and lost deep in the barrenness. I was gone to his tortured mind, closing my broad wings and, resuming my fresh disguise of decrepitude, I stumbled before him.

My heart ached, for he was become a wretched thing, brain filled with fever, all sense subject to the twisted will of his mother's rapist.

'Child, when did you realise your destiny?'

He turned to me, sallow and harried by starvation's dreams. 'What would you know of destiny, ancient one?'

I smiled, the toothless aspect of a sage, and said, with an all-embracing sweep of withered limbs, my staff a seemingly heavy extension of myself: 'I know nothing. For destiny is a lie.'

He smiled then, and I saw the power that had emanated from him when he had been but a babe. Even though his human body had been tested by the fierce sun and frigid moon, he stood before me in a state of emaciated glory. He knew God now, and I considered felling him forever, a quick slice with my staff become a blade. How would that count with his father?

But I would not, for there was hope in him, and my mind held the vision of his lovely mother and his good father.

'Destiny is my father, the one and true God,' he spoke, still

beaming beatifically, and I reckoned that felling him would
have been a small mercy.

I pressed a hand to my constructed withered chest. 'I am
Yesh, old hermit from the cave yonder. Who art thou, and what
ill chance has brought thee to this pass? For you would seem to
me, him that our new baptising prophet honoured as God's son,
at Jordan's ford.'

'As I told.'

I drew closer, struggling to maintain the disguise, weakened
as I still was by Mulciber's chemicals. 'Then thou hast been
here a good while, and must be more inured to thirst than the
camel, and must be -- and I see it be so -- starved, for there is
naught but tough stubs and roots to subsist upon.' I paused a
moment, leaning on my staff as if wilting in the blazing sun.
'Yet if thou be truly the son of God, turn these hard stones at
thy feet to bread, that thou may be saved and that we might
eat.'

Jesus said: 'Is it not written that Man lives not by bread
only, but by each word proceeding from the mouth of God?'

I sighed, for I had no desire to listen to mystical ramblings,
had only wished to see an example of the extent of his powers,
if he yet had any.

His drawn visage had darkened and he said, 'You think I do
not know you that my father foretold would come to tempt me,
as you tempted my mother and wormed with deceit into my
father's heart? You are he that lied and called himself uncle to
me, arch-tempter.'

With relief and a sigh I let the deception fall away, become
again the dragon, the gnarled staff my straight sword. 'It is true
I am that unfortunate free soul that leagued with an army of
likewise fallen and rebelled against God's tyranny.'

'No tyranny, serpent. You and your angels went against the
good, and for that my father imprisoned thee.'

'And yet,' said I, 'I enjoy the liberty of this globe, and of its
airs.'

'Your boasts of freedom are lies to thyself, for I feel your
grief and it is well deserved: for thou were composed of lies
from the beginning; and in lies will end. Thou art in the service
of Heaven's King, whether acknowledged or not.'

There were grains in his words that stung me, but, despite
the strength of his speech, I sensed confusion with this new-

found position of his, and I willed myself to be the man, dressed in fine silks and well-groomed that he had known as his kindly uncle, Jeshua.

'Do you not remember how you sat on my knee, when you were the child Emmanuel, and would listen to my tales of adventure? My words were true, Jesus, and your father -- and I reckon to be less of that monster in you than He would have you believe -- has told you naught but lies. Remember the man you are, not the god you would darkly strive to be. You have some aspects of what other men might deem holy, for I sense in you a mastery over matter that only angels and their creator possess, but thou art a man and as such subject to a man's passions and needs. I beg of you, Christos, feed your hunger, indulge your passions; be a man of substance, not a puppet of Heaven's dictates.'

With a flourish that drew me unsteady, threatened to fell my sickly form, I conjured before God's son the vision of a table richly spread in regal mode, replete with meats and game and good wine. And I drew from my mind scantily clad beauties, male as well as female, for I could not discern the taste of Christ's groin, to act as servants. If he would but reach for the phantom food, move to caress the alluring spectres, then his faith, in himself and his father, would be weakened enough for me to plant my seeds of self-determination in the spoiled soil of his mind. My spirits surged, for there was desire in him, for the meats that caused him to unconsciously slobber and for the rendered serving folk that rushed the blood from his mind. I saw and felt him fighting these base and wonderful needs.

'Does the son of God doubt to sit and eat, though naught is forbidden to He that is master of all men?'

He wiped with contempt at the saliva on his chin, casting his eyes from the nubile beauty that had foxed his resolve. 'I would sit and eat and enjoy your gift, Satan, but that you said naught is forbidden me. Why then accept your false gift, when I could summon aught that I would require? I have come to fast, and to commune with the Lord, and your tricks are as nothing to me.'

He swept his right arm upwards and my conjured glamour vanished, and I staggered, dropping to one knee.

'Thy powers are weak, old fiend.'

'And yours are strong, and burgeoning still, and would be of such aid to poor Man in his brief and terrifying existence. What a leader you would be, young Jesus, if thou would only cast off thy father's ugly yoke.'

'All you have, ancient devil,' said Jesus, 'are weak words. My Lord and father visits my mind and reveals the truth of His glory to me. I am not bound to His will, but act with free will in delivering His message.'

'If your will be free, then God is not all-knowing. If your will be free then, for the sake of argument, thou should act against your father's will, to ascertain that thou are no puppet.'

'I would not.'

'For why? It would be but a test. Have you so little faith in yourself, and by extension in Him on High?'

He wavered and I drew strength from his weakness, again the dragon, wings unfurled, fresh potency coursing my form. 'And what be His message, Christos?'

He stumbled over his words, smug sanctimony fled. 'I would start a new ministry to draw Man back to God's rule, with Heaven as the goal of those few good followers.'

He spoke weakly here, I think, because he had a fine mind for argument, and knew that he was on unsteady ground, for I was surely a better judge than he in matters of Heaven and Hell.

'Yet what of those that do not follow, those bad many?' I asked slyly.

He forced words from his lips, and I felt from his now unde-fended mind that he either did not believe his own words, or wished them to be untrue. 'Then they shall be damned, for eternity, in the fiery furnace of Hell.'

I laughed, scornful mockery, and advanced on the boy be-come a man that I had once entertained such high hopes for. 'Am I not a denizen of Hell.'

He stepped back, away from my shadow, as if it might con-sume or infect him. 'Thou art; thou art Hell's ruler.'

I bowed humbly. 'No ruler I. Hell is no kingdom, with no reflection of Heaven's intransigent monarchy. Yet I have been in Hell since its beginning, and never a bad man's soul have I known to come to that place. And neither in Heaven do good men reside for eternity, cravenly worshipping that vile king that forced himself into your mother. Men die, and that is the end of them as thinking creatures. There is no resurrection, Jesus.'

He had turned his narrow back to me. 'You will suffer, ser-pent, my father tells me so.'

'Yet where shall I suffer? In the place I call home, that is of comfort and well-used to me? That would be fine suffering in-deed.' I knew not his powers of mental divination, so I kept my mind tight shut lest he discern that I was now Hell's refugee, fair trapped on this Earth.

Jesus turned back to me, manufacturing bravado well, spreading his arms as if addressing the world entire, and I saw that in time he would become a greater demagogue than even I. 'Yet I will be the resurrection, and will deliver Mankind from evil unto the bosom of the Lord. And they shall hate me for it at first, for they have as a kind come to distrust love; but they shall come to love me, for they will know that I take their countless sins upon myself and show them the path to salva-tion.'

Words were done for the moment, for he had withdrawn into vainglorious rhetoric and so, feeling suddenly strong, I swooped on him, gathering him to me and bearing him aloft, through wispy clouds to a high peak where the sun was pleas-ingly merciless. He was visibly shaken by the ascent, clinging to a rock lest he tumble to oblivion.

I cast a sway over the vista that was below and reached to the shimmered horizon. I made the panorama as if populated with the cities of Man, smoke of industries hanging in a pall beneath the heavens' cope. And I painted armies over this landscape, warring men in their multitudes, showering one and the other with plagues of arrows, rending limb from trunk and head from neck with bloody sword.

'Thou could end this,' I said. 'Could limit, at the least, the warfare that is committed in the name of thy father.'

Jesus looked to me, a great sadness in his eyes. 'It is the way of Man to set himself at war with his fellow.'

'Nay, it is the way of God.'

'If my father would be gone, Man would still kill Man.'

'Perhaps,' I mused, 'but it would be over things such as ter-ritory or politics, things made by Man. Wars would not be fought for the entertainment of Jehovah, so that He could en-sure worship with genocide.'

Further weakened, he stumbled and seemed so close to

tumbling from the peak that I rushed and caught hold of his wrist, and altered in a breath the illusion below us. Now Man traded with his own species, and great cities had risen, with academies such as had been founded in Greece, where youngsters could be taught, girls as much as boys, to live well and love well and pursue science and reason. Informed chatter and unfettered laughter sailed up to us from this Utopia I had conjured.

'This could be, Christ,' I said. 'All the kingdoms of the world could be as I show you, if Man were emancipated from God.' I squeezed his wrist as hard as I dared. 'All of this I would share with thee, if thou would join with me.'

'Away from me, Satan,' he managed, but his words were but a whisper. 'I join only with the Lord God.'

'Very well,' said I, and again gathered him up and took to the wing. Christ felt so light now as to be almost insubstantial, and power surged through my bunched fibres. Mulciber's poison had been driven to the deepest reaches of my system, but even as a sense of giddy triumph had overtaken me I was dimly aware that the drugs would return with a vengeance once this fervent moment was passed.

And so we alighted on the highest pinnacle of Jerusalem's great temple.

'Here thou art surely closest to thy father, and would know Him best and be best in His care,' said I. 'Cast thyself down; safely, surely, if son of God. But no, you stand bowed and unsure, for you have no absolute faith, and rightly so, in resurrection. You are but meat, Christos, and meat is a fine thing to be. It was I that cut you from your mother when your father was content to let you throttle. I was your saviour, Jesus, and can be such again.'

He shrugged me off in flailing desperation. 'You lie, and filled my mother's mind with your corrupt falsehoods. I have faith, and it is everlasting, and it is not in thee.'

The son of God pitched himself from the high tower, the move taking me so by surprise that I was frozen aghast for a breath and was then rushing to the brink to stoop and swoop him to safety, but other wings, stronger than mine for not fizzing with venom, were beating to my rear, and the flat of a sword of divine construct cracked my skull and felled me with my head and shoulders hanging over 'Salem's far-below streets, blood running over my face and dripping to be lost to sight. Only the weight of my laggard wings saved me from following Jesus in his plunge; and my plummet would have been unrescued.

I saw the diving rear of the angel that had bested me yet again, that old foe that had felled me in the realm of God of which I had little remembrance. Grandiose Michael caught the plunging man that would be a god a moment before his weak flesh was pounded to impact-pulp, and bore him away through the blithe air.

With a great and despairing groan I drew myself back from the edge, the poison, as I had anticipated, surging my system as my immune system had collapsed alongside my spirits. 'Michael, old nemesis, one day I will best thee... and all days I better thee...'

Night found me indeed fallen, spread-winged and feverish on the temple's pinnacle. I thought of all the Hebrews who worshipped in the cavernous vault of the fine construct that lay beneath me, and I pitied their faith. And I was envious of their mendacious comfort. I was poisoned indeed. Vultures circled above, drawn from their roosts by the promise of easy flesh. I must be gone from this land, back to where Lilith waited, but that place, where the Empire held sway, was an age away. I could not help but admire these Romans that controlled the city below me and a third of the world. No wonder that adventurers such as Beelzebub and Moloch had disguised their demonic forms and joined such an artless yet pragmatic army.

Enough with this, the addled rambling of a disordered mind. I pitched to the edge of the tower and over, plummeting through the hot air, wings trailing. 'Strength Devil!' I roared at myself, and my sails beat, weak at first, then correcting my drive, pitching me up into the starry sky so that the marketers below, and the sweet revellers, and the stationed Latin soldiers, cried out -- in fear or ecstasy I know not which -- as a great winged dragon passed overhead, blotting out the stars and even the sliver of the moon.

I was aloft now, on nocturnal thermals, my sails bearing a form that was always on the verge of unconsciousness. Up to the stratosphere, where the winds roared in opposition to those at lower levels, where ice formed on my sails and the Earth was a map below me, dark but lighted more now by the lights of human civilization than I had hitherto witnessed. The lack of oxygen and the chill promise of the outer abyss seemed to imbue me with newfound strength that I understood must be utilised if I were not to drift in an orbit of repose, and so I set my compass for Italy, for where my Lilith was encamped before the Hellmouth and pitched back through the thickening atmosphere to crash within sight of the shelter where my wife had nursed me back to temporary health.

She came running now, barefoot and billowing silk, hair trailing behind her like the tail of a silver comet, and dropped to her knees beside me, concern etched on her face, and there was rebuke in her tone when she spoke. 'You risked too much, taking the Christ to the summit of the temple. In your wretched state you were in no condition to put your physical self in the way of peril.'

I was confounded. I had just returned and yet news had reached Lilith from far Judea ahead of me. Had she learnt the talent of flight in my absence, or become as adept a reader of minds as any angel? And now the thought entered my feverish mind: how had she known that Jesus had been baptised and had entered the desert when the news could not have reached this wild portion of Italy in so short a time?

'How... how?' I rasped, but she pressed two fingers to my lips, stilling my words.

'Not now. There is telling to be done, for I have an informant, and his identity might not be to your liking. But that is for later, when you are somewhat recovered. For now we must get you into shelter, lie you at the fire's side.'

I nodded, unable to focus my mind on the questions that threatened to snag at the edges of my mind, bearing all my will on drawing myself to something like an upright position. Lilith was there, slender but strong beyond her mass, supporting me into the shelter at an ungainly stagger, where at the fire's side I did indeed lay.

The sound of muted voices drifted through my haze of unconsciousness and I flickered into gradual, misty wakefulness. The conversation must have passed, or been a figment of my mind, for Lilith was now alone and naked and upon me. She kissed my body, and the pleasure seared my nerve endings, and yet, as was often the way with this glorious woman, there was pain also. She worked over my torso, to my throat, over my shoulders and down over my abdomen to groin and I groaned with pleasure and pain. I forced my head to raise once, and it seemed that her face was a mask of darkness, and in that instant I knew the terrible truth of what dreadful manner her nursing had taken.

'Lilith, no!' I strained, my voice a broken and lost thing.

Her face was over mine then, smeared with my dark arterial blood, a white and strained smile cutting through the mask. She stroked my brow with consummate tenderness. 'Worry not my love, I spat almost all out, swallowing only a drop here and a dribble there. Calm now. I think you almost drained; now you must feed.'

With her strong teeth she tore with sudden viciousness at her white and slender wrist, her own dark blood bubbling. I thrashed my head from side to side in negation, but she forced her wrist resolutely against my closed lips, straddling me with her lithe form, whispering forcefully to me.

'Drink of me, let my good blood fill you, spread from your gut to your veins, replace the poison.'

I tried to struggle, honestly I did, but after a while sweet drops of her fluid seeped onto my tongue, to the back of my throat and such was my damnable weakness that I began to gulp my love's lifeblood, lost to a strange rapture where all thought and reason and awareness of time's passage was lost. I became aware at length that Lilith was fighting against me, beating at me with her free hand.

'Too much,' she was sobbing. 'Release me.'

Eyes that had been closed in reverie sprang wide with shock, my sharp demon teeth releasing her wrist. She kicked away from me, collapsing supine, breast rising and falling at an alarming rate as she snatched for air. I rolled on to my side.

'Forgive me,' I implored. 'I was lost.' And my voice was stronger, deeper, more the voice of Satan than it had been since I was vanquished from hell.

I reached for her, terrified lest she turn from me, but her hand folded into my claw. There was pain in her grey eyes, a blanched and unhealthy paleness to her skin beyond even her usual marble tone.

'How much did I take?'

She smiled, such a horribly weary expression, and said, 'Never worry, I have enough to survive, and my marrow will generate enough to flood my veins, as will yours, with the blood I have given you as a source pure enough to restore your health in time.'

She was sitting up then, trembling slightly, my blood caked black round her mouth as hers must be round mine. She trembled slightly as she drew herself to her feet, yet only slightly.

'I will leave you now, for I need the feel of the night's wind on my skin. I am not as weak as I thought, and will take a stroll in the moonlight.' She looked down on me with sorrow dimming her eyes. 'You may not see me for a while, Devil, but it will be a short while for such as we that have endured ages apart.'

I struggled to rise as she made for the doorway of the shelter, but debilitating nausea wracked me of a sudden, leaving me gagging on my knees, rightly genuflecting in the wake of my wife.

She looked over her shoulder before slipping into the night, that terrible smile once more on her lips. 'Patience, Lucifer, you have alien blood in you and your system is fighting to assimilate it. Rest, rest, and I shall see you in a while.'

She was gone, my saviour, and I rocked back to sit on the earth, spreading my wings to stabilise me. It was then that I felt the presence of an angel, and I knew who Lilith's informant was and that she had made some dire deal with the enemy.

Gabriel stepped into the shelter, resplendent in his holy armour, white wings that sprouted from his shoulder blades carried with high pride. He came and stood over me, a pious smile at his lips.

'Oh how the unmighty have fallen,' he sneered. 'You have become a parasite, Satan, feeding on the blood of your own wife. Her love for you is indeed strong; though your love, as ever, is a self-directed vain and ugly thing.'

'What know you of love?' I snarled.

'I know of true love,' responded the sanctimonious bastard. 'I know God's love, so all-encompassing that He even extends a measure of divine compassion to you, and lets you live.'

'He lets me live because it pleases Him to toy with me, to see me broken. That is not compassion, that is sadism.'

Gabriel stooped towards me. 'How art thou fallen, Light

Bearer,' he mocked. 'Self-pitying snake.'

My abject fraud had drawn the archangel within striking distance and I slashed suddenly with my sword, my bloodless muscles screaming agony. But Gabriel whipped back, and crashed his lance across my forearms, sending my blade skittering across the shelter's floor. I threw up an injured arm in defence, raking talons at his abdomen with my free claw, aiming for evisceration. But he was strong and confident and dodged my slash with lazy ease, driving the point of his lance into my shoulder where my flesh burned with exquisite agony. He pitched me then, like a stuck pig, onto my belly, astride me, feet planted firmly at the base of each wing, sliding his lance easily free and repositioning its point at my nape.

'On your belly once more, lowly serpent. That is your natural condition. You have no sense, Lucifer, old angel. Always you fight, when always you are lost. What little victories you scored early on with God's child have been more than discredited now. For the son has grown strong and his ministry grows strong with him. He works miracles now, and heals the sick that they would follow him. He would even raise the dead.'

I spluttered into the earth, enraged yet impotent. 'None, not even Jehovah could raise the dead, and the Christ's miracles are little more than molecular sleights, impressive to apes perhaps, but of no genuine worth.'

The lance's point broke the scaled skin of my neck, fresh fire surging there, and pain and frustration wracked me so that hot tears spilled from my eyes.

'You do well to weep, worm. How could God not raise the dead, He that created the universe from nothing?'

I yearned decapitation at that moment, so unbearable was the shame of my position. 'He created nothing,' I spat into the dirt. 'He lied, and you gullible bastards swallowed His vainglorious deceptions. He didn't make the angels… another lie. And the apes, He only altered them; I have had more effect on humanity than as He.' I was laughing then, my hilarity muffled by grit but a wonderful release all the same. 'Your god is a fraud, archangel, nought but a cheap charlatan. Fuck Him I say, and fuck you too.'

The lance's point was withdrawn and Gabriel stepped from off of me, allowing me to roll on to my side and scrabble back into a sitting position.

'You wish your words to fire me to destroying you, but that is not Yahweh's will. He sent me to save you after you failed in your temptation of Christ. It is I that have been instructing Lilith on the whereabouts and the doings of Jesus; I that instructed her that you could be saved by a transfusion of her blood, on the condition that she would not lay eyes on you again until after the reign of the Christ.'

I staggered upright on unsteady legs. Still Gabriel, for all his fine armoury and flashing hubris, took a step back. 'He is but a man, with a man's longevity,' I said.

'Long enough for what Yahweh has in mind for him.'

'Which is?'

Gabriel smiled, but it looked forced and with my burgeoning strength I could detect seething disquiet in him. The conscience of this one was rarely a still thing, which made his subservience to the grand Narcissus Jehovah even more disgusting.

He said: 'Jesus the Christ will bring about the ruin of the Roman Empire, and in its place will rise a Kingdom of Heaven here on Earth, and all of mankind will live only to serve the Father of the Universe.'

'Oh, very good speech. You do realise that you are in the service of a fucking lunatic?'

'Your blasphemy will bring you no harm, Satan. It is all that you have left, deserted by Hell, demons, and now your whore.'

I took a step towards him, growling and beating my wings, and he raised his lance to ward me off.

'No more fighting, worm. Yahweh is arranging something special for his son, something to make the Hebrews and the Romans quiver with fear and instigate the rebellion that will spread like a scourge through all the empire; and you are to be there when Jesus makes his stand against the might of Man's great empire.'

'For why?'

'So that you can try and fail to dissuade Christ from his path, and then the apes will know that there is none greater than the father of Jesus. You will be humiliated in the eyes of Man, and Christ will reign supreme at Yahweh's right hand.'

'I will have no part in this.'

Gabriel laughed. 'You think that you have a choice? Free will is an illusion. God knows all and controls all. You will take part. You might tell yourself that it is your own desire to turn Christ to your path, that it is your pride that compels you, but in reality you are as subject to his will as we all are.'

'We shall see.'

He nodded with fabricated sagacity. 'Indeed we shall.

With that he took to the wing, tearing off the roof of the shelter, and a storm -- natural or otherwise I knew not -- had risen and rain stung my wounds and drove me to a covered corner draped in a blanket, and I thought of Lilith out there in the storm in her weakened state, and I still too weak to seek her out. Lightning fizzed and thunder broke overhead, and I roared at the heart of the storm that I was not finished yet, and I set my own path, not that grand puppeteer that called Himself God. I did control my own unknowable fate. To prove such, I would venture no more to Judea, keeping a continent's distance between me and Christ. I swore then that that would be my plan of inaction. Pride be damned, no more would I be a pawn of Jehovah.

Yet still, some months later, restored to full health and brimming with hubris, I stood before the man that I had delivered from his mother's womb. It was night and we were in the Garden of Gethsemane, and still yet again I had decided that I could thwart God's design.

Chapter Fourteen

'I stood over you as you slept fitfully in the early hours of that fateful morning so few days ago,' said Will, 'and whispered the five words that would set in motion all that has unfolded: A History of The Devil.'

Neil passed the laptop wordlessly to Leonard, folded in the backseat. The long chapter had taken him moments to skim through, as part of his mind knew the story, anticipated the order of the words on the screen with exactitude.

'That was the code then?' he said at length. 'The key to unlocking my programming, to killing Neil Mann, was the title of my memoirs.'

Will looked to Neil, his face appearing jaundiced in the sodium lighting that lined the thread of tarmac along which the three angels bulleted west. 'Yes, and the story of who you truly are should have been one spread over months if not years, but the decision cast by the Council of Heaven meant that I had no choice but to rouse you from your waking dream of banal comforts.'

'Tell me of this decision, of the council --'

'You know I cannot,' snapped out Will. 'I've told too much already. You have to recall all yourself, for the sake of your reborn and vulnerable mind.'

Neil sighed, sinking back into his seat, watching the orange-lit tarmac unfurl before them. He was as if in a dream, caught between two states. He had the memories of a dull but relatively successful, until loss and booze, life of a man; and the snaking into prehistory somehow more intense yet distant recall of The Devil himself. He looked to his hands. Just a man's hands, no claws waiting to unsheathed, only badly bitten fingernails. He pressed his hands to the soft skin of his face, ran a palm over the lush and oily growth where only days ago there had been a spreading patch of bald skin.

'Is this how I looked in Heaven, Will?' And then, 'And why can't I remember Heaven?'

Will kept his sight fixed resolutely ahead, square jaw clamped shut.

'Yes, yes, I know, I have to discover my past all on my own, or my devil's mind might crumble and make me become just a man again, or worse still a dribbling cabbage and then, for reasons you can't tell me, the angels would kill me, although one of them, mad Mike himself, pretty much wants to kill me anyway, and did so even when the others didn't.'

Will could not help but smile. 'Yes, that would be about the size of it.'

'But surely there is something you could tell me that would make me stronger, more... Satanic? I am going to fight God's warrior prince and I still feel as a mortal man. What chance do I have?' Neil's eye went to the flash of the celestial blade slid beneath his seat, his newly sharpen sight trying to fathom the sharpness of its edge and failing.

'You have hope,' said Will, 'in that Michael has been badly injured, firstly by Lilith and little Ithuriel here,' (Mr Thomas looked up from the computer screen, blushed and returned his attention to the story before him) 'and almost certainly by Gabriel, for I doubt that the archangel of death would suffer such wounds as he did without inflicting some of his own on his antagonist. And Michael is insane, though I am not sure whether that is a weakness or a strength in battle.'

'So you can disclose some information to me?' said Neil.

'Only if it is not directly part of your own story.' Will indicated and left the road that had carried them from the east coast, and now the lights and ugly high rises of the city were spread before them. Eleven-thirty-seven flashed the clock on the car's instrument panel. He turned his head to fix his sight on Neil, driving the car flawlessly without appearing to lend any sensory attention to the urban roads. 'You do realise,' he said, 'that Michael may have already killed your wife.'

Neil shook his head in negation, fighting down the possibility of that dread prospect. 'No. I lost Maria before; it will not happen again.'

Calmly, as if explaining to a child, Will said. 'You never lost Maria. Maria never existed. Lilith is your wife, has been for thousands of years; Maria was her tamed alter ego that lived in your invented memories for a few months.'

'And my son never existed, except the one that breathed but a moment millennia ago. Two realities and none seem quite real to me.'

'Oh this one is real, never let your mind tell you otherwise, for we have arrived and to doubt the reality of the moment would certainly spell your destruction.'

Michael pulled to the kerb and killed the engine. Mr Thomas folded the laptop closed, done with his reading, and the three angels looked to the ugly edifice of Coventry Cathedral, bathed in yellow light, that rose before the ruins of the old cathedral that Nazi bombs had eviscerated. A great and wide flight of steps ran from St. Michael's porch, the grand structure that sheltered the entrance to the cathedral, and to the right of the porch, on the southern end of the east wall was mounted the imposing bronze statue of St Michael and the Devil.

'Are you certain this is the right place?' asked Leonard Thomas. 'For time is short if we have chosen ill.'

'This is the place,' said Will with certainty. 'Where else would a monster as vainglorious as Michael choose for his final confrontation with his nemesis?'

'It's the place,' said Neil, stepping from the car, reaching for his sword, careless of whether the vicinity was deserted. 'Can you not feel the fizzing in the air?'

Will and Leonard joined him on the pavement.

'That is Michael's work,' said Will, 'he's cloaked the whole building in a perception filter so that no passing humans would discern what was occurring in its vicinity. We are at the edge of the cloak, Lucifer: can your devil's sight pierce it and discern what adorns that vile statue?'

Neil accepted the title of the light-bearer unthinkingly and peered through the curtain of oscillating molecules before him, and with a squint of the eyes and a strain of the mind he saw what Will spoke of and he gasped in horror.

A form was bound to the lower part of the great statue, to the wingless figure of the shackled and vanquished Satan, its leg's spread over The Devil's torso, its head at the statue's groin as if in a perverse rendering of fellatio. Lilith, his Maria, the Devil's wife, hair cascading over the bronze Satan's thighs, was bound over and over to this depiction of her husband, watched over by the damning bronze of Michael, spear aloft in triumph.

'You will stay here,' said Neil, his voice become resonant and guttural, his words unopen to argument, but Leonard touched his shoulder and pointed to a vehicle parked in shadows along the road. It was the black Jaguar, as sleek and glossy as its namesake.

'I believe,' said Neil, 'that I will reclaim that vehicle from my wayward wife once this business is done, and will drive her home in it.'

With that, sword held aloft by muscles that had burgeoned to easily wield the mighty blade, he strode through Michael's glamour, strange electricities passing through his form, speeding his heart and crackling his hair. Onto the expansive spread of steps that rose to the cross-crowned porch, sight fixed on the hostage bound to that ignominious statue. And he tasted her mind, his Maria, his Lilith, and choked back an exultant cry as he knew that she lived still. But his grown mind sensed another, a festering serpent's nest of seething hatred and madness. Michael was here, and all was unfolding as the archangel wanted, and Lilith was but bait, her fate precariously balanced.

Neil stopped and steeled himself. He was afraid, but this fear was an emotion to be embraced, to be utilised; not to be undone as a mere man might be. He was The Devil and he had the wherewithal and the talents to defeat Michael, to redress that shame that the damn statue depicted.

'Show yourself, angel,' he called, and his voice was as a roar, pleasing in its potency.

The pale and bound hostage struggled her head up as high as it could, for Lilith was bound loosely at the neck, and her grey eyes found his and the woman -- oh for the love of that woman -- actually smiled.

'I see you're feeling yourself once more,' she rasped.

He cried out, racing the steps to her, careless sword flashing blue sparks from the concrete steps, slicing their matter as if it were butter. He stood beneath his wife, feeling her agonies, physical and mental. He looked up to her, and a tear fell from her onto his upturned face. There was terror in her; yet not for herself.

'I will fetch you down.'

She hitched a choked laugh. 'So you have rediscovered your wings?'

'Not yet. Not yet.' He laughed himself, in spite of the situation. 'But all is coming.'

'Keep revisiting your history, hey, Lucifer?'

How sweet, how right, that title sounded, from her lips.

'Do hurry husband. You're a lot more becoming as Satan the dragon then you are as Satan the man.'

Then to Neil's left, from the porch that bore his name, stepped Michael. The archangel was resplendent in Heaven's armour, and his wings were revealed, broad and pale limbs of a monstrous hawk. He held a flashing celestial sword in his right hand and -- an odd and disquieting sight -- an oily and snub-nosed pistol in his left. And he had no nose. Or left eye. Where Michael's nose had been there was a black, gore-encrusted gape. Where his sinister eye had rested there was a mess of tissue and protruding shards of shorn bone. Neil could almost picture the arc of Gabriel's sword, Michael just snatching his skull back in time to prevent his head being cleft in two, but not quick enough to save a quarter of his face.

How those two comrades of old must have fought: how crazed must Michael have been to force Gabriel to engage in mortal combat with his ancient ally?

'Not mortal, serpent,' sneered Michael, easily catching Neil's thoughts. 'Heaven's highest are made of stronger stuff than felled devils. Healing may be lengthy, but it is inevitable.'

'But Gabriel is no more. He died before me, slayer of your own brother.'

'You lie. Always you lie.'

'Search my mind. You know it to be true.'

Lilith was speaking, her words desperate and pleading, but Neil could not catch them, for Michael was advancing, flashing sword aloft, and the raging madness that coiled around him bound Neil's attention. Even wounded so, he was terrifying. Yet Neil would not step back, felt strangely thrilled as he raised his own sword in an instinctive motion that he had no hope but to trust. He would not fail, felt the surge of his true form swelling within, striving to burst free, shoulder blades aching with the promise of sprouting dragon's wings. And then the archangel's blade was slicing the night air, bisecting atoms and aimed at taking his head. Neil's blade drew an upward arc and the blades clashed and flashed a shower of white sparks, the jolt of impact racing through Neil's musculature, and it was he who thrust quickest, catching Michael at an awkward angle, the infinite point shearing Michael's breastplate and penetrating flesh below the clavicle.

Michael cried out and ducked and twisted from the blade,

shearing his collar bone in the motion, responding with a wild swipe that Neil easily danced away from, ending two steps above Michael, now taller than the great archangel, the higher ground claimed, his back pressed to the wall beneath the statue and his woman. He felt triumph configure a smile on his lips. Michael was too weak; and he was too instinctively Satan.

Lilith's words found him: 'Our daughter... you must save our daughter... whatever occurs.'

Neil foundered, for the briefest of moments, his sword dipping as recollection of what he had thought a dream came back to him: Lilith telling of the child she had conceived of him, and he, a poor and pitiful creature, feigning a middle-aged drunken ape, suckling his daughter's milk from his wife's breast. The child was true, unlike the boy his mendacious mind had fabricated, and he knew now that he had impregnated Lilith in that original dream that had been a truth: that in which he had attempted futile suicide and had been brought low and ravaged by his rightly raging wife.

'Oh, Lilith, forgive me.'

He was open to attack then, vulnerable to the killing blow, but Michael instead raised his ugly little pistol, pathetic machine of Man, and fired over Neil's head. A blue wisp of smoke hung coiled in the still air and Neil, purpose rejoined and redoubled, struck with speed he would have thought impossible only breaths before. The blade sliced the wrist of Michael's gun hand as if it were gossamer, and the feeble weapon clattered down the steps, the severed hand that had released flexing and closing its digits like a nailed spider. Neil aimed a kick instinctively and well, his sole satisfyingly crunching Michael's jaw, sending the angel reeling and falling, splendid armour clattering down the concrete steps.

The Devil looked above.

All was lost.

Lilith's head lolled over the statue's massive thigh, her white tresses hanging and running with darkness that seeped down the follicles and gathered and dripped at their limit, his wife's blood splashing onto his face. Half of her face was gone, the beautiful configuration, the flawless symmetry, destroyed to a glutinous pulp. One silver eye remained, balefully glaring at him even as it misted with death.

'Another dream,' beseeched Satan, hope fleeing to the bottom of an unendurable pit. 'I lost you before and found you again. I'll wake from this too.'

There was no awakening and the dread and despair cramped Satan's foundations, blackness piling onto him. To rediscover the truth of his love, a love that had endured so many ages of Man and of angels, and to have her so cruelly and bathetically taken from him... it was beyond endurance, beyond despair; and his rage was beyond compare. He roared to the night, from the base of his being, the sound of his agony almost visible as a bleak breath that looked to blacken even the impassive moon in its holding orbit.

There was the flap of beating limbs that he recognised from old, the roar of displaced air as his oldest and most hated enemy bore down on him. Lucifer turned to face his deliverance, sword down, defenceless. All his rage roared at himself, for his pride, his vain triumphalism, that had led to this pass: the end of the love of his interminable existence.

Michael came on, borne by his beating hawk's wings, yet the archangel trailed his sword, held his head up, throat exposed, remaining eye closed, a beatific smile on his ruined face. Lucifer brought his blade up in a splendid arc, splitting his atomic self-hatred between himself and this crazed creature. As the unfathomable edge of his blade swept through the matter of Michael's neck, Lucifer knew that he had failed and the other had won. The archangel was insane, but his victory was utter: extinct, he would be at peace, believing himself no doubt to be passing into God's glory; and the Devil would be living, existing, in eternal purgatory, his one and abiding strength and solace taken from him by a being he could exact no revenge on.

The lopped head spun and thudded to the concrete, rolling down the steps, its straw-coloured hair trailing it, an obscene felled comet. The decapitated body slammed into Lucifer, pinning him to the unprepossessing cathedral's wall, mindless arms gripping him in a cold and steely embrace, frantic wings beating about him, raising a roaring wind of the still night, until Lucifer drove his blade into the breastplate of the headless monstrosity, and his celestial steel found the creature's heart, and he twisted the sword so that the organ burst, and the massive body tumbled back, crashing down the stone steps, sparks flashing from the rent armour, wings beating death's tattoo.

The flesh was unknitting already, skin dissolving, muscle and sinew revealed and decaying at an accelerated rate as atoms bound for eons came undone and rose as smoke into the night air.

There was no pleasure in this dissolution for Satan; indeed the sight revolted him. Combustion, explosion or implosion would have been more suited to the end of this archangel, not this ignominious decay. He strode past the almost gone form, bearing his sword before him.

'Beelzebub!' he cried, and his old lieutenant entered the bloody arena, seeming to stagger a little as he stepped onto the expansive stairway, Ithuriel beside him doubling over as if in a spasm of agony.

'Walk tall angels. What is with this weakness, when I who have failed yet again stand erect?'

It was Ithuriel that raised his sight to Satan's, and there was steel as well as hurt in the little angel's eyes. 'Michael's spell still holds, weak but still maintained.'

'Spell?'

'That which kept from human eyes unfolded events also kept all beings but you from joining the fray.'

The Devil strode down the steps to them, wielding his sword with fresh intent. 'Do you claim that Michael's barrier was what prevented you from aiding me?'

Beelzebub stepped between Satan and Ithuriel, producing a flashing sword of his own, held obliquely across his chest. His demonic visage seemed to be seething just beneath the surface of the mask of humanity he had worn for so long. 'Did you think we hung back through cowardice, or at your vain command that you would fight alone. We could not pass, even now with Michael's powers diminished it was onerous to walk through the glamour he drew around this place. If you would fight me to vent your rage at your own failings and your despair at this new and terrible loss, then I stand ready. It would not be the first time, and won't be the last I dare say, that your passions have got the better of your sense.'

'Look to your feet,' whispered Ithuriel from behind Beelzebub's bulk. 'See that your old nemesis still clings to existence, and still inflicts pain on his enemies. Your war is with him and his ilk, not with your most loyal friend.'

Wracked by confusion, the Devil did look down, and there

rested the head of Michael, right side up, blonde locks spread around it in a terrible halo.

The ancient mind lived, and the eye rolled up to meet the watch of Satan, flashing victory, and the mouth worked open and incredibly words were formed by that impossible tongue.

'Am I not victorious, Devil? Do I not go into eternity with the knowledge that Satan is a broken thing, the serpent brought lower than even God could deliver him?'

Satan felt for the archangel's diminishing mind, a talent that now seemed as natural and instinctual to him as breathing. Rage was a little thing in the monster now, replaced by a consuming and terrible pride. He knew that pride, that emotion which had been his own greatest failing and yet finest strength, was a thing waiting to be punctured and deflated. He knelt to the gloating skull, feeling the old magic he had thought a fiction working at his tongue that could stir agents to battle against insurmountable odds or destroy a mind, dependant upon the whim of the organ that instructed it.

'There is no eternity,' he whispered at the rolled-white eye of Michael, 'even for those as aged and divine as we. You know that, deep in your core. After life there is only an absence of existence. Your atoms will disperse, become part of the Universe to be bit parts in future complexifications, but once the consciousness has parted with the last breath, the final heartbeat, existence is done. You suffer still because of the truth of your own insignificance, your own mortality. It was that which God preyed upon with Man, that inability to accept that terrible yet wondrous incontrovertible knowledge that after life there is nothing but oblivion.'

The thing smiled. 'Yet I have faith.'

'And wretched lie is that delusion bereft of foundation in logic or reason or science.'

The head sneered and spat: 'Damn your science, recourse of your beloved apes.'

'Your damnation makes it no less the truth. Just as your proclamations of triumph make them no more the truth.' Lucifer leaned closer, lips almost touching the ear of the bodiless angel. 'I am not beaten,' he whispered. 'You have inspired me, old friend. Humanity shall have its hero once more. I will bring down the religions that poison Man and thwart human progress, and I will embrace that science which you despise so and show the people of this planet how they underestimate their own potential, how they can shape and mould their environment to their dictates with infinitely more wisdom and compassion than God ever did.

'And I shall have my wife back, for life is but a physical condition, and all physical conditions can be created and manipulated. You have won nothing , Michael, yet I, in my brief time of cowardice as a man, have learnt that humans are good and strong, and it is we angels that should look up to them, and give to them our talents that will enable them to better tend to their planet and all the peoples of it.'

Lucifer could find no sense of anything in the head he had whispered to, the good eye drawn closed, and so he stood, as desolate as he had ever been, yet more hopeful than he had long been.

But that mouth opened once more. 'Yet you will fail, demon. For you do not know the end of the story of your life that you have hidden from; and that revelation is what will destroy you.'

'Whatever it is, and it did drive me into hiding from myself, I will deal with and will utilise it to make me stronger. You murdered my wife. What could be worse than that? Yet still I go on, with fresh and greater resolve.'

'Oh, dear Lucifer, you must finish your history. You will be finished.'

The Devil shrugged. 'I think you wrong, and care less as you will soon be nothing but thoughtless matter.'

He brought his sword arcing sudden descent, and a rush of abject terror roared from the mind of Michael, a deathbed collapse of faith as he realised the imminence of his own non-existence, and he was screaming: 'God is --' but Beelzebub's blade caught the head even before Satan's, cleaving the skull in two and slicing through stone. Michael's grand and feverish brain sizzled on stone, unfolding its convolutions and fizzing to mist that was lost. The bone of the bisected skull, and the flesh it bore, were dust in moments.

Satan looked to his oldest friend, unsure whether he should be enraged or thankful for his interjection. In the end he simply nodded and handed his sword to Ithuriel and threw his arms around his lieutenant, holding him tight, hot fluid of emotion escaping him. 'Go fetch her, old friend. Cut her free and bring her down, for I am taking her with us.'

Beelzebub drew back, wiping angrily at his own eyes. 'Us?'

'Of course. Where would I be without you two unholy fools? If you would come with me while I finish my history I would consider myself humble and honoured.'

'Watch that slick tongue of his, Ithuriel,' said Beelzebub, 'it is not to be trusted, and will no doubt lead you on all sorts of perilous adventure.'

Ithuriel puffed out his chest, though he wept in agonies for the loss of his lady, bravely hitching out words of fortitude. 'Well, I have sampled adventure over the last few days, and have found it to my liking.'

Beelzebub smiled and spoke soft to Lucifer. 'Go to the car, your car, and I'll fetch her down. Be quick for we are no longer concealed, and the authorities will be abroad the night.'

And indeed sirens were wailing in the distance, drawing nearer.

Lucifer laid a hand on Ithuriel's shoulder. 'Come my little protector, let's do as instructed.' They strode off the cathedral's steps and moved through the shadow of the ruins of the old cathedral to where the black Jag rested. Lucifer heard the beating of dragon wings as Beelzebub rose to his onerous task, thought he heard the measured slices of the demon's blade as he undid the coils that bound his beloved's corpse.

'Where to next?' asked Ithuriel.

'Back to the house where I lived as Mann, and then...' mused Lucifer. '...And then... onwards... onwards and upwards.'

And with these words of strength and fortitude, Satan stumbled, his grief a black tide that could not be withheld. He fell against the Jaguar, the force of bleak reality bearing down on him. Was it not better to live a wretched and miserable lie as a pathetic wretch of an ape than endure the interminable agony of a fallen angel with its perpetuity of defeats and losses? He saw himself reflected in the car's rear window, his beautiful mask drawn into a visage of agony, his dark eyes pits of unendurable agony. He could lose this, return to shallow, human hurts. The spell of forgetfulness could be woven again.

Then, for the briefest of moments, his reflection blurred and the outline of his true form appeared as a ghostly aura, great wings spread wide, horned and terrible head with only those ancient eyes unchanged, and his preternatural sight pierced the gloom of the car's interior and he saw the Moses basket on the back seat, the fragile and pale babe within seeming to reach for him, a pitiful and desperate cry escaping her throat, her large eyes, so like her mother's, widening as if in recognition.

This was the child that he and Lilith had created in what he had thought a dream, when his wife had come to him at the house in Italy, had shown him the futility of his abject suicide attempt, and had fucked him with rage... and with love.

Satan pushed himself erect, turning to find Mr Thomas with his head bowed and Beelzebub striding towards them through the night with Lilith draped over his muscular arms, her ruined face hidden by a caul of matted and darkened hair.

'Put her in the back, old friend,' he rasped, 'with her daughter. Ithuriel will travel with me, and you shall follow in your motorised phallic symbol.'

Beelzebub raised a sickly grin. 'And then we shall rest awhile?'

'Not yet. Not yet. I believe I have one chapter of my history left in me this night.'

Death of a Demigod

Jesus was in torment in the garden called Gethsemane. A few of his followers were lost to slumber about the verdant grounds, spelled into unconsciousness, I could tell, by the man himself. His enemies were abroad and close, for he had become much the political agitator and insurrectionist against Roman tyranny in the months I had been away from him. He seemed to wish capture and internment, or worse, yet part of his fevered mind wished also his father's protection.

'My Father,' he spoke to the unheeding night, 'if it is possible, do not let this happen. However, I want to do the things that I desire. I choose not to do the things that you desire.'

Strange. He was become a rebel near as much as me; yet rebel first against his country's occupiers or against his own father I could not tell, and so I stepped before him and revealed myself.

'Satan,' he spoke, 'at the last you visit me again. My holy father told me it would be so, that you would tempt me again as in the desert. You come as a man, but are the same serpent that tempted weak Eve.'

Blood ran from wounds in his forearms where he had scourged himself and fell to spoil the soil of the garden.

'Never to tempt,' I said. 'To help. Perhaps to save.'

He laughed then, a bitter and lost sound. 'Oh, old pretender, I would save myself.'

'Then do so. Flee and live, for your enemies approach; or stay and fight, wake your disciples and make them fierce watchdogs, use your powers to bring down your would-be captors. What part in God's scheme can your meek submission play?'

He turned his back on me and my honest words of confusion.

'This is no scheme of God's; this is mine own plan.'

I saw it all then, the brave folly he was bent upon, and my heart went to him, for he truly was, in the end, his mother's son, and there was more man than god in him.

'You intend to die so as not to be Yahweh's instrument of

destruction. I salute your sentiments, though think your methods wasteful.'

'I will not be a pawn of war on Man. I have followed and pondered and then rejected my father's dictates. I trust that in Heaven he will forgive me, and take me to his right hand where I might sway Him to mercy on his subjects.'

I stepped closer and laid a hand on his bony shoulder. He did not shirk from me. 'There is no Heaven for you, brave Emmanuel, you are but flesh and shall die and decay. Stay in existence and use your powers to bring peace upon Man; work to plant compassion in your father's heart from here on Earth. Life is too splendid a thing to waste in misguided sacrifice.'

He turned his eyes to the starry firmament, his wretched consciousness lost to me. 'Heaven does await me. You have seen that glorious kingdom and yet deny its existence. Your lies are weak things, desolate one.'

'I would not lie to thee. Heaven does exist, though my memories of its grandeur are vague, lost to my mind since I was cast from that place, but it is not a spiritual plane. The good dead do not live on there; nor the bad in Hell. You have preached, as on the mount, that those that do not follow your laws shall suffer eternal torment in the fiery oven I call home, yet no damned soul has ever materialised in Hell. There is this life, Jesus, and this life only.'

He turned his gaze back to mine. 'I have no more need of your trickster words, Satan. I ask only one thing of you, one simple duty that you would perform me if you truly wish my salvation.'

I bowed my head then, a genuine gesture that none other except Lilith could have prompted me to. 'Ask what you will, and it shall be done.'

'My mother is in Jerusalem with a good companion that I have great affection for. I have wronged her greatly, treated her as a burden for she has tried to sway me from my Christ's duty as you have. Seek her out and ask her to forgive me, and persuade her to leave this place, to not pain her eyes with the sight of my terrible sacrifice.'

I nodded, sensing hope in Mary. Christ was desolate and desperate: if my tongue could not sway him to live then perhaps hers might.

'Go now, Satan, for my time is at hand.' He held out a

palm, his eyes steeling over. 'And let not your passions be stirred by my mother's companion, for she is a creature of scarce and breathtaking beauty and as good to me as a wife; not yours for the seducing.'

I withdrew a way and cloaked myself in darkness. Presently Roman soldiers appeared, headed by the Gnostic called Judas, working his duty as had been prearranged by his master. The Judas kiss sealed his fate and the soldiers fell upon him, waking the sentinel pawns who, fearful at the sight of Latin steel, fled in spite of their devotion to their leader. All was proceeding as the son of God dictated.

My mind and heart, as so often, were afire as I made my way through the moon-silvered streets. More even than the noble hope that Jesus could yet be saved by his mother, my brain seethed with the selfish memory of the son of God's last words to me: a creature of scarce and breathtaking beauty.

Could it be she? Surely no one in Hell or Earth better fitted that description?

I sensed Mary's good mind in time and was drawn to a humble letting. I felt no trace of my sweet wife, last driven from my side by Gabriel after saving me with her own sweet fluids. Was she cloaked in some fresh disguise, so skilfully woven as to be impervious even to the attentions of her husband?

It was not beyond her. Nothing was beyond my Lilith.

I stepped into the building, and Mary, seated at a table, was upright in a breath, sending her seat clattering, shock and tears in her eyes. She was white and lined beyond her years, as if the crushing burden of mothering Man's saviour had ravaged her past her time. But those eyes were still beautiful and wise and there was still hope in them, though it was a struggling thing.

'Good, Satan,' she spoke in a voice cracked with emotion, 'I have been too long without you,' and she opened her arms wide and I went into her embrace. I felt her pain.

'Too long indeed,' I said, and she drew back to appraise me with a sickly smile and wondering eyes.

'Time has no bearing on you, devil. You are as when I first laid eyes upon your good form, though I know this manly form to be an illusion. From whence comes thou?'

'From your son, in his despair at Gethsemane.'

She nodded bleakly. 'And is there news from him? Is there yet hope?'

'There is always hope, Mary. Always. I will impart Emmanuel's news, but first what of you? How is noble Joseph, and your family?'

She hung her skull, and her sad bearing found my mind before her words reached my ear. 'Joseph was taken from us in a swift fever two seasons past,' then light rose in her visage, 'but the rest of my family is well. Jesus has four strong brothers and two beautiful sisters.'

'My sorrow is with you, for your husband was the finest of men. Are your children with you?'

That wonderful emotion, anger, rose in her then. 'No. I would not bring them here to witness this travesty of suicide. Jesus is bent on destruction, and has no room in his heart for me or my loving words that seek to sway him from pointless martyrdom. He has become cold and cruel to me, yet still I follow his ministry to its bitter end across these lands.'

I laid my hands on her shoulders, waited until her eyes met mine. 'You are wrong, good mother. He sends his word with me, begging your forgiveness and beseeching you accept his enduring love.'

She sobbed then, and seemed near to falling, though I held her upright.

'Yet is he still intent on death?'

'He is, but all hope is not lost. Now, at the end, he realises how wrong has been his treatment of you and how he is more his mother's son than his father's. Your words could still save him. He is the son of God, and as such has great powers. While there is still breath in him he can save himself and escape his persecutors or bring them low.

'He will not fight, nor flee. He has great plans for after his death.'

I sighed. 'Yet there is no resurrection, on Earth or in Heaven. Not unless God uses His dark magic to rouse him from the sleep of destruction, which I do not believe will be part of His bleak plans.'

She shrugged meekly. 'His plans are for Humanity. It is for Mankind that he sacrifices himself.'

It was then that a new figure entered the room from a side chamber, tall and slender, her head low and hooded, bearing a tray of breads and wine. My heart rose, for this was Mary's companion, she of untold beauty. Yet there was no mental trace nor scent of my wife about. Still there was hope.

She raised her head and the hood fell away and hope died.

Not Lilith, but she was a beauty, sun-bronzed to Lilith's marble complexion, cascading tresses flaming red to Lilith's white mane, eyes dark as night to Lilith's silver-shot grey. She placed the tray on the table and sat on a chair, Mary and I following suit, emulating this gorgeous creature's grace.

Not Lilith. Not Lilith. Still my wife was out there in the world, separated from me. I fought risen despair down, locked it within, would not let it configure my features into etchings of grief.

'This,' said Mary mother of Jesus, 'is Mary of Magdala, my daughter-in-law, and high priestess of my son's ministry.'

I smiled in spite of my heavy heart. 'Good woman, you fill me with joy that Emmanuel should find solace and love with one such as you. Truly he is a man. How came the two of you to be together?'

'I was a whore,' she said, and such a statement delivered with such proud defiance, her sight unflinching, almost daring, to a male stranger quickened my admiration for her, and a prurient part of my mind wondered just how much it must have cost to lay with her.

'I was a whore and safe from prosecution due to my beauty and the fact that I shared my bed with great and powerful men. Yet when I heard the tale of the poor sister that Jesus saved, she who was taken in adultery and sentenced to stoning...'

'I have not heard that tale,' I said.

This fresh Mary let a slight smile dance over her lips, entrancing. 'Oh, they were to stone this poor creature for acting on her heart, according to the law of Moses and his god. But Jesus stood before these men of zeal with their ready boulders, and he drew in the sand -- of the transgressions against that same law of every man present, it is said -- and he spoke these words: "He that is without sin among you, let him first cast a stone at her", and on hearing those words they quaked and the rocks fell from their hands and the rabble dispersed.

'On hearing this story something moved in me, and I renounced my oldest profession and sought out this messiah.'

I nodded for it was indeed a fine and noble story.

'And now you are his woman.'

'And highest in his ministry, even above his male disciples,' she said proudly, and then, with unconcealed sadness. 'And it will be I that continue his teachings and found his church in the name of his eternal love.'

I groaned within, leaning towards her. 'Mary, there is no eternity. Jesus dies and all that he is dies with him.'

She herself drew herself closer, shadowing my motion, dangerous sparks flashing from her mind. 'But would it not be a noble and good deceit if Man were to believe that the son was immortal, could survive death to instil in humanity a love stronger than their fear of the father, could bind nation to nation and end all wars?'

I sighed. 'Methinks you might be aiming a little high.'

She laughed then, a fine and mocking sound. 'Oh, you should know all about aiming high, ancient one. He that would declare war on the Creator would chide my meagre ambitions?'

I leaned back on my seat, my surprise manifest before I could compose my features.

'You think I not know thee?' she lightly mocked, no fear or awe in her. Jesus had chosen well -- or been chosen -- this Magdalene was magnificent.

'She is wise beyond her years, with a fiery mind. Sometimes too fiery,' spoke Mary the mother, casting a warning look to the flame-haired beauty. 'But she is my son's chosen messenger. If he must die so as not be the instrument of a vengeful god, and perhaps to be an instrument in freeing Man from the yoke of fearful worship, then she shall tell of his resurrection, of his ascent to Heaven, from where he relays to her word of how he has calmed his father, made him a god of love.'

'Yet you would found your new church on a lie. And God would still deliver his wrath on to Man.'

The Magdalene stood, spilling her stool with a clatter. 'Who are we to say what are lies and truths? Christ would say that all is allowable in bringing harmony between men, and there is a germ of truth in all that is good. Let his father continue His persecution; if Mankind knows love then it will cast aside notions of damnation and eternal perdition.'

'I believe,' I snapped, anger threatening, 'that it was your sweet Jesus who, not very long past, was warning those that did not follow his teachings that the flames of Hell awaited them.'

She wheeled away from me, talking with imperious authority, much her husband's wife. 'Yet Jesus has learned much compassion of late. He has found his way and his true voice. God tortured his poor mind with such visions of bloodshed, insisted on his brain that he was his father's son and as such, instrument of his father's dreams of slaughter.' She turned to me then, and there was such pain in her eyes that my stirrings of anger dissipated in a moment. 'Can you not see, Devil, that he is now true to himself and has forsaken his father? Can you not see that the man in him has overpowered the monster? Can you not see that for this reason he believes he must die?'

I stood myself, laying a hand on the shoulder of Mary the mother, for the Magdalene's words had distressed her to tears. 'I do see,' I spoke. 'And it may be a good plan, to sacrifice oneself for a species, to become the ultimate martyr, and a great religion may be inspired by Jesus' sacrifice and the lies that you and your acolytes will spread after he is but carrion. Yet, his suffering might not be remembered at all, for Rome decrees that myriad "criminals" are tortured and put to the cross each revolution, and Jesus might become a name lost in a vast and ignominious crowd. And yet it might be worse: for God might infiltrate this good religion of Christ, might manipulate it to increase His worship, might have grand temples raised in the name of Himself and his son, temples with foundations of blood and pain and intolerance. God might split this new religion into opposing branches, invent heresies so that man will slay man in the name of God, believing they are murdering in the name of their own God, whilst all the time God is lost to laughter, revelling in the slaughter, revelling in the fact that all these humans, these noble apes, kill and die for love of Him.'

Mary hung her head low, her poor aged brow creased with shadow. The Magdalene held my gaze.

'This is the God you know,' she conceded. 'This is Yahweh that you raised an army against and lost. But Christ is greater than thee, and his mind is finer, and he will have reckoned that his is the way, the only way.'

'Girl,' I spoke, 'there is nary an only way, and greatness is decreed by history. Christ's mind is far blunter than mine, perhaps than yours, certainly than his mother's. Trust in my mind, for it is an ancient thing, and wisdom can come with age. Christ is but a babe, another innocent to be sacrificed on the altar of Yahweh; I am older than Man, and cleverer. Who wouldst thou listen to?'

Mary Magdalene was of bowed head, of sunken shoulders, yet her will was a force to reckon. 'I would listen to my husband, for he has achieved more, and suffered more, in earthly months than thou hast in celestial ages.'

'Suffered more?' I roared, freeing my dragon wings, letting my skull reconfigure itself into its demonic physiognomy. 'Achieved more?'

She flinched not a bit in her flesh, and her mind held strong. 'As you are, Satan. Slice me with those dread talons if you will, use those fangs to rip open my throat, eviscerate me with those horns.'

Laughter came to my ear, wild and pure, and I turned to Mary the mother, whose face was youthful and beautiful with hilarity, the lines of age and pain stretched away. 'She is fine and strong and lovely is she not, Satan? You cannot cow her, nor, I think, would you want to. See why she has claimed my son's heart.'

'Indeed,' I said, 'and I would wish that love to continue above all else, and wish for you, sweet Mary, to be in the ground while your son still lives and uses his powers and persuasion to set Humankind free.'

'Ah,' sighed Mary, 'a wonderful fancy.'

'Then,' said I, 'we must make it a wonderful reality.'

Emmanuel had truly suffered. He had endured the night in the Hebrew temple, beaten and tortured for his heresy, maintaining to his chief interrogator, Caiaphas, new high priest and keen to make his mark, that he was the son of Yahweh; then suffering flayings and fresh beatings at the hands of Romans, watched over by the Latin governor Pilate, who capitulated to the throng that screamed for bloodletting and were wont to revolt if such were not to be had.

How the crowd had turned. These screaming berserkers were the same apes that had welcomed Jesus with adoration and adulation as, only days previous, he had ridden into Jerusalem seated backwards on an ass. Had God planted this raging hatred in these people, changing their minds from compassionate thinking to murderous intent? I thought yes, for it would suit His plan; drive, He believed, His son to turn on the crowd, unleash his wrath on those that would drive him low. Yet still I felt nothing but commitment to his own scheme from Jesus, even now as he staggered, beneath a pitiless sun, the dusty trail towards the summit of the skull-shaped hill, Golgotha, the solid cross-beam of a crucifix stretched over his bloody shoulders, bound at each end to his wrists. As a final humiliation a thorny crown had been pressed into his scalp, so that blood matted his hair and ran into his eyes, leaving him near blind. A wretched king he made.

We, the two Mary's and I, made our way through the baying crowd that lined the climb, marking the ascent of Jesus. The mother tugged at my sleeve and I turned to meet her imploring, teary watch.

'When will you help him?'

I shouldered some bloodthirsty Jews aside, dragging her with me, next to the trail, now ahead of Jesus. He came on, staggering his rise towards us, flanked by a half-dozen armoured Roman convoy, the weight of the cross-beam intolerable but borne all the same.

'I could free him here,' I hissed low. 'I could cast off this disguise of humanity and spill the guts and open the throats of those soldiers that guard him, then bear him off into the sky and to safety.'

'Yes, Satan, do it.'

The Magdalene forced her way through the rabble to us, catching our words. 'Never. Not if it is not his will. All would be ruined. You promised us, Satan, that you would convince him to live, not abduct him against his will.'

'She speaks well,' I said to Mary the mother, 'and I, nay we, will make one last appeal to Emmanuel's judgement.'

She cried out then, for a rock hurled from the audience had struck Jesus on his brow and driven him to his knees, spine arched by his timber burden, bloodied face angled to the sun in undiluted agony. A boy, surely no more than twelve, ran from the crowd, dodged the soldiers, kicked the fallen Nazarene in his prominent ribs, spat on him and retreated.

'I must go to him,' cried the mother. The Magdalene enwrapped her in her slender but strong arms, pulling her trembling to her bosom, and turned her dark eyes of agony on me.

'And how, mighty, Lucifer, will we be granted a private audience with the Christ, how to sway his set mind when he is but steps from the cross and guarded by soldiers and surrounded by a mob that wants nothing but his destruction?'

'Come with me to the summit,' I spoke, 'and I will show thee.'

'But how?'

'Do you not yet know, woman, that I do magic?'

We rose to the summit of Golgotha, from where I surveyed the crowds that had gathered for the agonising demise of the one that would call God Himself his father. They stretched far, these blood-lusters, surely a more massed and cacophonous crowd than had ever before gathered for a crucifixion, Jews and gentiles and Romans, threaded along the path to this place of judgement, jostling en masse at the flat summit, where Christ would die, held at tremulous bay by Roman soldiers that emanated trepidation and bravado in equal measure as they kept the mob at hesitant bay with hefty blades. A figure, pitiful and broken, yet alive, was nailed to a cross, his legs smashed, a victim of the previous day's justice.

I looked to this wretch, feeling in his mind to ascertain his title and his crime: Dismas, a lowly thief. His lids sprang open as he felt my psychic intrusion, and I thought he knew me, for there was pleading in his gaze and in his mind, for an end to this torment.

'I cannot,' I whispered.

'Please,' his tortured mind echoed in my brain.

I sighed and altered the molecular structure of his heart, stilling the pump in the time it took this good thief to inhale his last torture of air. His head fell to his chest and he was no more than suspended carrion.

Jesus came on, staggering round the final turn, stumbling again, and a woman dashed from the crowd with a ladle of water, but a soldier crowned her with the flat of his blade, sending her sprawling and senseless in the hot dust. Another soldier took a whip, its tails barbed, to Christ's shoulders, curling the coils around his bunched forearms, drawing Jesus to his feet. Yet there was no premeditated cruelty in this soldier; there was fear, and the crazed pack mentality of one who had succumbed to a mass hypnosis that had made him more instinctual animal than conscious man.

'Act then, magician,' demanded the Magdalene, 'for the time is at hand.'

I gazed over the ocean of people, looked to the sky, darkening in the east where a tempest was forming, drawing energy from the hot earth and discharging stinging torrents.

'A storm is coming,' I muttered.

The Magdalene slapped me, a stinging blow across my cheek that actually rocked my head. 'Fuck the weather!' she screamed. 'If you have magic in you, use it now, for my lord is arrived.'

Jesus was indeed before us, and I found myself in a baying corridor of human-shaped bestiality, and I and the mother and the wife were in the way of Jesus and his crucifixion.

'Let me pass, Satan,' rasped this broken and bloodied messiah, 'and take my ladies away so that they not witness my final moments, lest I prove myself weaker than I hope and beg for mercy, or pray to my father.'

His mother flung herself to him, locking her arms around his neck in an embrace that must have been agony to him though he flinched not as she kissed the blood away from his poor face, her tears washing him clean. One of the armoured soldiers then, as if remembering his duty, moved to pull Mary from his charge, hand settling on the hilt of his sword in preparation of the unsheathing.

I reached then for the Magdalene and the Madonna that clung to her son, making a circuit of us. I intended to manipulate time, for it was a trick I knew could be done, had been done by Mulciber when I had been hostage in his home. We angels, fallen or not, had some mastery of the physics of space, and time and space were inextricably joined.

The Roman came on, blade raised over Mary's nape, and I willed time to halt in its convoluted motion, for all but we four joined by flesh. I reached with my seething mind to still the motion of all atoms in the vicinity, to freeze temporality by stilling spatiality.

Christ's eyes grew suddenly wide as he realised what business I was about, but I captured time itself before he could speak, bringing a moratorium on its passage but for us joined four.

The soldier was as a wondrous statue, his blade inches from

Mary's neck. All the crowd, thronging down and around the Golgothian hill, packed to the walls of Jerusalem, were like-wise petrified. Mouths gaped, caught mid-jeer, runners of ire-formed spittle depending from rotted teeth like slender icicles, eyes caught in the icy stasis of mindless hatred. Was this the true face of humanity, this snap-shot I had engendered?

'You should not have,' spoke Jesus. 'You have stilled the whole world, that it may not start again.'

Mary the mother loosed her embrace on her wretched son, the front of her dress and her palms and forearms wet with his blood, and ducked out of the shadow of the blade that had threatened to fell her, looking to the stilled forms with wonder in her eyes, gasping as she took in the sight of a dove, caught mid-flap, suspended in the air above her head, as if trapped in amber.

I reached to Jesus' wrists, revealing talons to slice the bind-ings there. The crossbeam that had been Emmanuel's burden had been touching his flesh and so fell to the earth, still subject to the forces of time and gravity -- though the earth itself, with all its molecules made still, gave out not a breath of noise on the heavy timber's impact -- and Jesus fell into the arms of the Magdalene, wrapping his scourged arms around her shoulders, his cheek pressed to her bosom, bloodying her breast. His eyes were on mine, the emotions therein shifting between baleful admonishment and something approaching gratitude.

'You should not have...' dwindled Jesus.

'Fear not,' said I, 'for it is only local time and space that I have stilled, and the effect will not last long: already I feel my synapses twitching and misfiring as I struggle to hold time timeless. See the storm that rages in the east, that still roils to-wards us? Still it comes. I have only subverted local nature, so that you might have a little time to speak your last with your good women and perhaps alter your intent. You could stay alive, young Emmanuel, could prosper and influence. Martyr-dom could be naught but a waste of good life.'

Jesus rose from his trembling rest at his lover's bosom and stood, blood trickling down his form to pool at his feet as a dark shadow cast by a bleak overhead star.

'Always this repetition, Satan. I have laid my plan, and my sacrifice will bring humanity together in a vast union of com-passion that my dread father will be compelled to capitulate to.'

'I think that thou does overestimate his father's capacity for empathy; and underestimates His capacity for self-centred destruction.'

Jesus smiled then, and there was that old madness of the divine-seeded demigod in his grin, as well as that so human fierce courage in the face of imminent destruction. 'You know my father only as an enemy, and for that I admire you: nemesis of He that is all-knowing, that cannot be defeated. Yet I have God in me, in my flesh, in my mind, and there is good in Him.

'Look to me, Devil, for I am a broken thing, god or man, and I am broken upon my own will. Would I suffer like this -- and I will suffer far more than has already passed, for I know of Roman mercy -- if I did not believe with utter faith that my father could be turned?'

'Faith is a dangerous concept, Nazarene, that which is accepted as immutable truth without evidence or logical foundation.'

He spread his arms, always the demagogue, even when his audience was so slender. 'If my faith is a lie then even that matters not. If God is ultimately unforgiving and callous of Man, then my legacy will remain: humans will be compassionate, be assured that I died for them, making a tabula rasa of their transgressions, and Yahweh will be powerless before their love and their goodness. His good would be made bad and He would be usurped from His high throne in the mind of Man.'

I turned from him, betwixt admiration and vexation. 'Fine rhetoric indeed, Christ, but rhetoric all the same. Me and thee speak in convolutions when perhaps unconsidered passion is required. I give thee thy women and their coarse and loving tongues.'

Mary the mother, seizing her cue with fervour, spoke first: 'I love you, my son. Do not die. Listen to Satan for he is not all wiles and machinations. You can do so much living, and hope of what you might achieve by dying might be misguided. Yahweh is a dangerous manipulator who would twist your message until it was a bloody coda for humanity. Live to fight, with the light-bearer at your side and the Magdalene and I and your good disciples as your council and guard. Your mind is great and your powers supreme among men. And live to love: consider beautiful, bowed Mary here, and all the love you two could share until your pleasant dotages, the beauteous children that you could raise with divine and rebellious blood flowing through their veins. You could inspire a new breed of Man, higher even than angels, equal near to God in power, and above him in compassion. Choose not death and its inherent risks to your purpose. Live, son, so that you might bury me in the ground, that I might pass to nothingness in painless peace with the knowledge in my mind that you still walk the Earth disseminating your goodness. I love thee so, my first and best child. Do not leave me.'

Jesus wept. His tears descended, cleansing his bloodied cheeks, and there should have been hope for me in this so human display of emotion, but my heart sank with his falling tears, for I perceived that his mind was still set, that some part of him even welcomed this pain of the psyche, found it a useful addition to the physical agonies that tore through his beaten form. He was become that most dangerous of beings: a martyr with absolute faith in his mission.

I turned to the Magdalene. 'And what would you say to the Christ, child? Quick, for I am losing my hold on time and space; atoms and photons itch to motion, to rejoin the universal expansion.'

And she turned her back on her love. 'I will say nothing. His will is supreme. He has my love entire, but never would I counter his will.'

'I thank thee, love,' said Jesus, wiping tears and congealed blood from his face. 'You are strong and true to the cause. Now, Satan, let us end this cessation of nature's course. Thou hast done his best, but still I go to my end with my mind set fast. I will be the saviour of Man, remembered for millennia as I would not have been if I had died in decrepitude.'

'In the end,' said I softly, 'it would seem that there was too much of your father's vain gloriousness in you, yet unfortunately not enough of His self-protective cowardice.'

I set time free with an unnecessary flourish of my arms, and the humans were reanimated, though jeers were absent from tongues revivified, confusion in eyes that had been filled with hate, as if they were aware, and shocked by the fact, that a miniscule portion of their existences had been stolen from them.

The Roman that had been about to strike Mary gazed stupidly at his blade poised over nothing but dust, and then to the cross-beam of the crucifix, stained with blood that lay at his feet, the cords that had bound it to the wrists of its bearer neatly severed. He looked to us, to Christ unbound particularly, and there was fear risen in his confusion.

'Prisoner,' he spoke, though his voice was a thing bereft of authority, 'you must bear your portion of the cross. It is law.'

Jesus turned his watch on the man, and I felt power stirring in him, even in such a wretched state. 'And what is your name, soldier, good servant of the empire?'

'Longinus,' spoke the Roman, and he seemed almost on the point of bowing, for the strength of Christ's mind had invaded and subsumed his own.

'Good Longinus, that once, no time past, would have felled my gentle mother, I ask you to share in my burden.' Jesus spread his bloody arms once more. 'For are we not both men? Is there not more to us than pain and fear? Are we not brothers, though you are splendid in armour while I wear blood-stained rags and a mocking crown that pierces to my skull, though you are strong and I am brought low? Would you not utilise that strength to make my end a little easier? Would that not be the strong and good thing to do, for I am so weak and feel that I have so much work still to do?'

Longinus holstered his blade and bent to gather the heavy cross-beam silently to his armoured shoulder, his eyes never shifting from those of his prisoner. The crowd held silent, the other Romans shifting and shuffling with confusion but none making move nor sound of remonstrance.

Oh Emmanuel, I thought, my heart and my hope goes with you and I shall work tirelessly for your dream.

As if in response to the workings of my mind, thunder rumbled and the first spots of blown rain found us, the sky darkening, the sun lost, and the procession reached the flat summit, stained rusty by the spilled blood of countless political prisoners and minor criminals, of Golgotha.

Here the fallen quiet crowd ringed the area where the condemned were crucified, soldiers there to hold them at bay should it be necessary. A few crosses stood, bare of their torn down erstwhile occupants, wood stained with blood and runners of gore. Jesus went meekly, flanked by Longinus and another soldier, to where his own long timber that promised torture and slow death lay on the earth, beside the crucifix that bore Dismas whom I had mercifully finished. Longinus, with a grunt of effort, lowered the cross-beam to its seating on the horizontal upright and two more soldiers appeared, bearing mallets and sacs of nails and hammered the cross together with swift professionalism.

Now Longinus and his fellow pressed the bloody Christ supine to the cross, pulling his wasted and torn and bloodied arms taut, pressing his legs to either side of the pole that would soon be erected to bear him in his agony. Like this he was held fast.

The first nail meant to penetrate flesh came out.

Mary the mother cried out, and grabbed convulsively at my wrist, and I grasped her to me, holding tight to her trembling form.

Emmanuel, I spoke silently, penetrating his brain, *still there is time. I would aid thee. Make good your escape, or free yourself to fight. It is not finished until death.*

His mind was still strong, and spat back at me: *Until death, it has not started. I will not yield. I cannot. Yet Satan, you have betrayed me, gone back on your word. Take my mother from this place. My wife is strong with belief and can endure, but gentle Mary must not see her son suffer so.*

Mary clutched tight to me, a mass of tremors, her mind and tormented maelstrom, and I clutched her even tighter to me, letting the wetness of her pain run down my torso, mixing with the rain that intensified suddenly in its lashing intensity, blue lightning fracturing the blackened sky, casting the sadistic tableau in etched relief.

I bowed my head, to Jesus though, not to the storm, and sent my words to him: *I break my word. For if your death is to save the world from itself and from your father, then who are you to deny she that loves you most witness to that sacrifice.*

Words formed in response, then became a scream in my skull, an agony tearing at my left calf as if celestial steel had lanced me there, and I staggered into the sand that the rain had mad muddy, dragging Mary with me, and the Magdalene rushed to our aid and struggled us upright, my lower leg still aflame.

A nail had been hammered through Jesus's left leg, above the ankle. Another tore through the right limb, pinning it to the wood of the cross, and I cried out in agony, my legs gone from under me, crashing me into the dirt, tears of pain blurring my vision. I flailed free of the women, dragging myself towards Jesus, and somehow he managed to raise his head and fix me with his dark eyes.

Forgive me, old one, for I know truly that you were never mine enemy, but I need to share my pain, pass it to another mine equal, or else it will go to my father that roils in the tempest overhead; and I feel if He should feel my torment then He might relish it and it might make Him strong.

I managed a nod, drool spilling from my pain-slackened gape. Next would be the palms transfixed to the cross-beam, now that the weight of the victim's body was supported by the nails at the calves.

The craftsmen wielded their mallets in unison and my hands curled like stabbed arachnids, the sudden agony clamping my teeth closed so violently that the tip of my tongue was severed, coppery blood filling my mouth, and I roared.

A sentinel soldier dashed forward and kicked me in the ribs, rolling me onto my back. 'Be done with your madness, holy fool,' he commanded, and spat on me.

I felt the dragon shift in me, yearning to cast off this wretched human disguise and tear this ape with my revealed talons, to laugh while his appalled eye watched his own innards slither from his opened gut to coil and steam at his feet.

You must not, spoke Jesus in my mind. *The worst is over now. He is but a pawn. Let me do this with no devilish distractions.*

And the pain was gone. The soldier that had kicked and spat on me watched with eagerness, hand on the hilt of his sword, for any hint of rebellion from me. The Marys came to my aid, struggling me to my feet, caked in sandy sludge that stank of blood. The soldier nodded as they drew me back to the front of the crowd, approving of my cowardice.

On that stormy plateau, rain lashing near horizontal, thunder roaring and blue jags of lightning splitting the atmosphere, the Romans, with the aid of a rope tied round the top of the crucifix's upright beam, raised Jesus, in all his bloody and battered dread-crowned glory until he loomed over us, a spread-eagled and dying messiah. A burly soldier put his broad shoulders to the base of the cross, shifting it effortful inches until it dropped into its designed seating, Christ crying out one last time at the jolt, his palms tearing.

I no longer felt his pain.

The Magdalene was at my ear, the true horror of the interminable execution at last piercing her shield of righteousness and purpose. 'Forgive me,' she cried, 'I was wrong. This cannot endure. We are not strong enough. Finish him, Satan; let him know peace.'

'I cannot,' said I. 'It is his will.'

'Yet the deed is done. End his pain, as you did that of Dismas who hangs beside him.'

I looked to her beauty, her hair afire even though sodden, her eyes cast cobalt as they reflected Heaven's cold fire. 'Dismas did not choose to suffer; Jesus did. I have no aid for him.'

And yet, another did. A Roman in resplendent armour, of massive physique, had shouldered his way to the foot of the cross, bearing a lance that flashed as no earthly metal could. His personality fizzed from him, more potent even than the storm and I gasped with recognition. An electric fork burned the atmosphere and met the spear, driving its bearer to one knee and he looked skyward into the heart of the maelstrom and spat some blasphemous defiance. His armoured fellows fell back from him, awe-struck as he regained his rectitude. His eyes found mine and they were filled with sorrow and scorn.

'How could you let him suffer so?' my oldest friend asked, his words finding me easily over the raging airs that separated us.

'It is his will.'

'I will have no part in such a perverse will. I was there as he breathed his first breath, and I will be the merciful instrument of his last.'

'Who do you speak with?' demanded Mary the mother.

'Good Beelzebub,' I said. 'He was with us at the birth of Emmanuel; you knew him as Balthazar.'

Her grip was as steel on my bicep. 'Let him wield mercy on my son.'

And so I nodded assent to Beelzebub, and the eyes of Jesus found him and he smiled, for he knew the nature of this creature and had seen him brought low but undefeated by God's harshest blast. Then he closed his eyes and spoke his final words, and though thunder exploded in a cacophony overhead, all in the crowd heard, and whimpered with risen fear.

'Forgive my father, for He knows not what He does.'

With a mighty roar Beelzebub drove the tip of his celestial lance into the side of Christ, up through lung and heart, ending a life and beginning a new religion.

The storm dispersed with the alacrity of no natural phenomenon. Some of the crowd melted away with the tempest, but many stayed, congealing into small congregations nervously muttering of what they had witnessed. Here the Magdalene would find the first members of her new church. They would take down the body, entomb it and then spirit it away with wholly physical methods. I disapproved of such mendacity, yet understood it: none would worship the memory of a man if they thought him but a man.

I looked to the body of Christ, hoping against hope, in spite of my hard won pragmatism, that there would be some flash from the corpse, some promise of resurrection. It was flesh, and only flesh; cooling carrion.

The Magdalene was not about the business of recruitment yet, for she and Emmanuel's mother were on their knees, sharing their grief with sobs and caresses, and so I left them to their sorrow.

Beelzebub had taken his leave unnoticed by me, but I knew that I should be reunited again with him soon, and I made my way through the motley gatherings of grown-penitent apes. When a person in beggar's rags appeared before me, I was so lost in my own thoughts that I felt not his divine nature nor recognised him in his disguise of humanity. He laid a not unkind hand on my shoulder, catching my attention, and I looked into the flashing eyes of Gabriel.

'Is your God pleased or cheated?' I asked, unable to feel rage or even contempt for this sorry creature. 'For His ways are lunatic, and I no longer know what is part of His plan or in spite of it.'

'All is God's plan, for He is all-knowing. Your part in all that has unfolded is part of His plan, for your schemes are His schemes, as are those of all Man and all Nature.'

'Yet still I feel that old agony in you, that inner part that doubts and reviles the evil He does, and that you do in His name. I envy you, archangel, for you have no self, and self is a terrible burden.'

'You speak of pride,' he spat.

'I speak of free will, of not being an instrument of another. Your God lies. He is the Father of Lies, not I. He is not all-knowing, for my mind is mine own. I envy you, Gabriel, yet I pity you more.'

I shrugged him off and hurried from the plateau of Golgotha, through crowds that milled aimlessly and breathed pious and fearful words around the walls of Jerusalem. Jesus had made the impact he intended, and I wished his memory well. Through these lethargic apes that I had come to admire, to love even, I made my way. Now they sickened me, for they were but beasts and I sought one like myself, one who was not transitory complexifications of carbon, one who would have all the time in the Earth. I cast around for Beelzebub, yet he was gone.

I found another.

Not a demon, nor angel, nor human even.

And so the crowds parted, as if at her dictate, and there, in the shadow of the walls of the holy city, stood my wife. She smiled so sweet, and her pale cheeks were wet with tears. 'My husband,' she spoke, 'never again let us be parted, by angel or demon or God.'

I fell into her arms, and my lips were on hers, my tears mingling with her own, and for too brief a moment all the pain of this world and the others I had known was forgotten.

Chapter Fifteen

The angel Ithuriel suckled the Devil's daughter from a teat that Beelzebub had manufactured him, altering his genetic code to manifest his left breast as a milk-expressing mammary. The child guzzled with closed-eyed pleasure, dehydrated and famished by her incarceration in the Jaguar. Such power coursed through the babe, such promise.

Beelzebub re-entered the room that he had recently left. The whirr of preternaturally depressed keys could be heard from the next room, where the angel that had so recently lived a wretched and ignorantly self-absorbed life as the drunken ape Neil Mann finished the first volume of his History.

Ithuriel looked up as Hell's second in command closed the door to the stairs gently behind him.

'Lilith?' he asked, looking back to the newly-motherless infant.

Beelzebub sat with a weary sigh. 'I have lain her on his bed, reconfigured and cleaned her face so that she is as pleasing to the eye as she ever was. If only I could reconstruct her life force as easily, Mr Thomas.'

Ithuriel bowed his head, kissing the crown of the baby. 'If only.'

From next door came the click of a disc being extracted, the whirr of a computer shutting down, and the Devil was on his feet and through the door to stand before them, and there was a fierceness about him, a combative aspect that was truly a reflection of the Satan of old. Surely he was not far from rediscovering the dragon and casting off this lie of humanity when he saw fit.

'How is my wife?'

'Dead,' stated Beelzebub, bluntly. 'I have fixed her flesh, cleaned her skin and hair, so that the bullet's work is indiscernible. She will not rot, but still she is as carrion. A dead thing. You must continue, old friend, must endure; it would be best to bury her and continue with your purpose.'

Ithuriel flinched and the baby withdrew from his manufactured breast, opening its grey eyes and looking to its father, gurgling pleasing nonsenses and smiling.

And Satan smiled. 'I will not bury her; she is coming with us.'

'Coming where?' asked Beelzebub, doubt creasing his brow and irritation sharpening his tongue.

'To Italy first, I think. To the house in whose grounds my daughter was conceived; grounds which no doubt hold within them, in some dark thicket, the gateway to Hell itself. We were happy there, I think. Then perhaps to Mesopotamia, Iraq now, to see what has become of Eden. I must revisit my History you see, for there is much of the tale still to be told -- much more. I still have barest of memories of before the fall, of Heaven and why we battled God and his minions. Can it have been just pride, would we have risked eternal perdition for that?' He held up a palm. 'I know, I know, you cannot answer. The story is mine to reveal as my mind is still a poor and weak thing, made fragile by the human condition I forced you to impose upon it. And why was that? For there is the biggest mystery to me. What calamity, after all we demons endured, would drive me to withdraw from my wife and a war I had waged for Earthly millennia? What could have been so terrible? The answer to that, I suppose, must be at the conclusion of my tale, for I know now that I could dive into your minds and extract answers but that might lose me all, leave me a gibbering ape with a fresh consciousness and title equally as wretched, or more so, as Nil Man.'

Lucifer reached for his daughter, trembling, overwhelmed by sorrow and love. Ithuriel handed the mite into her father's arms.

'Your mother is gone for a little while child,' spoke Satan, and the babe fell suddenly earnest, as if ingesting the gravity of his words. 'But I will bring her back.'

Beelzebub was to his feet. 'This is nonsense. This is the kind of supernatural shit you preach so fervently against. Our powers are finite; there is no resurrection.'

Satan flashed his old lieutenant a terrible, death's-head smile. 'Oh, we cannot know. Life is but a chemical reaction, and we are masters of chemistry. We have aimed too low, for too long. God? Pah! Fuck Him! That old fraud and monster. We will surpass His dubious achievements. His greatest angels are no more, and if He should bring the battle to us then He will find us more than His measure.'

Beelzebub shot Ithuriel a look of warning to silence tongue or mind, but Satan was lost in his reverie. His old audacity was back, and seemed to have grown, and the Devil was still far from being utterly himself.

Beelzebub groaned inwardly. What damn fool adventures would Lucifer drag them on now? He wanted to scream that God Himself was as dead as Michael and Gabriel. That Heaven's council would most likely have capitulated to discord and then chaos on hearing of the loss of those two archangels; especially if it learned that one had died at the hands of another. He wanted to scream that there was nothing left to fight.

Yet he knew that Satan would always find something to fight, and now it seemed that death itself was his newest enemy.

Lucifer had fallen morose, stroking the brow of his child. 'I invented a son in my man's mind, yet I had a real son once upon a time. But I was away at his birth and he perished. I should have dared to try and save him, to bring him back, but I had not enough of that quality the angels damn as pride yet I know as ambition. Always I dared not to hope that God could be bested, that my endeavours against Him were good and noble but ultimately doomed. I underestimated myself, and I underestimated my fellow fallen.'

The fervour returned, crackling from him. 'But now I feel reborn, as if from a period of restorative hibernation, and I have such hope for the future. I will finish my History, and uncover its prehistory, and the terrible truth that drove me to abandon myself will not shake me again to such cowardice.'

'Neil Mann is gone then?' asked Ithuriel.

'Oh yes, and all his artificial recalls: that imagined life and those imagined works.'

'And what do you now make of those works?' questioned Beelzebub, rising from his seat.

The Devil frowned. 'Meaning?'

'Come with me, look on your novels.'

Satan placed his grown-sleepy daughter gently down, and the three angels went back into the writing room, where the canon of Neil Mann had resided on a shelf above his computer, and his new eye took in the title that adorned each of the spines of the volumes that he had once recognised as fabricated works of an ape that had never existed. Each book was a different edition of Milton's Paradise Lost, and he laughed, for the irony was delicious: a version of some of his History had been there all along, right before his eyes as he had tapped away his more honest version.

'Your doing?' he said to Beelzebub.

'Of course. I was your literary agent after all, here to inspire your literature, whether you were conscious of it or not. You were always of the Devil's party, for the shortest of whiles you just didn't know it.'

Lucifer sat on the bed beside the corpse bathed in the silver light of a full moon that spilled through the chamber's window. Beelzebub had worked his craft perfectly, for she was as beautiful as ever in life, bathed pristine, her flawless face immaculately reconstructed. He wiped at his face, where some of her blood had fallen and dried to rusty powder and licked his palm to taste her desiccated fluid. A tear slid from his eye and fell onto her blanched cheek, frozen there by the coolness of her flesh. He wiped it gently away.

'So cold, Lilith. Look where loving me has brought you. Yet I will make you warm again. My absence has made me more audacious and I will struggle till the end of time in seeking out the science to rekindle the fire of life in you. God may have made you, but I will restore you to perfect health, and that is a finer trick.

'Forgive me, wife. Always I loved you. Always I love you.'

He kissed her cold lips once and rose from the bed in which he had lain as a man, where she had visited him only hours past, and he had drank from her and thought wonderful reality a dark and mortal dream.

He left the room and descended to the ground floor once more, past the room where his companions chatted in hushed whispers, and out into the back garden. It was a warm and still night, the sky clear and dazzling with its bodies. The full moon dominated, reflecting the sun's light as a silver wash over the portion of the world that faced it. A shooting star streaked the vault and fizzed to extinction, debris from an ancient collision igniting and dying as it entered the Earth's atmosphere. And to the stars themselves, nuclear furnaces whose existences were measured in such magnitude that in comparison his own span was as brief as a human's was to an angel's... or a god's. With his rediscovered demonic vision he could see farther into the universe, further back in time. But still the beginning of time and of all matter was beyond him, and he knew then with sudden surety that it was beyond God's reach too.

Yahweh was as insignificant to the universe as any angel, or man even, and this realisation, that would no doubt have inspired fury and even fear in insecure God, inspired the Devil. They were all but insignificant specks on an insignificant speck that circled an inconsequential star in an average system of a mundane galaxy that was itself a minor cog in the vast and mindless machine of the universe. There was wonder in such knowledge, that one's life had no bearing on the cosmos, registered not a tick on the universal clock, if one knew how to find such wonder. And the chance of being alive at all was vanishingly small, and yet here he was, tasting this warm air, gazing into the heart of the universe, and this tiny portion of the cosmos was where he had made his mark. Nothing to the vast and unthinking universe, but important to him and those he had touched and been touched by, those who were as unbelievably lucky as he to have lived.

He would resurrect Lilith, he swore silently, and it would matter not a jot to Nature, for he was bound by the forces of physics and would transgress no universal laws by reigniting life in her chemistry. He would improve Man's grasp of the sciences (which he had long talked of but never committed himself to, fearful that it would provoke God's wrath), and the apes would in time migrate to the stars and seed empires and sprawling civilizations. Yet still they would be insignificant in the vast ocean of the cosmos.

'To each other, though,' he spoke aloud to the heedless night, 'we are important. No matter that we are grains of living sand in a vast and sterile desert and there is nothing but life and non-life, no supernatural eternity. That is no reason to lose hope and inspiration; the opposite is true. We are all, by glorious chance, in the same boat... and what better reason could there be than that for feeling compassion towards one another.'

He laughed aloud, and it seemed that something within him fractured, and he stumbled to his knees, spasms coursing through him. And he looked to the east, where Venus rotated on her contrary axis, and the spasms increased. But he was not afraid, for there was no pain. And he looked to Mars, planet of war, a disc of red to his demon eye, and roared exultantly: 'You are wrong, God. It is hope and love that will govern Man, belief in the real and the present, not fear. When they work for the future it will be for later generations, not for reward in some imaginary afterlife. You are wrong, ancient one.'

Transformation swept through him, molecules oscillating, atoms reconfiguring.

Beelzebub and Ithuriel came into the garden, drawn by the furore.

'Where is he?' said Ithuriel.

But the demon had already looked to the sky, a knowing smile at his lips, and he saw the silhouette of the great dragon beat its powerful path across the disc of the moon, arcing up into the atmosphere, roaring euphoria at his condition.

Beelzebub laid a hand on his companion's shoulder.

'Brace yourself, Mr Thomas, for the adventure continues.'